The
Midwife
Of
Auschwitz

BOOKS BY ANNA STUART

A Letter from Pearl Harbor
The Secret Diary
The Berlin Zookeeper

The
Midwife
Of
Auschwitz

ANNA STUART

bookouture

Published by Bookouture in 2022

An imprint of Storyfire Ltd.
Carmelite House
50 Victoria Embankment
London EC4Y 0DZ

www.bookouture.com

ISBN: 978-1-80314-267-8
eBook ISBN: 978-1-80314-268-5

This book is dedicated to the memory of Stanislawa Leszczyńska and all those who, like her, laboured to keep hold of hope in the darkest days of the Holocaust.

PROLOGUE

APRIL 1946

There are cots everywhere. They fill the echoey, wooden-floored hall and from each one a small child peers, all eyes. There's not hope, the tiny infants aren't old enough for that, but there's a sort of longing that reaches deep into me and tugs, not on my heartstrings but deeper than that – right into my womb. It's been a long time since there was a child inside me but perhaps the feeling never quite goes. Perhaps every child I birthed has left a little part behind, a nub of the umbilical cord that will always make it easy for a pair of wide baby eyes to melt my heart. And perhaps every child I've ever helped ease onto this earth in my twenty-seven years as a midwife has affected me in the same way too.

I take a few steps into the room. The cots are rough and old but they are clean and carefully made. In one of them a baby wails and I hear a woman's voice lift in a lullaby, soft and soothing. The wails hiccup to a stop and only the music remains. Like everything else in this big room, it isn't shiny or smart but it rings with love. I smile and pray this is the place we've been looking for.

'Are you ready?'

I turn to the young woman who hovers in the doorway, her fingers gripping tight at the whitewashed wood of the door frame, her eyes as big as any of the orphans within.

'I'm not sure.'

I reach out for her hand.

'It was a foolish question. You'll never be ready, but you're here and that's enough.'

'What if it's not...?'

'Then we'll keep looking. Come on.'

I tug her forward as a kindly matron clips her way between the cots, all smiles.

'You made it. I'm so glad. I hope your journey wasn't too hard?'

I can't stop the bitter laugh. The journey this morning was simple, but the years preceding it have been a tangle of hurt and pain. We have been on the sort of dark, dirty road that no one should have to tread to get to this run-down place of dwindling hope. It has weakened us both and I'm not sure – whatever I've just said – how much further either of us can travel down it.

The matron seems to understand. She puts a hand on my arm and gives a nod.

'The bad years are gone now.'

'I hope you are right.'

'We have all lost too much.'

I look to my dear friend, who has crept forward, drawn by the cot nearest the window. In it sits a girl, blond hair wisping around a serious little face in the sunlight shining in on her. As she sees someone approach, the infant pulls herself up to standing, her legs wobbly but determined. My young friend crosses the last metres at speed and puts out a hand to the bar. The girl reaches through and my heart cracks at the sight – there have been too many bars, too many fences, too much segregation and division.

'Is this her?' I gasp out.

'She has something like the tattoo you described.' The matron shrugs awkwardly.

Something like... It's not enough. My heart sinks and suddenly it's me who's not ready, suddenly I want the dark, dirty road to wind on, for at least while we are travelling, we can travel in hope.

Stop! I want to cry, but the word sticks in my throat because now the young woman is reaching into the cot and lifting the child into her arms and the longing on her face is bigger than all these poor orphans put together. It is time to learn the truth. Time to see if our hearts can be healed.

PART ONE
ŁÓDŹ

ONE

1 SEPTEMBER 1939

ESTER

As the clock of St Stanislaus' cathedral rang out midday, Ester Abrams sank gratefully onto the steps beneath it and turned her face to the sun. The soft rays were warm on her skin but autumn was sending tendrils into the stone and it felt chill against her legs. For a moment she considered taking off her coat to sit on, but it was new and bought in a recklessly pale blue that her younger sister had said brought out the colour in her eyes, and she didn't want to risk staining it.

Ester flushed. It had been a foolish purchase really but Filip was always so beautifully dressed. Not extravagantly – an apprentice tailor had little more money than an apprentice nurse – but with care and pride. It had been one of the first things that had struck her on that day back in April when he'd first sat down on the far side of the steps and she'd felt every cell in her body fill up, like the blossom bursting into life on the nearby cherry tree. She'd looked down again straight away of course, fixing her eyes firmly on her pierogi, but had eaten her way through the little dumplings without tasting one morsel of her mother's finest mushroom and sauerkraut filling.

She hadn't dared look up again until, finally, he'd risen to go and she'd risked a quick glance. She could picture him now – his body long and lean and almost gangly, save for the purpose with which he walked; his jacket coarse but cut with style; his kippah intricately bordered as it clung to the back of his head. She'd feasted on the sight of him until, suddenly, he'd glanced back and his eyes had locked tight with hers and she'd felt not just her face but her entire body flush with something that should have been embarrassment but had felt more like... like joy.

The next day she'd been there early, tense with anticipation. Midday had struck but there'd been no young man, just an old one in a too-low hat, doddering up the steps on a stick. She'd rushed to help him, partly because it's what her mother would expect of her, and partly in the hope that by the time she came back out, the young man would be sat there. He hadn't been and she'd thrown herself down with her bajgiel, picking crossly at it as if the poor bread was to blame so that it had taken her until at least half the way through her food to realise that he was back in the same spot as yesterday. He'd been quietly eating his own lunch and immersing himself in a newspaper, save that whenever she glanced over, he'd seemed to be less reading it than staring through it.

For six long days they'd eaten at opposite sides of the steps as the people of Łódź had bustled and pushed and laughed their way along Piotrkowska Street below them. Every day she'd spent the whole time rehearsing sentences in her head that had tangled into agonising lumps whenever she'd tried to force them out of her lips. Then, finally, a woman had stepped between them and tutted loudly. Who knows what had annoyed her, for when they'd both looked up she'd already gone on into the church and instead they had found themselves looking straight at each other.

All the clever sentences had run round and round Ester's head, staying stubbornly within, and in the end he had said something asinine about the weather and she had said something even more asinine back and they had grinned at each other as if they'd just had the wisest ever debate, so perhaps he'd had other sentences inside his head too. Once those first words were out, others came more easily and soon they'd been, well, not exactly chatting, for they were neither of them the type to be extravagant with words, but sharing quiet, simple facts about their lives.

'I like your kippah,' she'd managed. 'The border is so pretty.'

He'd touched it self-consciously.

'Thank you. I embroidered it myself.'

'You did?!'

He'd flushed and she'd noticed that although his hair was dark, his eyes were as blue as her own.

'I'm training to be a tailor. It's mainly jackets and trousers and shirts but I like the...' He'd tugged at the edging of the cap. 'My father calls them the "fiddly bits". He doesn't approve. He thinks that embroidery is for women.'

'But you do it so well that he must be wrong.'

He'd laughed then, short but deep.

'Thank you. I think clothes should express something of yourself.'

Ester tugged at her pale blue coat now, remembering that comment and how much it had surprised her. She'd been brought up to believe that clothes should be neat, clean and modest, and had never thought about them expressing anything other than good housekeeping.

'Tell me more,' she'd invited, and he had, opening up as he'd talked so that she could have gladly sat there all afternoon, save that she only had half an hour for lunch and Matron was a tartar. If you were even a minute late, you'd find yourself on bedpan duty all afternoon, and although it might have been worth it to stay with the young tailor, her parents had sacrificed much to pay for her to train as a nurse and she'd owed it to them to do well. It had been so hard to pull herself away and she might as well have been on bedpan duty for all the attention she'd paid to her work that afternoon. But he'd been there the next day and the next, and she'd come to treasure those midday half hours like the finest jewels from the Russian mines. So where was he today?

She looked anxiously down Piotrkowska Street. Perhaps he had been held up at work, or perhaps there had been an incident of some sort. The air seemed curiously charged this morning, the people more animated than usual, the shops fuller. Everyone that went past seemed to be carrying bags rammed with groceries as if they were afraid they might mysteriously run out. The newspaper hawkers were shouting louder than ever but Ester had heard all the nasty jumble of words – Nazis, Hitler, invasion, bombs – too many times in the last months to pay them much heed. It was a beautiful autumn day, even if the step was rather chilly, and no one could, surely, do anything too terrible beneath such a blue sky?

There he was at last, weaving through the crowd outside the butcher's, striding easily between the myriad people. She half rose and then forced herself back down. For three months they had been meeting like this, eating their lunches closer and closer on the steps of St Stanislaus' cathedral as the blossom on the cherry tree had turned to fruit and the leaves had darkened and started to rust around the edges.

They had talked, growing in confidence with every shared piece of information. She knew his name – Filip Pasternak. She had, of course, tried it out against her own – Ester Pasternak –

though when her little sister, Leah, had done the same she'd snapped at her not to be ridiculous. He was training in his father's well-respected tailoring workshop, got no special treatment from him and said he was glad of it (though she wasn't sure that was entirely true), and he wasn't expected to marry yet because he had 'work to do'.

The conversation had hit a rut at that piece of information. Ester had managed to say that it sounded as if he had a lot of talent to give to the business and Filip had taken this and smiled gratefully and then said, in an unusually gruff tone, that 'fathers aren't always right about everything'. Then they'd both looked guiltily around in case anyone had heard such blasphemy and the clock had conveniently struck the half hour, sending them both leaping up. Ester had been on bedpan duty that afternoon but had barely noticed for the unruly thoughts bouncing around in her head.

She was pretty sure her parents would think her too young to marry, or at least too committed to her nursing and, to be fair to them, she'd spent the last two years saying she wasn't in any way interested in men and probably never would be, ever. Her mother had always smiled a wise smile that had annoyed her at the time but felt like a comfort now. Not that there'd been any mention of marriage, or even of dinner, or a walk in the park, or anything more than lunch on the steps of St Stanislaus' cathedral. It was like a rigid little bubble of a ritual they were both too shy to pop in case it had no other substance.

'Ester!'

He called her name across the crowd. There was a tram coming and for a terrible moment she thought he was going to try and cross in front of it, but despite the strangely wild look in his eyes he hung back and for too many agonising seconds it rumbled past. Then he was there again, bounding across the tracks and calling her name once more. 'Ester!'

She stood up.

'Filip. Is all well?'

'No! That is, yes. All is well with me. But not with the world, Ester, not with Poland.'

'Why? What's happened?'

'Haven't you heard?' She raised an eyebrow at him and he hit his hand against his forehead so comically that she almost laughed save that he looked far too worried for such frivolity. 'Of course you haven't or you would not ask. I'm sorry.'

He was standing two steps down from her and for the first time their eyes were level with each other. She looked deep into his, too concerned to be embarrassed.

'Please don't be, Filip. What's happened?'

He sighed.

'Germany have invaded. The Wehrmacht are swarming across our borders and we are none of us safe.'

'You will have to go and fight?'

'Perhaps. If there is time. But they are coming fast, Ester, making for Krakow and Warsaw.'

'And Łódź?'

'Who knows, but it looks that way. We are a fine city with much industry. Germans like industry.'

'But they don't like Jews.'

'No,' Filip agreed. 'They say some are leaving already, collecting up their gold and heading east.'

'Your family?'

He shook his head.

'Father won't leave his workshop for anything. And even if he did...'

He stopped, stared deep into Ester's eyes.

'Even if he did...?' she prompted.

She saw his chin go up, his eyes darken with sudden determination.

'Even if he did, I would not go with him. Not without you.'

'Without me?' she gasped, but he was taking her hands and dropping to his knees before her, his long legs clumsily balanced on the narrow steps.

'Ester Abrams, will you do me the very great honour of becoming my wife?'

Ester blinked at him, stunned. For a moment all of Piotrkowska Street seemed to stop its panicked bustle and turn their way. Two old ladies, dragging a wheelbarrow of shopping bags, paused and stared. She stared back and one of them gave her a wink and a nod, so that she turned her eyes back to the handsome man at her feet.

'I...'

'Because this is war, Ester; the moment I heard it, the moment I thought of soldiers and guns and an enemy marching into our city, I could only think of one thing – that it might rob me of you. And then I thought how ridiculous it was that I'd already wasted twenty-three and a half hours of every day of this summer *not* with you and I couldn't bear to waste another half an hour more. So, Ester, will you?'

'Marry you?'

'Yes.'

'Yes!'

The word exploded out of her and then she was tugging him up and he was taking her in his arms and his lips were touching hers and her only thought was that she, too, had been wasting far too much time. The world spun with the joy of him and a great noise buzzed in her ears as if God had set all the angels singing. Though if he had, he needed to pick a better choir, for it was more of a wail than a heavenly chorus and it was only when she finally pulled back that she realised it was an air raid siren crackling out of the rusty old speakers set along the street.

'Quick,' Filip said, taking her hand and pulling her up the steps and into the cathedral as, overhead, two German planes cut, dark and menacing, across the bright blue sky and Ester had no idea whether this was the happiest day of her life or the worst.

It was a question she was to ask herself again and again over the dark years to come.

TWO

19 NOVEMBER 1939

ANA

Ana Kaminski took her husband's arm as first Filip and then a blushing Ester were led up to the chuppah by their parents and faced each other beneath the pretty canopy. She smiled as the pair looked into each other's eyes, so clearly thrilled to be coupling their lives together, and felt her soul settle. Thank the good Lord she'd come. She'd hesitated when the invitation had arrived. Maybe, now she'd hit her mid-fifties, she was getting nervous, but she'd been uncertain whether God wanted her attending a Jewish ceremony. Bartek, bless him, had scoffed at her fears.

'Of course God wants you to go and see these young people celebrate their love for each other. There's far too much hate swilling around us at the moment not to seize such an opportunity with both hands, whatever building it takes place in.'

He'd been right, and she'd been ashamed of herself for even worrying about it. The Jewish people were earnest, kind and respectful, and that was to be valued, especially in a world in which imposing yourself on others seemed to be becoming the norm. It had been a hateful two and a half months since the Nazis had swept into Poland and imposed their rigid rules and ideologies on her beloved country. It made her want to rage at every one of the smug soldiers parading through her city, changing road signs and making new laws with no regard for custom, tradition or even, it seemed, any sort of common sense or decency.

Jesus taught her to turn the other cheek but the Nazis had come in slapping both cheeks at once and it was hard to forgive an offence when ten more were already coming at you. At times like this she felt herself more of an Old Testament Christian – yearning for fire and fury – than a New Testament one, which was perhaps ironic given where she was.

She looked around the synagogue as the rabbi began a low, mystical chanting that echoed off the painted walls. There had been a frost sparkling from the pavement as the guests had arrived but the sun was bright in the sky and slanting in through high-up windows, catching in the golden pillars and furnishings so that the whole place seemed to glow. It was not, she had to admit, dissimilar to their own beloved St Stanislaus' cathedral, and she hugged Bartek's arm, thankful again that he had insisted she come. This was the most peaceful she had felt all autumn.

She watched closely as Ester's younger sister, Leah, led her in a circle seven times around her groom, her sweet face solemn and her eyes fixed on the ground, though perhaps less in piety and more to be sure she did not step on her sister's hem. Ana remembered that feeling. Her own wedding to Bartek might have taken place twenty-three years ago but it was still vivid in her mind. It had been 1916 then, and in the middle of another war – the great war, they'd called it, the war to end all wars, but it hadn't been. Somehow, they were here again and once more the arrogant powers either side of poor Poland were rampaging across her peaceful towns and villages. Why could they not leave them alone? For centuries Russia and Germany had looked on Ana's homeland as something to carve up between them and at last, in 1918, Poland had regained her sovereignty. Now their neighbours were riding roughshod over her again – and this time with tanks and great big guns.

Ana shivered, trying to focus on the joyful ceremony as Ester came back round to stand before Filip and he tenderly reached up to lift her veil from the back of her head and over her face to symbolise that he cherished not just her body but her soul. This moment was a blessing, a day of love amidst the fear and a reminder that whatever the powers-that-be were battling to carve out, the people they were so unfortunately in charge of wanted simply to get on with their lives – to marry, to have babies, to become families. Was there anything more precious?

Instinctively Ana's hand went to the professional papers she always kept in an old toothpowder tin in her coat pocket. You never knew when you might be called upon and it was best to reassure labouring mothers that you knew what you were doing. She'd been a midwife in this city for the last twenty years and many was the time she'd been called from her dinner, or from drinks with friends, or even from the theatre to attend a birthing. If they ever stopped a play now, she tensed, waiting for the inevitable announcement – 'Could Midwife Kaminski please report to the foyer'. Bartek would sigh but drop a kiss on her forehead as she gathered her coat and the small bag of equipment that she carried everywhere and headed into the night.

A little of her would mourn the end of the play that she'd never get to see, but the moment she was caught up in the birthing, the trivialities of a pre-written drama would be swept away in the thrill of the unfolding natural one. It was such a privilege of a job. Every time that she helped to bring a new life into the world, her soul felt as if it were witnessing the birth of the Christ child all over again and any tiredness was dispelled by the joyous miracle. What power had guns and tanks against such simple renewal?

Ana looked closely at Ester, shaking her head at the passing of time. This lovely young woman standing before her groom today had been one of the first babies Ana had brought into the world. She'd been fresh out of midwife college in Warsaw and still awed that she was allowed to practise alone. Called to Ruth's clean and tidy home at dawn, she'd been greeted by her husband, Mordecai, huddled on the doorstep, drawing furiously on a pipe. He'd leaped up when he'd seen her, clasping her hands.

'Thank the Lord you are here. She needs you. My Ruth needs you. You will take care of her, won't you? You will keep her safe?'

He'd been babbling like a child and she'd felt the weight of his love pressing upon her. All his happiness, that day, had been in her hands, but those hands, she'd reminded herself, had been trained at the best midwifery college in Poland and, sending up a prayer to God, she'd hurried into the house.

It had not, in the end, been hard to fulfil Mordecai's wishes, for Ruth had been young and strong and aided by a no-nonsense mother who had forced her to grit her teeth and bear down when Ana had called for it. Little Ester had been born safe and well within an hour of Ana's arrival and Mordecai had come rushing in, showering her with praise. She'd assured him that the work had all been his wife's and then stood back as he'd taken Ruth's face in both hands, kissing her tenderly before taking the baby as if she were the most precious thing in the world. And now that baby was a woman.

Ana listened intently as Ester made her vows to Filip with a strong, clear voice. They were such a lovely young couple, both shy and serious about their chosen paths in the world. She saw something of herself in Ester. The girl was clearly passionate about her nursing and she hoped that she'd be able, as Ana had done, to keep up with her vocation while she had a family. Her eyes turned to Filip, standing so tall and proud as he pledged himself to his bride. The only blessing of being occupied, she supposed, was that their young men were not yet being called up to fight, so Filip could stand here with his best man, Tomaz, at his side. Who knew if the voracious Reich would choose to conscript them; but surely even Hitler was not mad enough to ask his enemies to fight for his cause, so perhaps Ester would keep her groom in her home.

Not that the poor man could work. The Łódź area had been 'honoured' with being taken into the Reich proper and two weeks ago the German commander had forbidden Jews from working in the textile or leather industries – a law that had forced almost 50 per cent of the Łódź community out of work in one swipe. Filip's tailoring apprenticeship had been terminated instantly and his father had been forced to hand his treasured workshop over to a big German with fat fingers and no talent.

The city would be the poorer clad for this senseless move and, meanwhile, the pigs in charge of Łódź had issued a 'compulsory labour' order for the poor Jews and were yanking them out of their homes and offices to break up Polish monuments, sweep pavements and change road signs. Just the other day Ana had passed two men openly weeping as they'd pulled down the noble old Piotrkowska Street signs to replace them with shiny new ones reading *Adolf-Hitler-Strasse*. The Nazis were doing the same to every street in the city, scrawling out the age-old names and writing arrogant German ones across them. No good Pole would use the new names, but they were there taunting them all the same.

And then there were the armbands. The order had come in just a few days ago – all Jews to wear a yellow armband ten centimetres wide directly below their armpit, a place designed for maximum discomfort. It was like the Middle Ages all over again. So many despotic leaders had enforced distinguishing badges on the Jewish peoples over the centuries to 'prevent accidental intermixing' – as if human beings did not talk to each other, or meet each other's families, or share their histories; as if it was up to the state who any individual chose to bind themselves to in holy matrimony.

Ana had met Ruth and Leah in the street the other day, wringing their hands over the impact on all their carefully chosen wedding outfits and praying that the wretched ruling would not be enforced until after the wedding but, no, the SS – the Germans' fiercest, most sadistic representatives – had been out on the streets all week pointing their guns at any poor Jew not marked out in yellow – and pulling the trigger sometimes too. Old Elijah Aarons, the most talented baker in the city, would make no more kołaczki or szarlotka to delight his myriad customers, for he'd been shot dead in his own shop for protesting that he had not yet found enough yellow fabric to go around his considerable bicep. So here they were, almost every member of the congregation, bar Ana and Bartek, bound around with bile. Even poor Ester had to wear one, though someone clever – almost certainly Filip – had sewn shining bands of gold around both arms in defiant obedience so that she looked more like a queen than an outcast.

The ceremony was reaching its conclusion and Ana pulled her mind away from troubled thoughts and into the glorious here and now as Ester's veil was lifted again and the rabbi took a glass and gave it to them to drink from in turn. Once it was emptied, he slotted it into a velvet bag, pulled the drawstring tightly and placed it on the floor before Filip. The young groom looked to Ester, who smiled encouragement and took his hand. The congregation moved forward as Filip lifted his heel and brought it sharply down upon the glass. Ana heard the first crack before it was drowned out in the joyous cheers of 'Mazel tov' and, joining in, she knew that, whatever the language and whatever the building, all cultures were united in the blessings of a happy marriage.

She turned to kiss her own husband as all around people chattered happily, hugging one another and crowding in to lift the bride and groom and parade them around the synagogue. The party would be held in the hall behind the pretty building, but it seemed it was starting already and the ridiculous yellow armbands were whirling into a hoop of gold around the young pair. Ana saw Ester laugh out loud as her hand was pulled from Filip's by Tomaz, who handed her up onto ready shoulders before moving to hoist Filip on high himself. The pair were borne in glory around the synagogue, but just as the clapping of their guests coalesced into one exuberant beat, the doors flew open and shots echoed around the building. The crowd froze as SS soldiers stormed in, shouting in coarse German: 'Raus, raus!' – Get out.

Ana heard Ester's laughter turn to horror as the SS pointed their guns at her, sat high on the shoulders of the crowd like a sitting duck, and instinctively she leaped forward.

'Please,' she said in German, 'this is a wedding.'

The officer looked at her in surprise. She'd been taught the language as a child and was all but fluent. It had stood her in good stead over the years for many of her clients had been Germans, resettled in Poland, but she'd never thought she'd have to use it with soldiers.

'A wedding?' The officer put an arm up to hold back his men as he looked around, which did, at least, give the frightened guests time to get both Ester and Filip down and into the relative safety of the crowd. The man laughed nastily. 'A Jewish wedding! That, lady, is precisely what we are here to stop. We cannot have these scum breeding. There are enough of them around already.' He looked her up and down, taking in her good coat, untarnished by an armband. 'What are you doing here?'

'Celebrating love,' she told him boldly.

The laugh was darker this time, more menacing. Out of the corner of her eye Ana saw broad-chested Tomaz standing guard as Ruth and Mordecai spirited the bride and groom out of the back door. She was grateful they'd got away, but the rest of the congregation were still in danger. Filip's parents, Benjamin and Sarah, were trying to calm everyone, but panic was rising.

'Do you need something, sir?' she asked, forcing herself to be polite, though the words seemed to tear at her very throat.

'Need something? Yes, lady – we need to tear down this blasphemous building and all the bastard Jews within it. Oi, you! Stay right there.'

He'd spotted the back entrance as other guests tried to sneak out and now he strode over and yanked Ester's bridesmaid back inside. Ana's heart squeezed. Fourteen-year-old Leah had looked so grown-up arriving behind her sister, her unusually blond hair twisted high on her head and a hint of make-up enhancing her features, but now she looked like a frightened child, and no wonder. The guns were so big this close, so furiously powerful. If the SS chose to unleash them in this contained space, there would be nothing Ruth and Mordecai's honoured guests would be able to do to hide.

'Please,' she said again. 'Just let them go. There are elderly people here, children.'

'*Jewish* children!'

'Children all the same.'

He looked at her, his face twisted up with hate.

'They are not the same,' he growled. 'The Jews are a plague on this earth and it is our duty to eradicate them.'

Ana felt as if all the air in her lungs had been sucked out of them. She'd watched Jews being forced to fill puddles with sand, had seen them shut up their shops and hide in their homes, but she had not, until this moment, realised the depth of the hatred pitted against them. This was not just mockery and spite; this was pure evil. She gasped for breath, her vision swimming, and felt Bartek's arm around her waist, strong and determined.

'And we thank you for it,' he said calmly, his German not as good as hers but clear enough. 'But what are your orders for today?'

Ana wanted to beat at his chest for his apparent complicity but as she fought to compose herself, she saw the soldier's shiny boots shuffle awkwardly. Orders. Bartek was right, that was what these automata responded to.

'We have orders to blow up all synagogues in Łódź.'

'But not people?'

'Not yet,' he spat, but Ana could hear the hesitation in his voice and clung to Bartek as he spoke again.

'Then perhaps, for now, you should let them out into the street where they can watch their sacred building collapse around them.'

'Yes!' The officer seized on this. 'A humiliation and a warning of the might of the Reich. Raus!' he cried, and his soldiers picked it up instantly. 'Raus, raus, raus!'

Leah led the scramble for the doors, everyone falling over themselves in their hurry to escape before the temple was pulled down around their heads as it had been too many times in their history. Bartek crumpled against a pillar, his head in his hands, and now it was Ana's turn to wrap an arm around his waist and guide him out with the rest.

'What did I say?' he moaned. 'It was horrible, horrible!'

'It was bold and brave and it saved the lives of all these people,' Ana told him.

'For now,' Bartek said darkly and, as they all rushed off towards Piotrkowska Street – Adolf-Hitler-Strasse – the wedding in disarray, Ana knew that he was right. The invaders had taken their city and now they were going to divide its people. Some fool man had decided that the baby Ana had brought into the world eighteen years ago, naked and innocent, was in some way less valuable than any other and was out to eliminate her and all her kin from the earth. This was surely not just war, but the end of civilisation, and as she made for home, all the peace of the beautiful wedding ceremony was wiped from Ana's soul to be replaced with a terrible sense of foreboding. She could only pray that Ester and Filip had a happy few days together, for they would need all their strength in the weeks and months ahead.

THREE

8 FEBRUARY 1940

ESTER

'Filip – I'm home!'

Oh, how Ester loved saying that. Never would she have thought that the simple act of walking through a door would feel so wonderful. Although this apartment was small and roughly furnished and up an awful lot of stairs, it was all theirs and she treasured it like the finest palace.

'Dinner's nearly ready,' Filip called back, and she giggled as she hung her coat up and went through into the galley kitchen to see him at the stove with a pinny wrapped around his waist and his lovely face flushed from the steam of the pot.

'It smells wonderful,' she said, stepping into his open arms and kissing him.

'It's bigos, or at least it's meant to be. My mother wrote her recipe down for me but I could barely find any of the ingredients in the shops. It should have seven different types of meat in it, but it's got two and, to be honest, I'm not sure either of them really count as meat in the purest sense of the word.'

She kissed him again, rubbing a smudge of gravy from his cheek.

'It will be perfect, Filip. Thank you.'

He smiled gratefully.

'I had to queue for hours and even when I got near the front someone would shove me back.'

'Did you not protest?'

'With the SS on every corner? I can imagine how they'd choose to come to my aid.'

Ester winced. Every day further into 1940 friends and family were struck or kicked or beaten by Nazis using them as their playthings. The other day one of Ester's friends, Maya, had turned up at their door weeping and begging for her help. The Nazis had made her ageing father carry bricks across the street with his bare hands all morning long, before ordering him to carry them back again. His poor fingers had been torn to shreds, his back bent almost double and his ribs blue where they'd kicked him whenever he had fallen down.

Ester had done her best to wash and dress his wounds but the next morning the SS had been banging on the door, demanding he get his 'lazy bones' out to work, and the nightmare had started up again. Her father was in hospital now and Maya was vowing revenge but what could they do? The Nazis had the guns and with them the power. The rest of the world had gone to war for Poland but it seemed that Poland herself just had to buckle down and pray for rescue. Many young men had fled abroad, looking for an army to join, and while Ester understood, she was unendingly glad Filip had stayed at her side.

'It's a bit upside down this, isn't it?' he said now. 'You going out to work and me keeping house.'

'I like it,' she said, grinning up at him. 'The apron suits you.'

He gave a funny half-curtsy and she giggled again and pulled him close for a longer, deeper kiss. She could hardly believe that it was not yet a year since this wonderful man had sat down on the steps across from her, and now they were married and living together. Already she couldn't truly remember what the world felt like without him in it, and she didn't think she'd ever tire of stepping into his arms.

'Is it ready?' she asked.

He tested the rich stew, frowning in concentration.

'I think it could do with another half an hour.'

'Good!' she said, taking him by the hand to lead him into the bedroom.

'Mrs Pasternak – are you seducing me?'

'Yes,' she agreed happily.

The physical side of their marriage had not got off to the best of starts with the horrors of being bundled from the synagogue just as their wedding celebrations had truly been starting. Filip's family had arranged for them to spend a few days in a charming chalet out in the Łagiewniki Forest but they'd been so upset that on their first night they'd been able to do little but huddle together, staring into the fire and wishing to be back with their families to be sure everyone was well.

Weary and uncertain, they'd finally climbed into bed, but a night's sleep in each other's arms had calmed them both and the next morning, with dawn light slanting through the trees, they had found their way to each other. After that, Ester would quite happily have stayed there forever. With Filip, she had discovered, she did not need to be shy. She trusted him so completely that shyness seemed pointless and, besides, they had come to their marriage as innocent as each other so it had been a journey they had taken together and would, she hoped, still be taking for many years to come.

'Bed then?' she asked, arching an eyebrow.

She saw his eyes darken in response.

'Yes please. Oh, but I've got something to tell you.'

'Can it wait? Oh!' She pulled back the bedclothes, ready to jump in, but found the mattress covered in clothing. 'Filip?'

He gathered the garments hastily up, bundling them into a hessian sack.

'Alterations. Everyone is losing weight so fast that they need their clothes taking in and word has got out that I'm prepared to do it. They pay in cash, or in food, which is even better, but...'

'But you have to keep it hidden,' Ester finished, her skin crawling at the thought of what would happen if they were raided. Working with textiles, even in your own bedroom, was banned.

'I can stop doing it if you want,' Filip said, clasping her tight against him.

She shook her head. They could joke about her husband's pinny, but she knew that being stuck at home all day was hard for him and this work might just keep him sane. Besides, people needed it. The armband had been replaced by a yellow star of David, to be sewn on both the breast and back of every item of clothing. With all Jewish savings accounts frozen and a cash withdrawal limit imposed, it was becoming increasingly hard to dress well but no one wanted their dignity taken by the immaculately uniformed SS. If tailors like Filip could help with that minor victory, then so much the better.

'You're just sewing on stars, right?' she said, pointing to the pile of them on one side.

'Right,' he agreed. That, at least, was permitted and some of the richer Jews had even been commissioning fancy ones, making fashion of misfortune, until the Germans had put a stop to that. Still, their pettiness had gained Filip more commissions, replacing them with the coarse patches their enemy preferred, and if he happened to take in a seam, or embroider a hem, or add a frill while the clothing was being branded, then who was to know?

'Then how can the Germans complain? They have enough of us already, don't they, without taking our clothing too?'

Filip shifted uncomfortably in her arms.

'I really do have something to tell you.'

She looked at him, surprised.

'It wasn't the clothing?'

'No.'

'Oh. Can it wait?' she asked again, but she was starting to get the uncomfortable feeling that whatever 'it' was, it had already ruined the mood. 'Go on then.'

'No, no, no. It can wait. Come here.'

He started to unbutton her uniform but his fingers were shaking and she stopped him gently.

'You better tell me, Filip. A problem shared...'

'Is still a problem,' he said gloomily.

'As long as we're here, together, then—'

'That's just it.'

Ester's heart thudded.

'What? Is it the apartment? Is the landlord—'

'Not the landlord, no. Just... Oh, hang on a moment.'

He darted back through to the kitchen and returned clutching the *Lodscher Zeitung* newspaper. Slowly he uncurled it and passed it over to Ester. Plastered across the front was a map of the city, a dark area shaded around Baluty Market with the words *Die Wohngebiet der Juden* below.

'Wohngebiet?' she asked Filip.

'Residential area,' he translated, adding bitterly: 'Ghetto.'

She sank onto the bed, only half aware of Filip hovering at her side as she battled to understand the German words. The order, written in the imperious style of the occupiers, denounced the Jews as a 'race lacking a sense of cleanliness' and stated that it was therefore an urgent matter of public health to separate them before they could infect the 'good people' of the city. Ester read the words over and over, only half taking them in.

'"Lacking a sense of cleanliness"', she spat out eventually. 'How dare they?'

She looked indignantly around their apartment – a little old, a little shabby even, but spotlessly clean.

'It's not true, Ester,' Filip said gently.

'I know! That just makes it even worse. How are they allowed to say those things about us? Isn't there a law against defamation? Why isn't anyone stopping them?'

Filip bit his lip.

'They're the conquerors, my love. That means they can do what they want.'

'Including putting us into a, a ghetto?'

Even the word was nasty – short and snappish, like an angry insect.

'It seems so.'

'When?'

He swallowed.

'We have three days.'

She stared at him in horror then got up and went to the bedroom door to look out into the kitchen/diner. Her coat was on its hook in the hallway where she had hung it when she'd come bouncing in to the smell of bigos and the glorious sight of her husband in an apron. One moment she wanted to batter at his chest for letting her even try and tease him into bed when he'd known about this, and the next she wished he'd kept it from her until... Until when?

'What do we do, Filip?'

He came over, wrapping his arms around her waist, and she leaned in against him. His lips brushed a soft kiss across her neck.

'We hold onto each other super tight, my love. I like this apartment as much as you do but home for me is wherever you are and if the Germans think they can break us by shifting us around our own city, then they have another think coming. Let's eat our bigos and climb into our bed and tomorrow we will find our families and make a new home – a home better than any fancy German palace because it will be filled with love, not hate.'

They tried. Both of them tried really hard but the bigos could have been sawdust in their mouths and it was impossible to sleep knowing that it could be their last night in their tiny marital home, so they were both relieved when dawn crept between the curtains, grey and damp. They could hear shouting on the streets already and huddled together, delaying the last safe moments, but then a knock on the door heralded the arrival of her parents and sister and there was no choice but to get up and face the nightmare.

Everyone was rushing around panicking. The ghetto was apparently to be set up in the area around the great Bałuty Market in the north of the city, where many Jewish people lived already but just as many did not. No one seemed to know where they were going to go.

'There's a housing bureau on Południowa Street,' Tomaz came to tell them, but when they got there the crowds were fifty deep.

'What will happen about school?' Leah asked, looking eagerly around. At fourteen she was the only one of them to see this as an adventure.

'School?' A passing German man laughed. 'What use is school for the likes of you? Just a waste of good teachers.'

Leah put her hands on her newly curving hips.

'I'll have you know I'm top of my class.'

'Yeah? Tell you what, come over here and I'll give you the sort of education the likes of you are good for.'

He made a lewd gesture and his mates cheered him loudly. Leah took a furious step forward, but Ester yanked her back.

'Leave them, Leah. They're not worth it.'

'They can't speak to us like that,' she shot back indignantly.

Ester smiled sadly at her. What could she say? Leah should be right, but the hideous truth of occupied Łódź was that their conquerors could speak to them however they wanted.

'Let's just get in the queue.'

It was a long, fearful wait until they finally reached the housing bureau. The desks were staffed by exhausted-looking clerks, watched over by Chaim Rumkowski, who had been appointed 'Eldest of the Jews' by the Germans last month and was apparently to run the ghetto. He had soft white hair and an encouraging smile, but his old eyes were sharp as they raked across the crowds of 'his' people, and he had two SS guards at his side. Ester was glad when they were pointed to a young woman at the furthest desk from his high-backed chair.

'We need a small house for my husband and I and another for my parents and sister,' she said. The woman looked up at her, started to laugh, and then her face crumpled. 'Are you well?' Ester asked.

'As well as you can be when you have to give every single person bad news,' she said wearily. 'You will have to share a house.'

'All of us?'

She sighed.

'All of you and others besides.'

'You want us to live with strangers?'

'I'm sorry but the ghetto has half the houses we have families to accommodate. And most of them still have Poles living in them.'

'What will happen to them?'

'They'll be resettled.'

She used the word with assurance, but Ester couldn't help

thinking it was misplaced, for there was nothing settling about this whole situation. She looked to Filip in horror. Their apartment had been tiny but it had been all their own. Now they were expected to share like children and to live with strangers, too!

'My parents,' Filip said. 'What if we add in my parents?'

'So there will be seven of you?' the woman asked, and they nodded. God knows, their parents had only met a handful of times, but Ester and Filip's presence would bind them. 'I do have a place here, on Kreuzstrasse.'

'Where?'

The woman leaned in.

'It used to be Krzyżowa,' she whispered, as if even mentioning the Polish name was a crime. 'It has two bedrooms.'

'Two?'

'And an attic.'

'We'll take it,' Filip said. His hand squeezed Ester's and he leaned in to whisper in her ear, 'Attics are very romantic.'

Ester loved him more than ever for his optimism but as they were handed the key to some unknown property they were to share with both sets of parents, she couldn't help thinking that she had scarcely heard of anything less romantic in her life. Some interloping German couple would be given their precious apartment while they were off to the ghetto. Her heart cracked and as they fought their way back out of the bureau, she clutched so tightly at Filip's hand that his knuckles turned deathly white.

FOUR

9 FEBRUARY 1940

ANA

Bang, bang, bang!

Ana pulled herself reluctantly from sleep and fumbled for her uniform, hung permanently ready on the back of the bedroom door. A sliver of light was creeping around the curtains so it must be almost dawn, but she didn't feel anywhere near ready to face the day. So many babies seemed to insist on coming out at night. Someone had told her once that it was the body's way of making sure it delivered the baby before the household duties of the day kicked in, which sounded about right. Sometimes, dearly as she loved Him, Ana wished God had been a woman, then pregnancy might have been better organised.

'Coming!' she called as the banging started up again. Clearly some poor mother was in need; in her head she ran through the list of patients near to their time. She'd not been expecting anyone this week, but that was babies for you – always came when they were ready, not when you were. She yanked on her thickest stockings, fumbling to attach them to the belt and wondering if it was time to start wearing trousers like some of the younger midwives. It looked so much more practical, but it didn't quite sit right with her. She was getting old, that was the problem, old and staid and slow at getting out of bed in the early hours.

'Coming!' she cried again.

She told everyone that it would take her some minutes to get to the door in the middle of the night, but fathers in a panic rarely remembered. Their thoughts were all for their precious wives and arriving children and, really, that was exactly as it should be. At last she was ready and made for the stairs. Bartek stirred and blew her a kiss and she blew him one back, though his eyes were closing again already, lucky man. He had another two hours before he had to get into the printing press where he worked as a typesetter – a far more sensible career choice. Even so, Ana felt a familiar stir of excitement at the thought of the new life she would bring into the world; you didn't get that setting letters onto a board.

She smiled in the direction of the firmly closed door of their sons' bedroom. Bronislaw and Alekzander had chosen to follow her into medicine, with Bron in his first year as a doctor and Zander still studying at medical college. Their youngest, Jakub, had asked to be apprenticed to Bartek and she knew his father was quietly delighted that one of their three was following his path.

She glanced at the family photo, proudly mounted at the bottom of the stairs. Oh, the fuss there'd been the day that had been done, but it had been worth it. They all looked a bit stiff, perhaps, a bit unnatural, standing staring into the camera instead of tearing around, laughing and teasing and wrestling with one another, but they were there, preserved forever – her family.

'Open up!' a coarse voice shouted through the door, and she hesitated.

That did not sound like an expectant father. Even so, she grabbed her coat, picked up her medical bag and turned the key. Instantly the door flew open and she stepped hastily back as two men stamped into the hallway. Her heart sank as she saw the SS uniforms, but she reminded herself that German women had babies too – indeed, she'd helped to deliver many in her time – and fought to compose herself.

'Can I help you, gentlemen?'

They looked taken aback.

'Where is your husband?'

'He's in bed.'

'He lets you answer the door in the night?' They looked to one another with a rough laugh. 'Poles!'

'I *choose* to answer the door in the night because it is always for me. I am a midwife.'

They took a step back and looked her up and down, taking in her uniform and bag. The older of the two gave her a funny little bow.

'Apologies, madam. A noble profession.'

'Thank you.'

The younger soldier looked at his companion curiously.

'My mother is a midwife,' his senior snapped at him. 'Stand back.'

They both shuffled towards the door, still open and letting the icy February air seep into Ana's home.

'What can I do for you?' she asked nervously.

'Oh. Yes. Erm...' The older soldier looked abashed and his compatriot stepped forward and whipped a paper out of his hand, thrusting it at Ana.

'You are to be resettled.'

'Sorry?'

'Moved. You cannot stay in this house.'

'Why not? This is my house, has been for nearly thirty years. My husband and I own it. We have paid in full.'

'It is needed by the Reich.'

Ana felt her whole body start to shake and had to reach for the wall to steady herself. Her hand connected with the family portrait, sending it skewing sideways, and she forced herself upright again.

'For what purpose?'

'You are in the area that is henceforth to be established as a residential quarter for the Jewish scum.'

'We can't be.'

Ana had read about the ghetto yesterday. She and Bartek had pored over the order in the newspaper, horrified by the callous tone, the ruthless efficiency, and the whole idea of segregating human beings based on arbitrary decisions about 'racial purity'. Her heart had broken – or so she'd sentimentally thought – for the Jews who were being uprooted from their homes and shoved into the area around the Baluty Market, just a few roads away, but it had never crossed her mind that she could be uprooted too. How arrogantly complacent of her. Her heart had not been breaking at all; but now it was.

'Please. What can we do? Is it money? We can—'

'It is not money, madam. It is orders. Your house is in the resettlement zone so you must move out. Do not worry. You will be given another house. It may be a better one. Some of these Jews have been living very richly on the profits of their leeching businesses.'

'Leeching? Half this city would be naked without Jewish tailors.'

The younger soldier tittered and the older one glared at him.

'Nonsense,' he said. 'There would just be room for good German tailors to get work. Poles too,' he added, as if this were some sort of kindness.

Ana felt her blood starting to boil and, with relief, heard the doors upstairs flinging open and her menfolk emerging. Bartek came charging down the stairs in his dressing gown, throwing a protective arm around her, and she leaned gratefully into it.

'What's going on?'

'We're being "resettled",' she told him bitterly.

'Where to?'

'Across the city,' the German said, clearly grateful to have a man to address. 'You are to pack up within two days and report to the housing bureau on February twelfth between' – he consulted his leather notebook – 'ten a.m. and midday. You will hand over your keys and be assigned a new set somewhere else in the city. Somewhere clean.'

'It is clean here.'

'But it will not be when all the Jews are living around you.'

Ana looked at him incredulously.

'Do you really believe that?' she asked.

The soldier frowned.

'It is the truth, madam. Our great scientists have done many experiments.'

'Experiments on how clean Jewish mothers keep their houses?'

'Of course not. It runs far deeper than that. It is about blood, about racial purity. You will not understand.'

'Why not?'

Ana felt Bartek's hand tighten on her shoulder and saw her boys looking at her with concern, but she could not stop herself.

'Because you are a woman.'

She glared up at him.

'I may be a woman, but I am medically trained.'

'Only in babies. Not in real science.'

'Not in real...! Let me tell you, young man, that without my branch of science you might have died twisted up in your mother's womb before you ever drew breath. Or you might have come out with the cord trapped around your neck, turning you blue and damaging your brain, although, on reflection, perhaps that is what happened if you believe that—'

'Enough, Ana!' Bartek's voice was urgent in her ear. The soldiers had both turned angry red and were reaching for their guns. He took the paper from her and waved it like a white flag between them. 'Thank you for this. We will read it carefully.'

'And do as it instructs,' the older soldier growled, 'or suffer the consequences. It is for your own good, even if...' he looked pointedly at Ana, 'you are too stupid to know it. Good day.'

Then they were stomping out of the house and Ana ran to the door, slamming it shut and pressing herself against it as if her ageing body might somehow keep the ferocious agents of the merciless Reich out of her home.

'How can they do this?' she wept. 'How can they throw us out of our own home?'

'It seems,' Bartek said bitterly, 'that they can do whatever they want. Come – breakfast, and then we had better start packing.'

It was a horrible two days. No concession was made for leave from work so Ana, Bartek and the boys were up most of their last two nights in their precious home, packing clothes and bedding, kitchenware and furniture. The Reich was handing them a new house but no allowance for removals, and they had to spend some of their meagre savings on an exorbitantly priced cart for a move none of them wanted to make.

Ana wept as she wrapped her wedding china in sheets of paper bearing the hated announcement of the ghetto. In theory they, too, were being moved into a Polish 'residential quarter' but their neighbours were being given houses all over Łódź, so that did not seem to be happening yet. How, though, were they to settle with the threat of another move hanging over their heads? A home was a nest, a place your family could feel safe, and now it seemed the Nazis were even taking that from them.

On the last night in their home, they sat among the packing crates sharing bread and cheese and a nice bottle of wine Bartek had been saving for a special occasion. Ana had hoped it would be there for a celebration – Bronislaw's engagement, perhaps – but Bartek determinedly announced that this *was* a celebration, of their family, their togetherness, their strength.

'We'll need it,' Ana said darkly, but the boys teased her out of her misery and they all sat up far too late talking over memories of happy times past and assuring each other of happier ones to come once this madness was over.

'We beat the Germans last time,' the boys said with the optimism of youth, 'and we will do it again.'

They did not have such big tanks last time, Ana had wanted to tell them, but she'd refrained. Optimism was about all they had to hold on to right now, however misplaced.

At their appointed hour, they took their overpriced cart and reported to the housing bureau. A cold-faced female SS officer snatched their keys from them without even looking into their faces and made a satisfied tick on her long list. Cross-checking, she produced another set and handed it over.

'Ostpreussenstrasse,' she snapped. 'Make sure you clean it well before you move in. It'll be crawling with disease.'

Bartek yanked Ana away before she could contradict her, and together the five of them walked across the city to their new home. On the other side of the street, lines of Jews, with carts just as laden as their own, and families just as frightened, stood waiting for admittance to the ghetto. Ana stared at them, wondering which of them would be assigned to her house – which couple would sleep in her and Bartek's room tonight, which children would run around their kitchen. She sent up a prayer to God that they would be happy there, but it was clear already that there were more people heading north to the

Jewish quarter than south away from it, and she feared there would not be much space for running. Already men were being press-ganged into erecting giant fences, and as they trudged along the road a great truck came rumbling down it bearing rolls of vicious barbed wire. Ana stopped, tugged on her husband's arm.

'This isn't right, Bartek. We shouldn't do this. We shouldn't just cave before them. What if we say "no"? What if we all just rise up and stand together in the middle of the street instead of processing down either side of it in obedience to a despicable ideology that is tearing us apart? There are far more Poles than Germans.'

He looked around, thinking about it, but then his eyes went to the ranks of SS guards lining the way, huge guns over their shoulders and great belts of ammunition slung across their chests.

'We have no weapons, Ana. Most of us would die.'

'But the rest would be free.'

'Until they sent reinforcements, and then the rest would be dispatched too and the Germans would have the whole city to themselves, just as they want.'

'So we are simply going to give in?'

He leaned down to drop a sad kiss on her lips.

'For now. But there are other ways to resist, my dearest – slower, more patient ways.'

Ana sighed. Patience had never been her strength. She was too forthright, she knew, too impetuous, too keen to act. She had learned patience in her trade, for babies worked to no schedule but their own, but she still found it hard in the rest of her life.

Bronislaw leaned in on her other side. 'I am already in contact with people, Mother.'

'People?'

'Sshh! There are plenty of us who feel the same way as you.

Compliance is but a shield. We will walk these streets with our heads bowed to their ridiculous orders, but underground...'

He grinned at her and she felt a rush of emotion – pride and relief and, swift on the back of both, fear.

'It will be dangerous.'

He shrugged.

'This is war and it isn't all fought on battlefields. Now come, Mother...' He raised his voice, straining to sound positive as they passed two dark-browed SS men. 'Let us go and find this wonderful new house that our kind masters have granted us.'

The SS looked at him suspiciously but Bronislaw gave them a low bow and they let him pass unmolested. Bartek hurried them on for they only had the cart for two hours before some other poor wretches needed it, and far too soon they were turning into Ostpreussenstrasse – the name scrawled in black paint across the Polish original, Bednarska – and stepping up to the door of someone else's treasured home. Truly, the world had turned upside down.

FIVE

30 APRIL 1940

ANA

Ana waved a cheery goodbye to a thickset mother and the new addition to her considerable brood, then let herself out of their house on Gartenstrasse, picking up her steps as she noticed the pink tinge in the spring sky. It would be dark soon and it didn't do to be out after dark these days, whatever your profession. Tonight was especially worrying for it was Walpurgisnacht, the festival of darkness where evil spirits were said to roam the skies before spring was born at dawn. Ana held no truck with such ancient superstitions, but the German youth did. They were abroad in blood-smeared costumes, bearing knives and miniature guns like parodies of their Nazi fathers, and they needed little excuse for violence. Bartek would be worrying about her, but at least another baby was safely in the world. She pictured the mother's face as she'd put her new son into her arms, and hugged the image close. The Nazis had taken much from them, but they could not take a mother's love.

She thought of her own sons, grown-up now but still as close to her heart as if they were newly out of her womb, and walked even faster. Her family had not, in the end, done badly out of the strange house-swap. Their new apartment had graciously high ceilings and long sash windows facing east to catch the morning sun. It had a large fireplace, a very well-appointed kitchen and even a third bedroom which Bronislaw had delightedly claimed. It wasn't home and she still felt, every day, as if she were treading on another family's memories, but it was warm and safe and all theirs – which was far more than could be said in the cramped Jewish quarter.

She glanced across to the ghetto. Gartenstrasse was fronted by a green area, crossed by the Lodka-bach stream, but on the other side was ugly fencing – high wooden struts topped with twisted barbed wire, guarded at about twenty-metre intervals by rough watchtowers manned with SS guards with long guns. In this south-western corner by the brook, the lighting was poor and the watchtowers further apart so Ana could move closer unnoticed and now she saw, at the end of the street, two giant gates being fixed into place. She gasped and a Polish woman hurrying past with two children in tow paused and looked at her.

'They're sealing them in, poor bastards.'

'Totally?'

The woman nodded.

'No Jews to go in or out. Even the main streets that cross the ghetto are fenced off and they're only allowed to cross them at set times. I heard the other day that the Nazis are making them build bridges so that they don't "taint" the highways.'

'Madness,' Ana muttered.

'Cruel madness,' the woman agreed and then, with a frightened glance to the shadows of the watchtowers, she hurried her children on.

Ana stood there as the skies turned purple above her, staring through the fence to the teeming crowd beyond. She wondered again who was living in her house and her feet carried her of their own volition down to the stream. It was low yet, for April had been unusually dry, and she was able to clear it with a single bound and move right up to the fence, shadowed by a clutch of bushes. Putting out a hand, she felt the rough surface of the cheap timber – a pitiful barrier for the poor souls within. Behind her, two German children dressed in devil-capes whirled past, and she jumped but held her ground, transfixed by the true evil before her.

'Ana?'

The voice was soft and gentle but made her jump far more than the children had. She looked fearfully around and saw a figure emerging from the milling crowd in the ghetto.

'Ester? Ester, is that you?'

'It's me,' she confirmed, stepping up to the fence and putting out her own hand. Ana gladly relinquished the splintered wood and clutched at the young girl's fingers.

'Are you well?'

'Well as we can be. Filip and I are sharing with our parents and Leah, but we have an attic room all to ourselves and it is very... romantic.'

Her voice caught on the last word and Ana's heart turned over.

'It does not sound romantic.'

'As long as Filip is there with me, it is,' Ester said, firm again now.

Ana glanced down the dark lines of the fence.

'They are shutting you in?'

'"Sealing the ghetto", yes. You will not see Jews dirtying the streets of Litzmannstadt any more.'

They both winced at 'Litzmannstadt'. The Germans had renamed Łódź after some German military hero and were slowly removing any traces of the Polish language from the city. It was unpleasant but not nearly as terrible as removing any traces of its Jewish inhabitants.

'Are you... safe?'

Ester's fingers trembled within her own but she gave a brave nod.

'We've set up our own hospitals, so I'm nursing again. And Filip is back at his sewing machine so that's something. Rumkowski says that we must work to survive, for the Germans will only want us while we are useful to them.'

'And then...?' Ester shivered. Ana cursed her foolish tongue and hurriedly added, 'I'm sure there will be plenty of work. The Nazis love their fine uniforms and their wives are mad for nice clothes.'

'So while we make their lives comfortable, they will allow us to hold onto ours? They are most gracious, our rulers.'

'Oh, Ester...' Ana hated the new sharpness in her young friend's voice. Ester was such a gentle, kind girl – but this place, this ghetto, would surely harden even the sweetest of natures. 'What can I do to help?'

'I'm not sure, Ana. We need—'

'Oi, you, Jew girl! Away from the fence.'

Ester leaped back as if already shot.

'I have to go. Stay safe, Ana.'

Then she was off, back into the relative safety of the crowds.

'And you,' the German snarled at Ana, 'away from the fence if you know what's good for you.'

A bullet ricocheted off the ground barely a metre away and, heart pounding, Ana turned and ran down to the brook, losing her footing and landing in the mud. The guard laughed and fired another shot just behind her as she scrambled away. Her ankle was throbbing but it was nothing compared to her heart, screaming with pain for the poor people crammed in at the mercy of these monsters.

SIX

JUNE 1940

ESTER

'Goodnight, Nurse Pasternak.'

'But...'

'Goodnight. Go home. See your family. Sleep.'

Ester let out a sigh she didn't even know she'd been holding in and smiled gratefully at the doctor. It had been a long hard shift, one in a run of many, and she was so tired she couldn't see straight, but leaving was hard. Dr Stern was an elderly man with a shock of white hair protruding from beneath his kippah, and should have been enjoying a well-earned pension, but medical staff were thin on the ground in the ghetto and he'd been called back into service. Ester felt like she was letting him down by putting on her coat and going home, but Dr Stern pressed her arm kindly.

'Think of it like this, Nurse – if you look after yourself, you can better look after them.'

He indicated the rows of people crammed into the ward and Ester nodded sadly. The warm weather had felt like a blessing in the ghetto at first – a chance to get outside and escape the overcrowded houses – but then had come the fleas and with them, typhus. The disease had raged around the streets until every second person had been doubled up with stomach pains and running a fever that could not be controlled in these burning days of June 1940.

There was a permanent queue at the water pumps and some had started digging their own wells. Worst of all was the diarrhoea. The ghetto had no sewage system. Excrement was carried away in carts by the poor people who could get no other work. It had been a reasonable system before the population of the area had been forcibly doubled and typhus had dug into their bowels, but now it was a mess. Everywhere smelt, everywhere was dirty, and that brought yet more disease. Ester had drilled into her own family that they must wash and scrub and disinfect their tiny home and so far they had escaped the worst of it, but disinfectant was running out and with supplies into the ghetto controlled by a central board there was no way of getting more. Letters from outside had recently been banned and an internal currency, 'ghetto marks' – swiftly named 'Rumki', after Rumkowski, their creator – had been introduced, available at crippling exchange rates. Conditions were spiralling downwards and no one seemed to care.

Ester fetched her hat and, resisting the urge to pinch her nose, plunged out into the streets. It was nearly nine o'clock at night and all were inside, on a curfew imposed by Rumkowski's new Jewish police. This internal force was meant to bring a gentler style of law and order than that provided by the Germans, but half the new officers were giddy with their authority and imposed their petty power every bit as ruthlessly as the SS. They had no guns but were brutal with their truncheons and, with networks of family and friends in the ghetto, far more open to corruption. Already it was clear that many of the best supplies coming through the gates were going to a select few and resentments were building.

Ester looked around nervously, glad of the nurse's uniform that served as her pass to be out after curfew. The sun was low in the sky and golden light was slanting down the streets, making them look deceptively pretty. She felt her spirits lift and looked up to the skies, searching for God. He was hard to find these days. The synagogues had all been torn down and, although Rumkowski had managed to get permission for prayer houses to be opened, few attended regularly – they were too cramped and dirty, and people were more afraid of the fleas than of God. Who could blame them, when it seemed that they were in hell already?

Ester shook herself and marched determinedly around the corner, making for her own house before anyone could call out for her. The other day a young man had darted from his doorway to clutch at her arm and beg for her help. His wife had been in labour but the only midwife in the ghetto had been shot in a skirmish over potatoes a few days before and the man had pleaded with Ester to assist.

'I have no training in birthing,' she'd told him.

'But you're a nurse,' he'd countered, looking at her so trustingly that she'd been unable to say no.

Luckily it had not been a hard birthing. His wife's mother had, it transpired, died of typhus just the week before and the poor girl's main problem was her fear. Once Ester had calmed her down, the birthing had gone relatively smoothly and the couple had showered her with thanks and, better still, pressed a fresh loaf of bread upon her. The new father worked in the bakery so was able to 'liberate' small loaves; several had found their way to Ester's door since. She was very grateful, but word had got round of her 'brilliance' as a midwife and she feared being called to a less straightforward delivery. She'd smuggled a note out to Ana via the young Polish boys who dared the SS guns on the other side of the fence to do favours for cash (real cash, not worthless Rumki). She'd begged for a book, or even some basic advice, but had heard nothing yet.

She paused just inside the door, gathering herself. She could hear Ruth and Sarah squabbling in the kitchen over the best way to tenderise beef – as if that mattered these days! – and she leaned against the hallway wall for a moment to compose herself.

'Ester!' Filip came running down the narrow stairs and swept her into his arms. 'You're back.' The joy in his voice was so pure that she felt tears prick at her weary eyes. He reached down and tenderly wiped them away. 'Don't cry, my beautiful girl. All is well, for we are together, are we not?'

He held her so tight against him that it was almost as if they were one. She felt her body flare and threw her arms around him, trying to pull him in even tighter. Her desire for him had not been dampened by their straitened circumstances. If anything, it had become sweeter and more urgent and her only fear was conceiving for, dearly as she would love to bear Filip's child, this hungry, dirty ghetto was no place to do it. Filip agreed and last week he had come home from his tailoring workshop with 'protection'. It had been awkward, but she'd loved him for his care of her and enjoyed their coupling all the more for it.

'Shall we go straight up to the attic?' she whispered.

He kissed her long and hard.

'I wish we could, but our mothers have been waiting for your return all evening. We have meat!'

'Meat?!' Ester's mouth watered instantly and now she understood the bickering. She looked cheekily up at Filip. 'Well in that case...'

'You love a side of beef more than me?'

'I love a single morsel of beef more than you!'

He clutched at his heart.

'I'm wounded.'

She giggled, the woes of the ghetto forgotten.

'A good job then, that I am a nurse and can heal you.'

'Oh yes...?'

'After the meat!'

He groaned, but gave her a quick kiss and, taking her hand, led her through to the kitchen.

'Ester!'

She was greeted with unusual enthusiasm, her arrival heralding the dishing up of whatever was bubbling in a pot on the stove. Everyone took up their places around the table, crammed in so that elbows forever bumped, but tonight no one cared. They all watched, eyes wide, as Ruth carefully ladled out stew, the usual potatoes and turnips made rich and enticing by the addition of juicy lumps of beef. Sarah handed out chunks of bread – it seemed Ester's grateful new father had been by again – and her eyes filled with tears once more at the sight of such a feast.

'How come we have meat?' she asked as she dipped her spoon into the broth and tasted its heavenly richness.

'Your sister's new job is going well,' Ruth told her.

Ester turned to Leah. Her sister, now fifteen, had recently secured a job in the administration offices in Baluty Market. They'd all been nervous about it, for the offices were crawling with Germans, but she'd settled in happily and was at least working in a clean, orderly building without the harsh conditions of many of the workshops Rumkowski was setting up all over the ghetto.

'You were paid in... beef?'

'Not paid, silly!' Leah gave a tinkling laugh. 'I'm paid in bloody Rumki like everyone else.'

'Leah, language!' Ruth snapped, and Leah flushed.

'Sorry, Mother. Everyone swears in the offices.'

'That doesn't mean you should. Standards must be maintained.'

Leah gave Ester a sideways glance and Ester suppressed a giggle, remembering an afternoon when the pair of them had hidden in the laundry cupboard (a room almost as big as the bedroom her poor parents were crammed into now) and tried out all the swear words they knew. There had not been many, but they'd felt deliciously naughty whispered to each other within metres of their scrupulous mother.

'So if you were not paid in beef,' Ester persisted, 'how did you get it?'

Her bowl was emptying horribly fast and she forced herself to slow down. Her father had finished already and was looking at his bowl as if he might pick it up and lick it out if it were not for 'standards'. Filip was savouring every mouthful and his parents were chasing their last morsels around with bread and peering hopefully into the pot – the empty pot. Leah popped her last delicious lump into her mouth with a smile.

'Hans gave it to me.'

Ester froze.

'Hans?'

'He works in my office. Well, runs it really. He's a German but he's quite nice. That's to say, he's not as nasty as the others.'

Ester looked to her mother, who avoided her eyes.

'How old is Hans, Leah?'

'Oh he's old. At least thirty.' Sarah choked on her bread. 'Don't worry – there's nothing to it. He just said that I work very hard and deserved a treat.'

'You work hard?'

'Yes!' Leah was indignant. 'I can, you know, Ester. It's not just you that's capable.'

'I know, I know. It's wonderful of you, Leah, really.'

'Thank you.'

Leah preened and Ester looked at her, realising just how pretty her sister had grown. Her features were soft and delicate and her hair even blonder than Ester's own. Her mother said it was a throwback to a Danish grandparent, but where Ester's was a sort of muddy straw, Leah's shone like gold. She could see why this Hans might choose to bestow his favours upon her.

'What particular work is it Hans was so impressed with?'

She could feel the others at the table tensing but Leah was oblivious.

'He says I type beautifully and he loves watching me doing the filing.'

'Does he?'

'And he says I dress the best in the office – which is nonsense because some of the women have really lovely clothes and I just wear the same thing all the time, but it's nice of him anyway, isn't it?'

Again Ester looked to her mother. Ruth cleared her throat.

'Lovely, dear, but do remember he's a German – keep your distance.'

'Why?' Leah demanded. 'That would be stupid. If he can get us meat, then I should be nice to him, surely? Look at you all – you loved that meal. Why not have it again?'

Ruth wrung her hands but did not seem to be able to find any words.

'It's a matter of price, Leah,' Ester said carefully.

'He did not charge me.'

'Not yet,' she started, but Leah was looking furious and it was a relief to them all when someone banged on the door.

Then fear sucked in.

'Who on earth can that be?' Mordecai asked, pushing himself up. Benjamin rose too but it was Filip who was first to the door. The rest of them looked nervously at each other but he came back with a young lad bearing a small package.

'It's for you Ester,' Filip said. 'From Ana.'

Ester leaped up and took it, offering the lad the last hunk of bread as a thank you. He tore into it right there, clearly eager to eat it before he returned to his pals in the shadows of the ghetto.

Ester opened the package, delighted to find a small volume enti-
tled *Practical Midwifery*. There was a note too and, reading it
swiftly, she glanced to the clock.

'Ana says she will be on the other side of the fence at ten
o'clock. I must go.'

'But it's after curfew,' Ruth protested. Ester indicated the
uniform she was still wearing, but Ruth shook her head. 'It's not
safe.'

'Neither is giving birth with no midwife,' Ester told her. 'I
need advice if I'm to help the mothers in the ghetto.'

'It's not your job.'

'It has to be someone's, and why not me? Besides, if we get
more grateful fathers, perhaps we will need less grateful
Germans.'

Ruth looked pained but, with a glance to Leah, gave a
sharp nod.

'I'll go with her,' Filip said.

'You have no pass,' Ester protested.

'And you have no escort. I'll go with you.'

Ester smiled gratefully at him, for the skies were dark now
and the ghetto far too full of shadows. Taking Filip's arm, she
thanked her family for her delicious meal and headed back out
of the door.

'Are we ever going to get to our attic tonight?' she asked
sadly. Her legs were almost buckling with tiredness and her
eyes stung, so desperate were they to close, but at least her
stomach was full. Gathering her resolve she forced herself
south, towards the place where she'd met Ana before. Her
uniform was pale in the moonlight and she gratefully accepted
the coat Filip had snatched off its hook to shield her from the
attentions of the guards.

As she reached the designated spot, she noted several SS in
the nearest tower, sitting around a flickering lantern with a
bottle of vodka and a pack of cards, thankfully far more inter-

ested in each other than in two nurses meeting in the darkness below.

'Ana?' she whispered through the fence.

'Ester?' The older lady emerged from a bush and reached out a hand. Briefly, they touched fingers. 'You got the book?'

'Yes. Thank you so much.'

'It will tell you all the basics, but midwifery is in the feel. It's about reading the mother, keeping her calm, working out when she is moving into a new stage.'

'A new stage?' Ester asked, lost already. Filip was standing a few steps away, keeping watch, but they did not have long. How was she to learn a skill that took dedicated women two years in a few snatched sentences through a fence?

'The mother is likely to be most agitated and feel the most pain just before it is time for her to bear down. That is when you must check to see if the baby's head is crowning – showing. If it is, she can push. Do not let her do so unless she is feeling the cramps. In between, she must rest. It could take five minutes or five hours – usually something in the middle. The key is not to panic.'

'The mother or me?'

'Both,' Ana said with a low chuckle. 'If Baby is slow to come out you can help him or her with your hands, but be very gentle and watch for the cord – it must not be round Baby's neck.'

'Or...?'

'Or it might strangle them.'

Ester swallowed.

'Ana, I'm not sure I can do this. Or if I must, I wish I could work with you. I'm not a midwife. What if I make things worse?'

The older lady's hand closed around hers, warm and sure.

'You will not make things worse, Ester. If there are going to be problems, they will happen anyway and you might be able to ease them. Babies are good at being born and it is a blessed miracle every time.'

Ester swallowed.

'If a new baby is such a miracle, then losing it must be the greatest tragedy of all.'

Ana smiled at her in the gloom.

'You must not let that stop you, child. This is a good and brave thing you are doing and God will bless you for it.'

'Your god or mine?'

Again the chuckle.

'Both. He is the same figure, we just have different ways of listening to him.'

To the side, the SS guards let out a roar as, presumably, someone won a hand at cards, and they both shrank back.

'You should go,' Ester said to Ana. 'It's not safe being this near us.'

'Not true,' her friend shot back. 'It is not safe being this near *them*.'

She glared at the guards but drew back all the same and Ester felt a rush of sorrow. There was so much to say, so much to learn. She stood staring at the space the midwife had vacated, but then Filip pulled her into his arms and hurried her behind the buildings at the edge of the ghetto as a guard staggered past. Heart pounding, she pressed gratefully against him until the street was clear again.

'I love you,' she whispered, gazing up into his dear, kind face.

'I love you too. Now – how about that attic?'

Ester nodded eagerly and together they traced their way home. Ester thought of babies and wished she could give herself to him, womb and all, but this was not the time for a child and it was enough, for now, just to have each other.

SEVEN

CHRISTMAS EVE 1940

ANA

'Stille nacht, heilige nacht.'

The carol drifting up from the street below Ana's apartment was being sung in German but still sounded beautiful. Going to the window, she peered down at the singers, their breath white in the frosty air as if the music were actually taking shape around them, and sighed. They looked so innocent as they gazed up at the giant Christmas tree set at the end of the street. These were not Nazis but normal German people who had been making their life peacefully in Łódź before the soldiers had marched in and told them they were superior to everyone else. Who didn't want to hear that?

It didn't mean she forgave them though. They might not be the ones changing the city's name, and making new laws, and pushing anyone different behind barbed wire, but they were not standing up to those that were. They were not saying 'No, this is wrong, this is not Christian.' Oh no! Even as they sang their songs of peace, they were quite happy to be on the right side of a war that was going to deliver them the world, no matter what it cost anyone else. Grinding her teeth, Ana turned away from the hypocrites and back to her own family.

Her heart squeezed as she saw the laden table. They had been fasting all day, but now the traditional feast awaited. The table was covered with hay beneath a white cloth, to symbolise the stable. Twelve dishes were laid out to represent the apostles and her mouth watered as she saw the beetroot soup, the delicate pierogi, the herring in cream and, at the centre of it all, the classic fried carp. The special fish had been hard to find this year but yesterday Jakub had come running home saying that a friend of his friend's father was selling some out of a tub at the back of Karolew (now officially Karlshof) and Bartek had gone running. They had cherished their 'catch' in the bathtub last night and now here it was, golden and delicious at the centre of their table.

The boys were dressed in their Sunday suits and looking so handsome and strong that she could not resist hugging every one, though Jakub protested that she was ruffling his hair. Working at the printing press was making him vain, perhaps because of the girls in the typing pool, and she hoped he might start courting. It was not an ideal time for a wedding – had poor Ester and Filip not proved that? – but all joy must be snatched at and she kissed him again. He surrendered graciously enough and moved to the table.

'It looks amazing, Mama.'

'It looks a large amount of food.'

The table seemed almost ridiculously opulent after the privations of the last year. Rationing was in place and the Poles were always last in the queue behind the pushy Germans, so their diet had been meagre. Even so, she knew from her occasional stolen conversations with Ester that things were far, far worse in the ghetto. The people in there were living on rotten potatoes and the vegetables considered unworthy of being dispatched to the Reich. With the temperatures well below zero, it was not enough and, even if it had been, there was a dire shortage of fuel with which to cook so they were having to eat them raw. Children trekked out to Marysin, the open area in the north of the ghetto, to dig in the soil for stray lumps of coal and people were so desperate for warmth that they were burning their furniture. Ana looked uncomfortably to the golden carp.

'It's Christmas, Mother,' Jakub said. 'And we've not eaten all day.'

'True,' Ana agreed, trying not to spoil the moment. She had put so much effort into this meal that it would be a shame to waste it with regret. Even so... 'We have, at least, been eating all week.'

Jakub froze, halfway to his seat.

'You are thinking of the Jews?'

Ana nodded and Alekzander, her most serious child, stepped up at her side.

'I see them when I go through on the trams,' he said.

Recently the Nazis had brought a load of German students into the hospitals and Zander had been told there was only space for him to work there three days a week, so he had taken a second job as a ticket collector on the trams. Bartek had moaned that it was below him, but Zander said it 'got him about the place'. Ana had a feeling he had friends in the Resistance and was quietly proud but had not dared to ask more.

'Are conditions as bad as they say?' Bartek asked his middle son.

'Worse. The streets are permanently dirty and if work groups try to clean them, the water freezes and makes it treacherous for any but the sturdiest to walk. And few are sturdy now. I see the food deliveries arriving – carts of vegetables so foul you wouldn't feed them to your cattle, but the poor people clamour for their ration before it is even unloaded. The typhus has gone with the cold weather, but TB is rampant. Every street rings with wracking coughs. And worse...' He looked around furtively, although they were alone at home. 'I hear whispers that this isn't the end of it, that they are sending some Jews to their deaths.'

'They are killing them?' Jakub gasped.

'With gas, yes. It makes me furious that I, a doctor – or nearly one – am stuck taking the tickets of stuck-up Germans as they ride between the fences keeping these people caged like animals, when I could be in there helping them. It's cruel – no, worse than cruel. It's barbaric.'

Ana squeezed his arm. This was her fault. She had brought up the ghetto and now they were standing around their beautiful Christmas meal feeling guilty.

'Shall we sit?' she suggested.

They did so but even Jakub was slow to his seat and they all looked awkwardly to the sixth place, traditionally set at the Christmas Eve table for any passing traveller who might need succour.

'We should offer aid,' Bronislaw said. 'I can get medicines from the hospital if we can find a way to smuggle them in.'

'Ester might help,' Ana said. 'If it's not too dangerous.'

'What's *too* dangerous?' Zander asked.

Ana swallowed.

'Might they shoot her?'

'They might.' He bit at his lip. 'But not if she's careful. I know people.'

It was said so low Ana did not think she'd heard it at first.

'People inside the ghetto?'

'People inside and out. Good people who want to help.'

'And to stick a finger up at the bastard Nazis,' Jakub added.

'Jakub!' Bartek protested.

'Well they do. Don't you?'

Ana saw her husband shift at the opposite end of the table

and watched him intently. The conversation was taking a risky turn and suddenly their family meal felt like so much more.

'Not so much "stick a finger" up at them,' Bartek said, 'as, as... beat them into oblivion.'

Ana sucked in a breath; rarely had she heard her peaceable husband speak so fiercely. He looked at her, his eyes a swirl of emotions – fear, perhaps, and pride and a need for approval. She smiled at him.

'Beat them out of Poland at least.'

He snatched at this.

'Exactly, my love. Out of Poland, out of Germany, out of everywhere that decent people are trying to make a simple living. There is no need for all this... this hate. Did the Lord Jesus not say, "Love thy neighbour"? Did he not exhort us to be like the Samaritan and help those in trouble, whatever their creed? Was He not born to bring peace into the world?'

They all looked at each other. Between them the soup glowed ruby red and the carp shone like gold. So many riches on their table while just a few streets away others were starving. Jakub leaped up.

'Oh, come on – we all know what we must do.' They looked to him, the strapping eighteen-year-old who just moments ago had been rubbing his hands at the feast before them.

'What?' Ana asked, dazed.

'We must pack up this food and take it to the ghetto. It's Christmas, a time for giving, and there have never been people more in need. Besides,' he added, as they all stared at him in admiration, 'I won't enjoy it now anyway.'

Bartek leaped up too and hugged his youngest son.

'You are a good boy. You are all good boys. Come – even the SS won't shoot at us on Christmas Eve.'

· · ·

He was right. The guards were at a minimum in the watchtowers and those on duty, softened perhaps by the carols still filling the streets of Litzmannstadt, looked the other way as they approached the fence with their bundles of food. They had made up as many as they could with a taste of all the dishes. The soup had had to stay but they'd opened the box of chocolates sent by Bartek's parents to add one into every parcel and make up the twelve treats. Silly really, when they'd been sending it to Jews who would not know their Christian tradition, but it had felt important all the same. When they'd had them ready, they'd stood in a circle as Bartek had blessed them and then headed nervously out into the night.

They were not alone. Many others were making for the wired fences with similar parcels and Ana was warmed by the love she felt from the group forming outside the ghetto. This was, surely, what Christmas was all about and she was glad that their precious carp was going into needier bellies than her own. She noticed Alekzander saying hello to a number of people and watched carefully, but as they reached the fence, people crowded to the other side, pressing desperate hands through and she had to pay attention to distribution. All too quickly their parcels were gone.

'Ana!' Ester came running up to the fence. 'I'm so glad to see you. I'm on my way back from a birthing, a hard one. The baby was back-to-back with the mother.' Ana winced in sympathy. 'But I managed to help turn her on the way out and all was well.'

'That's amazing.'

Ester beamed.

'A Christmas miracle,' she suggested. 'Or a Hanukkah one on this side of the fence – if only we had the candles to mark it. Still, we have food now and God will smile to see it, thank you.'

She gestured to the people scurrying away to their homes with their food parcels and Ana felt awful.

'Oh Ester, I'm so sorry. I have no food left.'

The girl waved an easy hand.

'Don't worry, we have some. Leah has... contacts in the offices and brings us enough to get by.'

'Contacts?'

Ester flushed.

'A German officer has taken to her. I do not like it, but so far he has just given her food and, in truth, things would go worse were she to refuse. All we can do is pray God will watch over her.'

She glanced to the starry skies and Ana took her hands.

'I will pray for you.'

'Thank you.'

Ester smiled at her but for once, dearly as she trusted in God, it did not feel enough. Ana spotted Zander talking earnestly with three other young men and drew in a deep breath.

'And we will help you.'

'How?'

Ana swallowed.

'I'm not sure yet. Could we get you out – you and Filip?'

Ester shook her head.

'They need me in the hospital and Filip is doing well in his workshop and keeping his father safe there. We couldn't leave our parents, or Leah.'

Ana nodded. She understood but that didn't mean she liked it.

'We'll do our best for you, I promise. Keep an eye out for my boy.' She indicated Zander. 'He works on the trams and has ways to get things into the ghetto. Food, fuel, medicines.'

Ester's eyes lit up as if she had just listed the finest goods in Christendom and Ana felt a flash of guilt – what if she was making promises she could not keep?

'Anything you can do would be appreciated,' Ester said, 'but will it not be too dangerous?'

'What's *too* dangerous?' Ana said lightly, echoing her son but, as if hearing her, the SS guards suddenly decided enough was enough and picked up their guns. The shots went into the air but it sent the crowd flying for cover and, with a tiny squeeze of her hand, Ester was gone. And Ana's mind was made up.

Later, they sat together over the beetroot soup, a quieter, more solemn family.

'I want to meet your friends, Zander,' Ana said.

'And I,' Bartek agreed.

'And I.'

'And I.'

The family looked at each other. Ana reached out her hands and they responded instantly, joining their own in a circle.

'We must be very, very certain of this,' Ana told them. 'If we join the Resistance, we may lose our lives.'

'And if we do not,' Bartek replied, 'we may lose our souls.'

It was no competition. Together they bowed their heads to God and swore themselves to the fight against evil.

EIGHT

OCTOBER 1941

ESTER

'Room, please – you have to give me some room. This woman is giving birth!'

Ester used her most commanding voice (something she seemed to be getting better at every day) and the crowd in the house moved back. Not nearly enough but, to be fair to them, there wasn't much more space to move into. She stamped her foot.

'Some of you are going to have to leave. You cannot all live here and the sooner you realise that, the better.'

The new arrivals looked at her but their eyes were clouded with exhaustion and Ester could see that they weren't understanding the situation. These were well-dressed people clutching fancy luggage who could not comprehend the deprivations of the Litzmannstadt ghetto even as they stood in the middle of it. They were hanging around, clinging onto their rights and waiting for some nice person with a clipboard to sort them out. It had been the same all this first week of October 1941. Rumkowski had announced that they were going to be having 'a few new arrivals' from smaller ghettos in the east that were being disbanded, but 'a few' had been Rumki-speak for thousands.

The poor people were being shoved off overcrowded trains at the siding up in the Marysin district and marched into the centre of the ghetto where the housing bureau was so overrun that most of the time they were simply told to go and find themselves somewhere to live. Needless to say, they all headed for the nicest houses, like the one this poor woman was trying to give birth in, only to find them – like this one – bursting at the seams. Those already in residence were not keen to give up their meagre living space and many fights had ensued.

At home Ester and Filip had been forced to move his parents into their precious attic and although Filip had rigged up an old curtain between their beds, it was still horribly embarrassing to sleep so close together. There was no need for protection any more, for no night was a good night for lovemaking when your parents-in-law could hear your every breath.

Behind her, the labouring mother cried out in pain and Ester lost patience.

'Right! You five, take that room there. The two of you already in it are going to have to move upstairs. I know, I know, but we're all sharing now so you'll just have to make the best of it. The rest of you, I'd get out there before all the other houses are snapped up too. Go on – go!'

She made small shooing gestures with her hands as if they were recalcitrant sheep and they began shuffling towards the door and off to hassle other poor residents.

'Good.'

Ester turned her back on the stragglers and paid attention to the real job in hand. The poor mother had been in labour for over a day and was growing weaker, but Baby was staying firmly inside.

'Actually, wait a moment!' She shot back to the last people

and grabbed a woman holding a child by each hand. 'Do you have food?'

'No.'

The woman tried to pull away but Ester had a firm hold.

'Yes you do. No mother travels without food.'

'We need it.'

'As much as she does?'

Ester pointed to the mother, who was laid on the bed, her huge belly a grotesque contrast to her emaciated form. The woman sighed.

'Not as much as that, no.'

She opened her bag and took out a pastry. It was squashed but perfect.

'Thank you,' Ester said. 'Thank you so much.'

The woman shifted.

'Do you need help?'

'You're a midwife?!'

She put up her hands.

'I'm afraid not, but I've pulled more nieces and nephews into the world than I can count.'

'Then, yes!' Ester cried. 'Yes please.'

'Come on then. I'm Martha, by the way.'

'Ester. Very, very pleased to meet you.'

Martha shook her hand, then shouted down the street after her husband: 'Noah, bring the baby back. We've a job to do.'

Noah looked uncertain for a moment but was clearly used to obeying his wife and dutifully turned back. He was a handsome, broad-shouldered man with a mop of dark curls and, grinning at the frightened father-to-be, he took him off into the kitchen with his three children.

'Don't worry, lad,' Ester heard him say in a gruff voice. 'Women are good at this stuff. Got any beer? No? None? What, not in this whole place?'

Ester didn't know whether to laugh or cry at the poor man's

naivety. Beer was the least of their worries in the ghetto. They'd heard tell that ration books were on their way, but they would be a joke as there wasn't enough food to go round – or clothes, or blankets or fuel. It was only thanks to Ana and her family that Ester had managed to get supplies for the hospital as the Nazis had no interest in providing medicine for Jews.

They had a system going where Ana and her son Bronislaw got basic medicines from kind doctors in the hospitals in free Litzmannstadt and Zander flung the packages up to kids posted on the bridges as he went past in the trams. If a guard was looking there was nothing Zander could do; some of the kids waited hours for him to come round at a safe – or *safer* – time. Ester knew what a risk the Kaminski family were taking to help those stuck in the ghetto and blessed them for it. Without them and others like them, the suffering in here would be even worse, especially with winter starting to bite.

For now, though, she had to focus on the job in hand so, praying Noah was right about women, she fed Martha's pastry to the mother morsel by morsel. The sugar seemed to kick in almost immediately and the young woman pushed herself up on the bed and stared at them, wild-eyed.

'Get this wretch out of me, ladies!'

Her spirit was strong, but her body still weak. She pushed the head out and Ester and Martha shouted in triumph, but that effort seemed to have been too much for her and she fell back on the bed, apparently spent.

'The cord,' Martha cried. 'The cord is round its neck.'

Ester recalled Ana's words from the other side of the fence and knew she had to act fast. Kneeling down, she left Martha to try and talk some energy back into the poor mother, and eased her hands as carefully as she could up and around the slippery body. Thankfully, the baby was small and she was able to painstakingly unwrap the cord but it still needed out.

'Push,' she cried as she saw the belly pulse. 'One more push and you can hold Baby in your arms.'

With a great cry, the mother bore down. Ester pulled as hard as she dared on the fragile body, praying they were not too late, but then, with a gush of fluid, she was out.

'It's a girl! You have a beautiful baby girl.'

The mother gave a happy sob, but Ester looked in horror at the child, who was limp and blue and not in the slightest bit beautiful.

'Here!'

Martha was at her side in a moment. Seizing the baby and turning it upside down, she gave it three sharp slaps on its bottom. Ester gasped in horror, thinking the woman had gone mad, but magically the tiny creature sucked in a breath and let out a long, blissfully loud wail.

'You did it.' Ester stared at Martha as she cradled the baby in her arms.

'I did it,' Martha agreed, sounding every bit as stunned.

'You didn't know it would work?'

She shrugged.

'I saw a midwife do it once with our Johanna's middle boy, but I haven't done it myself. Even so, I couldn't see that we had much choice but to try. Now, what do we wrap Baby in?'

Ester apologetically handed over an old shirt. Martha frowned but then expertly swaddled the crying child and handed her to her mother. The baby rooted for the breast and, to Ester's amazement, seemed to find some milk. She sighed in relief; the resilience of the female body always awed her.

'Thank you so much,' she said to her new helper as the afterbirth slid out. 'You have a job.'

'But no house,' Martha replied.

Ester sighed. 'You'd better come with me.'

They still had a living room after all, and how could they be mean enough to hold onto space to sit at leisure when people were sleeping in the streets?

On the way across the city, they had to pass through Baluty Market and Ester noticed a crowd gathered in the big square. A lectern had been set up at the front and she could see Chaim Rumkowski mounting it and readying himself to speak. A few people jeered, others cheered, most just stood there, numbly awaiting whatever new pronouncement was to come. Ester watched the Eldest of the Jews, trying to work him out. On the surface, Rumkowski looked like a kindly old man, but it was hard to ignore the fact that he was immaculately dressed and had cheeks plump enough to suggest he was not sharing his people's many privations.

He had driven the opening of more and more workshops, stating over and over that work meant life. It seemed that he might have a point, for the leisured new arrivals had been kicked from their less purposeful ghettos, while the Litz-mannstadt one still stood. Ester was grateful as, despite the tough conditions, Filip was glad to be wielding his needle. True, he was having to use it to make warm, smartly trimmed Wehrmacht uniforms while all their own clothes slowly wore away, but he was good at it and both he and his dear friend Tomaz had been promoted to 'special workers' which meant that most vital of all privileges – extra soup at lunchtime. That, in turn, meant that Filip could give up his evening meal for their mothers who, as non-workers, were on official rations barely sufficient to feed a mouse.

Filip's father was working alongside his son and bravely claiming the large workshop reminded him of his days as an apprentice. Mordecai had secured a treasured job peeling vegetables in a factory kitchen that enabled him to sneak a few extras back home; with that and Leah's gifts from the worrying

Hans, the family were getting by. Others were far less fortunate and seeing their leader standing smart and well fed before them was unlikely to make them content. Ester moved to push her way round, but Martha held her back.

'What's he saying?'

'I don't know, but it won't be good news. It never is.'

But the crowd was too great to get past and Ester was forced to stand there as Rumkowski cleared his throat self-importantly into the microphone.

'Ladies and gentlemen – good news.'

'See,' Martha said, nudging Ester.

'I, the Elder of the Jews, have seen your struggle for space and am glad to report that I have found a solution. Very soon there will be opportunities for people to leave Litzmannstadt and move to camps in the countryside. The Germans have told me of one they are calling Auschwitz where there is more space, cleaner air and wholesome outdoor work.' The crowd looked uncertainly at each other and began muttering. Rumkowski raised his voice. 'And more food.'

That captured their attention.

'How much more?' someone demanded.

'Plenty. You will be working on farms, so it will come direct from the fields.'

'Not rotting and trampled like it is here?'

Rumkowski gave a tight smile.

'Exactly. The first trains will leave in two days' time. Report to the central offices tomorrow to reserve your place. First come, first served.'

'Why not now?' someone demanded, and others joined him. The crowd started to push forward and Ester seized the chance to move around them and escape the square.

'That sounds good, do you not think?' Martha said to her husband.

Noah was less sure.

'I've heard about these labour camps,' he said, raking his hand through his dark curls, 'and they sound like dark, dangerous places. It's more building roads and crushing rocks than it is tending pretty vegetables – and that's if you're lucky. I say we wait.'

Ester agreed with him. The ghetto might be cramped and under-provided but it was safe – for now.

'Here we are,' she said brightly, guiding Martha into their street, 'home.'

It was a poor word for it, with one set of strangers already moved into Filip's parents' room and now another family to join them. Everyone's faces fell when she walked in with her five charges, but they soon perked up when Noah opened a case and produced several tins of beans and, unbelievably, a bar of chocolate.

'A feast!' Filip cried, ushering them in, and Ester loved him for his kind welcome.

'Martha helped me birth a tricky babe today,' she told him, as everyone budged up to try and make room for the newcomers. 'I thought it was going to die, truly I did, but then she—'

Her words dried up as Leah came flying into the room, hair all over the place and eyes red-rimmed. Ruth rushed to her.

'Leah, what is it? What's happened?'

'Ha... Ha... Hans,' Leah stuttered out.

Their father was on his feet instantly, fists clenched.

'What did he do to you?'

Leah gulped in big breaths, as if she couldn't find enough goodness in the air.

'He tried to kiss me. He said he was going away on second-ment to Berlin and he'd miss me. He said would I miss him, so of course I said I would because I had to be polite. But then he pushed me up against the shelves in the supply cupboard and tried to kiss me. I pushed him away. I don't know how because he's much bigger than me, but I must have caught him by surprise. I think he thought I'd be hon... honoured that he wanted me. But I wasn't. I was just scared, so I pushed him and he tipped backwards and fell down. Hard. He was furious. He leaped up to come after me, but I was round him and back down the corridor to the main office before he could grab me.'

They all stared at her, horrified.

'Is he a senior officer?' Benjamin asked.

'Who cares?' Mordecai roared. 'Senior or not, I'll bust his jaw for this.'

'You will not,' Ruth told him crisply, 'or who knows what will happen to us all.'

'But he's going to Berlin, right?' Ester asked, trying to stay calm. 'You said that, Leah, didn't you? You said he was going on secondment to Berlin?'

Leah nodded.

'He is. Tonight.'

'So that's all right then.'

'For now.'

'What do you mean?' Everyone was staring at Leah. Poor Martha looked more bewildered than ever and her children's eyes were as wide as if they'd been brought to live in a zoo. 'What do you mean?' Ester repeated.

Leah swallowed.

'He collared me again when I was leaving at the end of the day. I was trying to stick with the other girls but he said he "needed a word" and I had no choice but to go.'

'What did he do?' Mordecai growled.

'Nothing,' Leah said hastily. 'I didn't let him, Papa. I didn't—'

'It's not your fault, Leah,' Ruth said, stroking her hair. 'None of this is your fault.'

That was true, Ester thought guiltily. Leah was too young to know better, but Ester had realised what this Hans' intentions were. She and her mother had both realised, and probably her father besides, but they'd all been too busy gorging themselves on German beef to warn her off.

'What did he say, Leah?' Filip asked gently.

Leah looked to him, her lip quivering.

'He said I was a, a "nasty prude" and a, a...' She blushed.

'It doesn't matter,' Ester told her hastily. 'Whatever it was, it isn't true.'

Leah looked at her gratefully.

'But then – then he told me I should just wait till he got back from Berlin in the new year. He said then he'd be a senior officer and he'd, he'd "Germanise" me. What does that mean, Ester? How would he do that?'

Ester grabbed her sister in a hug, her eyes scanning the others for something to say. Sarah stepped forward.

'Probably just that he'll change your name, Leah, like they've done to Łódź.'

Leah stared at her for a long moment but then she shook her head.

'No. I felt him hold me. I felt his breath on me. It's more than that, isn't it?' She looked to Ester. 'Isn't it?!'

Ester clutched her even tighter.

'It's more than that,' she agreed, realising again how horribly fast her fifteen-year-old sister was growing up. She'd had a lucky escape today but if this Hans came back, she was on borrowed time. 'I think we need to get you out of here.'

'The transports?' Martha suggested tentatively.

Ester looked at her. She wanted to believe Rumkowski about the space and the fresh air and the good food but it just didn't sound right.

'We've got time,' she said. 'Let's wait, ask Bronislaw to keep his ears to the ground for reports on these camps and then decide. Yes?'

'Yes,' everyone agreed.

'I don't want to leave you,' Leah said, clasping at Ester. 'I don't want to go to a camp.'

'No one's going to a camp,' Ester assured her. 'Now come on, let's eat.'

Martha tentatively picked up the beans but, for the first time since the ghetto was sealed up, no one had any appetite.

NINE

JANUARY 1942

ANA

Ana let herself out of the beautiful house just off Piotrkowska Street (she would never call it Adolf-Hitler-Strasse), clutching the wad of marks she'd been given as a tip and trying to focus on the beauty of what had been a really lovely birthing – healthy twins, born to a strong young woman, already mother to a two-year-old son. The toddler had come running into the room once it was all over, so sweetly rapt with his matching pair of sisters that it would have been hard for anyone not to have been moved. The fact that they were Germans, newly arrived from Austria and handed this house because the proud new father was an eminent professor of chemistry, should not matter.

But it did.

Ana looked up to the warmly lit windows, glowing in the snowy dusk. Not so long ago this house had been the treasured home to hardworking Jews who were now cowering with ten others in the ghetto, possibly in Ana's own home. It was hard not to look at the many German families playing in the newly created parks, spilling out of the newly financed theatres, and filling the newly expanded schools, without feeling bitter. Sometimes, despite her fifty-six years, Ana wanted to throw herself onto the ground in the middle of this wretched 'Adolf-Hitler-Strasse', pound her hands like a toddler and scream, 'It's not fair!'

Tonight's mother had been charming. There had been little, beyond the usual obligatory picture of the weasel-faced Fuhrer, to indicate any strong Nazi views, and her husband had been a quiet, earnest gentleman. They'd been delighted she could speak fluent German and had even, between contractions, asked her all about the history of their new city. They were just a family who had got lucky, but she bet they never went north to see the suffering of the people who had, in the harshest possible way, given them this life. Almost she'd said something, almost she'd asked them if they thought it was fine for some to suffer while others lived in luxury but was that not an age-old question?

Not like this.

Never before had the line between the haves and the have-nots been so stark. Jewish wealth was being systematically stolen for the Reich and now there were rumours that their lives were being stolen too. Ana shivered and drew her coat closer around her as snow began to fall. It was already thick on the ground and had been for some weeks. The Germans had seen in the new year of 1942 eating sugary doughnuts and spiced gluhwein in the 'pretty' whiteness before hurrying inside to their big fires and warm meals. Meanwhile in the ghetto, the Jewish people were burning their beds to try and keep their very bones from freezing. Ignorance was no excuse.

Ana felt a surge of hatred so overpowering that it almost knocked her off her feet. A couple approached, the woman in a big fur coat and the man in SS uniform. As they passed, he said something that set her off in a delighted peal of laughter and Ana felt a sudden, desperate urge to throw herself onto his broad back, pull on his blond hair and scream at him to open his ignorant blue eyes and see what evil he was imposing on the world.

Her breath came hard and fast, clouding in the cold air, and she put a hand to the rosary at her waist, fumbling with the beads as she muttered a Hail Mary beneath her breath. For once the familiar prayer did not soothe her. God forgive her, but she was churning with hate.

Disorientated, she looked desperately around and, to her relief, saw coloured light spilling welcomingly onto the snow just metres in front of her. St Stanislaus' cathedral! Closing her eyes, she stilled her breath and sent a thank you up to God, who had seen her despair and was here for her. Clutching her medical bag, she hurried up the steps, picturing Ester and Filip sat here eating their lunches last year. She'd seen them occasionally as she'd passed on her duties, and watched the shy progress of their romance as they'd got oh-so-slowly closer and closer to each other. The pair were growing into fine young people and she just hoped they could keep getting supplies into the ghetto until all this madness was somehow over.

The church was suffused with calm and Ana genuflected gratefully and slipped into a pew to pray. A monk was intoning Psalm 37 and as she dipped her head and let the music swirl around her, he reached verse 11: 'But the meek will inherit the land and enjoy peace and prosperity.'

'Oh Mary, Mother of God, let that be right,' she murmured. 'Look kindly on those who serve, who help each other, who do not go out and try and impose their warped, cruel, *evil* view on the world...'

She cut herself off, trying to focus on the blessed meek and not the cruel oppressors, but it was hard. Opening her eyes, she looked up to the altar, trying to draw calm from the beautiful

House of God. Here, at least, there were no soldiers, for the Nazis believed only in their damned Führer. Their religion was themselves; they worshipped their own misplaced sense of superiority. They...

'The meek...' she told herself out loud and then flushed as someone in the next pew frowned. Goodness, what must she look like – an old lady muttering away to herself? She'd have to be careful or they'd cart her off to an institution and then the Nazis would 'euthanise' her – a word carefully chosen to hide the ultimate cruelty beneath a veneer of care.

'How dare they...?'

She was muttering again. She should go home, but it wasn't home, was it? Restless, she pushed herself out of the pew and went slowly to the altar, gazing up at the suffering Christ above. Had he really died for man, just to have him turn into this? It must be so very disappointing. Heart aching, Ana turned away, furious with herself for not finding the peace that God had so clearly intended when he had shone His light onto the snow outside. And that's when she noticed the small group.

They were standing in the Lady Chapel, murmuring angrily – just as she had been doing a moment before – and they were clutching a copy of a newspaper. Ana squinted in the candlelight and saw the name: *The Polish Fortnightly Review*, an underground paper. She hastened forward. The group looked up guiltily but then a young man Ana recognised as one of Zander's friends stepped forward and smiled at her.

'Mrs Kaminski, welcome.'

The others murmured greetings, but the paper was gone, no doubt behind one of their backs. She moved closer.

'May I see?'

'Sorry?'

'May I see the newspaper?'

'What—'

'Just show me it, please. I want to know what's happening in the world – what's *really* happening, I mean, not just what the Nazis choose to tell us.'

The youngsters looked at each other and Zander's friend shrugged.

'We can trust her. She's working with the ghetto group.'

Ana felt a tiny flush of pride then told herself not to be foolish. This wasn't about her; it was about the people they were trying to save.

'It's not nice though,' a young woman said, looking at her with concern.

Ana folded her arms.

'Young lady, I pull gunky, bloodied babies out of women every day of the week. I don't need "nice".'

The girl blinked and then let out a half laugh and produced the forbidden newspaper. Ana took it as one of them moved to guard the chapel entrance.

'Gas vans at Chelmno,' the headline screamed and went on to describe, with eye-witness reports and grainy photographs, how the Jews sent on the transports out of Litzmannstadt were being herded into sealed vans and gassed with carbon monoxide from the engines. These killing chambers were then conveniently driven deep into the forest where the bodies were tipped into pits and burned to ash before being scattered into the river. Human life, cast away on the stream in less than an hour from start to finish. It was too hideous to conceive.

'Can it be true?' she gasped, looking around the group.

Their faces told her that they were struggling to believe it too, but this wasn't just one person's scandalmongering. The village of Chelmno was being used as a centre for this barbaric operation and, while many were scared witless by the Nazis who had brought guns into their homes, a few were daring to get away and speak out. Their stories were all the same: gangs of Jews brought in by train, barns used to keep them in and then the vans – the killing vans.

'They're exterminating them,' the young woman whispered. 'Efficiently and systematically exterminating them, and it's the same at this place they call Auschwitz. There are *no* labour camps, Mrs Kaminski. Or if there are, the people of Łódź are not being sent there. They're being sent to their death.'

Ana crossed herself and looked back to Christ, tormented on the cross. This, then, was why God had brought her into his sacred cathedral – not to find peace, but purpose. She thought of all the Jews in the ghetto, putting their hands up to go and farm for the Reich and finding themselves herded to their deaths. Unfair didn't come close to describing it, neither did cruel or barbaric or even evil. There were no words for what was happening here.

Ester's face popped into Ana's head. Her friend had grown thin with a lack of food and an excess of worry, but her eyes still burned brightly as she worked to help her people. Ana had tried, several times, to convince the girl to let the Resistance help her to escape but she was always adamant that she had a job to do in the ghetto. Ana was sure she was right; those poor people needed brave, good souls like Ester to keep them going. But what did that do to Ester?

They were considering sending her sister, Leah, out at least. Ana recalled Ester saying something about the transports and a threatening SS officer. She'd not paid enough attention, too focused on Ester's questions about midwifery, but she did now. She had to get word to her friend. She had to tell her not, on any account, to let her sister get on those trains, and she had to figure out another way to get Leah out of the ghetto, whatever it cost.

'Thank you,' she said to the young Resistance workers, pressing all their hands in turn. 'Thank you for your work. It is vital, *vital*. These Nazis think they have won with their tanks and their guns and their insidious brand of hate, but we will undermine them with patience, quiet strength and care. May the Lord bless you all.'

And then she was gone, out of the cathedral with a last, grateful bow to God, and home to Bartek and the boys to somehow find a plan to get the Jews away from their persecutors.

TEN

FEBRUARY 1942

ESTER

'Parcel for you, Nurse.'

'For me, but I didn't...'

Ester cut herself off at the urgent look in the orderly's eyes, and took the package. Trying to look routine, she walked briskly down the corridor and into the storeroom where, door safely locked behind her, she prised it open. Inside were the usual medicines but then a large letter. Ester opened it, turned the strange, stiff piece of paper over, and gasped in horror.

'Death Certificate' it read across the top, and just below it, in the firm, barely legible hand of a doctor, was a name: Leah Kaminski.

'Leah!' she gasped, fighting to make sense of this.

Her sister had been at home this morning, getting ready to go to work. She'd been increasingly nervous over the last few days in case Hans came back, but so far there'd been no sign. Thousands had left on the transports over winter and every time a train had gone the family had wondered about putting Leah on it but every time they'd agreed they were better together. They had prayed to God to keep their dear girl safe and so far He had answered, but they were well into 1942 now and if Hans was coming back, time was running out. Ester read the hideous words again, her hands shaking. Surely even Nazis could not kill and certify someone in two hours?

Fighting for breath, she pulled out the rest of the letter. It was written in stiff capitals but the words throbbed with meaning:

THIS CERTIFICATE IS YOUR SISTER'S TICKET OUT OF THE GHETTO. SHE MUST NOT LEAVE VIA THE TRANSPORTS FOR THEY ARE NOT ALL THEY SEEM. THERE ARE PEOPLE WHO WILL HELP. A CART IS DUE INTO YOUR HUSBAND'S FACTORY IN TWO DAYS' TIME TO PICK UP A LARGE CONSIGNMENT OF WEHRMACHT UNIFORMS. IF YOU HIDE YOUR SISTER BENEATH THEM, OUR DRIVER WILL TAKE HER THROUGH THE GATES. YOU WILL PRESENT THIS CERTIFICATE TO THE AUTHOR-ITIES AND MOURN, BUT BENEATH IT I PRAY YOUR HEARTS WILL BE LIGHTENED FOR WE WILL PERSONALLY ENSURE HER SAFETY WITH A NEW IDENTITY AND A KIND CARER UNTIL SUCH TIME AS YOU CAN, PRAY GOD, BE REUNITED WITH HER IN PEACE AND SAFETY. THE LORD BE WITH YOU.

Ester read it over and over. Hide your sister beneath them. Present this certificate. Mourn. Could they do it? Your hearts will be lightened. Of course they could.

It was all she could do to keep up her duties until she could find an excuse to get away from the hospital, then she ran home at full tilt, tumbling into the house to find her mother.

'We can get Leah out. In two days' time. We must get word to her now. Tell her to feign illness, to come home. And we must talk to Filip.'

Her mother was confused, afraid. Ester knew how she felt but they'd been offered a lifeline and had to seize it with both hands. She sat Ruth down and read her the letter as patiently as she could bear, then she tore it into tiny pieces and buried it in the ash of their once-a-week fire and hid the death certificate high up above one of the rafters in the attic. Two days! They had just two days. Her heart was pounding in her chest and she feared it would not stop until she saw the cart drive out of the gates of the ghetto with her sister safely inside.

That night they made their plans. Ruth had reached Leah's office with whispered word she was to start up a cough and, as Leah had overheard two SS officers talking about their friend Hans' imminent return, her resulting 'illness' had been at least half true. Her boss had sent her home early – an almost unheard-of command – irritated by her wracking coughs and now she was huddled in a worn blanket, looking so wan that Ester almost believed she was at death's door herself.

'You must be brave, Leah. You must be brave and you must be calm. Very, very calm. Can you do that?'

Her sister looked up at her, grey eyes wide with fear, but she nodded.

'I can do it, Ester. Will I be alone?'

'Just for a little time, sweet one. Once you are out of the ghetto, Ana will take care of you.'

Leah nodded again.

'Out of the ghetto,' she repeated in an awed whisper.

'Only if we do it right,' Mordecai warned, wringing his hands.

'We will,' Filip said calmly. 'We will.'

But it was hard. Two days later, with the cart due at any moment, Ruth and Ester walked Leah round to the back of the workshop, their arms linked tightly into hers.

'You must lie very still,' Ester told her. 'You must barely breathe.'

'Barely,' Ruth repeated. 'But do breathe, Leah. Do keep on breathing, every day of this hideous war.'

Leah clutched at her mother.

'Come with me. We can both go. We can be happy together.'

Ruth shook her head.

'One slim girl will go unnoticed beneath all those great-coats, but two is far too risky. I'll be happy here, Leah, just knowing that you are safe. And when this is over, when these monsters are beaten, we will find you and be happy together.'

Leah nodded, tears sparkling in her eyes, and Ester hurried them on. It would not do to draw attention to themselves when Leah was meant to be dying at home.

'Here.' The factory door was very slightly ajar, left that way by Filip. 'This is it.' She clasped Leah's arms. 'You know what to do, Leah?'

'Slip inside and hide behind the third door on the left until someone comes to find me.'

'Good.'

Behind them there was a rumble on the potholed road and they all turned to see a large cart heading towards the factory. This was it; this was Leah's passage out of the ghetto. Ester seized her sister, trying to squeeze all her love into one hug but there was no time for more and she pushed her almost roughly to the door. Tears spilled down Leah's cheeks.

'I love you,' she said.

'We love you too. Now, go!'

And she did. She slid through the gap in the door and closed it behind her with the tiniest clunk. Ester and Ruth stood there in the melting snow, staring at the blank metal rectangle. They had done their job and now it was all up to Filip. Ruth fell to her knees, hands clasped and eyes turned to heaven but there was no time, even, for prayer, and Ester jerked her up and marched her away.

'Let me watch,' Ruth begged. 'Let me watch her go, Ester. Let me see her safely out.'

Ester looked at her mother. She longed to see it too but they could not afford to jeopardise the plan. More lives than just their own were at stake.

'You cannot cry, Mother. You must be strong, calm.'

'I know.' Ruth straightened herself, pushed the tears from her cheeks and adjusted her headscarf. 'I know.'

They joined a queue outside the bakery nearest to the main gates of the ghetto, ration coupons in hand, and for once they were glad of the hideously slow progress towards the shop. All their attention was on the road from the factory and at last the cart rumbled out, laden with carefully packaged uniforms. Ruth's hand tightened on Ester's arm but other than that she made no obvious movement and Ester clutched her back, her heart pounding so hard that she swore the guards would hear it from twenty metres away.

The cart moved to the gates and four SS men stepped up to it. The driver offered papers and one of the guards perused them as the other three stalked around the cart. One pushed at the top packages, half-heartedly lifting a few. Ester's breath stuck in her throat. The main guard was handing back the papers, waving to the men on the gates. They were swinging open. It was going to work! But then, as the driver took up the reins, Ester saw something move in the cart.

'No,' she whispered.

One of the guards pointed.

'Halt!'

The driver did as he was bid, though Ester could see his

shoulders stiff with tension. The second guard turned, lifted his gun from his shoulder and calmly fitted the bayonet. Ester pictured Leah somewhere in the middle of all that fabric. How deep in was she? How far would the blade go? They had been so close and now...

A shout from the people behind her in the queue made her jump.

'Your poor mother. Help her!'

Ruth had fallen to the floor and was jerking horribly in the mud. Others in the queue were pointing, crying out, and Ester dropped to her knees at Ruth's side.

'Make a fuss,' Ruth hissed to her. 'Make a huge, bloody fuss.'

It was the first time she had ever heard her mother swear and it galvanised her.

'Help!' she shouted, leaping up and running towards the guards. 'You must help us – my mother is having a fit.'

'A fit?' The guard with the bayonet looked around, his lip curled. 'Bloody filthy Jews. If they're not coughing or running with pissing diarrhoea, they're having bloody fits.' He shoved his gun at his companion and came striding towards them, his face red with fury. 'Do you know what helps with fits?' he snarled.

Ester shook her head helplessly but the other guards, more interested in the drama than a dull consignment of uniforms, waved the cart through. Ester watched as it rumbled off down the street, away from the factory, away from the ghetto, with her sister, surely, safely inside.

'A good kicking, that's what.'

'No!'

Ester flung herself in front of her mother as the guard's jack-boot came swinging viciously in. The blow caught her arm, sending pain searing through her, but her intervention only incensed the officer further. Yanking her by the same arm, he threw her aside and this time his boot connected with her mother. Ruth curled herself into a ball, as the people in the queue fell back, hands to their mouths, helpless to stop the torment. Again and again the boot plunged into Ruth's frail frame before, at last, he kicked himself out and, with a harsh laugh, turned away. Ruth lay there, unmoving.

'See,' he tossed over his shoulder. 'No more fit – worked a treat.'

His fellows gave a grotesque cheer and they were gone, back to the gates, leaving Ruth broken in the mud. Ester ran to her, cradling her in her arms.

'Mother?'

Ruth's eyes were clouded with pain but she was breathing still.

'Did she get away?' she gasped out. 'Did Leah get away?'

'She did,' Ester told her, stroking her hair tenderly from her face.

'Then it was all worth it,' Ruth said with the sweetest smile before her eyes rolled back and she went limp in Ester's arms.

ANA

On the other side of the city, Ana ran forward as the cart pulled into a dark side street.

'Leah,' she hissed. 'Leah are you in there?'

No answer.

'Leah, it's Ana. You're safe. You can come out.'

Around her, Bartek and the boys began lifting up the top packages. There were a lot of them and they looked heavy. What if they had crushed the girl? What if they had suffocated her? What if—

'Ana?'

'Leah!'

They scrambled to lift a few more packages and then Leah

was clambering out, shaky but whole. She looked around her, as if in a fantasy land.

'Am I out, Ana? Am I really out?'

'You really are,' she assured her. 'We're going to get you right away from the city. Here.' She handed her a new set of identity papers, fresh off Bartek's clever press. 'You're Lena Kaminski now, my second cousin once removed, helping your Aunty Krystyna on her smallholding in the countryside to ensure she can produce as many vegetables as possible for the honourable Reich.'

Leah – Lena – scanned the papers, blinking furiously as she fought to take it all in.

'When do we go?'

'Now.'

Already the boys had reloaded the cart and it was pulling away to meet the train that would take the uniforms to the front. The Germans had shocked everyone by invading Russia last summer and now their poor little soldiers needed warm gear to cope with the Soviet ice. For a moment Ana was tempted to burn the whole lot and let the ice take them, as it was taking the Jews in the ghetto, but she had to stay true to the Resistance plans – patience, quiet strength and care. Letting the uniforms go, she led Leah to another, far smaller cart.

'You've brought vegetables to the station to fulfil the quota demanded of you by the local council and now you're taking it home with your cousin, Alekzander here.' Leah looked nervously to Zander, sat tall-backed at the reins in rough farmer's clothes. Ana leaned in. 'He's not as rough as he looks. Alekzander is my son and a doctor.'

'A doctor?'

Ana smiled.

'We are none of us quite as we seem these days.' She took a neat pair of scissors from her pocket, snipped the threads holding the hateful yellow star to Leah's coat, and tore it away.

Leah looked down at her chest in something like wonder and Ana kissed her. 'Now go, sweet one. Be free, be safe, be as happy as you can. And try not to fret about your family, for they will be thanking God daily for your escape.'

Leah nodded, tears in her eyes, and stepped bravely up into the cart at Zander's side. He handed her a blanket against the cold and, though it was only an old thing, Ana saw her stroke it in wonder and hated the Nazis all over again for what they were doing to these poor innocents. *The meek will inherit the earth*, she reminded herself, but she knew now that they would only do that with help. *Her* help. Today they had got Leah to safety and that was a victory to be celebrated, but there were far too many people still stuck in the ghetto, and with death-vans stalking them, it was no time to be complacent. They had to do more, so, so much more.

ELEVEN

1 SEPTEMBER 1942

ESTER

Ester carefully unclipped the last of the stitches on old Mr Becker's leg and looked proudly at the slim scar.

'That's healing beautifully, Mr Becker.'

'Thanks to your stitches, Nurse.'

'And the thread coming in from the Resistance.'

He winked at her.

'Should know not to try and tear apart a Jew, hey? No one better with a needle. Fast as they try to take us apart, we put ourselves back together.'

Ester smiled and nodded, wishing that were true. They were saving maybe one in every twenty Jews taken by the cold, or by malnutrition or, like poor Mr Becker here, by a casually callous beating by a bored SS officer. And then there were the transports...

They'd had word from Ana not long after Leah's dramatic escape from the ghetto that she was safe in the countryside with her cousin Krystyna and had offered up prayers of thanks every day since. At least one of them might make it to the other side of the war alive, but the hostilities had showed no sign of abating through the summer of 1942 and with the Germans apparently close to taking Stalingrad it was beginning to look as if they might win the war. If the Nazis took over the world, it would surely be the end of the Jewish nation.

Rumours were coming in every day about Rumkowski's Auschwitz 'farm' with its fresh air and plentiful food. A few of the hardier Jews were, perhaps, being sent there to labour, but the rest would go straight into gas vans. There were no longer any volunteers for the transports but with so many already dispatched, there was some space in the ghetto. Martha, Noah and their three children were still in their one-time living room, but the other family had moved out of Benjamin and Sarah's room and so Ester and Filip had their attic to themselves once more.

Tonight would be the third anniversary of Filip proposing to her and they had a treat planned. For two weeks they had been saving and swapping rations so they could make bigos again and eat it in their room together. They even had a fresh roll and a half bottle of wine, a gift from a grateful new father with a very well-hidden cellar. Ester could not wait.

'There you go, Mr Becker,' she said, cleaning the stitch-holes with a tiny dab of precious antiseptic. 'Good as new.'

'You're an angel. Not many would treat gas-van fodder like me.'

'Mr Becker – don't!'

He shrugged.

'It's true though. If I don't get back to work, I'll be a goner next time the soldiers come calling.'

'Nonsense,' Ester said briskly, though more for herself than for her patient.

Her poor mother had outwardly recovered from her beating back in January but Ester feared there was more insidious damage, for Ruth struggled to draw air into her lungs and her appetite was poor.

'It's a blessing not to be hungry,' she would say cheerfully, sliding her bread onto Filip's plate, but they all knew that wasn't true.

Ruth's skin was grey and her hair falling out. It was only by hiding away in her bedroom that she'd escaped typhus this summer, and with winter already starting to whistle down the ghetto streets, Ester feared that TB would take her. Sarah was faring slightly better but she, too, looked wasted and far older than her fifty years. Filip had secured her a job in the 'mattress factory' that had opened up in an old church, but the feathers and wood dust that they used to stuff the soldiers' rough bedding got into every cranny of the workers' lungs and Sarah found it very hard.

A system had developed, whenever the Jewish police came calling for 'volunteers' for the next transport, of hiding the elderly and frail a few streets ahead of the officers, keeping them moving round with the help of watchful kids on the street corners until they could safely bring them back into their already-searched houses. It wasn't foolproof and too many were still snatched away but so far both Ruth and Sarah had escaped deportation. Even so, no one ever went to bed or left the house without a fond goodbye these days, just in case it was their last chance.

Ester looked up at the clock but it wasn't even midday yet – hours until she could tuck into the attic with her husband. Her hands cleaned her workstation automatically but in her mind she was picturing Filip on the other side of the table they'd made out of a metal crate he'd 'liberated' from the factory and she'd covered with the sewn-together edges of a worn-away sheet. She had no present to give him save herself but she knew that, with their privacy restored, that would be more than enough for both of them.

'Nurse!'

It was Mrs Gelb calling from the far bed, no doubt needing to relieve herself yet again, poor woman. Ester closed the lid on her daydream, knowing it would be reality in just a few hours, and went back to her duties. But Mrs Gelb didn't need the latrine. She was sitting up and pointing agitatedly out of the open window. Even before Ester could see what was bothering her, she heard it: 'Raus! Raus!' Below them, on the main floor of the hospital, she heard the crack of the doors being flung back and the unmistakably chilling noise of jackboots moving at pace across the tiled floor. 'Up now! Everybody out! Time to go!'

'Go where?' Mrs Gelb asked.

No one offered an answer but they all knew. So far the hospitals had had immunity from selection for the transports, but it seemed that had come to an end. Ester stood frozen with fear as the footsteps clattered up the stairs and four SS officers burst into the ward.

'Raus! Raus!'

Dr Stern moved forward, running an agitated hand through his white hair and knocking his kippah askew.

'What is the meaning of this, Officer? What do you want with these sick people?'

The head officer leaned over, so close to Dr Stern that spittle flew into his face: 'We want rid of them.'

'But they are unwell.'

'Exactly! This is a working ghetto, for working people.'

Dr Stern squared his old shoulders bravely. 'They will work again when they are better.'

'How long will that take? Your turn-around times are appalling, Doctor.'

'Because we have no supplies, no medicines, no—'

The officer cut him off with a harsh slap and the doctor staggered back.

'Better. Now – what are you waiting for? Get up. Go!'

Some of the patients began to shakily clamber out of bed. The SS ran round, prodding them in the back like cattle and forcing them to the stairs. One poor lady stumbled and was wrenched to her feet. Another, struggling to limp on a broken leg, was simply pushed so that she rolled down the steps, clattering into the wall at the bottom in a sickening heap.

'Please,' Ester said, hurrying forward. 'Let us help. It will be more...' She sought for a convincing word. 'More efficient.'

It worked. The head officer nodded and Ester and the other medical staff ran to help the invalids down the stairs. It felt terrible escorting them to what would surely be their deaths, but at least they could go with some dignity.

'And you,' a German voice snapped behind her, 'now!'

Ester looked back to see Mr Becker sitting in his bed, arms folded and a defiant scowl on his face. 'No.'

'No?' The SS man looked taken aback. 'No what?'

'No, I'm not going with you. I don't want to die scratching at the sides of a gas van in agony. I'd rather you just shot me here, in my bed.'

'Shot you?' The German laughed. 'I wouldn't waste a bullet on you, Jew. Now get up.'

'No.'

Ester watched, frozen in admiration for Mr Becker's bravery, but now the officer was striding over to him and yanking him bodily from his bed.

'You don't want to take the stairs out of here?'

'No,' Mr Becker repeated, though his voice was hoarse.

'Fine. You can take the window.'

With that, he lifted Mr Becker, strode to the window and, without even breaking stride, threw him out. Ester closed her eyes against the horror of it but still heard the crack of his ancient bones on the pavement below and could only pray that he had died instantly.

'What are you standing there for, Nurse? Do you want to go after him?'

Shaking her head, Ester spun round and ran down the stairs. Out in the street it was chaos. Not just the hospital patients but all the elderly were being rounded up and herded through the city towards the railway siding up in the Marysin district. The air was filled with wailing and cries of 'have mercy' but they were reflex only, for everyone knew that the Nazis had no mercy. Ester's thoughts flew to her mother and she darted down a side street and cut across to home. She was stopped just outside by Delilah, a kindly woman who had once been as round as a sugar-doughnut and whose skin now hung like strange flaps from her wasted body.

'I have them hidden.'

'Sorry?'

'Your mothers, Sarah and Ruth. I have them hidden with my own. My Ishmael is a carpenter and we have a panel, a fake one. They are behind it and will hopefully stay that way, but best not to draw attention to the house.'

'Of course.' Ester pressed her hand. 'Thank you so much.'

'We must stick together, Ester. It's the only way any of us will come out of this alive.'

Then she was off, heading back inside to hide Ester's loved ones. She prayed her fathers were safely at work with Filip and thought of Leah with a warm sense of relief, but then Martha came spilling out of the house, all three of her children clutched to her. Ester rushed to help.

'Where are you going?'

'There's going to be a speech. Rumkowski is going to tell us what's happening. Oh God, Ester – what will he say?'

Ester thought back to Martha naively listening to the Eldest of the Jews on the day they had first delivered a baby together. There had been many more births since and Ester had been grateful to have stoic Martha's assistance, but today she looked panicked and a sickness rose in Ester's stomach as she worked out why. *This is a working ghetto,* the SS officer had said in the hospital, *for working people only.* And who did not work? Children.

Surely not, Ester thought, but even as she did so she saw the SS officer tossing Mr Becker out of the window as easily as if he were dirty dishwater. There was nothing these people would not do. She took Martha's youngest from her as they moved towards the square.

Almost everyone in the ghetto was massed there. She looked around for Filip but it would be impossible to find one man in such a crowd and already Rumkowski was stepping up to the lectern and clearing his throat into the microphone. This time even he looked worn down and Ester found herself stroking baby Zillah's hair over and over as she waited for him to speak.

He held up a hand and a tense silence fell.

'Today,' he said gravely, 'the ghetto has been struck a hard blow.' He looked around the crowd, his hands clutching at the lectern as if he needed it to hold him up. 'They demand what is most dear to it – children and old people.'

'No!' Martha cried at Ester's side, and the terrible wail echoed up and down the ranks.

Ester sought for words to comfort her friend but there were none. Surely he could not mean this; not the children. She fought to focus on the Eldest of the Jews, but his words were ones no man or woman should ever have to hear.

'In my old age, I am forced to stretch out my hands and to beg: "Brothers and sisters, give them to me! Fathers and mothers, give me your children..."'

Martha fell to her knees, clutching her children to her and clawing almost blindly to have Zillah as well. Ester bent to pass her down, only half listening to Rumkowski talking on about the order he had received to send away more than twenty thousand

Jews and how he and the council had chosen to take the terrible decision about who went for themselves.

'We were guided not by the thought *How many will be lost?* but *How many can be saved?*' he said, his voice rising over the terrible wailing. 'I cannot give you comfort today. I have come like a robber, to take from you what is dearest to your heart. I must carry out this difficult and bloody operation, I must cut off limbs in order to save the body. I must take away children, and if I do not, others too will be taken.'

He spoke on, pleading his case, trying to explain how hard he had worked to change Nazi minds, but no one was listening now. All anyone could hear, round and round like a siren from hell was, 'Give me your children, give me your children, give me your children.'

TWELVE

12 SEPTEMBER 1942

ESTER

An eerie silence sat on the ghetto. Today was the holy festival of Rosh Hashana but no one was celebrating. Family tables had families around them no more and all appetite was gone. No child ran down the street, held a skipping rope for friends, or threw pebbles on a chalked-out hopscotch. No old women sat on the steps, watching the little ones and peeling the meagre vegetable rations for supper. No babies cried and the only tears were those of the mothers from whose arms they had been ripped.

All week long the Jewish police and their SS masters had terrorised the ghetto, driving out all those who were not registered to work. They had emptied homes, ticked off lists, turned children from lofts, toddlers from barrels and infants from drawers and wells and any other place people could think of in which to try and hide them. They had rammed bayonets into every mattress and sofa, had shot holes into walls and sent vicious dogs into cellars and sheds. The streets leading to Marysin had been filled with bewildered children clutching the hands of staggering grandparents and every dark day train after train had taken them mercilessly away.

Now the only sounds on the autumn air were the rumbles of sewing machines, leather stampers and looms as the ghetto worked to live a life that no one was sure they wanted any more. For what was a life without a generation to lead the way and another to come behind? What was anyone working for, save another few days in this miserable non-existence?

Some had survived. Ruth and Sarah had crept out of their sliver of a hiding place yesterday and were home again, but Martha had gone, refusing to let her children ride the train without her, and Noah just sat in the corner, tugging on his dark curls and weeping. He had tried to follow his family but been roughly pushed back from the crammed cattle trains, his broad shoulders worth too much to the Nazis to let him go with those he loved.

The Pasternak-Abrams family gathered around the dinner table but no one cared to eat.

'They will get us next time,' Ruth said, her voice quavering but sure.

'Next time,' Sarah echoed, her eyes on the floor. 'You should get out, Ester. You and Filip should get out, like Leah did. I would die to get you out, truly.'

'And I,' Ruth agreed. 'A thousand times over.'

Their husbands put their arms around their wives, nodding solemnly.

'We have lived,' Mordecai said. 'We have had our youth, have had our children, have known the joys of many years but you – you are young. Get in touch with Ana and Bartek, Ester. Get out of here and live – for yourselves, for us, and for the children that will carry on both our lines.' He reached out his hands. 'Please,' he said, his voice cracking. 'For us, you must try.'

Ester looked to Filip. For so long she had resisted leaving, sure that the people in the ghetto needed her, but what use was a nurse with no patients? A midwife with no mothers? Still, though, she felt guilty at even contemplating escape. Filip put an arm around her, warm and sure, and dropped a kiss on her lips.

'It is time,' he said. 'Is it not, Ester?'

She shook her head, tears welling in her eyes, but in truth she had no idea what to do any more and everyone else seemed so certain.

'It is time,' she agreed.

THIRTEEN

FEBRUARY 1943

ANA

Ana unfolded the delicate cardboard and checked the details for what must be the hundredth time. There was Ester's face, looking solemnly out at her above the solidly Polish name: 'Emilia Nowak'. Emilia was listed as a good Catholic girl from Łęczyca, working as a nurse in Warsaw. Ana had contacts in the hospital there from her time in midwifery college and had secured Ester/Emilia a position so that she and 'Filip Nowak' would have somewhere to go once they reached the capital. There had been much deliberation about whether to list Filip as a tailor, given that most of the textile workers in Łódź were Jewish, but he needed to work and there were a number of bespoke tailoring companies in Warsaw so he had become a Warsaw native travelling to Łódź for supplies. The only thing missing from their identity cards were their fingerprints, which they would have to do themselves once they got out of the ghetto – *if* they got out of the ghetto.

Ana folded the card up again and placed it into a cash box with a sigh. This was the fourth time they had planned an escape for the young couple and, yet again, it had failed. A clever carpenter in the Resistance movement had fashioned a fake bottom for one of the carts that took goods in and out of the ghetto and a number of people had escaped that way over the last two months but it wasn't easy. Carts usually went into the ghetto laden with vegetables and came out again with goods made in the workshops but, with the rise in escapes in these first two months of 1943, both the Jewish police and the SS officers kept a close eye on them so that it was often impossible to find a moment to get escapees into the secret compartment.

Four times Ana had stood waiting anxiously for the cart to pull up in the side street and four times the driver had approached sadly shaking his head. She was beginning to think they would never manage it and the situation was getting desperate. The word on the Resistance grapevine was that the killings at Chelmno had ground to a halt. That had seemed like good news until they'd heard rumours of suspicious activity in Nazi concentration camps, most notably the one they called Auschwitz. Rumour had it they were building giant crematoria there which could only mean one thing – that the Nazis had stopped trying to 'contain' Jews and were starting to eliminate them on a grand scale. Smaller ghettos all around Poland were being disbanded and it wouldn't be long before the larger ones followed suit, however hard they worked. She had to get Ester and Filip out, and fast.

'Perhaps, if they're keeping such a close eye on the carts, we need a new way,' Alekzander said.

'Such as?'

'There's a girl who's got a group working on a tunnel out of an old wine cellar. It's got to be long to get past the perimeter but if we could get it finished, it might be a route to safety for lots of people. I'm trying to find out more.'

Ana's heart lurched. Her middle son looked so fiercely determined and she loved him for it, but she feared for him too.

'You will take care, Zander?'

'Of course, Mother. Don't worry about me. Jakub is doing a great job on the ID cards, so it's my job to liberate people to use them.'

Jakub beamed. He had, indeed, become expert at the fake cards, using the printing press to run off spares and then working to fake details and signatures. He had personally created a near-perfect replica of the official stamp. The sticking point was getting people out.

'Don't worry, Mother,' he said, echoing his brother, 'we'll get Ester and Filip out very soon and off to Warsaw to see out this damned war. The Russians are fighting back hard and they've got the Nazis on the run. The tide is turning, I'm sure of it. Give it another year and we'll all be visiting Filip "Nowak" for designer suits to celebrate the Allied victory.'

Ana smiled at them both.

'You're good boys. God blesses you, I know, and your father and I are very proud of you. Now let's get these papers hidden away again so they're safe for next time.'

Alekzander stood up and lifted the loose floorboard but as Ana bent to stash the locked cash box safely beneath it, a loud knocking shook the front door.

'Quick!' Jakub urged.

'Open up!' shouted a voice with an ominous German accent. 'Open up now!'

Ana shoved the box into the gap.

'Just coming,' she called and stomped noisily towards the door, fumbling elaborately with the catch to give the boys time to get the floorboard back in place. The door shook with more knocking and she finally pulled it open.

'I'm so sorry. My fingers aren't as nimble as they used to be,' she said in fluent German. It took them aback and the front one actually doffed his hat, but there were three others behind him and Ana felt her breathing quicken. Four SS was a significant visit indeed. 'Can I help you?'

An older officer stepped forward.

'We believe you can, Frau Kaminski. We believe you are in contact with members of the Resistance. We believe your family' – his eyes raked over Zander and Jakub, who had come to stand at her shoulders – 'are at the heart of a forging operation that is both illegal under Polish law and an act of deliberate sabotage to the Third Reich.'

'Forging?' Ana said, fighting to keep any tremor from her voice. 'Me?'

'Your family,' the officer said, pushing his way inside and commanding his men, 'Search the place.'

The other three stomped in, turning over furniture and pulling pictures off the walls with callous disregard. Ana winced. This smart apartment was not their true home but over the last two years they had made it theirs and she hated seeing it torn apart by these SS animals. She felt a renewed surge of hatred towards their oppressors and it gave her strength to stand up to them.

'There is no treachery in this house. We are just honest working people, getting on with our jobs.'

'Which are? Papers please.'

He looked at Ana's, then Zander's but paused for longer over Jakub's.

'You are at the printing works?'

'I am.'

'And what do you print there?'

'All sorts, sir. Books, papers—'

'Identity cards?'

'We have done those, yes, if they are ordered by the Reich.'

The SS man grabbed Jakub by the collar and rammed him back against the wall.

'Or by illegals.'

'No,' Jakub choked out, 'only by the Reich, sir.'

Out of the corner of her eye, Ana saw that one of the soldiers had reached the floorboard under which the identity cards were stashed. She forced herself not to look, not to draw attention to it in any way. If they found Ester and Filip's pictures, they would hunt them down and kill them without a moment's hesitation. Her attempts to save them would turn into the surest way to send them to their deaths and she could only pray that Zander had had time to replace the board securely.

The officer dropped Jakub as suddenly as he had pushed him.

'Found anything?' he demanded of his team.

They shook their heads and Ana noted with relief that the soldier had moved away from the crucial floorboard. They thundered through to the bedrooms and although she hated the thought of them rifling through her personal effects it was better than finding the incriminating evidence.

'Not that it matters,' the main officer said, pacing around the three of them like a big cat. 'We have information that this family is involved and that's enough.'

'Information from where?' Zander demanded.

'From a source. A very helpful source.'

'A very beaten source,' Zander shot back.

Ana reached out a hand to take his and try to calm him, but the officer just gave a thin smile.

'It's amazing what people will tell you with some... persuasion.' He stuck his face up against Zander's. 'As you will find out.'

Ana saw Jakub glance at the door and willed him to make a break for it. Three of the SS were in the bedrooms and the other one would most likely not leave her and Zander alone to pursue him. He might just make it away. But, as if sensing her thoughts, the officer suddenly grabbed her, wrenching her arm behind her back so that a sharp pain shot through it and she gasped out loud.

'Make any rash moves, boys, and your mother dies.'

He drew his pistol from a halter at his waist and put it to her head. Ana felt its ice-cold kiss and fear shuddered through her, but so what? She'd take death if it got her boys away. Now, though, the other officers were returning and any chance had gone. She was just grateful Bartek and Bronislaw were out.

'Anything?' the leader snapped at his men.

'Just this, sir – nasty-looking tools.'

One of them presented Ana's medical bag, lifting out her forceps and snapping them in the air.

'Those are for drawing a baby out of a woman,' Ana told him, and almost laughed when he dropped them as if they were scalding. 'And that,' she went on, nodding to the knife, 'is for cutting the umbilical cord so that Baby can be swaddled and the afterbirth safely ejected.' All four soldiers looked disgusted and Ana hated them even more. 'It would have happened to you all,' she said, 'when you were beautiful, innocent newborns, when—'

'Enough!'

The lead officer pushed her arm upwards again, so hard she felt it almost pull from the socket.

'Hail Mary, Mother of God,' she started, searching for strength, but the prayer only gained her a kick in the calf.

'Shut up with your religious mumbo-jumbo. This is the Reich now – no place for foolish superstition. Out!'

He shoved her towards the door and Ana, for all her hatred, felt suddenly weak with fear.

'Where?'

'To the cells. Perhaps a night or two courtesy of Gestapo hospitality will make you all more helpful.'

'But she's done nothing wrong,' Jakub protested. 'Take us

but leave her. She's just an old woman, a midwife. She's innocent.'

'Then she has nothing to fear,' the man said nastily. 'Out!'

He pushed Ana onto the stairs and a rush of cold air hit her.

'My coat,' she said. 'Can I take my coat?'

The officer grunted and one of the others lifted her coat off the hook and patted it down. Victoriously he produced a small tin from the pocket and gave it to his superior.

'Ah-ha! What's this?'

To her huge relief, he let go of her arm to fumble with the lid of the toothpowder tin.

'It's my medical papers,' she told him. 'The tin keeps them dry.'

'A likely story,' he snarled but then he lifted the lid and found, as she'd said, the simple papers proclaiming her qualification as a midwife. Face falling, he shoved it back into the pocket without another word and pushed the coat at her. 'Out!' he snapped again and this time there was no way of delaying it further.

Ana found herself marched down the steps and shoved into a dark van with her two sons. Neighbours peeked warily from their doors and she prayed someone would get word to Bartek and Bronislaw so that they would not come back to an SS trap. As the doors slammed shut on them, she wondered if she would ever see her dear husband again.

The only blessing was that the cash box had gone undiscovered – they might have her, Zander and Jakub, but at least Ester and Filip had not been betrayed. Neither, however, had they escaped the ghetto and with the threat of extermination camps looming, that failure dug into Ana, as sharp a pain as those she feared were about to come in the dreaded cells of the Gestapo.

PART TWO

AUSCHWITZ-BIRKENAU

FOURTEEN

APRIL 1943

ESTER

'Here, Mama, try and drink this – it will make you stronger.'

Ester lifted the broth to her mother's lips and willed her to take some. Ruth did her best, but she was so frail now that it seemed to be too great an effort to even swallow. Ester prayed for patience. She was due back at the hospital, but this particular patient was too precious to leave.

'That's good, Mama. A bit at a time, that's all we need.' Ruth's eyes were apologetic in her horribly thin face. Ester saw her focus on the broth, forcing herself to take some more, and smiled at her. 'Good. That's really good.'

A little more went down Ruth's throat and Ester allowed herself to feel a morsel of hope. It had been a long, hard winter with TB stalking through the ghetto, snatching up people with reckless abandon. They'd lost poor Sarah at the start of January in a wrack of hideous coughs that had sucked them all into her suffering night after night so that it had been almost a blessing when God had taken her to his rest. Ester had mourned the mother-in-law she had only got to know amidst hardship and suffering, and battled to comfort Filip, holding him beneath the blankets at night as he had cried his grief into the darkness. Ruth, however, had somehow clung on to life and with the spring weather upon them, Ester was sure she could recover – if only she would eat.

The one luxury they didn't have was time. The transports out of the ghetto had dropped off over the winter – perhaps the poor German soldiers didn't like herding people to their deaths in the ice and snow – but last week they had started up again and anyone not working was at risk. There was a plum job waiting for Ruth in the bakery – a favour to Ester from the grateful grandmother of a boy born on the first day of Hannukah – so if she could just get her out of bed, all would be well.

'Eat the rest, Mama, please.'

Ruth rolled her eyes but sipped some more.

'I don't know why you bother with me, sweet one.'

'Because I love you, Mama.'

A tear sparkled in Ruth's eye and she reached up a thin arm and gave Ester a surprisingly strong hug.

'You're a good girl, Ester. I wish we'd got you out of here.'

'I'm glad we didn't, or I wouldn't be here to care for you.'

That much was true, but Ester had to admit that her heart ached when she thought of how close she and Filip had been to escaping this hellhole. Four times they had cowered in the back of Filip's factory looking for a moment to leap into the cart but every time the weaselly Jewish police had been strutting self-importantly around, leaving not a moment's space for a young couple to clamber on board. And then had come the terrible message: 'Abort'.

Ester still wasn't sure what had happened but she'd heard nothing from Ana since and her son Zander did not ride the trams any more. Every night she and Filip got down on their knees in their attic room and prayed for the Kaminski family's safety, but she feared the worst. If the Gestapo had caught them helping Jews, they would show no mercy, and it tormented Ester that those poor, good people might have died for her.

'We must be sure to live,' Filip said to her, 'to honour them.' And they tried, they really did, but it was hard when life was one long grind to simply survive.

The only place they truly found any joy these days was huddled beneath the covers together and Ester flushed now, remembering the tender way Filip had caressed her last night. 'You are my feast, Ester,' he'd murmured against her skin. 'You are my concert and my party, my night out and my day in. You are all I need.'

'And you, I,' she'd murmured back, arching to meet him.

'Ester!' She jumped, pulled out of her pleasant remember-ings at the sound of her name being hissed up the stairs. Running to the top, she saw Delilah, their neighbour, staring up at her, eyes full of fear. 'They're coming. The police are coming and they have a list.'

Ice ran through Ester.

'Where are they?'

'Back towards my house but moving fast. There's no way we can get Ruth behind the panel. Can you move her on? Vera on Marynarska has a cellar. She might— Oh!'

Ester watched in horror as a policeman grabbed Delilah and unceremoniously shoved her aside.

'Ester Pasternak?' he demanded. Ester nodded dumbly. 'Good. I have a list here of persons who are a drain on the Reich.'

'A what?'

The young Jew had the grace to blush but he stared her down and pushed on with his vile job.

'A drain on the Reich. Germany cannot afford to keep people in the ghetto who are not contributing to the economic viability of the community.'

'Pardon?'

'Workers. You know this. Please don't make it harder than it need be.'

'For who?' Ester demanded. 'For you? It hurts you, does it, to ship poor defenceless people to their deaths? It troubles your conscience, perhaps? Or – no – just annoys you if it drags your day out longer than need be before you can go home to your warm house and your filling stew, provided by the Nazis you kowtow to.'

'Ester!' Delilah warned from behind the man, but Ester did not seem to be able to stop herself.

'Why?' she asked, coming down the stairs to face him. 'Why do you do this? Why do you sell your own people to the enemy?'

'Germany is not the enemy,' the policeman said stiffly. 'The Fatherland is our protector.'

'That's what they tell you, is it? And how is putting our people into gas vans protecting them?'

He shuffled before her.

'Sometimes we must sacrifice the individual for the greater good of the whole.'

'Sacrifice? Is that what our faith teaches us? Is that what the Torah tells us?'

'Well, I—'

'I can tell you exactly what the Torah preaches: "In the presence of the elderly you shall rise, and you shall respect an elder." Leviticus 19, verse 32. So tell me, is it respecting elders to drag them from their sick beds and post them onto trains into oblivion?'

Ester could see Delilah backing away, worried about being associated with her, but was she just meant to send her mother to her death without any resistance?

'Look,' she said, fighting to modulate her tone. 'My mother has a job in the bakery. She's due to start next week and just needs a few more days to regain full strength.' It was a lie and they both knew it but the policeman hesitated and Ester threw herself on her knees before him. 'Please, sir. I'm a nurse. I know how to make her well. Give us a week. If I've not got her to the bakery by then, you can add her back on to your list.'

The policeman looked down at his notepad, then reached for his pen, and for one glorious moment Ester thought he was going to strike out her mother's name, but then an SS officer marched around the corner and he snapped to attention and rammed the pen back into his pocket.

'All well here, Officer?' the German demanded.

'All well. Just getting this young woman to fetch her mother for transport.'

'Excellent.' The Nazi turned his piercing blue eyes on Ester and put a hand menacingly to his gun. 'Hurry up then. We don't have all day.'

Ester glared at him but then a frail voice said, 'I'm here, Officer. I'm ready,' and she turned to see Ruth working her way down the stairs, leaning heavily on the rail.

'Mother!' Ester ran to help her. 'We can't let this happen,' she hissed. 'We can't—'

'We can't risk you,' Ruth said calmly. 'Tell your father I love him, my sweet, and take care of him for me until I can see him again on the other side.'

'No, Mama.'

'Move along please,' the policeman said sharply, with a glance to the SS commander. 'It's time.'

A straggling parade was coming down the street, shepherded by Nazis with big sticks, and the policeman gave Ruth a shove towards them. She caught her foot on a loose stone and went flying to the ground.

'Get up!' the SS officer barked, kicking her.

Ester saw red.

'Leave her alone,' she cried, pushing past him to help her

mother up. 'Isn't it enough that you're sending her to her death without having the grace to at least let her walk there with dignity?'

'Oooh – this one's got fire,' the commander said. 'A right Jewish wildcat.'

'I'll tame her, sir,' one of the stick-wielding underlings said with a leer, and Ester cowered back, clutching Ruth tightly to her.

The commander sneered.

'Don't sully yourself, Officer. And you' – he jabbed his gun at Ester – 'if you're so keen on your mother walking to her death with dignity, you can accompany her.'

'No!' Ruth shrieked. 'Ester, no. Say sorry. Step away. Go back inside. You mustn't come with me. Please – you mustn't come.'

'Too late,' the commander growled. 'Fall in.'

'But—'

'Fall in!' He poked the gun into Ester's back and wiggled his finger on the trigger. Ester stepped hastily in with the poor band, dragging Ruth along with her. 'Good little cat. Have a nice trip.'

He gave her a mocking wave as they were marched off towards Marysin.

'Don't worry,' Ester whispered to Ruth. 'I'll get away at the station. I'll just say I was getting you to the train. They'll see my uniform. They'll let me go.'

But even as they were hustled up the road, she could see the policeman taking out his pen again and, instead of crossing out her mother's name, writing in her own. She was on the list now and would have to fight with all she had not to be on the train as well.

At the station all was chaos and Ester was horrified to see that amongst the elderly and infirm were a number of younger people. She did not recognise any of them and assumed they must be Jews in transit from other ghettos but their presence meant her own would not stand out as she had hoped and dread began to clamp itself like iron around her heart. So many times she had watched others being marched to the stark wooden cattle trucks and now she was amongst them the full horror of the inhuman transports hit home.

'Filip!' she cried. She couldn't leave him; she couldn't die. She pictured his face when he got home and found her gone and hated herself for doing this to him. Only last night they had been wrapped up so tight in each other that there was no knowing where one began and the other ended, and now she had torn them apart with her foolishness. Why couldn't she have kept quiet like Ruth had said? Why had she picked today to find her voice? But a look at her mother, weak and terrified at her side, told her exactly why. She could not have sent Ruth off alone with these monsters.

'Where are we going?' she asked one of the policemen herding them towards the wagons. He was young and dark-eyed and was swigging from a flask, as if to dull the pain. She felt no sorrow for him but might, at least, be able to exploit his weakness. 'Is it Chelmno?'

'Not Chelmno, no.'

'Then where?'

He looked down at her, eyes cloudy.

'Some place called Auschwitz. It's a camp.'

'A camp?' she snatched at this. 'What sort of camp?'

He shrugged and turned away, but Ruth grabbed his arm.

'My daughter isn't meant to be here. She's a nurse. An important nurse.'

He gave a dark laugh.

'She's Jewish, woman. No one Jewish is important in this lot's eyes.'

'Can we just see...?'

'But he'd gone and they were almost at the trains. The cattle wagons were a metre off the ground and there were no steps. Two strong SS men, standing either side of the gaping doorway, were reaching down and yanking people up into them and on instinct Ester lifted Ruth to spare her their rough attentions. Ruth sat on the edge for a moment, legs dangling like a toddler, and Ester felt herself brimming with love for the kindly woman who had brought her into the world, but already she was being pushed deeper into the wagon as more and more people were shoved in.

'Go,' Ruth called to her. 'Push backwards. Get away. Go back to Filip.'

Ester nodded, fighting against the crowd. Her heart broke all over again to leave her mother but there was nothing she could do for her now except try to secure her own survival. Planting her feet firmly in the muddy ground, she let others board before her, praying that somehow the train would run out of space and she would have time to plead her case. Theirs was the last wagon and suddenly the engine started up and the driver let out a viciously jaunty toot on the whistle. The guards began shouting and shoving but it was clear not everyone was going to get on.

'Go!' Ruth called again before she was swallowed into the depths of the crowd.

Ester nodded, tears streaming down her face, but at that moment she caught sight of someone in the doorway, pushed to the front by the new additions being shoved inside.

'Ana?'

She must be mistaken. The woman looked like her old friend but she was so thin and her face was so beaten and scarred that it was impossible to tell. It couldn't be her, Ester told herself. Why would she be on this train with the poor Jews?

'Ester?'

They locked eyes and the moment Ester saw the firm,

caring look behind the beaten lids, she knew for sure that it was the midwife.

'What are you doing here?' she cried.

The guards were trying to push Ana back to make space to close the giant door and Ester instinctively stepped towards her as she cried out in pain. The next thing she knew someone was grabbing her around the waist and lifting her bodily into the carriage.

'No!' she screamed, kicking against him, but the door was closing, pushing her into the press of bodies and shutting them all into a dark, fetid, fearful space.

Panic welled up inside her and she felt her heart ping against her ribs as she fought to breathe. She thought of Filip and her whole body caved in on itself so that she would have jack-knifed to the floor save that she was held torturously upright by all the other poor souls rammed in around her.

'I'm sorry, my love,' she gasped out. 'I'm so, so sorry.'

Tears ran down her cheeks into her mouth, clogging her already closing airways and she felt her head start to spin nauseatingly. But then an arm was around her, not pushing her this time but holding her, secure and safe.

'I've got you, Ester,' Ana's voice said in the darkness. 'I've got you and, wherever they take us, I won't let you go.'

FIFTEEN

APRIL 1943

ANA

'Come, Ester.'

Ana put out her arms to the young woman as she tried to clamber from the train still holding her mother's body. Ruth Pasternak had died in the night and the only blessing was that she had been safe in her daughter's arms when she went. Once the train had moved away from Łódź, people had shuffled around in the cramped space. Someone had torn a loose board from the side of the cattle wagon, letting in blessed fresh air and some light so that the two of them had been able to find Ruth. Already it had been clear that she'd been fading and Ana had stood, praying quietly, as Ester had soothed her mother into her eternal rest. Just before the end, however, Ruth had reached out and touched Ana's arm, lightly but with intent.

'Will you look after her?' she'd beseeched. 'Will you look after my girl?'

'Of course,' Ana had assured her. 'It will be my pleasure.'

Ruth had given a nod. 'She's your daughter now.'

And then, reaching up to press a kiss on Ester's cheek, she

had let go of life. Ester had wept in quiet, contained sobs but the long hours of their journey, for all its discomfort, had at least offered her time to mourn. Now, it seemed, that was at an end.

'Put that down,' an SS officer snapped at Ester, waving contemptuously at her mother's corpse.

'I need to bury her, sir.'

'Bury her!' He gave a bark of a laugh. 'Where would you *bury* her in Birkenau? Leave her there and she can go in the pit with the rest.'

'The rest?' Ester asked, looking around at the people stumbling from the train.

'Don't ask,' Ana urged. 'I'm sorry, Ester, but you must leave her. We have to keep up.'

The train seemed to have dropped them in the middle of nowhere and the deportees were being pushed onto a rough road, vicious dogs snapping at their heels. Already they were drawing too much attention to themselves, so gently Ana prised Ruth's body from the young woman's arms and laid her on the earth. Her eyes were closed, sparing her the sight of the bleak place her daughter had been delivered to. Covering Ruth's face with her own scarf, Ana took Ester's arm and hurried her away. *She's your daughter now.* Well, dearly as she loved her boys, she had always wanted a daughter and if this was not the ideal place to have acquired one, it was the place all the same. God moved in mysterious ways.

Thoughts of her sons threatened to swamp Ana and she held tight to Ester, as much for her own support as for the girl's. She had no way of knowing what had happened to Bartek and Bronislaw and could only pray they had escaped Łódź. They'd held whispered talks over dinner sometimes about what they would do if they were caught, and Bartek had made contact with Resistance cells in Warsaw that would take them in should the need arise. She liked to imagine the two of them in the capital and pictured them in her old midwifery college. It was foolish, she knew, but it was the part of the city that was most vivid to her and somehow it kept them alive in her hearts.

She had no idea where they had taken Zander and Jakub. They had tormented her with it time and again in the interrogation room. 'Tell us all you know, or it will go badly for your boys.' They'd agreed though, over those whispered dinners, that if they were ever caught they would say nothing and, above all else, give no names. Ana had not, in truth, been sure that she would be strong enough to withstand Nazi brutality, but God had been with her in that room full of hatred and His light had got her through it. Eventually her tormentors had snapped and told her she was a stupid, ignorant old hag and could get off to a camp to 'learn good German ways'. Now here she was.

The rough road stretched ahead of them across marshy land and in through an archway in a big, brick building, from which huge, double fences ran out on either side. The vicious barbed wires were supported by great concrete pillars and guarded at regular intervals by giant wooden watchtowers. Large signs warned of electrocution when the lights were on and this boundary made the Łódź ghetto fence look like a child's construction. Ana shivered at the thought of being trapped inside.

'So that's the camp?' Ester said, raising her head at last. 'Birkenau? I thought we were coming to Auschwitz.'

'Auschwitz-Birkenau,' a nearby guard told her with a leer. 'It's a lovely new, all-purpose, super-efficient camp.'

He gave a nasty laugh and forced them into a line with three other women. Ana saw they were being arranged into two columns, women and men, all in lines of five, to start marching inexorably towards the wires. She wanted to push back, to resist, but the Germans set a relentless pace and hit out at anyone who stumbled. It was hard not to, for they'd had no food or, worse, water in the train and Ana felt dangerously light-headed. For a moment she almost envied Ruth her passage out of this hell, then she told herself off for such weakness. She was here for a reason; God had just not revealed it to her yet.

The road they were on was clearly being dug up for new railway lines and workers were chased to the side, forming a curious welcome guard, spades over their slender shoulders. Ana looked at them, taking in their emaciated forms and the haunted look in their eyes and wanted to plant her feet in the earth and stop this forced march through those dark gates. Why were they all letting themselves be herded so meekly? Why were they allowing the Nazis to push them into their sick ghettos and camps? There were far more prisoners than guards; if they all just took a stand, they could stop this.

One look at the guns, though, and she knew it wasn't true. They would just shoot them down and throw them into the pit with Ruth and 'the rest' and what would be gained by that? Staying alive was the only weapon they had right now. She locked eyes with one of the prisoners as their pitiful column halted before the gates and he took a small step forward.

'Look well,' he hissed. She stared at him, startled. 'You must look well,' he insisted. 'Especially you.'

He pointed to the yellow star on Ester's coat and Ana noticed a yellow triangle roughly sewn onto his uniform alongside a number. A glance down the line told her that most of the men had the same branding though there were a few with triangles in red and green as well. They were all horribly thin and wearing strange striped uniforms, far too meagre for the cold day.

'Or what?' she asked.

In reply he nodded through the opening gates to the back of the camp where five big chimneys were rising up out of the trees. Ana sucked in a breath, realising what the guard had meant when he'd said 'super-efficient'. She recalled the rumours on the underground network of crematoria being built at the camp they were calling Auschwitz, of a Nazi 'final solution' to the so-called Jewish-problem. It was one of the reasons she'd upped her efforts to get Ester out of the ghetto and now, in some dark twist of fate, she was arriving at the death camp with her.

She's your daughter now.

Ana glanced behind her, feeling a sudden urge to rush back to Ruth and shake her to life, to say she couldn't do it, she couldn't keep Ester safe, but of course that was a nonsense. The gates had swung open with a mocking clang and they were being shoved through. She looked around, curiosity momentarily taking the edge off her fear. The camp was vast. Ahead of them the road they had come in on pushed forward, bisecting vast living areas, and in here railway tracks were being laid – the Germans were clearly readying themselves for many new arrivals.

To the left, long lines of barracks ran parallel to the road behind more wire fences. They seemed to stand six deep, the first three lines made of wood, those behind of brick, and each one looked capable of housing maybe fifty people. Ana tried to calculate the total likely population of this hell, but she could not see how far back towards the trees on the skyline the rough barrack buildings went and lost count fast.

To the right, the camp was at least five times as big. Here the barracks ran perpendicular to the road in fenced-off sections disappearing further than the eye could see. The earth in between them was churned to mud but the whole place was eerily empty. She glanced at the nurse's watch on her lapel and saw that it was nine in the morning. Maybe they were at work? The thought gave her hope but then she remembered the man's hissed words – 'look well' – and her eyes moved up from the barracks to the far side of the camp where green trees sat incongruously bright above the stark lines of the fencing. The five great chimneys were belching out thick grey fumes and her nose caught the tang of charred meat on the air.

'God have mercy on us,' she muttered and clutched Ester's arm tighter. 'Stand up tall, Ester. Look fit and strong.'

'What?' The girl was clearly still clouded by grief and peered at her in confusion.

'Just do it,' Ana snapped.

They were reaching the front and she could see a man in an SS uniform decorated with braids. As each prisoner was pushed forward, he scrutinised them and then pointed with a stick to the left or the right. It was clear from just one glance at those to the right that they were being designated as unfit for work. Ana looked again to the dark smoke and steeled herself to push her shoulders back and stand tall. Much like in the ghetto, the Nazis only wanted people who might be of use to them.

'You!'

Her heart thudded as she was prodded forward. The man looked at her curiously, taking in her bruised face.

'She looks rather old, Herr Doktor,' someone said behind him and she knew, with searing sharpness, that this moment was critical.

'Old but strong,' she said, pleased to hear no waver in her voice. 'I am a nurse, sir, and a midwife besides.'

'A midwife!' The underling chuckled but the doctor looked at her with something like interest.

'You can prove that?'

Heart thumping, Ana took the tooth powder tin out of her pocket and fumbled to open it. The doctor snapped his fingers and his underling grabbed it from her and yanked it open. Her papers fell out and the doctor unfolded them and gave a quick nod.

'Very well. Left.' He glanced back to his assistant. 'Block 17.'

'But Herr Doktor...'

'Block 17!' he roared and the man cowered.

'Yes, Herr Doktor.'

Ana took her courage in both hands and faced the doctor a moment longer. His hands, she noticed, were shaking slightly and his eyes had the hazed patina of a man who had been on the drink. At this time in the morning that surely meant he found this task distasteful and, crossing her fingers behind her back for God's protection, she spoke again.

'This young woman is my assistant.'

'This one?' He gave a flick of his hand and Ester was shoved forward. 'She's very slight.'

'And very talented.'

'Very well. Left.'

The underling was going purple.

'Herr Doktor...'

'Be quiet!' he roared at him. 'There are new directives you know nothing of, fool. Step back and let me do my job.'

The underling was puce with rage but that mattered little to Ana. Grabbing Ester's arm, she hurried into the left line, hating that she could not save those poor creatures struggling to stand in the other one, but counting their own survival a small victory. The only question now, was what happened in Block 17.

'You – the pair of midwives, in there!' The female SS officer gave them both a vicious prod in the back with a cackle of a laugh. 'It's a noble calling, midwifery, right, Klara?'

A thickset woman with forearms the size of marrows and a mottled, angry face strode to the door and faced them down.

'Very noble, Aufseherin Grese,' she agreed with a sneer. 'Life is sacred and all that.'

Ana tried to see behind the woman into the wooden barrack but she was filling the door frame and it was impossible.

'This is Schwester Klara,' Grese told them. 'She's a midwife too. Or was.'

'Stripped of my licence,' Klara told them proudly. 'Infanticide.'

Ana felt her blood run cold.

'Infanticide?' she whispered.

'Abortions,' Klara said casually. 'It's a crime – though not for the women I treated, I must say. Why give up your own life for some mewling brat?'

'Quite right,' Grese agreed, smiling slyly at Ana and Ester. 'Schwester Klara has perfected her art here in Auschwitz-Birkenau.'

'Perfected it,' Klara agreed smugly. 'I can dispose of any child now.'

Ana glanced to Ester but they both kept their faces straight. Already they were learning how the camp worked. Their 'processing' had been an exercise in callous humiliation. Hustled into a big building at the rear of the camp, just past the two long, chimneyed ones, they'd been ordered to strip. The officers – most of them male – had not hesitated to 'encourage' speed with leather whips and there had been no choice but to shed their clothes and stand there, denuded.

Agonisingly slowly they'd been shuffled past the leering Nazis as prisoners with big clippers had shaved their heads and more, with cruelly blunt razors, had perfunctorily shaved the rest of their exposed bodies. Ana, having birthed three children, had simply closed her eyes and borne it, but she'd seen the furious embarrassment in Ester's young eyes and felt hatred, ever simmering just below the surface, threatening to explode. Thankfully the job had been done fast and they'd found themselves before a small prisoner with a needle.

'Arm.'

'What?' she'd asked, confused.

'Give me your arm.'

He'd taken it surprisingly gently but his grip had been firm as he'd dug a number into her skin: 41401. So, she'd thought, over forty thousand women had been herded through these cruel gates before her. How many were still alive?

The question had made her want to snatch up the horrible needle and fight but before she could muster the strength, they'd been herded into a dark room for a 'shower'. The rumours in Łódź had been that the gas chambers operated like shower rooms and Ester and Ana had clutched at each other as the doors had closed and the pipes had clanked. She'd never been more relieved than when water, cold but blessedly clean, had fallen down on them.

Once that was done, they'd been back in a queue to be handed striped tops and ill-fitting skirts. Ester's had been far too big for her slender frame but she'd been allowed no belt or tie and in the end Ana had fashioned a rough knot in the back of the skirt to stop it falling perpetually around her ankles. There had been no underwear and no socks – just clumsy wooden clogs that were already chafing at the edges of her feet from the march to Block 17 – and now this: a murderous midwife.

'I came into the profession to save the lives of babies and mothers,' Ana dared to say.

Schwester Klara leered down at her.

'Sweet.' Then her face hardened. 'Time to retrain, blöde Kühe.'

Ana flinched but she'd been called worse than a 'stupid cow' in her time and she wasn't going to let this bitter woman intimidate her.

'You better show us around then.'

'Won't take long.'

At last Klara stepped back and with an exaggerated sweep of the hand showed them into the hut. Ana took a few cautious steps and reared back in horror. The smell was terrible – blood mingled with sweat, excrement and the stink of unwashed bodies. Something ran across her foot and behind her Ester screamed.

'A rat!'

Klara kicked out at it with feet which were, Ana noticed, clad in large, comfortably worn-in boots.

'They love it here, vermin,' she said, almost fondly. 'Lots to eat, you see.'

She gestured to a row of bunks and, as Ana's eyes adjusted to the gloom inside, she realised that she was looking at around a hundred women, all crammed in together, maybe five or six to a double bunk. Most of them were in the advanced stages of pregnancy and their bumps protruded like obscene bulges from their emaciated bodies. She stepped closer and saw that one of them was crying out against fierce cramps.

'This woman is in labour,' she gasped.

'That happens,' Klara agreed, examining some dirt under her fingernails.

'Get her out of that bunk,' Ana snapped.

'Why?'

'She needs to move to ease the pains, of course. Ester.'

The girl came running to her side and together they helped the poor woman down from the bunk. The others looked up, only half curious, and Ana hated the helpless lethargy she saw within them.

'Here,' she said to the labouring woman, 'walk with me. It will ease the cramps.'

The woman looked at her in confusion but leaned gratefully on her arm and began to walk. The corridor between the crammed-in bunks was narrow and the hut only about forty paces long but by the time they had made it to the far end and back she was walking more easily.

'Where do they give birth?' she asked Klara, who was leaning against the wall watching her with apparent amusement.

'Wherever they fall.'

Ana bit her lip and looked around her. There was nothing

bar a rough chair with a woman lounging upon it. She wore her uniform sewed curiously tight and cut low to expose a large if sagging cleavage. Her hair stood out amongst the shaven-headed women, first for being still there, long and luxurious, and second for being flaming red. Her black triangle marked her out as an 'anti-social' – a prostitute.

'Could you get up, please,' Ana said to her. 'We need that chair.'

'What for?' the woman drawled.

'For this poor labouring mother.'

'This poor labouring *Jew*,' she corrected, her pretty face twisted with hatred.

'It makes little difference.'

'You think?' She rocked back on the chair, her red hair thrown dramatically back. 'Hear that, Klara? "It makes little difference." Who are this pair of dummköpfe?'

Ana stood her ground.

'The chair please.'

Klara let out an exaggerated sigh.

'Let the dummkopf have the chair, Pfani, and let's see what she does with it.'

Pfani got up ostentatiously slowly and, picking up the chair, slammed it down in front of Ana.

'Thank you,' Ana said, then, turning her back on her, she guided the poor mother onto the chair and showed her how to lean forward to take pressure off her back. The cramps were coming fast and it was clear there wasn't long to go. Ana crouched before her.

'Breathe through it,' she urged. 'Like this.' She showed the woman how to pant against the pain and saw a speck of hope come into her eyes as she responded to the care. 'Good. That's very good. What's your name?'

'Elizabet,' she panted.

'Lovely. Now, Elizabet, when the pains ease, I'm going to check where you're at.'

'Thank you,' she gasped out. 'Owww!'

Ester stepped up at Ana's shoulder and she gratefully relinquished her position to her, moving down to edge the woman forward on the seat and hitch her skirts up.

'Baby's on the way,' she said excitedly, spotting the crown. The dirty hut faded around her, the scratch of her ill-fitting uniform dissipated and the pain of the wooden clog against her foot was nothing as she settled herself into the birthing. 'When I tell you, Elizabet, you push. Three, two, one – push!'

Elizabet braced against Ester and, with a roar, bore down. All around them women were sitting up in their bunks, offering weak encouragement.

'Fantastic,' Ana encouraged. 'The head's out. Almost done, my love. Rest a moment and we go again. Three, two, one – push.'

Elizabet half rose, leaning against Ester and bearing down with all her strength.

'It's coming,' Ana called. 'Baby is coming. One more push, Elizabet, and you will be holding your child in your arms.'

Behind her she heard Pfani and Klara give a mocking laugh but Klara did order Pfani to 'fetch the bucket' so perhaps they were readying themselves to give some sort of assistance. She focused on the mother.

'Last push.'

Elizabet let out another roar and her baby was born, small but perfect.

'It's a girl,' Ana cried, looking round for a towel and, finding none, wiping the child on her skirts. 'You have a beautiful baby girl.'

Elizabet sank back in the chair and gave a smile.

'Thank you,' she gasped. 'Thank you so much.'

She held out her arms and Ana looked around for scissors to

cut the cord. Pfani offered her a knife. It was blunt and slightly rusted but in the absence of anything else, Ana rubbed it against her skirts to try and clean the surface muck from it, then gritted her teeth and cut the cord.

'Very good, Nurse,' Klara said. 'Very... instructive. And now, let me teach you.'

She reached down and snatched the baby from Ana, dunking it unceremoniously in a bucket.

'Careful,' Ana beseeched. 'You'll hurt her. Klara. Stop!' She leaped up, grabbing at one of Klara's meaty forearms as Ester grabbed the other but the woman was strong and held the tiny new life tight under the water. Ana felt as if her own lungs were filling. Behind her she could hear the mother screaming, the horrified eyes of the others filling the bunks loomed in on her and in the centre of it all was Klara, pushing the beautiful new baby further and further down in the filthy metal bucket until the bubbles stopped and it was still. Forever still.

Ana let go and fell back against one of the bunks, fighting for breath.

'I told you,' Klara drawled. 'Retraining.' Then, lifting the tiny corpse out of the water, she took five big strides to the door and flung it out into the mud. They heard it land with a dull thud and Ana fumbled for Ester's hand as the world spun around her. She'd feared Auschwitz would be hell but had not known hell could be so very deep or so desperately inhuman.

Elizabet was weeping and Ana watched, stupefied, as hands reached out and pulled her into a bunk where she lay in the arms of others, her sorrow all the sharper in its terrible resignation. All Ana had done was given her a painful moment of hope to be dashed out with her baby's fragile life.

'No!'

The shout came from deep within her and she could no more have stopped it than she could have stopped the poor doomed baby being born.

'No?' Klara asked, menace in her voice as she stepped in front of her, crossing her meaty arms.

'No,' Ana insisted. 'You cannot do that, Sister. You cannot betray our profession in this way. We have been granted authority to bring life into the world, not to snuff it out.'

'When will you see, dummkopf? This is Auschwitz-Birkenau and it is a world all of its own. Play by its rules or die.'

'No.'

'I see.' Klara snapped her fingers and Pfani came scuttling to her side. 'We have a rebel in the block, Pfani. Rebels unsettle the community and we can't have that, can we?'

'We can't, Klara,' Pfani agreed, rubbing her hands. 'We must teach her how to behave.'

'No!' This time it was Ester, throwing herself in front of Ana, but Klara just reached out, took one of her wrists in her big fingers and squeezed until she twisted to the floor with pain, then shoved her aside.

Ana's fingers reached for her rosary but it was gone, taken from her with everything else by her cruel guards, and now she was at the mercy of the vicious block kapo. 'Hail Mary, Mother of God,' she muttered.

Klara cackled.

'God won't help you in here. Now...'

She lifted a fist but at that moment the door swung back and boots rang out across the dirt floor.

'What's going on here?' a deep voice demanded and Klara spun round and gave a curious bow.

'Insolence, Doktor Rohde.'

It was the man from the road, the one who had sent her and Ester to the left. Ana almost wished he had not bothered; she could have been halfway to heaven in a cloud of dark smoke and spared the horrors of Block 17. Perhaps she yet would be, but she would at least go speaking out for justice. She took a step forward.

'Herr Doktor,' she said in clear, steady German. 'I have just helped a mother give birth only to have this, this... *woman*...' (the word was a travesty but she fought to spit it out), 'drown the child before all our eyes. That is a dereliction of our sworn duty and runs counter to every fibre of the Hippocratic oath that we, like you, have taken.'

Doktor Rohde blinked down at her.

'The Hippocratic oath?' he said, almost as if being reminded of something from an ancient past.

'Why are babies being murdered?' she demanded.

The women in the bunks around sucked in their breath at her choice of word but the doctor seemed to consider it.

'This is a work camp,' he said. 'Ergo, people are here to work. A mother with a baby cannot do so.'

'She can. Many is the woman you see in the fields at harvest time with a babe strapped to her back.'

That startled him.

'True,' he agreed reluctantly. 'I have seen it myself in my youth.' Again the words seemed tinged with nostalgia, as if he were ancient, though he looked to be forty at the most. He gave a shake of his head. 'But the work here is not simply gathering in corn. There are roads to build, railway tracks to lay, fish and fowl to farm. Babies have no place in Auschwitz.'

That Ana could only agree with, but sending them out of there in a bucket was not right.

'Surely a kindergarten...'

The word was drowned out by another cackle from Klara and Pfani. Doktor Rohde frowned at them.

'Enough,' he snapped, and their laughter died instantly.

'As it happens,' he said, 'we have a new directive from Herr Himmler himself. The euthanasia programme is, henceforth, only to apply to the mentally deficient. The Reich needs labour and we cannot be wasting pregnant women any longer. From now on neither they, nor their babies, are to be... removed.'

Klara looked furious.

'The babies are to live?' she asked with dark incredulity.

'The babies are *not* to be killed,' Doktor Rohde corrected.

He cast a look around the dirty hut and even Ana, after only hours in this hellhole, understood that any newborn would have the tiniest chance of survival. But she felt Ester's hand slide into hers and squeeze it and knew that it was a start.

'Thank you, Herr Doktor,' she said.

He gave her a curt nod.

'You may do your job, Midwife. And you,' he looked to Klara, 'will alter yours.'

Klara glared at Ana but there was little she could do.

'Yes, Herr Doktor.'

Ana felt a flash of triumph. This, then, was why she was here. This was the mission God had set out for her and she must seize it with both hands. Whatever it cost her, she must battle to save the life of every single baby born in Auschwitz-Birkenau from this day forward. She looked to Ester, still tight at her side, and dared to give her a tiny smile. They would do this together.

But Klara had not done with them yet.

'Not the Jewish ones, though, Herr Doktor?' she said slyly as her superior reached the door.

Doktor Rohde looked around.

'Oh no,' he agreed without a moment's hesitation. 'The Jewish ones die.'

SIXTEEN

JUNE 1943

ESTER

'Up! Up! Come on, you dumme Kühe – up!'

Ester battled to the surface of consciousness as Klara ran her treasured baton along the bunks, startling everyone out of an uneasy half sleep into even more uneasy wakefulness. It was 4 a.m. and even in the height of summer the sun was not yet peeking over the horizon so Block 17 was in darkness. Ester pushed her fists into her eyes to stop the ever-ready tears coming; she couldn't afford to lose the moisture.

'Hail Mary, Mother of God,' she heard Ana mutter into the darkness and drew brief comfort from the now familiar prayer. At first she had found the words strange but these days she let them wash over her and drank in their resonance, as if it were a rabbi chanting in the synagogue. Her poor, weary mind had no idea any more if God was watching over them in Birkenau, but she knew for sure that, if he was, he must be weeping. She shifted against the women with whom she was crammed into the bare wooden bunk and felt, as ever, her body ache for the comfort of Filip beside her. Would she ever see him again?

'Come on, you filthy whores – up and out.'

Ester tore her thoughts from her husband and forced herself to clamber down. Klara hated getting up and took out the discomforts of the camp regime on those unfortunate enough to be set beneath her. She was prisoner 837 – a number so low in the sequence that she was, as far as they knew, the longest standing female inmate in the camp. Delivered straight to newly built Birkenau from a German prison in 1942, she'd been singled out as a woman suitably sadistic to lead and as block 'kapo' she had a tiny room of her own just inside the door, with a mattress and a blanket all to herself – luxuries indeed. Not that they improved her temper.

'Special day today,' she said, striking out randomly at women as they tried to clamber down from the three-tiered bunks.

'Your birthday is it, Klara?' one older woman asked and got herself a clout on the back of her thighs.

'Shame someone didn't drown *her* in a bucket,' Ester heard someone else mutter and smirked.

'Or just treated her with kindness,' Ana suggested, and she felt instant shame. Her friend was right, but it was becoming almost impossible to imagine anyone – except dear Ana – treating people with kindness.

Impossible, too, to conceive of what a 'special day' might entail as every one in the camp passed in a blur of routine – roll call, the dishwater they called coffee, work, rotting soup, more work, another roll call, and a crust of bread meant to serve as both supper and breakfast. The evenings offered such joys as queueing for the latrine pits, picking lice out of your hair and fighting for a half-space in a hard wooden bunk. At least Ester was spared being marched out of the camp to work on one of the many farms in the area, for those women came in worn down to nothing every evening. Her nursing work, however, although not physically tough, was emotionally battering. She and Ana were employed across the four barracks currently designated as hospitals, and with typhus raging through the women and almost no medicines, disinfectants or even water, trying to care for them was soul-destroying work. Which was exactly what the Nazis wanted.

Everything their tormentors did, from the shaved heads, to the matching uniforms, to the use of numbers instead of names, was designed to turn them into tallies on a stick instead of actual human beings. If women died in the night, their fellows had to carry them out to the dawn roll call so that they could be accounted for and tossed onto piles of corpses awaiting a cart to the crematoria. Ester swore the SS left them there longer than necessary just to remind the living how close they were to nothingness and had learned fast that you had to fight that with every inch of your former self you could possibly hold onto.

As she tumbled out into the first tendrils of a misty dawn for roll call she fought against the sickness that seemed to forever roil in her poor, empty stomach and battled to pull the threads of herself together. Shuffling into her place in line, she closed her eyes against the ranks of half-starved women, the prowling SS and their snapping dogs, the bodies of the dead being carried out to take their place for the tally. Pushing every cell inside her head to work with her, she carried herself to the steps of St Stanislaus' cathedral and suddenly the sun was warm on her head and the step teasingly cold against her thighs. People were bustling past her on Piotrkowska Street, buying groceries for their families, eating lunch with friends, window-shopping for glamorous shoes.

She thought of the lunch that awaited her. Her mother's home-made twarog cheese with a simple but oh-so-delicious bajgiel was sitting in the paper Ruth had lovingly wrapped it in that morning and she could open it slowly and take a bite. She lingered there, ignoring the shouts and the wails and the barks that threatened to penetrate her perfect daydream, and let her other self savour the cheese on her tongue before finally she allowed herself the very best sensation of all – to look up and see him, Filip, bounding towards her, hair mussed, satchel banging against his long legs, smile broad across his kind, open face.

'Filip,' she whispered, and half lifted her hand as if her fingers could actually clasp his through the great chasm of time and space that their oppressors had carved between them.

Instead, she got a sharp elbow in the ribs.

'Ester!'

She blinked her eyes open to see Ana staring imploringly at her.

'Number 41400.'

'Here!' she called quickly.

The guard's eyes narrowed and, as she marched over, Ester saw with a sinking heart that it was SS-Aufseherin Irma Grese, a woman whose perfect Aryan beauty was matched only by her cruelty.

'Are you sure, 41400?' Grese demanded, a curl to her cupid's bow. 'Because you looked to be very much somewhere else.'

'Here, Aufseherin,' Ester said, fighting to stand up as straight as she could.

Grese hated weakness. The only thing she hated more, it was whispered around the camp, was attractiveness, as if it in some way challenged her own hourglass perfection. She'd been known to flay off the breasts of a comely woman in a fit of envy and for once Ester was glad that almost all trace of her own womanliness had been eroded away in the last three months of starvation and fear. Thankfully Grese was distracted this morning and satisfied herself with a slap across Ester's cheek. She wore a heavy signet ring and it cut into her cheekbone but Ester forced herself not to react and, with a small grunt, Grese turned away.

'Good – because you need to be sharp today. You're moving.'

'Moving?'

The question came from a woman behind. Grese's eyes narrowed further and, with an almost animal scream, she pounced.

'How dare you question me?'

Her stick came down on the woman's back again and again as the other prisoners cowered away and the SS looked on with bored detachment. Ester fumbled for Ana's hand, knowing full well it could have been her whose bones were cracking beneath the sadist's irrational fury. She longed to take herself back to St Stanislaus where Filip had just been arriving, but she did not dare. She needed all her wits about her.

Finally, Grese wore herself out and stalked back to join her fellows, leaving the poor woman in a broken heap. Every fibre in Ester wanted to bend to help her but she did not dare; Birkenau had stripped even the humanity of helping others. As Ana always said to her, their only weapon now was staying alive. Kindness had become an underground movement.

Grese's superior, Lagerführerin Maria Mandel, stepped forward and the whole camp snapped to attention as best it could.

'Today,' she said in her stark German, 'is a day of reorganisation.'

The women stiffened, terrified this was a new euphemism for selection. Periodically the SS, whether on orders, working to quotas, or just for their own amusement, used a roll call to 'select' prisoners to be sent up the dreaded chimneys. If there was not yet room in their vast ovens, they shoved them into the feared Block 25, the 'antechamber to the crematorium', where they were kept without food or water until there were enough poor wretches to make up a 'full batch'.

The lucky ones died before they ever had to make the

journey to the back of the camp, for no one knew exactly what went on there. Every so often men were hauled into the crematoria Sonderkommando – labour unit – but they were kept totally separate from the other prisoners so only snatches of information ever made it back. Some people said poison gas was delivered in Red Cross ambulances, stolen for the purpose, others said they just shoved people into ovens and burned them alive. The 'lucky' new arrivals who were sent straight there were lulled with the pretence that they were going to showers but the regular inmates did not have that luxury. Death hung over the camp in physical clouds, tainting the very air they breathed with a barbaric smell that always made Ester feel even sicker than usual.

'Today,' Mandel went on, pulling Ester back from the coils of her stomach, 'the men are moving across the tracks and we will have twice as much space for the women.'

There was a shuffle of something close to excitement at the words 'twice as much space'.

'Those fine women capable of working will move to B1b.' She gestured left to the back end of the camp where, now they looked, they could see parades of men filing out of their barracks and over the road to the far side. 'Those drains on the Reich who need time to get back to usefulness, will stay here in B1a. Your kapos have more details. Do as they tell you and do it fast. There will be no rations until the move is complete. Go!'

The women looked at each other in confusion.

'Back to your blocks, Schweinedreck, to be assigned to your new ones.'

Everyone scrambled. The sun was coming up now, kissing the wires of Birkenau a deceptively pretty pink. Looking to the skies, Ester saw not the radiance of nature but the thirst that a day of moving beneath a hot sun was sure to bring. Already her lips were chapped and her tongue sticking painfully to the roof of her mouth and without even the mug of so-called coffee that was normally served after roll call, there was hell ahead.

'Gather your goods,' Klara snapped (presumably a joke as all anyone had to their name was a part-share in a filthy blanket). 'We're off to Block 24.'

'The hospital?' Ana asked.

'One of them, yes. I'm to be overall kapo and you're to get a maternity section.'

'Really?' Ester saw Ana's eyes light up, and so did Klara.

'Oh yes. State of the art it will be. Clean floors, lovely padded birthing beds, sterilised tools...'

She cackled madly and the light shut off in Ana. Ester hated to see it. Asking them to offer medical aid in these conditions was like asking a man to dig a road with his hands. Mind you, she wouldn't be surprised if the Nazis did that as well – everything was designed to make them fail and they had to fight against it time and again. All her midwife friend had to tend her patients was filthy, lice-infested blankets, dirty water and a rusting pair of manicure scissors. Every baby that was born in the camp was a tiny victory– a bubble of air in the cesspool – and if it ended in heartbreak as the tiny life leeched away, at least there had been joy for a moment.

'Your hands are all the comfort a labouring mother needs,' she whispered to Ana. 'Come on, let's go and find our new ward.'

Block 24 was teeming with women. Some lay helpless in bed, on fire with typhus, the others had apparently been drafted in to help 'thin them out' as Klara put it. It emerged that thirty bunks were to be cleared at the far end as the maternity section, but it would take some time to move the poor women battling for their lives. Someone, no doubt Klara, had decided to assign Ana the area currently occupied by the worst sufferers, and the poor women were too weak to do anything but lie in their own – and each other's – bodily fluids. There were mattresses of a sort in here, but the stuffing was so thin as to be useless and the fabric merely soaked up the filth.

'We need water,' Ester said, and Klara laughingly sent Pfani across with a bucket of something that was surely more dirt than water and that was, besides, cracked so that even as they tried to use the filthy fluid, it leaked away into the untiled floor.

Ana sank to her knees, as if her spirit was leaking away with it, and Ester rubbed helplessly at her back.

'What's the point?' Ana asked, lifting her brown eyes up to Ester's. 'What on earth is the point of even trying?'

'Because if we don't, they've won,' Ester said, crouching next to her.

Ana pressed her forehead to Ester's own.

'They *have* won,' she whispered.

'Not yet,' Ester said fiercely. While Filip was still clear in her mind's eye, she had something to fight for and she wasn't going to give up on even the slimmest chance to see him again. 'Come on.'

She lifted Ana to her feet and as she did so a woman came towards them, wearing a white blouse that was almost clean and, rarer yet, a smile.

'Ana Kaminski?' She put out a hand, talking in Polish. 'I'm honoured to meet you. I've heard much of your skills.'

'You have?' Ana stuttered, also in their native language.

'Of course. It's rare in this place to bring life instead of death and I honour you for it. I'm Dr Węgierska – Janina. I was a GP in Warsaw what feels like a very long time ago. I was sent to this place for the "crime" of treating Jews – and I'm determined to keep on doing it! I'm trying to bring some order to the hospital barracks. Will you help me?'

Ana looked to Ester and, to her huge relief, Ester saw her ageing back straighten again.

'We would love to.'

All morning long they worked, cleaning bunks with water Janina somehow managed to produce and moving patients across, slowly freeing up space so that the poor women had some room to move, some air around their fevered bodies and slight relief from the lice. The SS kept their distance, afraid of infection, and for the first time since she'd come to Birkenau, Ester felt almost as if she were working for the common good. Around midday they reached the middle bunks where a sorry bunch of women were huddled.

'We're here to help you,' Ester told them, reaching out a hand.

They cowered back as if she might strike them and Ester looked at them curiously. They had sun-darkened skin and eyes like black olives and they babbled to each other in a language she had never heard before.

'Where are you from?' she asked in halting German.

No answer. She tried again in Polish but still nothing.

'They're not rude,' a voice said behind her, in heavily accented Polish, 'they just don't understand. They're Greek.'

Ester spun round and found herself face to face with a young woman with a heart-shaped face, striking green eyes and the beginnings of curls springing determinedly from her shaven head.

'Naomi,' the girl introduced herself, putting down two buckets of water and offering Ester her hand. 'Number 39882.' She grimaced at the number on her arm. 'I'm Greek too but my mother was Polish so I have an advantage over my poor friends. I've spent time with my grandparents in Krakow, so the climate here is not such a shock.'

Ester glanced out the window where the sun was beating down and Naomi laughed. It was such an alien sound in the camp that it made Ester laugh too and the bubble of it in her throat tasted like the finest champagne.

'Today is a good day,' Naomi conceded, 'but when we first arrived it was shocking. We come from Salonika and never have we seen so much rain.'

'I envy you.'

Naomi grinned.

'You will have to come and visit then, when this is all over.'

Ester stared at her, amazed at her simple optimism.

'You think it will be?'

'One way or another it has to be, and what's the point in thinking the worst?'

Ester grabbed her hands.

'Bless you, Naomi. You are right.'

'I wish I could tell my mother that.' For a moment the smile slipped and Naomi cast a glance out to the chimneys, but then she pulled it firmly back into place. 'She always said I was a bit of a dunce and I think she was right, but perhaps sometimes it's a blessing to be stupid.'

'Naomi! You don't seem stupid to me.'

'Oh, believe me, I am doing my very best to be, for if you allow yourself even a moment's truly rational thought about this place you would surely lose all sanity.'

'True,' Ester agreed. 'I like to take myself away from it.'

'Away?' Naomi's green eyes widened. 'How?'

Ester flushed.

'Oh, not in reality, just in my mind.'

'Where do you go?' Her interest was so genuine that it surprised Ester into telling her.

'I go to the steps of a cathedral in my home town.'

'A cathedral?' Naomi squinted at her. 'Are you not a Jew?'

Ester pointed to the yellow triangle on her ill-fitting uniform.

'I'm very much a Jew but the cathedral was close to the hospital where I worked and I used to sit there to eat my lunch and watch the people on Piotrkowska Street. Then one day this young man came there to eat his lunch too.'

'And you got talking and fell in love!'

Ester's smile widened, stretching out the cracks in her lips.

'Well, it took a bit longer than that – we were both rather shy – but yes.'

'That's soo romantic. What's his name?'

'Filip.' Speaking it aloud was a joy so tender that she almost cried.

'Is he... is he here?'

Ester shook her head.

'No. At least, I don't know that for sure. I don't know anything for sure. I picture him all the time and I have this idea that while I can do that, he must still be alive, but that's silly, is it not?'

'Not at all. If your souls are connected then they will call to each other.'

'You think so?'

'I know so,' she said firmly, 'but if you want a bit more detail, I could talk to Mala.'

'Mala?'

'Mala Zimetbaum. You must know her?'

Ester shook her head.

'Oh, Mala's fabulous.' Naomi looked surreptitiously around but the SS were still staying away and even Klara was out, sitting in the sun with Pfani, ostensibly supervising the cleaning of blankets. 'She's a Polish Jew but she's lived in Belgium for, like, forever and she can speak all these different languages. She's very sophisticated too so the Germans use her as an interpreter and courier.' She lowered her voice even further. 'That means she gets in and out of the postal offices all the time and while she's there she can... liberate letters.'

'Letters?' The word was like the finest promise.

Naomi nodded eagerly.

'The other day she brought me one with a picture in it of my family. Not my mother...' Again the shade, but again she shook it off, 'but my Papa and my sisters. They got away, you see, when the Nazis came. I was working in a factory so they got to me first but Papa had time to take my little sisters into the hills. They're in Switzerland now. They're safe.'

'That's amazing. And they wrote to you? Here? And it got through?'

'Oh yes. It all gets through. The Germans love it because people send money and food that they can keep for themselves. They let the non-Jews have their stuff – some of it at least – but not us. Mala, though, Mala can find it. What's your name?'

'Ester Pasternak. That's my married name. Filip's name.'

'If he's written to you, Ester, Mala will find it. I'll talk to her tomorrow, I promise.'

'That's so kind of you.'

'Anything for romance. I so want to fall in love.'

Ester looked around the barrack full of sick women.

'I'm afraid you might have to wait a while.'

'It looks that way. The only men around here are Nazis, though some of them don't seem too bad.'

Ester stared at her in horror.

'Naomi – they're all awful!'

'Some of the younger ones can be all right.'

'Which younger ones? Where?'

She shrugged.

'I've got a job in Kanada and they can be quite nice in there sometimes, especially if they think you've found something interesting. One of them let me keep a lipstick the other day. See.'

She gave a funny pout and Ester saw that she did, indeed, have the remains of a dark pink gloss on her lips. She'd heard about people working in 'Kanada' – the great run of blocks next to the crematoria, where the clothes and goods of new arrivals were sorted. It was an enviable task, done under a roof and with endless possibilities for 'organising' supplies if you had the nerve for it. Naomi seemed to have plenty of nerve but, looking at her more closely, Ester realised she was very young.

'How old are you, Naomi?'

'Sixteen,' she said, chin jutting up in a way that suggested she might be less. Ester didn't push it. Something about the girl reminded her of Leah and she felt a surge of protectiveness.

'Don't talk to the SS, Naomi, however nice they might seem. These are the men who are keeping you imprisoned against your will, feeding you next to nothing, killing your friends and relatives.'

Naomi's brow shaded.

'I suppose they're only obeying orders,' she suggested in a small voice.

'No,' Ester said, sure on this one. 'Everyone here is in the SS or the Gestapo – paid-up members of the Nazi party. It's thanks to men like them that Hitler got into power. It's thanks to their support of his sick ideas on racial purity that the likes of you and I are deemed "lesser" and sent to be kicked around like animals. It's thanks to—'

'I get it!'

Naomi put up her hands and Ester stopped herself.

'Sorry. I get a bit angry.'

'Don't we all.' Naomi threw her arms around Ester in a hug so spontaneous and pure that it sent tears leaping from her eyes. 'Oi – don't cry.'

Ester scrubbed at her face.

'I can't seem to help it. I do it all the time. If I'm not feeling weepy, I'm feeling sick.'

'It's this place,' Naomi said, giving her another hug but Ester sensed someone else hovering over them and, turning, was relieved to see it was only Ana.

'Ana – you must meet Naomi. She's been carrying water for us.'

'So I see. Thank you, Naomi.' Ana offered a half smile in the girl's direction but her eyes were all on Ester. 'Sick and weepy?' she queried.

Ester nodded.

'It's just hunger, Ana, and tiredness.' She saw the old woman's face. 'Isn't it?'

'Of course,' Ana agreed quickly. 'Bound to be. Now, shall we scrub this bunk?'

She gestured to the newly cleared bed and Ester went to help but she'd seen the hesitation in her friend and pressed her hand surreptitiously to her forehead. Did she have typhus? It wouldn't be surprising, surrounded by it day and night, but so far she'd escaped. She looked at the poor women, writhing with pain all around the barracks, and prayed – to her God, to Ana's God, to any god who might conceivably be able to hear her over the cries – to keep her well.

Naomi's lipstick-bright optimism had stirred hope within her and, as she picked up a worn scrubbing brush to set to work, the picture of Filip was brighter than ever in her mind's eye. Her body filled with love and she pushed the nausea fiercely aside. She *would* stay fit, she *would* stay alive, and she *would*, somehow, get out of here.

SEVENTEEN

JUNE 1943

ANA

'Still alive? Interesting.'

The new doctor made a neat note in a small leather notepad and Ana suppressed an urge to snatch his fancy fountain pen off him and ram it into his Nazi eyeball. The 'interesting' subject was a tiny baby, born four days ago to Mrs Haim, a Jewish woman who had lost her three older children to the gas chambers on arrival in camp. Being of ample proportions, her pregnancy had been well hidden until five months of hard labour dredging the fish farm had cut away enough of her flesh for her belly to protrude. There had been terrifying talk of her being taken to Doktor Nierzwicki, who was carrying out hideous experiments to abort and sterilise women, but then this new doctor's eye had fallen upon her and she'd been marked out for a different but equally cruel bit of speculative science.

Doktor Josef Mengele, head physician at the Roma camp across the tracks, wished to know how long a newborn could live without food and had been idly monitoring Rebekah Haim's son since he had come into this dark corner of the world.

These days any babies born to non-Jewish mothers were registered as camp inmates and given their own number, tattooed onto their thigh by Pfani, who took a curious pleasure in the task. It was not, as far as Ana could see, to do with inflicting pain on the babies but rather to do with the artistry. Sometimes, in an idle hour, Pfani would etch pictures onto her own skin, or that of anyone foolish enough to let her and, although rough, they had a certain style. 'Auschwitz-art' the prostitute called it; that said it all.

Not that Pfani's numbers helped the babies much. Few mothers could keep them alive for more than a week or two, though even that was more than the poor Jewish children could hope for. Klara and Pfani still had permission – indeed orders – to kill all Jewish babies at birth and prowled Block 24 whenever they knew a Jewish mother was near her time. Occasionally Ana had been able to keep one hidden if it was born in the dead of night when the despotic pair were snoring in their private room, but only ever for a day or two – those women could sniff out babies like the rats could sniff out rotting flesh.

Only Rebekah's baby had been 'spared' for Mengele's evil study; and to make matters worse, his chosen subject, unlike many of the exhausted mothers, seemed to have milk aplenty. Spotting this, Mengele had bound her breasts so tightly that it was a miracle her heart could still beat beneath them and, in truth, it might have been a blessing if it had stopped but four long, spiralling days later, both mother and baby were still alive.

Mengele tipped his head on one side, tapped his pen against his perfect teeth and then suddenly said, 'Enough of this. Block 25.'

Ana swallowed at the dreaded sound of the 'antechamber to the crematoria'.

'Beg pardon, Herr Doktor?' she tried.

He glared at her.

'Send them to Block 25, Nurse.'

'I'm the midwife, Herr Doktor.'

His head tipped the other way.

'Are you indeed? How curious.' He peered at her uniform, noting the green triangle that marked her out as a 'criminal'. 'You're not a Jew?'

'No, Herr Doktor. I am a Christian woman, but I believe in the sanctity of all human life.'

'Do you? How foolish. Do you think a rat worth the same as a horse?'

She blinked, seeing the trap instantly. Horses were beautiful, noble creatures and rats filthy scavengers. Every day she had to chase the bloated beasts off the patients as they looked for tasty edges to nibble on, little caring whether their helpless prey was alive or dead. But that was not the point here.

'I assume other rats would stand up for their fellows' worth,' she said carefully.

Mengele let out a laugh.

'Very good, Midwife. Your name?'

'Ana Kaminski, sir,' she stuttered in surprise, unused to say anything more than her number.

'And you are here for?'

'Suspected resistance, sir.'

'I see. Ah well, it shows spirit I suppose.' He looked her up and down and then gave a sly smile. 'You must be the woman who stopped Schwester Klara drowning the babies.'

'I am,' she agreed, though it was only partly true.

Every time Ana confirmed a Jewish pregnancy her heart sank. Nine months was a long time to carry the seed of a life that would be snatched from you the moment it flowered. And she had another reason to worry. Ester did not look at all well these days and Ana had seen the signs far too many times to be able to deny them, however much she longed to. She had to do something.

Swallowing down fear, she crossed her hands in front of her

and said, 'It is not in the Hippocratic oath to take life, Herr Doktor.'

'True, Mrs Kaminski.' Again the tip of the head, but only for the briefest moment. 'But it is also not in the Hippocratic oath to save rats. You – Block 25.'

He spun away from Ana to stand over Rebekah Haim as she heaved herself from her bunk, her baby clutched tight to her bound chest, and made for the door. Ana reached out and touched her arm.

'God bless you, Rebekah.'

The poor woman turned soulful eyes upon her.

'I'm sorry, Ana, but I think God gave up on us a long time ago.'

'But—'

'It's fine. I will take this one to meet his siblings far, far away from these devils.'

With that, she spat onto Mengele's highly polished boot and, head high, limped out and round to Block 25. Cursing, Mengele stomped away, and the moment he was gone Ana crossed to the far window that looked out onto the courtyard of the doomed block. If there were circles of hell in Birkenau, Block 25 was the lowest of all. Desperate women could sometimes be seen sucking at the stray blades of grass that made it out of the mud, trying to slake their thirst as they were left to wait day after day for enough of their fellows to be doomed to join them. Rebekah would be 'lucky' for both the hut and the courtyard were full of unfortunates and the trucks would surely be here soon to take them away.

Ana usually avoided looking out on this side but today her eyes were glued to Rebekah as she sat herself down in the sunshine, laid her baby in her lap and slowly but with furious determination unbound the cruel fabric from her breasts. Finally free, she lifted the child and put it to the nipple. His head lolled at first, too weak to even suck, and Rebekah squeezed a few droplets free and touched them tenderly to his lips until, like a miracle, he found the strength to latch on. They would, at least, have the consolation of this final bond but the waste of two precious lives was almost too much for Ana to bear and she sank down against the wall and wept.

'Please God,' she prayed through her tears. 'Please don't let Ester be pregnant.'

If watching Rebekah Haim go to her death was hard, watching Ester do so would be impossible. *She's your daughter now*, Ruth had told her that hideous night in the train to hell and Ana had to protect her with all she had.

The problem was – what if all she had was not enough?

She sank her head into her hands, wishing Bartek were here. So many times in their long marriage she'd brought the trials of her work home and he had listened calmly and stroked her hair and quietly put everything into perspective for her. She fought to think what he might say to her were he here or, better yet, were she somewhere – anywhere – else with him. Her fingers fumbled to her waist and met with the blessed comfort of an old set of rosary beads. Naomi had 'organised' – the camp slang for underhand procurement – them from Kanada, bless her, and Ana kept them beneath her skirt where the feel of the beads, worn beautifully smooth by years of someone's prayers, calmed her. Now she ran quietly through a Hail Mary as she reminded herself that her dear husband was still alive.

The magical parcel had come a few days ago. A tall, hard-faced prisoner, with the green triangle of a criminal, had stomped into the block shouting 'post for Ana Kaminski'. They'd all thought it was some sort of cruel joke, but when Ana had made herself known, the woman had indeed shown her a parcel – or rather the remnants of a parcel – with her name written on it in a hand so familiar that she had almost fainted.

'Thank you,' she'd gasped out, reaching for it, but the woman had held it high.

'There'll be a fee.'

Ana had spread her hands wide.

'I don't have anything.'

'Oh but you do.' She'd proceeded to open up the parcel, already torn apart and presumably searched and denuded of anything the Germans in the postal office had fancied, and rifle through what was left. 'I'll take this.'

Ana and all the other women in Block 24 had stared enviously as she'd extracted a bar of chocolate – small but desperately precious – and tucked it into her pocket. Then, finally, she'd shoved the parcel at Ana and stomped to the exit with her prize.

'Why has *she* got a parcel?' someone had called petulantly from a bunk and the 'postwoman' had paused to leer at her.

'Because she's not Jewish, is she, Sauhund.'

Then she'd been gone and all eyes had fallen on Ana. For a moment she'd felt like a mouse beneath a hawk and been grateful this was the hospital ward where the women were too weak to set upon her.

'I will share the food,' she'd told them, though Lord knows the remaining supplies would not go far. She hadn't cared. It hadn't been the dried meat that she'd wanted, so much as the news. The letter had been heavily censored, scrawled through with a thick black pen that obscured far too many of her husband's precious words, but she had got 'Warsaw' and 'Bron with me' and 'safe' and it had been enough. More than enough. Bartek and Bron were alive and well and no doubt fighting for freedom and that thought had filled Ana with joy ever since.

As she stood watching Rebekah Haim waiting to die, though, Warsaw felt so very, very far away. Even the village of Oświęcim, almost within sight of the camp, felt impossibly distant, as if the wire fences, buzzed full of lethal electricity at night, were set at the very edges of the known world. Anything could be happening out there and they would never know.

Their life was bounded by the trains coming in at one end and the smoke going out at the other; everything in between was just limbo.

'On your feet – all of you.'

Schwester Klara was back from wherever she'd been lazing around and by the sound of her voice, she was on her best behaviour. That did not bode well and cold dread settled around Ana as she forced herself up, stashing the rosary beneath the folds of her skirt.

'Ah, Schwester Ana.' Ana blinked – she'd never heard Klara offer her more of a title than alte Kuh – old cow – before. 'These officers are here to honour some of our babies.'

'Honour them?'

Ester had come up across from the main ward to see the new arrivals but looked as lost as Ana. There were two officers, a man and a woman, both in SS uniform and decorated with enough braid and badges to indicate the sort of superior rank that explained Kara's snivelling behaviour.

'They are here to select babies for the Lebensborn programme.'

'Lebensborn?' Ana queried. The word, as far as she was aware, translated as 'fount of life' but that helped little.

The female officer, a tall woman in heeled boots, looked down at her.

'It is a programme instituted by the Third Reich to ensure that all babies of valuable stock are kept safe and brought up in solid, Führer-loving homes.'

Still Ana struggled to work it out.

'You are here to take mothers and babies to Germany?'

It sounded too good to be true. If she could see one new mother walk out of this camp to freedom it would rejuvenate her faith.

'We are here,' the woman said sternly, 'to take babies to Germany.'

It *was* too good to be true.

'But the mothers—'

'Will stay here and work, as was intended when they were deported. Do not worry, Nurse, there are plenty of wholesome families in the Reich who will bring the babies up. And far, far better than these women could do.'

Her nose wrinkled as she looked around the maternity section. Ana, Ester and Doctor Węgierska had done their best to improve the new 'ward'. The pregnant women were separated from those in the hospital proper by a 'curtain' made of old bedsheets from Kanada, and with thirty bunks available they usually only had to share two or maybe three to a double bunk. The mattresses were so thin that the poor things might as well be sleeping on bare boards, but Ana had been granted permission to fetch water whenever she needed it so they usually kept them clean, partially lice-free, and with plenty to drink.

Best of all was the 'delivery suite' – a long, brick stove that ran the length of the block, fed by fires at either end. The fires were never lit in the summer but the area was long, accessible from both sides, and raised off the ground – a big improvement on the single chair they'd been using in Block 17. Even so, it must be a pitiful sight to a newcomer and Ana felt a sudden flare of hope that if these officers wanted their babies, they might be able to help.

'Conditions here are very tough for mothers,' she said.

The woman gave a crisp nod.

'Which is precisely why valuable babies must be removed as soon as possible. We will be visiting regularly and Schwester Klara here assures me that she will be sure to save any promising children.'

'Promising?' Ana asked.

'Blond,' the woman said shortly.

Ana looked to Ester, whose fingers went instinctively to her own unusually blond hair, growing back in golden tufts. Had God been listening to her after all?

'You want all blond babies? Even Jewish ones.'

'Don't be ridiculous, Ana,' Klara snapped. 'Why would they want...?'

But the male officer put up a sharp hand and Klara babbled to a confused halt.

'If the babies are blond,' he pronounced imperiously, 'they cannot be Jewish.'

It was twisted logic, but Ana let it go.

'And the mothers?' she dared to ask, but at that he shook his head in disgust.

'Oh no – not the mothers. There might have been hope for them, once, but they have been too steeped in dirty Jewish influences to ever truly be free. We are here to break that cycle.' He looked smugly around. 'I'm sure any Jewish mother will be delighted to have her baby released to live as a good German in the freedom of the Reich.' The Jewish mothers standing before their bunks – and indeed their Polish, Russian and Greek compatriots – cowered back, belying his words, but he did not seem to notice. 'Let us see the babies then,' he said with relish. 'Let us choose.'

The women looked nervously to each other but already Klara was pounding down the line, shoving those with their infants still safely inside them back onto bunks and forcing those with babes in arms to hold them out as the two SS officers moved along behind her like inspectors on a production line. Ana felt Ester creep in tight against her side and together they watched in frozen horror.

'That one!' the man pronounced, pointing to a four-day-old Polish boy whose downy hair was the colour of straw.

Klara snatched the baby from his mother's arms and marched behind him with it as the poor woman collapsed in a friend's arms.

'And this one.'

A Russian girl. This time the mother was forewarned and put up a fight but it was clear that Klara would rather tear a limb from the baby than give it up and she was forced to concede.

'Oh and definitely this one.'

The man took this baby himself, another girl who had been born in the early hours of this morning with hair so blond as to be almost white. The mother was Jewish and it was only thanks to Klara's obsession with sitting in the sun that she had made it this far into life. Now, it seemed, she was to be stolen away, not for death in a bucket but for life in a Nazi family. Ana wasn't sure which was worse. The officer looked almost tenderly down at the child, then peered curiously at the mother, a dark-haired girl, still weak from a long labour and quivering helplessly before him.

'How did *you* produce this?' he asked scathingly.

'My, my husband is Norwegian,' she stuttered.

'Ah! A mischling. Well, well done you. Don't worry – this will go to a good home.' He patted her head as if he was taking nothing more than a trinket from her and proceeded on down the line. 'No, no, definitely not. Hmmm.' He was almost at the end of the line and clearly not up to his expected quota. He prodded at a baby with hair the colour of damp sand and frowned. 'What do you think, Aufseherin Wolf?'

The female officer tugged on the baby's hair, as if to check it was real, and shrugged.

'It'll do, Hauptsturmführer Meyer. His hair might look brighter with these filthy Jewish lice washed out, and Himmler's desperate now the bastard Reds are killing all our boys so the officials at the centre won't look too closely. We'll have him.'

And with that, she seized the baby, carrying him out in front of her as if he might taint her which, indeed, he might, given that no one ever provided the maternity section with any nappies. The baby did nothing but the mother threw herself on Wolf, clutching tightly onto her legs so that she almost fell.

'Please,' she begged. 'Please don't take my baby.'

'You want to keep him here?' Wolf asked, lip curled as she looked pointedly around the dank ward.

'I want to keep him with me,' the mother said. 'He's mine.'

Wolf shrugged.

'And you, I'm afraid, are mine. Now get off me before I have to have you taken off.'

But the poor woman would not let go and, with Klara laden down with the first two babies, there was no one to force her.

'Mein Gott!' Meyer exclaimed and, pulling a pistol from his belt, shot her through the head.

She slumped at his colleague's feet and with a sniff Aufseherin Wolf lifted her heeled boots from the tangle of her limp arms and strode away without a backward glance.

'We'll be back,' she said, pausing in the doorway, a dark silhouette against the sun beyond. 'Keep the good ones for us.'

'Of course,' Klara said, actually bowing. 'It will be my honour.'

'It will,' Wolf agreed, and then they were gone.

A heavy silence settled around the corpse of the poor mother who had committed no crime save trying to keep her own child.

'What?' Klara snapped. 'You should cheer up, the lot of you, at least your babies are safe.'

'Safe?' the Russian wept. 'You call it safe being brought up by some Nazi from hell? What if they turn my baby into one of them? What if they corrupt her with their evil ideas and use her as a weapon against her own people? What on earth is "safe" about that?'

She ran to the door and they all spilled after her, but the SS were gone, off in their fancy car with the four unfortunate infants, their path crossing with three big trucks pulling up outside Block 25. They all stood and watched as Rebekah Haim stepped with calm dignity into the first one, her baby clutched tightly to her.

'At least she gets to die in peace with her child,' the Russian cried, as the other deprived mothers huddled in with her.

Ester took Ana's arm.

'What sort of world do we live in where *that* is the enviable option?' she asked.

Ana could only shake her head. Every time she thought they had reached the depths of Birkenau, a new pit seemed to open up. She leaned shakily back against the wall of the hut but Irma Grese was stalking towards the wailing mothers and Ester tugged on her arm.

'Let's get inside, Ana. I need to stay out of Grese's way. I think those snacks Naomi has been bringing us from Kanada are going straight to my breasts. Look.'

She patted nervously at her chest, which was indeed swelling, and Ana hurried her inside, her heart aching as the pit deepened inexorably beneath them.

EIGHTEEN

JULY 1943

ESTER

Ester lay in her bunk caressing the thin but infinitely precious sheet of paper tightly to her chest.

My dearest, most treasured wife.

It was a miracle. Somehow, Filip had found out where she was; somehow, he had smuggled a letter out of the ghetto; somehow, it had made it to Birkenau and right to her. She would bless Mala Zimetbaum every remaining day of her life for bringing her this much joy.

It had been a filthy day, with summer rain battering down from louring clouds, and Ester had been working with Ana to try and somehow rid the barracks of the lice running rampant over everything this damp, hot month. If it wasn't rats nibbling on their patients, it was lice digging into their poor, fevered skin and no one, however healthy, could sleep without the constant itch of their tiny bodies. Naomi had organised some disinfectant and they'd been trying to clean one bunk at a time but it was a hopeless task. Yesterday, Ester had pressed her forehead helplessly to the rough wooden walls, weeping that they were in such a state they couldn't even defeat creatures smaller than her fingernails, and that's when she'd heard her name.

'Is there an Ester Pasternak in here?'

The voice had been soft and cultured and she'd turned slowly to see a tall woman standing in the doorway wearing well-cut clothes, like a vision from a whole other time and place. She was thin but not as emaciated as the rest of them and she had hair – rich, dark hair cut in a swinging bob that Ester had instantly wanted to reach out and stroke. Best of all, she'd been holding a small envelope in her hand.

'Me,' she'd gasped out. 'Me, I'm Ester.'

The woman had smiled and crossed the barrack.

'Hi, I'm Mala. Naomi told me you've been looking for news of your husband.'

'Yes. Oh God, yes.'

Her reply had come out on an embarrassing sob, but Mala had just pressed the letter into her hand with a smile.

'Then I hope this brings you comfort.'

'Thank you. Thank you so much. You're an angel.'

Mala had smiled again and pushed her glossy hair self-consciously back.

'I'm no angel, Ester, just an ordinary woman doing what I can to help us all survive this madness until the world rights itself again. Keep that hidden.'

'Of course. Thank you. You don't know what this means.'

'Oh I do,' she'd said. 'We all have to know that there's something to live for.'

And then she'd gone, slipping away as quietly as she'd arrived and Ester had crawled into the back of her bunk, with the lice and the rats unnoticed as she'd torn open the envelope and devoured Filip's words after three endless months without him.

My dearest, most treasured wife,

I have no idea if this will find you, or even if you are still alive, but if prayers can protect someone – as surely they can – then I am working day and night to keep you safe. I ask God to watch over you as I eat, as I work, as I walk home, even in my sleep. You are the most wonderful thing that ever happened to me, my beautiful Ester, and I refuse to believe that the universe is going to take you away. We may be apart right now but it will not last forever. I will fight to stay alive and you, my darling one, must fight too. Life must be our goal in these dark times, for if we stay alive then we can find each other and life – real life, full of love and joy and care – can surely start up again.

I have not much space, for paper is hard to find and people prepared to deliver it even harder, but rest assured that I am well, that our papas are well and that Leah thrives. I had word the other day that she is courting a good man, a young farmer, and we can both take comfort that someone dear to us is living in peace. That will be us, Ester. A love as strong as ours is made to last and I only wish, now, that I had got down on one knee and asked you to marry me the very first morning I set eyes on you – for I knew then, Ester. I knew you were the girl for me and every day I curse my foolish shyness for robbing me of even a moment of happiness in your arms. But there will be more. Hold on, my Ester, hold on with all you have, for I love you with every inch of myself and, whatever it takes, I will be here for you when this is over.

Your ever-loving husband,

Filip

Oh, she had cried the first time she read it, and many times since, but they had been tears of happiness and of hope. He was safe, they were all safe, and he believed that there would be a life after this hellish limbo. It had made her joyous and it had made her ashamed. There he had been, praying for her safety with every moment sent to him, and she had been wasting hers in self-pity and despair. Well, no more.

In the week since Mala had pressed his precious letter into her hands, she'd set herself to her prayers with new energy, saying them deep in her heart, muttering them under her breath, and even, at times, singing them out loud. She felt a renewed energy. The sickness had gone at last and her body felt softer and less wasted. She was even, she was sure, getting a slight tummy, though it was perhaps simply the start of the mocking swelling of starvation that seemed to afflict so many in the camp. She had been here just three months but it had started to feel like the only life she had ever known. Hearing from Filip had reminded her of what was beyond the fences and nowadays she didn't just picture him on the steps at St Stanislaus' but in their attic room, in his workshop, eating with their fathers – living on, as she was now determined to live on.

'Up! Up! Up!'

Klara's horrible rattling cry did not start her from sleep, for she had been in a far more peaceful rest with Filip's words, but it was still with reluctance that she clambered from her bunk. Naomi had organised them a bale of hay to the barracks and they'd been able to stuff the threadbare mattresses in the maternity section into something approaching comfort. It gave the lice more to romp in, of course, but it was worth it not to have wooden boards digging into your fleshless hips at night and they were all eternally grateful to the young Greek girl. Ester could swear she was getting wilier at procuring things and every day she reminded her more of her own sister. Mind you, Leah's naive friendliness to Hans had not turned out well; she just hoped Naomi was being more careful.

'Everybody out,' a voice yelled from beyond the thin barrack walls. 'The doctors have prepared a treat for us today.'

Ester's flesh crawled with more than just lice and she shoved Filip's letter through a slit in the fabric, then scrambled to join the other women filing out into the open air for roll call. With July creeping to an end, the sun was only just sending its first rays over the scarred horizon but there was enough light to see large tubs standing before every barrack. The sharp tang of disinfectant filled the misty air and SS guards were pacing before them, dogs snapping eagerly on leads.

Doktor Rohde was there too.

'Strip!' he ordered, adding a surprising, 'Please.'

Ester looked at him, grateful for this small kindness, then remembered Naomi telling her that some of the SS were nice and how she had berated her for her foolishness in mistaking the 'gift' of a lipstick stolen from a murdered woman as kindness. Standards in the camp were so low that a simple please – attached to a humiliating order – was gaining her gratitude and she hardened her heart against the doctor, even as she started to remove her clothes. She hated them seeing her like this, stripped bare of everything.

Not of everything, she reminded herself, for they could not take away the love in her heart, and she sent up a silent prayer for Filip as her clothes puddled around her feet. They had been sent to have their heads shaved again last week in a futile attempt to keep the lice at bay, but thankfully Naomi had organised them two razors and the whole barracks had been able to attend to their own more intimate areas. The look on the guards' faces when they had seen their hairless bodies had been almost comical and Ester had found herself wondering if somewhere in Berlin an erudite, but utterly misplaced, paper on hair-growth in the malnourished would appear by one of the 'doctors' using the camp as their own sick laboratory.

'Line up,' Doktor Rohde ordered. 'When your name is called, you will step into the bath on this side, submerse yourself fully for thirty seconds, then exit it on this side.'

It was classic German efficiency but it did nothing to stop the sting. Janina Węgierska stepped up first and Ester saw the kind doctor wince as the high-strength disinfectant made contact with her raw, lice-eaten skin. Her eyes streamed as she clambered out again, but she knew better than to cry out. Why add bruises to your sores?

'Will it work?' she whispered to Ana.

'It might get rid of the lice from us,' she said, 'but they are all burrowed deep into the mattresses and clothes, so it won't take them long to come out again.'

Ester thought of Filip's letter, nestled amongst the lice, and prayed they would not get a taste for paper. But now her turn was coming and as she clambered into the tub, she bit her lip to keep herself from letting out her pain. Every inch of her felt as if it was on fire and she hesitated, unable to face dipping her face down through the scummy layer of dying lice. A hand came down, hard, on the top of her head and she was pushed under before she could even draw breath. Now it was not the fire on her skin that mattered but the fire in the lungs.

Hold on, my Ester.

Filip's words came to her and she forced herself not to struggle as she was held under, for there was nothing an SS liked more than imposing their dominance. Her head swam and she knew that in a moment she was going to have to open her mouth and let the dirty, alkaline fluid into her lungs and then all would surely be lost.

Hold on, my Ester.

The hand released her and she shot to the surface, sucking in air.

'Out!'

She scrambled to the edge, but was so dizzy that she could not find a handhold and it was only Ana daring to steady her that stopped her flopping to the ground like a dead fish. It earned them both a clout with a baton but then Ana was into the tub and ducking below the surface, Ester made it to the line of wet, shivering women, and the SS lost interest.

On and on the dunkings went, as every one of the one hundred women crammed into Block 24 were forced through the same stinking fluid and lined up in the early-morning air. The sun was fighting its way into the sky but the power of its rays was still blocked by the trees at the back of the camp and could not dry the moisture on their raw skin. Those with typhus could barely stand but any that collapsed to the ground were dragged off by the SS to the dreaded Block 25, so they did their best to hold the weakest upright.

Ester closed her eyes and prayed for Filip. She pictured him getting up in their attic, eating a crust of bread in the cramped kitchen, walking across the ghetto to his workshop. How she had hated that shut-off part of Łódź and yet, from the hell of Birkenau, it looked like an idyll. At least in Łódź she had been with her family, with her husband. At least in Łódź she had been ruled by other Jews and, oh, if they had known what true oppression looked like they would never have uttered a moment's complaint against Rumkowski.

If we stay alive then we can find each other and life – real life, full of love and joy and care – can surely start up again.

Was he right? Was it possible? Already her fingers itched to hold her husband's letter again, to trace the very ink that had come from his pen.

A loud thump pulled her from her daydream. Her eyes flew open and, to her utter horror, she saw male prisoners filing out of their block, carrying their mattresses between them. They dumped them all down in a long row on the ground, then picked up watering cans and, dunking them in the filthy tub, began pouring the disinfectant all over their surface.

'No!' Ester cried and it was only Ana grabbing at her arms that stopped her running forward and flinging herself in front of the cleaners. She looked wildly at her friend. 'They can't do that, Ana. They're making them all wet.'

'They'll dry, Ester. The sun is coming and—'

'My letter,' she hissed and saw understanding cross Ana's old eyes.

'You hid it in...?'

She nodded furiously and looked down the line of mattresses. They were identical and it was impossible to tell which one held her treasure, not that it mattered for they were all soaked through and his dear words would be turned to pulp.

'It doesn't matter,' Ana was whispering in her ear, her hands still tight on her arms. 'You know them all, Ester, you have them in your heart.'

Ester barely registered what her dear friend was saying. The world swam as it had when she'd been held beneath the surface of the fluid that was eating away at the one speck of hope she'd been granted in this bitter place and she felt herself sway.

'Ester,' Ana hissed, more urgently. 'Ester, look at me. Please, look at me. You have to stay upright or they'll ship you to Block 25. It's just a letter. Filip is safe and well. He wants you to stay alive, Ester, to stay alive for him.'

'Yes,' she managed, but it felt as if his words were being pulped from her head as well as from the pitiful mattress before them. She couldn't see straight, she couldn't find a way to make her legs hold her.

'Ester!' Ana's voice came as if from far away. 'Ester, do you think, perhaps, you might be pregnant?'

She blinked. Fractions of the world seemed to link up again and she clung to Ana.

'Pregnant?'

Ana looked frantically around but as Ester's vision steadied, she could see that the guards were too busy battering the poor men who were gathering up their clothes to pay them much attention. She put a hand to her belly, feeling the swell that she had put down to the start of starvation-sickness, then to her breasts. They were hardly the ripe mounds they had once been but they were there – there and ready, perhaps, to feed a child.

'Is it possible?' Ana asked her. 'We have been here three months, Ester. Is it possible? Were you with Filip before you left?'

Ester cast her mind back to their cramped attic room, to a soft bed and dark nights and the endless, beautiful comfort of her husband's arms. She remembered how they had come together just the night before the police had arrived for her mother and she'd found herself bundled into the cattle cart bound for Birkenau. Filip's voice came to her, low and sweet: *You are my feast, Ester. You are my concert and my party, my night out and my day in.*

'It's possible,' she admitted, though it seemed insane that the sweetness of that bed could be in any way connected into the horrors of Birkenau. Insane and glorious.

The men were leaving, taking the women's clothes with them. The mattresses were starting to steam as the sun poked over the treeline and the droplets of disinfectant were evaporating off their own skin too, but Ester could no longer think of anything but the new life inside her. She might have lost Filip's letter but she had his child. *Their* child. She looked to Ana in wonder.

'I'm going to have a baby?'

'I think so.'

It was a moment of perfect joy, but then a woman toppled

at Ester's side and a dog was released to clamp its slavering jaws around her ankle and drag her off to Block 25, and the true horror of Ester's fate was brought starkly home. She was a Jewish woman, in a camp where a crazed criminal and her prostitute of a helper drowned Jewish babies in a dirty bucket the moment they took their first breath. She might have the most wonderful midwife to help her, but they had the rest of this dark parody of a world against them. Filip's baby was not just a joy, but the greatest possible danger to Ester's life.

NINETEEN

SEPTEMBER 1943

ANA

The music lilted around Ana like a lullaby and she closed her eyes and for a moment forgot that she was in Birkenau, surrounded by the sick and the dying, and imagined herself in her own living room, back when there was no such thing as Nazi rule and no such thing as a ghetto and they had all just got on with their lives as best they could. Today was the Jewish festival of Rosh Hashana – New Year – and Alma Rosé, the leader of the Birkenau orchestra, had suggested that while the poor inmates might have none of the traditional cakes, or honey-coated apples of home, they should be offered the sweetness of their instruments. Ana knew nothing of the ceremony but certainly appreciated the music.

As the exquisite notes of a violin lifted through Block 24, she remembered Bartek playing his old fiddle. He had not been as talented as Alma Rosé, an Austrian musician, now a prisoner like the rest of them (her Jewish blood apparently being of more importance than her talent), but he had played with heart. She could still see the smile on her husband's face as he drew his bow across the strings faster and faster in his favourite jig, the boys fighting to keep up with the pace he was setting.

They'd all been talented. *Are* talented, she corrected herself. It had been eight terrible months since she had last seen all her beautiful boys but she refused to believe they were lost and thought longingly of them now. Bron's long fingers had been as well suited to the piano keys as to the surgeon's knife, Zander had loved his flute, and little Jakub had taught himself the guitar on an old instrument left to Bartek by his father. She tutted at herself. Jakub was not 'little' any more, and thank heavens, for he would need all the strength of a grown man to survive this war.

Word had crept in from a new batch of Russian prisoners that the Germans were taking a beating in the east. In Bartek's last package his letter had been more censored than ever, barely a handful of meaningless connectives surviving the cruel marker-pen, but he had hidden a message in a small pastry. The pastry itself had been mouldy by the time it reached her but that had, at least, kept it from the greedy grasp of the post-woman and inside had been the sweetest treat – a note, bearing words of love and hope: *Hold fast, we are winning, my love.*

Ana had no idea whether to listen to the rumours forever circulating the camp but Bartek's words she could trust. They were starting to see the evidence for themselves. The Soviets being shipped to the camps in this autumn of 1943 were from towns and villages taken on retreat not attack, and thousands of Wehrmacht soldiers were being killed every day. Ana had been overjoyed to hear it and then chided herself; no good Christian should rejoice in the killing of any man, whatever his nation. Even so, it was hard not to be pleased at news of Nazi defeats for it was the only way that they would ever get out of Birkenau.

The violin sang out again, the notes soaring confident and bright over the accompanying instruments. The orchestra had been put together not long after women first came to the camp, but Alma Rosé had taken over last month and the group was growing in both numbers and talent. The SS liked concerts on a Sunday afternoon and some of the other prisoners hated the musicians for playing for them. A Yugoslav viola player who had given birth last week had confided in Ana that she'd been punched, spat at and kicked by her fellow inmates for agreeing to play for Germans, but it had been the only way to save her life and, therefore, that of her unborn child. She had gone back to the musical barrack with her baby son hidden in her viola case and Ana could only pray that the privileges offered to the musicians enabled her to keep the child safe. She doubted it.

'Hail Mary, Mother of God, please keep my sons safe, wherever they may be.'

Her fingers felt for her beads but met only the dirty creases of her skirt. She had lost the rosary in the delousing and although Naomi had assured her she'd find another, she'd not yet had a chance. Ana glanced across to the girl, wedged onto the bunk between herself and Ester. It was evening so she was back from Kanada and had snuck into Block 24, as she so often did. The Greek Jews had been put into Blocks 20 and 21 with the Russians but almost all of Naomi's poor compatriots had died of typhus, starvation, or just overwhelming despair, and she hated it in there. Mala was working to try and get her reassigned, but these things took time and meanwhile Naomi joined them whenever she could. Sometimes Mala joined them too, chatting happily away in German or Polish and even working to learn Naomi's native Greek. She had a natural fascination with both languages and people, though rumour had it she was especially drawn to a young man called Edek Galiński, a skilled mechanic who did work in the offices.

'Is it true, Mala?' Naomi would whisper to her, over and over. 'Are you courting?'

And Mala would tut and say, 'As if such a thing would be possible in Birkenau!' But they all knew from her smile and from the flush in her pretty cheeks that such a thing *was* possible and they all felt just that bit better for it.

Recently, though, Naomi had shown less interest in Mala's 'romance' and Ana looked at her in concern. She seemed listless and had lost some of her beautiful bounce, so Ana was glad to see her lost in the music. She put out a hand to her and Naomi clasped it so hard Ana feared for her old knuckles.

'Are you all right, Naomi?' she whispered.

The girl released her grip.

'My mother used to play the violin.'

'And my husband. Well, the fiddle.'

'Do you miss him?'

'Every single day.'

'That must be nice.' Ana frowned and Naomi shrugged. 'To have a husband to miss.'

Despite herself, Ana smiled; the Greek girl always had such a sideways way of looking at the world.

'I suppose so. You'll have someone one day, Naomi.'

'I will,' she agreed, but her eyes slid to the floor.

Ana wanted to press her further but the orchestra were gearing up for the finale of their overture and it seemed rude to talk. She settled back and let the music wash over her again, each note a tiny trip out of here to be seized with both hands, and when the overture had finished, she joined the rest in spontaneous applause, almost surprised that her hands still knew how to express approval. She looked to the viola player who caught her eye and gave her a single, brief nod. The baby lived yet then; that was good.

'Stand by your bunks!'

They all jumped and looked nervously to the door. The SS were usually safe in their warm, comfortable barracks drinking stolen spirits in the evenings and even Klara had been enjoying the music. She scrambled to greet the new arrivals and Ana's heart sank as she recognised Wolf and Meyer, the two SS officers who had come before to claim babies for their ridiculously named 'Lebensborn' programme. She had not seen them since and had dared to hope they'd lost interest but here they were, on the hunt again.

She saw the viola player slide out of the door and noted at least one wily new mother crawl right to the back of her bunk to keep her baby in the shadows. For those nearest the door, however, there was no such escape and Klara and Pfani soon had them standing to attention, babies in front of them like human trophies, waiting to be claimed.

'They look a bit sickly,' Meyer said, his lip curling.

'Are you surprised?' someone snapped, and Ana turned round to see Ester had stepped forward, hands on hips.

There was a strange, translucent light in her eyes and the lines of her angular body seemed to ripple with fury. She was clearly pregnant now and regularly cradled her bump at night, muttering away to it in the darkness and making it heart-breaking promises: 'I'm going to keep you so safe, little one'; 'I'm going to get you back to your papa'; 'I'm going to give you the world. Not this world, but a better one, a decent one.' Ana never asked her how she intended to deliver, she just held her close and stroked her forehead and prayed for a miracle. But they were not in the darkness now and this was a time for silence.

'Ester!' she hissed, but she had been separated from the girl by the two SS and could not reach her without drawing too much attention to them both. Mind you, Ester seemed to be doing that all by herself.

'They have no clothes, no nappies and no milk unless their mothers can produce it, which few can as they have been trading their own rations for bedlinen and soap so they do not die on the birthing table.'

Hauptsturmführer Meyer barely glanced at her. 'A good job, then, that we are here to take them away. I'm sure they will soon fatten up with good German mothers to care for them.' He scanned down the line. 'We'll take all of them except that one.'

He pointed to a dark-skinned Russian baby whose mother almost fainted with relief. Before the rest could even react, Klara, Pfani and Wolf were taking their children from them and marching them out to the car and, just like that, it was done. One of the poor women, still recovering from a difficult birth, just stood there, staring down at her empty hands in confusion. Another leaned back against the bunk and began slowly and methodically tearing her hair out, and the third fell to her knees, begging for her baby in crude German.

'Bitte. Meine kleine infant. Meine baby.'

'*Meine* baby,' Meyer said with dark glee but at that Ester launched herself across the barrack and latched onto his back, hissing and spitting and shrieking into his ear. Ana watched in horror as the officer looked behind him, seeming at first bemused and then angry.

'Get this blöde Hündin off me. Mein Gott, it's like a zoo in here. The sooner we exterminate these creatures, the better. Get! Off! Me!'

It was Klara who obliged, marching back into the hut and yanking Ester off with her meaty arms.

'I'll see her punished, Herr Hauptsturmführer,' she said with relish.

'Be sure you do. These women have no idea what's good for them.'

'Well, it's not taking their babies,' Ester shrieked, still fighting in Klara's grasp.

Pfani stepped forward and slapped her, hard. Ana saw blood spurt from Ester's mouth but she just spat it back and the scarlet droplets caught in Pfani's auburn hair like jewels. Meyer looked at them with disgust, his fingers twitching for his gun, but then one of the babies cried from the car outside and he blinked, snapped his fingers at Wolf, and strode from the hut.

'Please,' Ana said, stepping between Ester and Pfani, 'let's all calm down.'

She heard the throaty roar of the SS car pulling away, but judging by the light in Klara's narrow eyes, Ester was still in danger. Schwester Klara had hated both of them since they'd put a stop to her baby-drowning and this was her chance for revenge.

'Oh, I'm calm,' Klara said, her voice simmering with malice. 'I'm very calm and I have my orders. Number 41400 is to be punished. Pfani – I will need my whip. The big one.'

Ana saw clarity return to Ester's eyes. She struggled in Klara's grasp but the German, well fed on kapo rations, was strong and she had no chance. Pfani brought her the whip, a long leather device with five vicious threads, beaded on the ends. Ana had not yet seen a woman survive it.

'Klara, please. We should stick together.'

'Oh, *we* are,' she shot back, nodding to Pfani. 'Strip her and bind her to the bunk.'

Pfani tore Ester's top from her, popping the buttons so that they fired at the women watching, terrified from their bunks. Ana saw Klara's eyes narrow as she took in the swell of Ester's belly and ice washed across her.

'Klara,' she begged, but Klara did not even glance her way.

'Bind her, Pfani. No, not like that.' She grabbed Ester and yanked her round to face her. 'This way. I'd say there's a nasty little Jew inside this nasty big Jew and that's what's making her so disrespectful to her betters. Time we had it out.'

'No!' Ester shrieked, trying to cover her belly with her hands, but Pfani had her wrists in her bony grip and was tying them to one of the bunks with a thin piece of cord. Ester fought against them, cutting welts into her skin, but Pfani just pulled them tighter.

'Not so fiery now, Jew girl.'

'Please, Pfani. Imagine if your baby was taken.'

For a moment a cloud passed across the prostitute's eyes but then she swiped it away with her hand, giving Ester a clout for good measure.

'Shut up. You put us all in danger with your fool antics and you need to learn a lesson.'

She stepped back and Klara raised her whip, stroking the five vicious strands like pet snakes.

'This is going to hurt,' she cooed.

'No!' Ana threw herself in front of Ester. 'Stop, Klara, this is madness.'

'The madness, Midwife, is that I have been forced to listen to you for so long. Stand aside, or I'll whip you too.'

Her hand flicked expertly back and the leather came down hard across Ana's arm, tearing her uniform and biting into her flesh so that she cried out in pain and fell to the floor. Klara laughed and lifted the whip again.

'Enough.'

It was Naomi this time, stepping boldly out to stand over Ana and in front of Ester.

'Who are *you*?' Klara spat.

'It matters little who I am, Kapo, and more what I have.'

'Pardon?'

Naomi lifted her striped uniform to reveal a soft silk shirt beneath. Slowly she untucked the hem, held it before her and ran a nail along the stitching. Klara watched greedily as Naomi made a hole and something small and hard ran down the seam and into her palm. Standing well back from the kapo, she unfurled her fist to reveal a diamond, sparkling in the last of the sun slanting through the grimy windows. Klara licked her lips.

'It's real,' Naomi said. 'I liberated it from Kanada. I've been saving it for something special, but Ester *is* special so it's yours, Klara, if you let her go.'

Klara looked from Ester, to Pfani, to the diamond. Ana could see calculations running through her nasty brain and forced herself to her feet to stand with Naomi. Several other women levered themselves off their bunks and came to join them, forming a guard around the precious jewel. Klara snorted then gave a dismissive wave.

'Fine. I'm knackered anyway. Give.'

Naomi shook her head.

'Not until Ester is free.'

Klara grunted but nodded to Pfani, who gave a loud sigh and began picking at the knots in the cord. They had pulled tight and there was a long, painful pause as she prised Ester free but finally it was done. Pfani shoved her at Naomi, who caught her in her arms and flung the diamond at Klara's feet.

'That stupid stone isn't worth even a tenth of this wonderful woman,' she said and, as Klara scrabbled for her prize, they all retreated to the back of the maternity section and piled onto a bunk together. Ana's arm ached but Ester was safe and that was all that counted.

'You were amazing, Naomi,' she said, hugging the young girl tight to her.

Naomi squirmed away.

'There's not much amazing about bribery.'

'There is to me,' Ester told her. 'You saved me, Naomi. You saved my baby.'

Still Naomi squirmed between them.

'No need to be so dramatic, Ester. Maybe one day you'll do the same for me.'

'Save you?'

'Or my baby, if I happen to have one.'

'Your...? Oh, Naomi.'

The two of them stared at the young Greek girl, who bit at her determinedly lipsticked lip, looking suddenly every inch the child she truly was.

'What's happened?' Ana asked her, but Ester was quicker.

'The German, the one you said was nice.' Naomi gave a small nod. 'He forced himself on you?'

'He... he said he'd make it worth my while. And he has done, hasn't he? Look at all the things we've had – the disinfectant, the straw, the diamond.'

Ana looked at Ester and saw her own horror mirrored in the younger woman's eyes.

'You did that for us?'

Naomi shrugged.

'I told you, no need to be so dramatic. I didn't have much choice in the matter anyway, so I might as well make the most of it, right? And it's not, you know, terrible. He's not meant to do it, is he, so he has to be very quick.'

It was said so bravely that Ana's heart turned over in her battered body. A year ago Naomi had been living with her family in Salonika, no doubt heading off to school every morning beneath a benign Greek sun, with the sea sparkling a cheery hello. Battle must have seemed so far away, but this war was reaching into every household across the world and ripping people from their core.

'You should have said, Naomi.'

Again the shrug.

'Why? What could you have done, save worry about me?'

Ana leaned in, hugging her again.

'Worry *with* you.'

Naomi made a strangled sound, half sigh, half sob, and Ana felt her fold in against her.

'What a mess,' she said. 'What a tangled, nasty old mess.'

It was such a ridiculous understatement that Ana found herself laughing and then Ester was laughing and Naomi was laughing and they clutched at each other in the growing gloom and laughed until they cried.

· · ·

Later, the two girls slept and Ana lay awake between them, arms wrapped tight around their slender shoulders. Naomi should go back to her own barrack but, really, who would care? Lives came and went so lightly around here that one misplaced body in the bunks was of little consequence.

She held them tight, picturing the diamond glittering in the dust of the barrack floor as Klara scrambled greedily for it. *That stupid stone isn't worth even a tenth of this wonderful woman*, Naomi had said and she'd been right, so, so right. Naomi was young, Ester too, but they were both showing unbelievable bravery in this most fearful of places and Ana felt a rush of pride suffuse her old body. She missed Bartek and her boys every single day but these two, and all the other women in her care, were her family for now and as she lay there, with her adoptive daughters curled against her, she swore to God above that she would do everything she could as a midwife, a mother, and a friend, to keep them safe.

TWENTY

SEPTEMBER 1943

ESTER

Ester sat back against the edge of the bunk, cradling her belly and watching curiously as Pfani worked the tattooing needle across her pale thigh. The picture was beginning to form and Ester was intrigued to see that it was a tree of life, like something out of Norse legend. It had squirrels and hedgehogs around the base and birds in the branches and, strange as she found it to etch ink into your skin, she had to admit that it was rather beautiful.

'You're good at that.'

Pfani looked at her in surprise.

'Thanks,' she grunted. 'Something to do, isn't it?'

Ester looked around. It was Sunday – their nominal day off – and with the autumn sun shining outside, everyone who was capable of getting out of their bunks was making the most of it. The other day there had been a surprise frost nipping at their feet when they'd stumbled up for roll call and some of the longer-term inmates had started muttering about the horrors of winter in Birkenau so everyone was keen to soak up warmth while they still could. Ester had only come inside because she'd been feeling a bit giddy and wanted a moment out of the glare, but she found herself curiously mesmerised by Pfani's needle.

'Did you do a lot of art, you know, before...'

'A bit. I used to draw as a child but then my mama died and the home they chucked me into wasn't keen on "drawing silly pictures".'

'Oh, Pfani.'

Ester thought fondly of her and Leah's upbringing, strict but full of love, and reached out for the red-headed girl in front of her but Pfani put up a hand to ward off her sympathy.

'It's just how it was. Luckily Madame Lulu was kinder.'

'Madame Lulu...?'

'She ran the brothel. Took me in when I was fourteen. I was an early bloomer.'

She said all this in a flat, matter-of-fact voice and Ester fought to hide her shock. She'd known Pfani was here as a prostitute but had never really thought about why.

'And you, er, you did some art there?'

'The walls. Madame Lulu liked colour, so I did big pictures of landscapes. Sunsets and autumn trees and tropical stuff. She was big on reds and oranges. They're very, you know, fleshy.'

'Right.'

Ester sat watching as Pfani dug a falling leaf into her skin. Beads of blood puckered up where the needle dug in but she did not even seem to notice. Suddenly, she looked up.

'D'you know, I've been in camps of some sort or another since I was eight but this one is the worst. I'd take any idiot man's sexual perversions to get out of here.'

'There's a brothel in Auschwitz I,' said a voice from a door, and Ester looked up to see Naomi standing there.

'A brothel?' Ester asked, astonished.

Every so often they heard tales from Auschwitz I, the original concentration camp, adapted from Polish summer-workers' accommodation at the start of the war. The commandant there ruled over Birkenau too and occasionally people were transferred between the two. The political prison was in Auschwitz I, as was some sort of mockery of a court, situated conveniently alongside an execution wall, but Ester knew nothing else about it.

Naomi nodded.

'Mala was telling me about it the other day. They call it the Puff and it's there for the poor sexually starved SS, stuck out here with only us dirty Jews to violate.'

Ester went to Naomi and put an arm around her shoulder.

'Your guard is still...?'

'Yes. But he does get me food.'

'Prostitution,' Pfani said sagely.

'Hardly!' Ester protested, but Pfani wasn't listening. She was drawing a second squirrel onto her thigh and, as Ester watched it form, she suddenly realised that it was mating with the first.

'Pfani! You'll have that on you for always.'

'So? Clients will like it.'

'You don't have to go back, you know. There'll be other opportunities after the war—'

'After?' Pfani laughed and put the finishing touches to her male squirrel. 'I'm not thinking about after.' She looked to Naomi again. 'The Puff, you say, in Auschwitz I. Fascinating.'

Then she was up suddenly and darting out of the barrack, leaving her tattooing kit on her chair. Ester stared at it, seeing not the ridiculous squirrels of Pfani's broken mind, but the parade of numbers she had dug into so many babies' tiny thighs. Jewish babies, destined only for the afterlife, did not get a number and neither did those infants intended for 'Germanisation'. They were to be unblemished, untraceable.

An idea formed in Ester's head. Stepping across to the tool, she lifted it up and tested the needle against the back of her hand. She had to press harder than she'd expected but then the ink bit and a tiny blue dot appeared on her skin.

'Ester, stop!'

Naomi darted forward and pulled the needle away. Ester turned to her and smiled.

'Pray Pfani gets into her precious Puff, Naomi, because I have a plan. They might take our babies from us, but one day, when this is all over and our lives are no longer bounded by wire, we will find them again.'

'How?'

Ester took the needle back and returned it to the chair. For the first time in ages she felt something like hope.

'Secret marking, Naomi, my sweet – secret marking!'

'What?'

She pulled her close.

'We take any baby put on the list for the Lebensborn programme and we tattoo them with their mother's number – small and neat and somewhere it won't be noticed by the officers. Then, when this is all over, we will have a way of identifying them, finding them, taking them back into our arms.'

Naomi looked at Ester with admiration.

'Clever,' she said, but Ester shook her head sadly.

'Not clever, Naomi, just desperate.'

TWENTY-ONE

ESTER

'You're doing what?' Klara shrieked.

'Moving,' Pfani said calmly, rolling her rough mattress up off the floor of the kapo's private room.

'Moving where?'

Klara's solid body twitched and she tried to reach for Pfani but the redhead dodged out of her way and headed down the barrack.

Ester nudged Naomi and Ana and they looked round from tending Zofia, a horribly skinny young Polish girl who was labouring on the brick stove. All summer long the cattle trains had kept bringing women into the camp, many of them pregnant. Those showing at initial selection were sent mercilessly into the death-queue but some escaped detection and ended up in Ana's maternity ward alongside the poor girls who were preyed upon by the guards.

They came from all over, many from Russia and Belorussia, taken as hostages to the bitter German retreat. Those women, at least, had some strength, but birthing in Auschwitz was precarious for even the healthiest. Poor Zofia, sent in from the disbanded ghetto of Rejowiec a few months ago, was struggling even in the early stages. Ester moved to shield her as Klara marched furiously after Pfani.

'Moving where, Pfani? You won't get a kapo who treats you better than me, you know.'

'I know.' Pfani grinned and tossed back her hair. 'I'm off to the Puff – soft beds, pretty clothes and all the baths you want.'

The other women sighed in envy.

'What's the Puff?' Janina asked, coming up from the hospital end of the block.

'It's the brothel,' Naomi informed her curtly, 'for the Nazis.'

'No!' Janina looked at Pfani in horror. 'You can't go there – you'll have to have those monsters all over you. Inside you!'

'So? Didn't you hear me – soft beds, pretty clothes and all the baths I want. That's worth a bit of German sausage, I'd say.'

'No, Pfani. What about your dignity? Your pride?'

Pfani sneered at the doctor.

'Dignity and pride don't keep you alive. I learned that a long time ago and it's even more true now. I'm going.'

'You're leaving me?' Klara looked so distraught Ester almost felt sorry for her and then remembered the kapo, beaded whip raised above her own pregnant belly, and hardened her heart.

'Of course I'm leaving you,' Pfani laughed. 'What have you ever given me, Klara – a space on your floor and the chance to do your dirty work? Well, thanks, but find yourself a new skivvy. I'm off to do dirty work of my own.'

With a wave to Block 24, she strode out without a backward glance, her red hair flaming in the setting sun framed in the doorway. They all heard a Nazi car gun its big engine and then there was silence.

'Owww!' Zofia whimpered, snapping them back into their own world.

'You're doing really well,' Ana assured her soothingly.

Ester wasn't sure that was true. Tiny Zofia had arrived mourning a husband who'd been shot dead in front of her and a sister sent straight to the gas; she had never truly recovered so labour might be the last straw. However, Ana had not lost a mother in a birthing yet, so Ester had to trust to her friend's skill, especially as she had other business right now. She gave the girl a soothing stroke then forced herself up to face Klara, keen to seize her moment while the cruel kapo was at her weakest.

'Oh dear,' she said mildly. 'Who's going to tattoo the babies now?'

'Tattoo?' Klara looked hazily at her, then shuddered. 'Not me. I hate needles.'

Ester dug her nails into her palms, willing herself to get this right.

'Me too. The poor babies. That tool sends shivers up me every time it runs.'

Klara's eyes narrowed.

'Does it indeed? How weak of you, Number 41400.'

'Yes, but—'

Klara picked up the tattooing kit where it was still sitting on Pfani's vacated chair and shoved it at Ester.

'You just got yourself a new job, Jew. Starting tonight.'

'Klara, I—'

'Tonight. And I don't want to hear any complaints, ever.'

Ester took the kit and drew in a deep, satisfied breath.

'No, Klara.'

But already the kapo was gone, stomping down the barracks and slamming the door on her private room. The flimsy wood did little to mask the sound of her sobs and Ester smiled. Her plan had worked.

. . .

Zofia's baby came into the world, small but bawling loud enough for someone twice her size. Ana blessed her, as she always did, and Zofia asked her to name her Oliwia, after her sister. The women gathered for the improvised ceremony and Zofia kissed her daughter over and over on her downy hair – her blond, downy hair. Klara was straight out of her room at the sound of her cries, though her eyes were red and bleary and she swayed with the effects of the schnapps that seeped out of her every pore.

'One for the Lebensborn, I see. Excellent!'

Zofia clutched Oliwia close.

'Please, Klara,' she babbled in Polish. 'Don't take her away from me.'

'Speak German, peasant! You should thank God your child's blond hair will save its filthy Jewish life. And that it is going to have a better chance in life than you.'

'*I'm* mother,' Zofia stuttered in rough German. '*I* give best life.'

'Not for more than a day or two,' Klara gloated. 'She's on my list. And you...' She pointed shakily at Ester. 'Don't you dare tattoo this one. It goes to the Reich unsullied.'

'Of course, Klara.'

Klara narrowed her eyes and Ester cursed herself but luckily the kapo's brain was too addled to pick up on anything and, with a growl, she teetered back into her room.

Ester swallowed and looked to Zofia.

'We have to do it,' she whispered to her in Polish. 'We have to tattoo her.'

Zofia nodded and, tears in her eyes, handed her precious bundle into Ester's arms.

'You mark my Oliwia and I'll find her. One day, I'll find her.'

'Exactly.'

It sounded so straightforward like that, but as Ester laid

Oliwia down on the stove beside her mother and lifted the tattooing needle, her hand shook. That would not do. They had agreed that the best place to hide the mark was in the armpit, but it would need to be small to stand a chance of going unnoticed, and accurate to be of any use at some impossibly distant moment in the future when they might be free enough to go looking.

All evening, as Ana had guided Zofia through her labour, Ester had been practising on the arm of a dead woman laid outside the barrack. It had been gruesome work, but she'd been sure the poor lost soul would not have begrudged them her lifeless skin if she had known the importance of the mission and so she'd pushed on. Now though, with a live child before her, it felt a very different prospect.

'I can't do it,' she whispered.

Ana was at her side instantly.

'You can do it, Ester. You are brave and kind and strong. It will only hurt Oliwia for a moment and it will give her a chance of seeing her mother again, so it is worth it. You know it is.'

Ester nodded, swallowed hard and lifted the needle. The baby's blue eyes stared up at her and she looked straight into them, imagining this to be her own child. Ana was right – it was worth this and so much more.

'I'm sorry for what I'm about to do,' she whispered to the baby, 'but I pray you will see the good of it one day.'

Gently Ana lifted Oliwia's arm, holding her tiny body tight as Ester took the needle and checked Zofia's number: 58031. Oh God, she thought, why couldn't it have been something easy, but she pictured the run of numbers down the dead woman's arm outside (now cut away to avoid suspicion) and, taking a deep breath, leaned in. At the first touch of the needle Oliwia gave a startled cry and Zofia gasped but Ester heard her murmuring words of comfort and encouragement to her child and let them wash through her too as, tongue between her teeth, she slowly carved out the numbers – small and neat – into the crook of the baby's armpit.

'Done.'

She stood back, relief flooding through her. Ana checked the number and nodded approval.

'Beautiful.'

'That is beauty in Birkenau?' Ester asked, her heart straining at the thought.

'Not directly,' Ana conceded, 'but *that* is.'

Ester looked to where she pointed at Zofia gathering her child to her breast, dropping kisses onto her forehead as she rooted at the nipple, the needle already forgotten, and knew that it was true. She smiled at the thought of the tiny mark, known only to them, that would form a gossamer thread into a future of which they had to keep dreaming.

TWENTY-TWO

CHRISTMAS EVE 1943

ANA

'Are you well? Baby safe inside?'

Ana paced the maternity ward at speed, desperately trying to get some feeling into her frozen feet and hands as she checked on the expectant mothers. How would she deliver a baby with blue fingers? She looked yearningly to the long brick stove running the length of the barrack – solid, efficient and utterly without fuel. The temperature had been below zero for weeks and they had long since run out of the meagre coal and wood the Nazis had seen fit to provide for the winter.

Sometimes the local Polish underground threw logs over the fence but you had to be quick to secure them for your barrack and as Block 24 was full of sick and pregnant women they had little chance. Naomi, still thankfully without child, could sometimes grab some, or trade it for the vital matches she liberated from Kanada, but Ester was huge now and Ana's old bones were too creaky in the cold to be a match for camp-hardened women. She groaned and rubbed furiously at her hands, willing life into them. No one was in labour at the moment but at least three women were close and it was always a blessing to bear a baby on the same day as the Christ child so Ana had to be ready to assist.

She glanced out of the window, shaking her head to see yet more snow falling down from the starry sky, stark against the tall lamps that flooded the camp with light every night. Evening roll call would be upon them soon and they would have to leave the marginal protection of the wooden barrack walls to stand out there, the icy air biting through their meagre clothing, the snow mounting cruelly around feet bare in wooden clogs, the shivers so intense that she swore you could hear some women's fleshless bones shaking. The Nazis didn't care. Anyone who collapsed, whether dead or just unconscious, was thrown onto a pile of frozen corpses to be taken away by the death cart.

Ana and Ester were lucky because Naomi had organised them some warm jumpers to wear beneath their uniforms but with little flesh left they would have needed five apiece for true warmth. The travesty, of course, was that in Kanada lay mountains of clothes, stolen from the poor inmates on arrival and sorted to be shipped back to the Reich for German citizens. The workers, labouring in the frozen fields in thin uniforms with no coats, hats or even socks to protect them, had to watch trucks piled with furs, woollen sweaters, soft scarves and gloves go past day after day, heading to people who already had plenty. It was a starker, harsher cruelty than any beating and Ana had no idea how any of them were going to make it to spring.

'Are you well? Baby safe inside?'

They were foolish questions, she thought crossly, as she asked them over and over, for nothing was well in Birkenau and sometimes in these last days she'd looked almost enviously at the dark smoke coming from the crematoria – at least it would be warm in there. She shook herself furiously. Life was a gift from God and if He saw fit to keep her alive, it was for a reason and she must embrace that.

Another parcel had arrived from Bartek the other day and

while that thin thread existed between them, she had to fight. It had held sausage, wizened from who knew how long in the post but still a rich, luscious delicacy after the increasingly thin and rotten turnip soup that seemed to be all the camp authorities were prepared to provide against the frozen days. Even more warming had been the tiny message slotted carefully into the centre – I love you. There was a letter too, heavily censored and with the same words scored out for no reason bar basic cruelty, but Bartek had got them through to her anyway – three tiny words with the power of a thousand times that many. A power the sadistic Nazis would never understand.

Looking out at the snow again, Ana realised that on any other year she would have pointed to the Christmas Eve flakes with joy, saying how pretty they looked against the street decorations and the big tree in Łódź marketplace. She would have laughed at the snowmen the children had built in the parks and gone out to Widzewska Hill to watch the boys throw themselves down the slope on hand-made toboggans. Then they would all have hurried inside for steaming glasses of grzaniec galicyjski and mouthfuls of sweet kołaczki. Ana's mouth watered at the memory of the fragrant wine and cookies on her tongue and for a moment she was back there. God help her, she had known that those were happy times but until she'd come to Birkenau, she'd had no concept of how unhappy it was possible to be.

Not unhappy, she reminded herself sternly, just permanently, impossibly uncomfortable – cold right through to her bones, hunger so consuming it was hard to think of anything past the next crust, and an endless ache in her ribs where she feared she had never quite recovered from her beating in the interrogation room almost a year ago. She missed her family like a hole in her soul, but she had Ester and Naomi and the women who came and went from her maternity section. There were moments of joy but every one was undercut with the pain of loss. So far she had brought over a thousand babies into the camp and, bar those who'd been snatched away for 'Germanisation', only one had survived.

The act of creation was still beautiful but every birth was bittersweet. Some of the stronger Russian women managed to keep feeding their babies for weeks but as soon as they were sent back out to labour, the children languished. Some days you could hear them wailing endlessly from the barracks where they had to be left while their mothers senselessly built roads or moved bricks around, and eventually even the strongest would give up.

Many of the mothers, having survived their birthing in Ana's care, did not cope with the heartbreak of losing their child. Zofia's Oliwia had been taken away two days after her birthing and Zofia had just laid down on her bed and refused to get up. Ester had held her as her poor, tortured soul had departed her body, and Ana was dreading Ester's own birthing. She cared for all her patients, labouring in such dire circumstances, but Ester was special.

She's your daughter now.

Oh Lord, she prayed, *give me the strength to aid her in her travails.*

But already she knew that, however hard the birthing, the true struggle would come once the baby was born and every night she begged God for a Christmas miracle for Ester's baby. There was hope in the one survival she knew of. The viola player's son had been smuggled into the 'family camp' – a new area that had been set up to take an influx from the ghetto at Theresienstadt two months ago. Mothers and children were allowed to stay together there, fathers too sometimes. They had easier work and more generous rations and children played with skipping ropes and hoops. No one had known why these particular Jews were so favoured until Goebbels' gang of publicity bandits had brought cameras into their idyllic section of Birkenau and the rest of the prisoners, faces pressed up against the fences, had understood that these people were here to present an acceptable face of the camps to the world.

'At least it means the world is showing some interest,' Mala had said, always positive. 'They only need to look closer to realise that we are not all living that way.'

But the world was fighting a war and would most likely be too busy to probe the Nazi's lie of a film. Certainly no one had come calling and the rest of the inmates could only look enviously into the 'family camp' as their relative privilege mocked everyone else's hardships. But if the viola player's son was living in there, within reach of his mother, then maybe Ester's could too? It was a thin thread of hope, for sure, but a thread all the same and Ana was holding onto it with all she had.

The shouts went up for roll call and a groan ran around the maternity section. Those in Janina's hospital were spared standing before the SS, but the pregnant women were deemed capable and all began heaving themselves off the bunks where they'd been huddled, bumps sticking up like a human mountain range as they pressed close together for warmth.

'Raus, raus. Come on, ladies,' Irma Grese called, poking her icily beautiful head into Block 24. 'It's Christmas! We have a treat for you.'

No one fell for it. There were no treats in Birkenau and it was with a dread as cold as her gnarled fingers that Ana dragged herself out of the door after her charges. Ester looped an arm through hers and she attempted a smile at her but as snowflakes were whipped into her face, it rapidly turned into a grimace.

'What will Bartek be doing, do you think?' Ester whispered to her.

It was their trick, these days. If they spoke of home – of the people they loved and the foods they might eat and the everyday acts they might be carrying out, it took them away from here and kept some tiny part of their minds halfway sane.

'Cooking up kołaczki,' Ana told her, without hesitation. She pictured the biscuits warm from the oven, sparkling with jewel-coloured jams.

'He can cook?'

'Not many things, but kołaczki is one he can do. He used to say it was his contribution to Christmas and he'd put on my pinny and set to. Oh Ester, he was hopeless. It would take him forever and the kitchen would be coated in flour and egg. It would be on the floor and across the table and in his hair.' Almost she laughed but the icy wind whipped it into something more akin to a sob and she clutched tighter at her young friend's arm. 'Will we ever get back, Ester?'

'Of course,' she said. 'Your St Nicholas is going to come in his sleigh and carry us off.'

Naomi slid into line next to them.

'Fantastic,' she said, 'I'll get the wine on the stove.'

She sent Ana a cheeky, carefully lipsticked grin and Ana looked to the skies and blessed God for sending her these two amazing young women, for without them she would surely have let Birkenau steal her spirit. She would turn fifty-eight next March, if she made it that far, and some days it was only sheer force of will that kept her poor, weak body moving.

Our only weapon is staying alive, she reminded herself, and stamped her feet against the ice.

'Here,' Naomi said, pushing something into her hands. 'Happy Hannukah.'

Ana blinked, remembering that this was the time of the Jewish festival of light – a horrible irony in the darkness of Birkenau, but Naomi was light enough. Ana felt the ripple of silk against her fingers and gasped. 'It's a slip,' Naomi whispered. 'Pretty thing. Cost a fortune back in someone's home-town, I bet, but no use to them now. The lace won't help you much, but silk is meant to be really good at keeping in warmth.'

'Bless you, Naomi,' Ana said, feeling a shimmer of joy at the girl's kindness. That was what they had to hold onto. That was how they would survive in here. That—

'See!' Irma Grese cried into her thoughts. 'A Christmas treat.'

She waved and to their astonishment the women lined up in the snow saw that someone had lugged a fir tree into the middle of the camp and SS guards were solemnly lighting candles on the branches, as if they were gathered on a village green to sing carols. The women looked to each other, unsure what to make of this. It was a travesty of a gift of course, far less use than just one extra helping of soup, but as the candles flickered bravely in the snowy night a few sighed softly, drinking in the reminder of happier times.

Ana thought back to that fateful Christmas Eve three years ago when she, Bartek and the boys had lifted their feast from their table and taken it across town to the poor Jews in the ghetto. They had made a decision that day – a decision not to hide in their own safe lives, but to step up and help their fellow men. They had all known it was right, but they had certainly not known what it would entail. If they had, would they have acted differently? Ana prayed not, but if she had spent even one night in this place, it would have taken all her faith and courage to step onto the path that had led her here.

'Happy Christmas!' Irma Grese cried out gaily, stamping up and down in front of them in her giant overcoat and big, padded boots. 'Especially all you lovely Jews. Missed out on this one, didn't you? Didn't see the signs. Well, don't worry – the Christians have got it wrong too. You've all got it wrong. Do you still think there's a God?' She stopped and rammed her baton into the air. 'There is no God. We are on this earth alone and the strongest of us wins. *We* win.'

She threw back her golden hair and laughed like a twisted angel, then strode back to the tree and pulled a sheet away from beneath it. A few people looked enviously at the sheet but then the true horror of what was beneath permeated and they could only stare. The Nazis had arranged a pile of corpses under the sparkling fir, the top ones trimmed with sick red ribbons.

'A present for you,' Irma cried, 'from us!'

She joined the other SS, who smirked at their dark joke as they looked along the line of the frozen inmates, shivering before their dead friends. Ana felt pure, unadulterated rage well up inside her. She remembered Ester flinging herself at the Lebensborn officers, claws out, and wanted to do the same to the vicious woman who had been set over them all, not because of any personal strength but because she had guns and tanks and a whole dynasty of evil behind her. Well, perhaps winning did not always look the way they thought it might.

Opening her mouth, Ana sang the first line of 'Silent Night'. She was, as her boys would be the first to tell you, no great singer, but so what? The other inmates looked to her, eyes frightened at first but then filling with something warmer, deeper, and as Ana moved into the second line other voices joined her, tentative at first but growing in volume. Even the Jewish women joined in, stumbling over the words but lending their voices to the music that swelled up and around the camp, singing to the candles on the tree not the bodies beneath it.

The SS shifted and Grese's eyes narrowed but the singing seemed to hold them bound and not one raised their weapon. The music rose up around the emaciated women in a halo of warm, swirling breath, pouring out their humanity, their togetherness, their refusal just to lie down and die in the dirt of the Nazi regime. Ana felt her heart swell and pump her blood out to her frozen fingers at last. She felt the silk of Naomi's gift, and the warmth of Ester's arm through hers. She felt Bartek smiling at her from somewhere in Warsaw where, even now, he would be plotting with others to bring about the end of this misery.

Our only weapon is staying alive.

The carol was winding to its end and Ana clung to the last

notes, wanting them to linger, to hold them all in peace, but then Irma Grese stepped forward and shook at the tree so that the candles were tipped into the needles and the whole thing began to burn. There was a ripple of shock amongst the prisoners and at Ana's side Ester gave a sharp cry.

'It's not that bad,' Naomi said to her. 'At least it's... Oh no!'

She grabbed at Ana, pointing down to the ground, where fluid was gushing from between Ester's legs onto the snow in a cloud of steam. Ana sucked in a deep breath.

'Sssh!' she warned Naomi, clutching Ester's arm even more tightly.

As the prisoners were released back to their barracks, they hurried her as fast as they could to Block 24. With the SS gone to the warmth of their Christmas feasts, the more daring prisoners could dart up to the burning tree and grab branches to take back to the stoves. Naomi led the charge and even the heavily pregnant mothers went with her, keen to find some warmth for the woman who had helped so many to birth their babies and whose own turn had now come. They fed the burning fir into the fire at the maternity end of the barracks and slowly, as Ester's cramps increased, the brick began to warm. It wasn't much, just a glow in the frost, but they laid a blanket on it and in between battling her pains, Ester could try and rest. Everyone else drew close and someone carried on the carol singing so that Ester laboured to soft tunes of peace and love.

But poor Ester, although young, was far too thin and low on energy and her labour ground on as the last of the fir burned itself out in the stove and the other women drifted into sleep. Ana and Naomi stayed awake, talking with Ester, rubbing her back, offering encouragement. Ana dug the last of Bartek's sausage out of hiding and Ester sucked gratefully at it as the cramps upped in ferocity. Morning roll call came and they were forced outside but it was Christmas day, for the SS at least, and the junior officer was peremptory in her duties so that, praise

God, they were all back inside again within half an hour. Ana had been forced to stand by while women laboured in line before now, battling not to cry out against the pain for fear of having more inflicted upon them by an SS baton. One woman had even given birth, her baby dropping onto the mud below, and had taken a battering for daring to pick the tiny thing up into her arms. That had been terrible, but with Ester it was hell.

'Not long now,' Ana promised her, helping her gratefully back to the stove. 'You're almost fully dilated. Baby will be coming soon.'

'I don't want it.'

'What?'

'I don't want it to come out. I want it to stay inside. I want it to stay with me.' Ester was wild-eyed. Her body was drooping with the effort of battling the cramps, but she clutched at Ana with surprising strength. 'Keep it inside me, Ana. Keep it safe inside me.'

'That's the one thing I can't do, my sweet,' Ana said. 'Baby wants to see you and we have to get him or her into your arms.'

'My arms aren't strong enough.'

'They are,' Ana assured her.

It was not her friend's arms she feared for but her heart. But the time was come and, like a million women before her and a million women to come, she had no choice but to work with the pain and drive her baby into the world.

'Push, Ester. Push hard.'

Ester closed her eyes, almost weeping with fear.

'Mama,' she wailed. 'Leah.'

Ana wanted to weep herself for the poor girl, so far from those who should be supporting her in this vital time, but Naomi, released from duties at Kanada for two whole days for the 'festive season', stepped up in front of her.

'We're here, Ester,' she said. 'Ana and I are here for you.' Taking Ester's hands, she placed them on her own shoulders and pressed her forehead to her friend's. 'Come on, girl, we're going to do this together. Push!'

Ester opened her eyes and, looking deep into Naomi's, nodded. Then, drawing in a long, shaky breath, she bore down.

'It's coming,' Ana urged. 'Again, Ester. It's coming.'

She prayed this stage would not go on too long for Ester was already low on strength, but thankfully her baby was keen to be born and it took only two more big pushes before the head was out.

'Baby's here, Ester,' she cried. 'One last push.'

With a roar, Ester pushed against Naomi as the other women, waking again, shouted encouragement and then, there she was in Ana's hands – a tiny, utterly perfect baby girl – and no cold could permeate her old bones now.

'You've done it, Ester. You have a daughter, a beautiful daughter.'

Ester sank back on the stove, Naomi tucking herself round beneath her to provide a pillow for her weary head as Ana cut the cord with the nail scissors that were her only tool, and handed the baby into her arms.

'A daughter,' Ester breathed.

'Born on...' Ana started but then cut short her observation, for Christmas Day would mean nothing to the young Jewish mother. Even so, Ana sent up her own prayer to God for seeing Ester's baby into the world on Christ's birthing day and fifty more begging Him to keep her there.

'What will you call her, Ester?' she asked gently.

'Filipa,' Ester said without a moment's hesitation. 'Filipa Ruth.'

'Perfect,' she said, then ducked down, ostensibly busying herself with the afterbirth but in truth burying sudden tears in Ester's skirts.

Filipa Ruth. It was a name that cried out to Ester's lost mother and her husband Filip, who was hopefully still battling somewhere far too far from here. Ana prayed that, somehow, they could both hear it. Ester was caressing her baby's downy head and murmuring softly to her, all fear lost in the wonder of motherhood, all cold driven away by the warmth of love, and it was both wonderful and terrifying to see. The two-day 'holiday' would at least keep the SS from Block 24 but they would be back. All too soon they would be back and then the ice and the pain would return with a vengeance.

TWENTY-THREE

27 DECEMBER 1943

ESTER

'There, there, sweetheart. Mama's got you. Mama's got you safe.'

Ester dropped a kiss on Filipa's tiny head and watched as her eyes fought sleep to meet her own. She stared into them, trying to feed all her love to the baby, trying to fill her right up with it against the time when...

She refused to even think it. She'd had two blissful days with her daughter. A little milk had come in and as the news of her birthing had spread, many women had come to Block 24 with scraps of their own food – tiny items but a huge proportion of what they had to give. They were mothers at whose own births she had assisted and although Ester had tried to refuse, they had pressed the crusts, the scrapes of margarine and the morsels of beet upon her.

'Feed her, Ester. Feed her and love her while you can.'

The last words had been the gall in the loving offerings – the dark knowledge that this would not, could not last. Every one of those women was without their child now but every one had told Ester that their brief days with their infant had brought them a belief in the inherent hope and goodness of the world that had bolstered them, despite their intense grief, against the fear and hatred of the camp. With Filipa in her arms, Ester understood. The rest of her bitter existence had faded into the shadows in the dazzling light of her baby girl and she had let herself bask in it, but already the shadows were creeping back in.

'It's you and me, Pippa,' she whispered, calling her by the pet name that was both an honour to her father and her own precious identity. 'Whatever they do to us, wherever they force us to go, we are joined as surely as if the cord between us is still intact and we *will* be together again.'

Pippa's eyes were closing but her tiny fingers clutched tightly around one of Ester's own as if she understood how hard they were both going to have to cling on to each other in this evil world. Ester sat, drinking in the sight of her. Her face, she could swear, had the lines of her father and already she had a tiny dimple to the left of her pursed mouth. Ester prayed it meant that she would be ready to find joy in life, for she was going to need that.

'I love you, sweetheart,' she murmured, glancing nervously to the door where Klara was lurking, waiting for Wolf and Meyer to turn up with the gifts they brought her for handing over other people's children.

The kapo had emerged from the bottom of her Christmas bottle of vodka yesterday and leered at Pippa like a wicked witch in a fairy tale.

'What a pretty little thing, Number 41400. The spit of her father, no doubt.' That had dug at Ester's heart, precisely as it had been meant to, though she had refused to rise. But then Klara had leaned in so close that the vodka had rolled off her tongue and straight into Ester's face, sharp and sour. 'And so beautifully blond.' She'd let out a low chuckle. 'I'll add her to my list.'

'Klara, no. *Please.*'

Ana had told her that the viola player's son was thriving in the family camp. There were mothers in there with strong arms and milk-filled breasts who could keep Pippa alive until the war came to an end. It tore at Ester's heart to think of another mother nursing her baby, but better that than she died. Mala was trying to find a way to move her in secret, but it would not work if Wolf and Meyer got to her first.

'No?' The kapo had pretended surprise. 'You want me to dunk her in my bucket instead?'

'No!'

Ester had clutched Pippa tight against her and Klara had laughed.

'I thought not. The SS will be so pleased. They're due any day, you know, and this beauty will make the perfect New Year's gift for a nice young couple, don't you think? Really start 1944 off happily for them.'

It had been impossible not to react and it had only been Pippa in her arms that had stopped Ester flinging herself at the hideous woman.

'Have you no compassion, Klara?' she'd begged, but Klara had just shrugged.

'Nope. I may have had some, once, but it's long gone – and thank heavens for that. Compassion is worth nothing around here.'

'That's where you're wrong,' Ester had hissed, as Ana and Naomi had closed ranks at her shoulders. 'Hate may burn brightly, but love burns far longer.'

'Then I suppose it will hurt longer once she's gone too,' Klara had thrown at her and been off to write poor Pippa's name on her list and condemn her to be snatched from Ester's arms.

'We have to do it, sweetheart,' she said to her now sleeping daughter. 'Mama has to mark you. She has to mark you so that she can find you again and sweep you back up in her arms one day, however big you've grown.'

A sob wrenched from her at the thought of the bleak months, maybe even years, ahead without her daughter, but tattooing her number in Pippa's armpit was the one tiny way in which she could tie a thread across that horrible future to a brighter one beyond. It was time.

'Ana,' she said, her voice hoarse.

Ana turned from where she was checking on another mother, surely past her time and growing larger every day.

'Ester?'

'Will you hold Pippa for me?'

Ana looked at her for a long moment and then nodded. With a reassuring pat to the other mother, she came across and took Pippa so that Ester could clamber from her bunk. Even those brief moments without her baby in her arms felt like agony and she could not begin to imagine the black hole of having her gone from Block 24 forever.

She fetched the tattoo needle, her legs horribly wobbly beneath her. She should be up, really, and returned to nursing. Some poor mothers had been sent back out to the farms just the day after giving birth, blood still trickling down their legs, but Ana and Janina were in charge of Ester's work-rota and had spared her. There was one job, however, that she could not spare herself.

She nodded to Ana, who gently lifted Pippa's tiny arm to expose the soft, secret curve of her armpit beneath. Ester glanced to her own number, roughly tattooed across her forearm and forced tears from her eyes. She had to do the best possible job. Biting her lip, she checked the ink in the needle and pressed it to Pippa's skin. The needle bit, Pippa's eyes flew open in shock and she let out a bleat of a wail.

'There, there,' Ester soothed. 'It won't last long. It'll be worth it. It will make you truly mine.'

It was all a nonsense of course, a babbled, manic nonsense, but she kept on spurting the words as she forced herself to mark out the numbers: 41400. The double o was like Pippa's confused eyes peering out at her in reproach but at least her numbers were easy to form and she pushed on to the end. Dabbing the beads of blood with the cleanest bit of her skirt, she gathered Pippa up into her arms, crushing her against her heart.

'I'm sorry, Baby. I'm so, so sorry.'

Already Pippa was settling, already she had forgiven her, and it broke Ester's heart that her tiny daughter's troubles were only just beginning.

They came two days later, roaring up to Block 24 with an arrogant thrum of engine and the rap of boots on laboriously cleared paths, bringing ice sweeping through the door to lock around Ester's swollen heart. The poor overdue mother was in labour, but crept into the back of her bunk, biting down on the wood to keep herself quiet and avoid the Nazi leeches. There was no such chance for Ester, her name written large across Klara's list of just three mothers, and she was forced to stand with them while the hard-faced officers peered at their babies as if they were fruit in a market.

Ester willed them to say no and allow her the chance, however slight, to smuggle Pippa across Birkenau to the relative safety of the family camp, but Wolf prodded at her with an unnerving smile.

'Not bad.' She glanced up to Ester and, as recognition registered in her eyes a sly smile crept across her lips. 'Well look who it is – the wild cat! It will be a pleasure to tame your kitten. Give her to me.'

She put her hands around Pippa and Ester saw them magnified. Wolf's skin was creamy with health, her veins rich with blood, her nails glossy with polish but still they looked like the most vicious talons in the world.

'Don't hurt her,' she moaned.

'Why would I hurt her?' Wolf sneered. 'She's a good daughter of the Reich.'

'She's *my* daughter,' Ester wailed. 'Please, let me keep her. Let me come with you. I'll be her nurse. I'll never say a word, I promise. I'll let—'

'You?!' the woman snapped, cutting her off. 'Why would we let you into a good German home, Jew? You're lucky your baby is getting this chance, but if you don't like it – if you're not grateful – we can dispose of her. There are more where this comes from.'

Ester's whole body quivered and it was only Ana putting gentle hands on her shoulders that gave her the strength to let go of her baby. She leaned down to press a kiss on Pippa's precious head but she had already been whipped away and Ester stumbled.

'She'll be better off without you,' the woman said, and then she was gone and, just like that, so was Pippa.

Ester fell to her knees in the frosty mud of the barrack, tangled her hands in her hair and wept. She knew for sure that her baby would not be better off without her and that without her baby, she just might fall apart. Then warm arms went around her and someone was cradling her, stroking her terrible blond stubble and whispering words of love.

'Mama,' she murmured and felt a kiss drop upon her head.

'I have you, Ester. I have you and I will keep you. Remember – our only weapon is to stay alive and to stay alive we must love and we must give and, I'm afraid, we must hurt.'

Ester nodded and let herself be folded away and rocked until the pain was evenly distributed across her broken body and not digging an endless hole into her heart. Every last fibre of her ached for her stolen baby but, somehow, she must fight on and she must pray that one day she would find Filip and they would find Pippa and they would be a family. It was a desperate hope but the only one she had, and she would cling to it with every dark day ahead.

TWENTY-FOUR

24 JUNE 1944

ANA

Ana lifted the rusty pail and, back groaning in protest, turned to carry the water to Block 24. Usually Ester or Janina did this for her but with typhus raging across the camp again they were too busy tending to the dying. She eyed up the walk down the long central path in the burning heat and her whole body protested. It was amazing, though, how much a person could endure. She'd found that out, over this last year and a half in Birkenau. It should have been inspiring, really, the resilience that was possible in the face of extreme suffering, but in truth Ana was beginning to find it faintly ridiculous.

She was not, perhaps, entirely sane. The weather had been so hot for so long and her skin was so thin that she could swear her actual organs burned when she was out in it for any time. She should be grateful that she didn't have to work outside but gratitude, like inspiration, was hard to find. Every day she helped mothers to birth babies that would be lucky to see out their first week in the camp. Every day she stepped over corpses in the simple course of doing her job. Every day, trains pulled into Birkenau – where the new platform stood testimony to the efficiency of the German killing machine – and rattled the walls of Block 24, as if issuing a warning: Your shelter is shaky, your protection slim; you could be next.

Would it matter?

Ana had not had a parcel from Bartek since Easter. There could be any number of reasons for that, but Mala had been keeping a close eye out, so she knew that the packages were not being blocked here in Birkenau. That meant that they were either being stopped somewhere else, or Bartek was not sending them. And if he was not sending them...

Ana set down the bucket, fighting to draw breath into her lungs. She'd always prided herself on her strength, on her ability to work hard, to sleep little, to stay in good health, but Birkenau had robbed her of all of that. She still worked hard, still slept little and was still, at least compared to so many in the camp, in good health, but her ageing body was slowly caving in on her. She needed this to end.

Stretching out her back, Ana looked to the skies, praying for planes. A rumour had reached them that the Allies had invaded Europe. Someone in the men's camp had installed a secret radio and could tune into the BBC. Naomi had heard about it in Kanada but no one knew if it was true. No one even knew if it was the real BBC, but the increasingly nervous behaviour of the guards seemed to suggest that the reports might hold some validity.

It was a hope almost too delicious to bear and the prisoners all looked to the skies, hoping that through the smoke of a thousand souls a day being dispatched, they might see an Allied plane; hoping that they might all watch as first one and then the next crematoria went up in their own flames; hoping that, somehow, parachutists might float down from the blue and shoot the SS out of the watchtowers. They had, perhaps, seen too many action films in the cinemas, back when cinemas had been more a part of life than lice and rats and endless queues for rotten soup.

'If they come in the next month,' Ester had said the other day, 'Pippa will only be six months old. She might still remember me. Do you think she would, Ana? Do you think she would remember me?'

'Of course,' she'd told her. 'A baby will always know its mother.'

She had no idea if that was true. She doubted it, but she knew Ester doubted it too and there was no point in either of them saying so. The girl was smart – smart enough to know which truths to avoid if you wanted your mind to stay at least half intact. For the first two months of this grinding year of 1944, she had strayed constantly to the track-side fence, not to look at the endless new arrivals but beyond them to the family camp where, for a few brief days, they had all hoped Pippa might go.

But then in March, in one of those cruel strikes of which the Nazis were so fond, the entire camp had been emptied out and marched up the road into the crematoria. They had heard the viola player wailing all across their own section of the camp and known the worst. Her son had survived Birkenau for nine whole months – the longest on record – but now he was gone. Ester had pulled herself away from the fence and these days she just wandered the camp in a daze, as if she had sent a large part of herself off with her daughter.

The only thing that had sparked any true life in her was poor Naomi's swelling belly. The young girl's pregnancy had become apparent as the buds had formed on the trees around the edges of Birkenau and burst defiantly into blossom. Naomi had apparently suffered no sickness and seen only a small drop in her formidable energy levels and, to Ana's shame, she hadn't picked up on the girl's condition until she'd started complaining about fluttering motions in her stomach two weeks ago. An examination had confirmed that she was already around five months pregnant and the next day her German officer had dropped her, horrified at the news. To Ana that seemed a relief, but Naomi had taken it hard.

'It's not that I liked him,' she'd told her and Ester in the dark of the night, for she regularly slept in their barracks these days. 'It was just good to have someone on my side.'

'*We're* on your side,' Ana had told her fiercely, but the girl was more fragile than she let on and she was trying to keep a close eye on her.

Naomi, she knew, was transferring all the needy affection she'd had for the German to the child in her belly, but its father had been a classic blond Aryan and Klara had already reported her unborn baby to the Lebensborn officers as a 'target for Germanisation'. Wolf and Meyer were coming more and more often now, sometimes as much as once a week, and Klara had been toadying expertly. Ana had seen bottles slipped into her greedy hands and knew that in this warped world of Birkenau, tiny new lives were being sold for mouthfuls of vodka. Their only hope of keeping Naomi's baby from the same fate as Ester's was that the camp might be liberated before the birth.

Back in April two Slovaks had escaped after spending months collecting evidence of the killings in Birkenau. Brave people across the camp had helped. The Sonderkommando in the crematoria had dared to copy out records from the gas chambers and steal labels from the sinister gas canisters that were delivered by the appropriated Red Cross ambulances, and someone had even managed to take a photograph to pass to the Slovaks.

At the appointed time, Rudolf Vrba and Alfréd Wetzler had hidden in a woodpile in the outer perimeter for three whole days – the usual time the guards spent searching for escapees. The whole camp had held their breath waiting for the news that the pair were gone and when it had come – or, rather, when

they had not been marched back through the gates to public execution like all the others who had tried it before them – there had been quiet rejoicing. Surely, people had whispered across the work gangs and the food queues and the latrine pits, once the two men handed over their evidence, the Allies would come running. There had been nothing for ages but then, last month, planes had been spotted circling the camp. American planes. Someone had sworn they'd seen a camera lens and excitable rumours had swept around Birkenau once more. But still nothing.

Two more men had escaped since and last week Mala had come to sit in Block 24 and, under cover of a particularly vocal labouring mother, had confided her own daring plans. She was to leave with a porcelain washbasin over her head, disguised as a workman on the way to install it under the supervision of an SS officer – or, rather, Edek, who had acquired himself the uniform of an SS officer and was prepared to risk all to get out of there with Mala.

'So you *are* courting!' Naomi had exclaimed triumphantly, and Mala had shaken her head shyly and said, 'I suppose I am.'

The whole barracks had oohed at that, taken for a moment to happier times when love had been forever popping up between people, and Klara had come pounding out of her room to see what was going on.

'Just admiring Mala's new hair-do,' Naomi had told her and Klara had tutted.

'Jews shouldn't have hair,' she'd shot at them. 'And you shouldn't be in here anyway, Mala.'

'Just leaving, Klara,' Mala had said sweetly and sashayed out with a wink to everyone else that had set hopes soaring.

If anyone could make it out of Birkenau, it was Mala, and she might actually have the drive to force the people beyond the wire to do something about their plight. Ana thought back to the resistance's reports of the killing vans she'd read in the cathedral way back at the start of 1942. She thought of the rumours they'd picked up about Auschwitz long before she'd been shipped out here. That had been two and a half years ago. Why did no one come? Did they not care? Did they not believe? Ana would not blame them because the scale of the inhumanity in Birkenau was beyond the imagination of any decent human being, but it would take only a few days of counting the trains into this place to work out that not everyone who arrived was making it into a barrack. Imagination could be questioned; maths could not. It had to be that they did not care.

With a sigh, Ana picked up her bucket again and forced herself to walk back to Block 24. There was a mother in the advanced stages of labour who would need her. Ana had chalked up around 2,000 births in Birkenau and had still not lost either a mother or a baby in the birthing itself. Closing her eyes for a moment, Ana thought back to the day that she had graduated from midwifery college. She had gone into St Florian's cathedral in Warsaw, overwhelmed by the ceremony, and had sought the sanctuary of the Lady Chapel. There she had vowed to Mary, Mother of God, that if she ever lost a baby she would stop practising. Bartek had scolded her when she'd told him later, had insisted that it was an impossible aim and that resigning would only result in more losses, but the vow had been made by then and, to her pride, she had, as yet, had no reason to resign – not even here.

One step after another, that's all she had to do – get the water back, get the baby out, keep the mother comfortable while her son or daughter was robbed of the precious life she'd battled to give it, the Jews by Klara's murdering hand and the non-Jews by the gentler but more painfully prolonged death by starvation. If this was what God needed of her, then she must deliver it.

But why had she not heard from Bartek?

Where was he? Where were her boys? Would they be there

to go back to if the Allies ever did their maths and came to free them? A train rattled into the camp, pulling up not fifty metres from Ana. Doors squealed open and people were pushed onto the ramp in a tumble of confusion and fear. Ana looked across and saw Dr Mengele striding out to take up his position before them. The poor people. Mengele was the only doctor who did the selections sober, and he seemed to enjoy them in the way that a scientist might enjoy looking at bugs through a microscope. She'd heard horrible rumours about the labs he had set up in the Roma camp, about the experiments he did on women and children, about his fascination with twins. The other day she'd even watched a distraught Jewish mother, who'd given birth to two tiny baby boys, smother one of them in case Mengele came looking. The second baby had died too not long after but not, at least, beneath a scalpel.

Ana shook herself – she could not dwell on these everyday tragedies, or she would lose what remained of her will to carry on. She hurried towards Block 24 but then something else caught her eye and she stopped once more, her breathing broken this time less by exertion and more by fear. Or was it excitement?

A figure was shuffling down the path towards the gate, a large basin held over its head and a tall SS guard in attendance. He was hurrying the inmate along with a rough hand on his elbow but something about the hold caught Ana's attention and she looked more closely. It was Mala, it had to be. She was in baggy clothes and sagging beneath the weight of the basin but if you looked closely there was a curve to the hips and the officer was supporting her as much as hassling her on. Was that, then, Edek?

Ana froze, watching the pair with bated breath as they approached the perimeter gate. Edek, like Mala, spoke fluent German but would his accent pass muster? Would the gate guard demand to see the inmate's face? She could only imagine how hard their hearts must be beating beneath their borrowed clothing and she leaned forward, willing them on as the guard came out.

The men saluted each other, Edek looking very crisp, then words were exchanged. Edek grabbed Mala's elbow again and tossed his head to the other man, clearly exchanging Nazi banter about the poor prisoner between them. Ana realised she wasn't breathing and forced herself to suck in air, but the guard was waving them through and Edek was saluting again and prodding Mala forward and they were, it seemed, walking out of the camp. Mala, Ana knew, had a smart dress beneath that uniform that Naomi had organised from Kanada. Once they were far enough away the plan was for her to transform from basin-carrying inmate into elegant SS girlfriend. She would take Edek's arm and they would stroll like any happy couple, on and on and on until, just like that, they were away.

'Go, Mala,' Ana whispered. 'Go. Get away. Get help.'

Maybe God heard her, for Mala kept on staggering into the distance until even the white basin on her head disappeared over Ana's horizon. Ana grabbed her bucket and suddenly she was moving at pace, ignoring the sun, ignoring the quiver of her legs and the ache in her shoulders, ignoring even the labouring mother waiting for her return. She burst into Block 24 and, casting an eye to Klara, curled into her bed as she so often seemed to be these days, she grabbed the first woman she came to.

'Mala's out,' she whispered.

The woman's eyes widened and she turned to her neighbour, who turned to hers and so on until, like the whisper of a summer breeze through the stifling sickness of the camp, the news was all around and, doubtless, on its way to the next barrack too. Mala had escaped and hope flared quietly through them all. Perhaps, Ana thought, as she finally took the water to her patient, it would not matter that Bartek wasn't sending parcels any more, because perhaps within weeks she would be on her way to Warsaw to find him herself.

'Come on, my love,' she said to the mother. 'Let's get this baby out and hope it's the start of something wonderful for us all.'

Three days later, the SS brought Mala and Edek back into Birkenau in chains. Ana watched them being marched past Block 24, bloodied and beaten, and felt pain flood across her own body as sharply as if it were she bearing the purple bruises of SS brutality. She'd thought Mala gone, free. She'd thought that she would walk herself right out of Poland and find someone and make them listen. She'd thought she would stride around offices telling important men about the atrocities in Auschwitz-Birkenau and they would come running to save them all. How naive she had been, how ridiculously, foolishly, unbearably naive.

Suddenly it was too much to bear. Ana wanted to tear herself apart before these merciless Nazis did it for her and, running back inside, she flung herself against the wooden wall at the back of the dirty, cramped, barbaric excuse of a 'maternity ward'. She heard voices cry out to her, hands reach for her but she threw herself at it again and again until she had battered herself to the floor. The darkness, when it finally came, was a relief and all she heard as she surrendered to it was Ester's sweet voice.

'There, there, Ana. I've got you. I've got you safe.'

They were the words Ana had heard Ester say over and over to Pippa in the five short days she'd had with her, and they had been lies. Sweet lies, perhaps, well-meant lies, but lies all the same. No one was safe in Birkenau, or, it seemed, beyond it.

TWENTY-FIVE
5 AUGUST 1944

ESTER

Pippa would be seven months and eleven days old today, Ester thought, rubbing at the windows with a small cloth. The torn fabric had been wrapped around a baby until it had died an hour ago and was still damp with the mother's tears but at least they were having some impact on the grime. Before she'd left for Kanada this morning, Naomi had ordered Ester to 'get some light into this damned block' and although neither Ester nor Ana had seen a problem with the kindly gloom, she was doing as instructed. It was the best way.

Thinking for herself had become such hard work. Her brain just seemed to be a fog of hunger, loneliness and grief. Her family seemed so far away and she struggled to picture the dear faces of her mother or father, or even her bright-eyed sister. The one picture that still stood out clearly in the jumbled mass was that of her little girl's eyes turned up to her, as wide as the oo in her armpit, but that was an image already long out of date. Pippa would be seven months and eleven days, she thought again, and would look so different that Ester might not even recognise her. Was that possible? Surely something inside her would instinctively know her own child? But, then, she'd once thought her soul so in tune with Filip's that she would know if he had died, but she knew nothing any more.

Even her love for her husband, once so pure and bright, felt as grimy as the windows. When she closed her eyes and tried to picture him on the steps of St Stanislaus' cathedral, she could never get past the brutal rows of barracks and bunks that criss-crossed her vision. She was scared that even if, somehow, she got out of here and found him again, her love would be as hard to polish up as it was to clean these damned windows.

She rubbed harder but only succeeded in chasing the grime around the glass. There had been a minuscule improvement in the barrack since a work party had been assigned to fit brick tiling to the floor. The tiles were rough and chipped but they kept the dust down and as the weather turned, they might help with the endless mud. Ester shivered at the thought of a second winter in Birkenau and let her cloth drop. What was the point of this? She needed water and soap but both were in desperately short supply with the summer sun still beating down on them, typhus-strong. The other day, as she and Janina had carried yet another corpse from the block, Ester had actually caught herself wishing she could catch the disease – a fever might at least send her blood chasing around her veins in the way it had used to do – but she had nursed so many with it in the last year and a half that she must surely be immune.

'God doesn't want me on the corpse heap,' she'd told Ana and Naomi last night.

'Good,' Naomi had said hotly.

Ana had said nothing. She rarely did these days, bar when she was helping at a birthing. That she still did with her customary calm and kindness but it sat like a veneer on her, polished but only skin deep. She still cared, Ester knew she did. Every baby was still a blessing, but it never lasted and bit by bit they were learning how dangerous caring was. There was only such much loss a woman could take and something seemed to have broken inside Ana the day poor Mala Zimetbaum had been brought back into the camp. Mala had disappeared now, apparently off to the prison in Auschwitz I. Someone had told them that she and Edek could be heard singing to each other from their respective cells, but it was almost certainly not true. Who sang in here?

A train rattled into Birkenau and Ester watched it idly through the small patches she'd wiped out of the dirt. She wouldn't clean the windows on the Block 25 side, preferring to mask the view of the poor women in the antechamber to the crematoria, although now, with three or four trains coming in every day, the antechamber rarely filled up. There was always, it seemed, a procession trailing up the road towards the chimneys so no one had to wait long for a 'full batch' for the ovens.

The new arrivals came from Hungary mainly. No one was sure why that country had suddenly decided to tip its Jews into the Nazi pit but it might have something to do with the Allies invading France. News of that miracle had whispered across the camp like a beautiful breeze and more and more radios were being smuggled into the camp. Someone had told Ester the other day that Paris would be liberated any moment, but she feared all minds in here were as damaged as her own and truth was long since lost.

All she truly knew was that Poland was still in the clutches of the increasingly vicious Nazis and that the Hungarians were coming in their droves, exhausted after days and nights in the cattle carts and more than willing to undress and get into a shower. She'd heard tell that the SS guards asked them to hang their clothes on numbered hooks and even handed them towels and soap to get them into the chamber without fuss. Ironic, really, that those going to their deaths got better treatment than those battling to hold onto their lives. A towel and soap would really help with these windows.

Ester pressed her forehead against the glass, hating herself for her callousness, her indifference, her damned lethargy, but when you looked death in the face day after day after day it was hard to let it move you. She was becoming as bad as them.

Get some light into this damned block.

Naomi's voice rang out in her head, clear and sure. The girl's belly was swollen with her baby now and already Klara had it on her nasty list, delighted to bag a child with actual German blood for her Lebensborn masters. Naomi had told Ester the other day that its father had been promoted. This had apparently softened him to her and although he hadn't resumed his attentions – was, in fact, busily providing babies for the Fatherland via various other poor girls – he made sure that Naomi got warm clothes and extra food. She shared it out every night but was the only one of the three of them who ate with relish.

'Staying alive is our only weapon,' Ana would still mutter sometimes, chewing grimly on a piece of Hungarian sausage, but Ester was beginning to wonder who that weapon was trained on. What, in reality, were they staying alive for?

The train was disgorging its goods and Ester looked half-heartedly at them, curious to see that the poor people were almost as emaciated as the camp inmates. Not Hungarians then. She rubbed harder at the glass and saw a scuffle in the back carriage – shouting and beating, not from the guards but from the prisoners. Jolted out of her lethargy, she dropped the cloth and ran to the door of Block 24. Others were coming, drawn by the noise, and they gathered as close to the fence as they dared, though the SS were paying no attention, their eyes fixed on the curious show before them.

An old man had been flung from the train and was cowering

on the ground as those tumbling out after him took it in turns to kick at his hunched figure. A woman was keening at his side and several people set on her too.

'Look at you – fat on our misery.'

'I kept you alive this far,' the man shouted defiantly, though his voice was ripped through with pain.

'For what? To die in a gas chamber instead of in the arms of our families?'

'To survive the war.'

'To keep yourself in rich clothes and fine wines and fancy horses, more like. We didn't see you burning your Louis XVI furniture to keep warm. We didn't see you scratching lice from your body or fighting over a rotten turnip.'

Recognition was beginning to swell in Ester and she crept closer to the fence.

'Oh no!' the leader of the kickers shouted on. 'You exploited us, Rumkowski. You may have kept us alive but you sure as hell kept some of us more alive than others.'

And with that the kicking started up again. Although the men and women looked horribly weak, anger gave them power and the crumpled-up figure of Rumkowski, Eldest of the Jews of Łódź, was battered into the ramp of Birkenau. One of the SS officers cheered and Ester sank to her knees. So it had come to this – Nazis cheering Jewish brutality; Hitler was truly winning now, whatever the leaked news claimed.

Slowly though, as she watched Rumkowski, a man she had last seen riding a white carriage into Baluty Market, tendrils of something like sense crept into her sluggish brain. If Rumkowski was here, then these people were from Łódź and if they were from Łódź...

'Filip!' She leaped to her feet, running to the fence. 'Filip!'

Prisoners turned to stare, guards turned to stare, but Ester didn't care. Her love for her husband was not grimy and dulled, but as bright and sharp as ever and it dug at her, urging her on.

'Filip – are you here? Filip!!'

'Ester?'

She stopped dead, tripping over her own feet as she spun round to look for the voice. It did not sound like her husband but who knew what the last year and a half had done to him. She peered wildly into the crowd as a man stepped out. Her heart dropped.

'Tomaz?' Filip's friend stood before her, his once-broad frame miserably thin and his left leg dragging. She looked eagerly around but no one else joined him. 'Tomaz, where's Filip?'

'He's not here, Ester.'

Behind them the SS had tired of watching Rumkowski die and were shoving the new arrivals into their customary lines. There wasn't much time.

'Where is he Tomaz? Is he...?'

'No!' Her heart leaped. 'Or rather, I don't know. He was taken away in April, to Chelmno.'

'Chelmno?'

The white heat of her renewed love seemed to turn to dark fire inside her. Chelmno was where the gas vans did their gruesome work. Her knees gave way beneath her and she fell against the fence. Barbed wire cut into her hand but she cared not.

'Then he's dead,' she wailed.

'No! Not necessarily, Ester. He went with a work party. To build barracks, they said and to... to dig.'

'To...?'

'You there – get in line!'

Tomaz looked around, confused. An SS man strode towards them, gun in hand, and Ester forced herself upright.

'Don't limp, Tomaz.'

'Impossible.' He lifted the frayed edge of his trousers to show her his foot, the toes mere black stubs. 'Frostbite. Last winter.'

'You – get in line. Last chance.'

Tomaz looked around wildly but his eyes came straight back to Ester.

'Filip told me,' he said urgently, 'that if I saw you I was to tell you he loved you, to tell you that finding you had been like finding the finest jewel the world could ever produce. He told me that his few months married to you were the happiest of his life, even in the ghetto. He told me there was no suffering for him because all he needed to survive was your love.'

'He has it still.'

'Then he will survive. And so must you. They are coming, Ester, the Allies are coming. I've heard it too many times to doubt.'

'You – insolent pig. Move.'

The guard came closer, gun raised.

'They will kill me, right?' Ester glanced to his foot and nodded. For the first time in a long time she felt tears in her eyes. 'Then I take death here, with you. Live, Ester. Live and love and—'

The bullet cut off his last words, slicing clean through his head and ricocheting off the fence post at Ester's side. She jumped and darted back, hands up, as the SS officer glared at her. Just a few short minutes ago she might have stood there and let him shoot, but things were different now. She could feel energy surging through her as if the electricity had been on in the fence and it had jerked through her, bringing her back to life.

She didn't know what else Tomaz had been going to say but it was enough. If the giant Łódź ghetto had been disbanded, the Germans had to be worried. They had to be in retreat. The Allies had to be coming. Suddenly, the ability to stay alive felt like a weapon again and, turning from poor Tomaz's body, she thanked God for giving him a quick death and ran, away from the chimneys, away from the Nazi death machine and back to Block 24 where her job was bringing life into the world.

Live and love. It felt, once more, like a task to cling to.

TWENTY-SIX

22 AUGUST 1944

ANA

'It will take place tomorrow at evening roll call.' Irma Grese's voice rang out around Block 24. 'Make sure they're all there.'

Ana paused at the door to Klara's room just in time to hear the kapo's reply: 'Yes, Aufseherin Grese, of course. It will be my pleasure. The woman should be made an example of and... Oh.'

Ana bit back wicked pleasure at the fall in Klara's voice as Irma Grese strode out of the room, not waiting to hear her toadying reply. Since Pfani's departure, Klara had taken to following the beautiful officer around like a puppy. It would be funny, save that she was getting increasingly violent in a vain attempt to impress her sadistic superior. Besides, nothing was ever funny in Birkenau.

Ana could feel her heart shrivelling. Ever since Mala Zimetbaum had been marched back into Auschwitz she'd found it hard to persuade the poor organ to keep pumping and she swore it was contracting with every day that passed. Even the love for Ester that had kept her going for so long felt more of an effort than a joy – a responsibility that she wasn't quite strong enough for any more – and still she'd had no parcels from Bartek.

'It will just be that the Germans have blocked all post,' Ester had told her so many times. 'They're on the run, Ana. Tomaz told me.'

'Tomaz was in a ghetto, Ester,' she'd point out wearily every time. 'He was as much a prisoner of Nazi news blockades as we are here.'

'So how did tales of their defeats reach him?' Ester would say triumphantly.

She'd been different since the transport from Łódź that had disgorged Rumkowski onto the ramp to be battered to death by his own people. Seeing Filip's friend had fired up her memories of her husband and the lethargy that so mirrored Ana's own had been replaced with an almost manic expectation of liberty that Ana worried was even more dangerous. Hope hurt.

'What are you doing lurking there?' Klara spat, bursting out of her room and startling Ana.

The kapo half-raised her hand and Ana flinched automatically back but although Klara kicked many of the poor patients around Block 24, she had never yet hit Ana. It was perhaps because, with her excellent German, she was the only one who dared to stand up to the Nazis. The other day Dr Mengele had rapped into the barrack amidst great fanfare to announce the 'dissolution' of the Roma camp and his own promotion to Chief Physician over the women in Birkenau. Ana had not been impressed.

'By "dissolution" you mean mass murder?' she'd challenged, her whole body shaking with anger at the cowardly choice of word.

Mengele's eyes had narrowed but he'd stepped up to her calmly.

'Do you think semantics useful, Midwife?'

'Yes, Herr Doktor. My medical training taught me to be

precise, as I'm sure did yours, so I think we should call things what they are.'

He'd considered this.

'I agree. We could take all the women in this hospital and categorise them as simply "dying" but what use would that be? How would that tell us symptoms or prognosis?' Ana had been forced to nod her agreement and he had gone easily on. 'It is the same with the Roma camp. Gypsies are a drain on society. They live by their own laws and off other people's land. They are not worth the same as a proper human being and so they cannot, by the letter of the law, be "murdered".' He'd smiled. 'Semantics, Midwife. Very useful.'

The sheer cold-hearted logic would have been chilling if Ana's blood had not long since been turned to ice by Nazi persecution. Even so, the casual words 'a proper human being' had itched at her skin even more than the ever-present lice.

'So you do not, Herr Doktor, consider me to be a proper human being?'

He'd been about to turn away and had tutted impatiently at the delay.

'Do not be boring, Midwife. You are a Catholic Pole, I believe, here only on suspicion of resistance. You have potential; do not waste it.'

'And this woman here, this nurse...' Ana had jerked a horrified Ester forward, but Mengele was gone, turning his smart SS back on them both.

'Ana!' Ester had hissed, pulling her away from the departing doctor. 'What are you doing? Mengele sends people to the gas with a wave of his little finger. You could have got us killed.'

'Does it matter?'

'It does to me. I thought you were a fighter, Ana? I thought you believed in the inherent goodness of people – most people. I thought you wanted to stay alive to spite the men and women holding us prisoner to their sick ideals?'

Ana had closed her eyes, the horror of what might have happened washing over her.

'I thought I did too.'

Ester had let out a sigh but then her arms had closed around Ana and she had held her so tight that Ana had wondered who was the mother, and who the daughter. She felt so old, so very old.

'*You* are good, Ester,' she'd murmured into the girl's bony shoulder.

'So fight for me, Ana. And I'll fight for you.'

She'd agreed, of course, but it was so hard. When she'd first arrived here, she'd been proud to fight for the right to help women to have their babies, but these days she was starting to suspect that the hard-won permission had just been a sick Nazi joke. She'd joined the medical profession to save lives, not to cast them to the bitter Birkenau winds, but those winds kept on blowing. And now some poor woman was going to be 'made an example of'.

'What's happening tomorrow, Klara?' she asked.

Klara gave her a sickly grin.

'Tomorrow, Ana? Tomorrow your precious failure of an escapee is going to be executed.'

'Mala?!' Ana gasped, reeling from this additional blow to her too-battered heart.

'The very same and, guess what – you all get to watch.'

They gathered in a long huddle, SS dogs snapping at their backs and a gibbet stark against a grey sky. Rain was falling, thin but determined, soaking into clothing with a taunting reminder of the winter ahead. Word had reached them that Edek had been hanged in the men's camp this morning and now it was poor, generous Mala's turn. It seemed almost too much to bear but Ana felt Ester's arm link through hers on her right and Naomi's on her left and surrendered herself to their youth. She did not want to watch this but Ester said they owed it to Mala to stand by her in her final hour, so here she was. Not that she'd had a choice. There was never a choice any more.

'Prisoners – attention!'

They did this sometimes, the SS, amusing themselves by shooting anyone who didn't stand ramrod straight in their torn clothes and splintered clogs. Today, though, the order was obeyed with unusual alacrity as the women stood, not for their persecutors, but for the woman who was being bundled out of a truck before them. Mala was dressed in a thin white slip and her feet were bare but her rich, dark hair was piled up on her head in a glamorous bun, making her look more film star than prisoner. Ana watched, spellbound, as she picked herself up from the ground and stood, looking out at them all. Maria Mandel, presiding over the gruesome proceedings, motioned a guard to hustle her forward to the gibbet but she resisted.

'Kill me,' she taunted the hard-faced Lagerführerin. 'Go on – what have I got to lose?'

She gave a mocking look to the gibbet waiting to 'make an example' of her, and the guard contented himself with a kick in her shins. She staggered but did not go down and as her eyes swept across the prisoners Ana was suddenly glad she'd been forced here. She did not want this warm, brave woman to die, but if die she must, she would not do it alone.

'We love you, Mala,' she shouted out in Polish.

The guards leaped forward but had no way of distinguishing who had spoken. In the meantime Mala was walking towards the gibbet, a smile on her face, so they scrambled to focus on her instead.

'Thank you,' Mala said, her voice ringing clear around the drizzly evening. 'I love you all too. A wonderful emotion is it not, love? So much more nourishing than hate.'

A guard shoved her onto the steps up to the gibbet but she took them readily, her eyes flashing.

'I tried to escape,' she shouted loudly. 'I tried to escape and I failed.' The guards gave a snigger and she pushed herself up taller. 'But others have succeeded. Others have made it beyond the wire and are even now talking to the Allies. Help will come, people. Help *is* coming. Today Paris has been liberated and more cities will surely follow, right up to Berlin itself. Germany will lose this war.'

Mandel howled in fury and the guards grabbed at Mala, trying to shove her into the noose, but she fought hard.

'They will lose it because they are inhuman, wicked bastards and God will make them pay!'

She jerked away from the guard on her right and put a hand to her hair. For a strange moment Ana thought she was going to loosen the bun and let it fall, starlet-like, but instead she pulled something from it and, fast as lightning, whipped it across the crook of both of her bare arms. Blood spurted, shockingly scarlet, blooming like poppies across her white slip and splattering the faces of the guards.

'Mala!' Ester called, soft and sweet, and she was not alone. One by one the prisoners' voices rose, chanting out her name.

Up on the gibbet, Mala was staggering but she reached up a hand, grabbing at the noose to steady herself and smiling around at them as her lifeblood leeched away.

'Resist!' she cried. 'When the time is right, resist! They are rising up in Warsaw. I heard it from my prison, heard it from Nazis – terrified Nazis!'

Ana stared, fighting to put the words together in her fuzzy brain: Rising up. Warsaw. She blinked. Bartek was in Warsaw. Bronislaw too. They would be fighting. They would be right there, at the front, fighting with all they had. She fixed on Mala as the guards tried to wrestle her closer to the gibbet.

'They are fighting in the streets,' she assured them, as if she was talking direct to Ana. 'The Soviets are marching west as fast as the Brits are marching east and the Varsovians are preparing their way. It *will* be over, my comrades. Your suffering *will* end.'

Still her name rippled around the prisoners like a spell, but Mandel had had enough and jumped up onto the platform, shooting two bullets into the air. Silence fell. She glared around and fixed on Ana.

'You – Midwife! Bind this woman's wounds. Now!'

Ana scuttled forward, grateful when Ester came with her.

'I need bandages, Lagerführerin.'

'Here.' With a single movement, Mandel tore Mala's slip from her and ripped it in two. 'Quickly.'

Ana stumbled up the steps to take them and bent over Mala, who had fallen to the wooden boards beneath the gibbet. She did not dare look up at the noose dangling its dark shadow over them and her hands shook as she wrapped the thin cotton around the condemned prisoner's arm.

'Not too tight,' Mala said, her voice a whisper.

Ana stared at her. She knew what her friend was asking but not how to deliver it; all life was precious in God's sight.

'Mala, I—'

'Please – let me die my own way, not theirs.'

Ana stared uncertainly at her, but now Ester was pushing past, taking the bandages and saying loudly, 'Let me, Midwife – I'm better qualified to bind wounds.'

Swallowing hard, Ana nodded, then moved back and watched, transfixed, as Ester efficiently, and utterly ineffectually, wrapped the fabric around Mala's arms. It stained red immediately and Mala smiled.

'Pressure here,' Ester said, loud enough for Mandel to hear and assume they were trying to stop the flow, but even as she spoke, she hunched over the prostrate prisoner, squeezing hard on the veins to encourage the blood out.

'The cuts are too big,' Ana cried as Mala sagged before her. She took the brave woman in her arms.

'I have you,' she whispered. 'I have you safe.'

Mala's eyelids flickered and a smile quivered at the edges of her lips.

'Oh, for God's sake.'

Mandel pushed Ana and Ester aside and grabbed Mala's wrist, feeling for a pulse. She glanced to the ranks of women shuffling before her, muttering amongst themselves, louder and louder. The SS guards looked nervous and Ana realised with a sudden thrill that they were scared of a riot. Would they? Could they? She looked around. There had to be a thousand prisoners here and less than a hundred guards. How many bullets did each gun hold? How many of them would have to die for the rest to break out?

Clearly the same questions were running through Mandel's head for, with cold precision, she took out her pistol, shot a bullet dead centre between Mala's bold eyes, and strutted away. The young woman's body went limp and the bullet buried itself in the wood, centimetres from where Ana's arm was cradling her. She froze, staring at it. That could have been her, could still be her. And suddenly she knew, with the clear, cold clarity of a winter's day out here in Birkenau, that she did not want to die.

Bending, she pressed a kiss onto Mala's forehead, right where the bullet had gone in, and then released her and stood back. Her legs were stiff and she struggled to stand but Ester took her arm and together they scrambled down the steps and back into the safety of the lines. The prisoners were stilling, the moment of revolution shot out of them, and the SS hurried to get them back into the barracks, away from the sight of Mala, naked and red with her own blood, sprawled beneath the gibbet that had been meant to take her life with Nazi efficiency.

Maria Mandel was boiling with fury. Mala had stolen German pride today and, in the process, gifted something back to those prisoners still clinging to life in Birkenau. Ana looked to the skies and prayed that God was taking this angel into his bosom for she had given Ana hope and, although it hurt like the blade of a razor to lose Mala, it would not strangle her like a Nazi noose.

'Come,' she said, leading the way into Block 24. 'We have babies to birth, babies who will live to escape Birkenau.'

Being a midwife was the one thing she truly knew and the one thing she would do until they were all, finally, liberated.

TWENTY-SEVEN

7 OCTOBER 1944

ESTER

'Push, Naomi. That's it, girl – push!'

Ester whispered the command, desperately trying to avoid Klara's attention. Naomi's birthing had progressed so swiftly that it had even taken Ana by surprise and she'd been off fetching water when it had become apparent that things were, quite literally, reaching a head. Ester had had to rush down from Janina's end of the ward to take command and she'd never been more relieved than when she saw the midwife come back through the door of Block 24.

'Goodness!' Ana said, with something almost like a smile. 'You do move fast, Naomi. Right, let's get Baby out, shall we?'

'Sssh,' Ester urged, nodding to the door.

Klara was outside, trying to make small talk with Irma Grese, recently promoted to SS-Rapportführerin. She, too, would not be expecting Naomi to give birth this quickly and perhaps, somehow, they could keep the baby a secret. Ester looked desperately around the barracks, empty of all but wooden bunks, paper-thin mattresses and torn blankets. There were no chests of drawers, no bedside tables, no laundry baskets – why would there be when all the residents owned was on their backs? And yet...

There were shadows at the rear of the lower bunks, if you guarded them carefully enough. And there were women aplenty prepared to help do so. Every day rumours came in of more Allied victories and there was panic in the German air. The trains were still arriving daily, but the guards hustled almost everyone straight to the gas and they looked furtive, as if they knew they were about to be caught in what must surely be the biggest ever crime against humanity.

Everyone in Birkenau these days looked to the skies and the fences in the hope of rescue from the advancing troops. Air raid sirens had started sounding again and they'd seen planes going over. They hadn't opened up their bomb ports over the camp yet, but they might at any time, and operations at the crematoria had been slowed, with dark irony, to keep the underground chambers free for the SS to hide in when the sirens sounded. These days, when trucks rolled up to the gate, everyone looked over in the hope that it might be Tommies or GIs, bursting into the camp with machine guns blazing and tins of meat in their pockets. It hadn't yet – but it might.

'Push, Naomi. You're nearly there.'

Naomi's baby was truly in a hurry and as the young girl bent over the stove and let out a strangled hiss of effort, Ana gave a triumphant cry, echoed by a lusty wail. Naomi beamed and spun round to gather her baby into her arms.

'Steady on,' Ana laughed. 'I've got to cut his cord yet.'

Naomi laughed too but all Ester could hear was the determined cry of the newborn and it ran through her like a knife. In that moment she was there, back on the stove herself, pushing Pippa from her womb. Suddenly she was holding her daughter in her arms again, tiny and red and shouting in protest at the world she found herself in – and who could have blamed her?

Ester fumbled for the edge of the stove as her vision clouded. She sat gratefully down but her arms cradled automatically around the empty air where once her daughter had been and she could not stop the tears.

'Ester?' Naomi asked, looking at her in concern over the top of her mewling son.

Ester blinked ferociously. 'Tears of happiness, Naomi.'

Naomi wasn't fooled. She leaned solicitously over. 'Here, you hold him.'

Ester threw up her hands.

'No. He's yours. You need to make the most of him. You need to make the most of every tiny, fast-moving minute that he's still here.'

She glanced fearfully out of the door but there was no sign of Klara. She could see Grese across by the fence, tormenting a poor group of men doing repairs, and the figure hovering in her wake looked very like their kapo. Her heart felt as if it was tearing apart all over again as she looked down at Naomi's son in her dear friend's arms and she couldn't bear the thought of him, too, being shipped away to anonymous parents. Birkenau was hell, but it was *their* hell. There had to be something they could do.

'What will you call him, Naomi?' Ana was asking.

'Isaac,' Naomi said instantly. 'After my father. He'll like that, when he meets him.'

When. Even after nearly two years in Birkenau, it seemed that Naomi held onto her lipstick-bright optimism. Ester admired that but she knew, too, that optimism needed a helping hand. She had not been able to keep her own baby in the darkness of last winter but things had changed. The Allies were coming and the Germans were scared. Fear for their own survival was making them careless in their duties, so there were gaps in the once rigid Birkenau discipline. Somehow, for Isaac's sake, they had to find a way to slide him into them.

Outside, Grese had tired of playing with prisoners and was turning away. Klara would be back in Block 24 and the moment she saw Isaac, he would be on her list. His hair was, at best, hazel but it wouldn't matter. If accounts were true, the Wehrmacht were being pounded into oblivion on both the Eastern and the Western fronts and the Lebensborn officers would be hungry for any young flesh they could grab for the imagined future of the Reich.

Ester pushed herself up and ran to the door. Klara, abandoned by Grese, was trudging back to the barrack and taking Naomi's baby from her would be just the sort of petty revenge she would be looking for.

'We have to hide him,' she said, running back to her friends, but Klara's big figure was already looming in the doorway and Naomi was right there, on the stove, in the dead centre of the barracks. Ester stepped in front of her but at that moment a huge boom sounded out across the camp. The walls of their flimsy wooden block shook and Klara turned and fled, keen to save her own skin if it was going to fall down.

'What on earth is that?' Ana asked.

Janina came running from the hospital end and even the weakest patients came tumbling out of their bunks after her. They all pushed outside, eyes turned hopefully to the sky, but no planes could be seen.

'There!' Janina shouted, pointing to the back of the camp.

Ester swung round to see flames leaping from Crematorium IV – not the usual flames, surging up the chimney high on human fuel, but wild, all-engulfing ones.

'Was it a bomb?' she asked, but the women who'd already been outside shook their heads.

'No bomb, unless it was set off from inside.'

Ester looked wildly around. Shouts were going up in fierce, angry German and SS guards were coming running out of every nook and cranny of the camp. Over by the burning crematorium, a group of figures had cut a hole in the fence and were making for the woods beyond. Already guards were after them, dogs unleashed and bounding after their prey, jaws dripping with excited slather.

'It's the Crematoria Sonderkommando,' someone said. 'They've been planning a rebellion for months and it looks like, finally, it's happening.'

Ester watched one of the first escapees reach the line of trees before the dogs and hoped that there were enough tangles beyond to give them half a chance. *Go*, she willed the man. *Run, climb, hide.* But they had their own problem to deal with, for other guards were heading their way, shouting people back into the barracks, and nothing would stop Klara finding baby Isaac. Anger surged through Ester, as hot as the flames in Crematorium IV. She had not been able to protect Pippa from the vicious Nazis but she would do all she could to protect Isaac.

Her eyes fell on the ever-present pile of corpses awaiting collection outside the block. Sitting atop it, like a grotesque cherry on a cake, was a tiny baby who had died in the early hours of this morning. Dared she? What had she got to lose? Glancing around, she made for the door of the barrack and, at the last moment, swiped the tiny body into her arms. It was limp and cold and she shuddered at the lifeless feel of it, but Auschwitz robbed you of all normal scruples and right now the important thing was saving the living baby.

Behind her, guards were shooing everyone into their barracks, and Janina was battling to keep patients ahead of the whips cracking through the autumn air. They would doubtless be stuck in lockdown now but Grese had given Klara a bottle of schnapps yesterday for services Ester didn't even want to know about and hopefully there was enough of it left to keep her locked in her room. This might just work. If, that is, they could convince the kapo that the poor dead baby was Naomi's.

'Here.'

She ran up to Naomi, taking Isaac from her and shoving the tiny corpse into her arms. Naomi recoiled in horror, but she was a sharp young thing, and as Klara stumbled in, shouting at them all to get into their bunks, she gave Ester a quick nod. Ana, not far behind, worked it all out too and put her arms around Naomi who, with the finesse of a highly trained actress, burst into loud sobs.

'What's this?' Klara demanded, homing straight in on Naomi's misery.

Ester, Isaac clutched tight to her chest, crawled into the lowest bunk and made her way to the back. It was cramped and grimed with the accumulated fluids of too many sick women but for once Ester found the horrific conditions a blessing, for there was no way Klara would burrow into this filth.

'Let me see,' she heard Klara snap. Peering out between the other women who had climbed into the bunks to shield her from view, she saw the kapo forcing Naomi's arms open and prising out the child. She held her breath. Would Klara recognise the corpse she had tossed onto the pile earlier? Apparently not. 'Ugly little thing, isn't it? But I guess that's no surprise.'

'With him having a German father, you mean?' Naomi shot at her, her voice thick with apparent tears.

'I'd say this is simply proof that bad Jewish blood does not mix with good German blood, wouldn't you?'

'No. I'd say the conditions in this place robbed my baby of his life.'

'His?' Klara queried, looking at the baby. 'This is a girl.'

Ester held her breath. There'd been no time to tell Naomi. No time for her to check.

'Poor Naomi,' Ana said smoothly. 'Grief has addled her. She'd been so sure it was going to be a boy. She'd promised its father, you see.'

Klara let out a sharp laugh.

'Well now you will have to give him a double disappointment, Naomi – it's a girl, and a dead one.'

Ester let out her breath and Isaac stirred in her arms and rootled at her chest. Her breasts ached, as if suddenly filled with the milk that had leaked out of her once Pippa had gone, but she knew it was a ghost pain and offered him her little finger. He sucked at it and she crawled further behind the women crowded on the bunk and willed him to keep quiet. There were other babies in the ward, clinging to life against all the odds but, even so, she couldn't afford to rouse Klara's ready suspicions.

Klara, however, had thought of something else. Dangling the poor corpse before her like a skinned rabbit, she advanced on Ana.

'Oh dear, Number 41401. I do believe this means that your precious record is gone. Finally, you lose a baby and what a one to choose – your precious Greek friend's brat. Poor Naomi. She put her trust in you, and you betrayed it. All that experience, all that care, all that *faith* – useless!'

'One baby, Klara,' Ana shot back. 'I've lost one baby in over two thousand and in this...' She gestured around the rough, dirty barrack. 'I'd say that's still something to be proud of.'

'Absolutely,' the other women agreed, leaning forward from their beds. Ester had no idea how many of them had spotted their deception but she knew, for sure, that not one of them would give it away.

'Didn't you make some sort of vow, though,' Klara taunted, 'to your dear old Mother of God? It seems she's let you down, Ana. Or you've let her down. Either way – a failure.'

Ester ached for Ana, but the accusation was not real, and she felt a rush of pride as she saw the ageing midwife stand up tall and face her.

'I'll take my "failure" over your "success", Klara.'

'Looks like you'll have to.'

She shook the baby in Ana's face but Naomi leaped up and snatched it from her.

'Leave my baby. I need to nurse her.'

Through the tiny gap, Ester saw Naomi cradling the poor corpse, rocking it and singing to it. Klara watched her for a moment and then, with a toss of her head, spun away.

'You're mad, the lot of you, stark, raving mad. I should beat you for this, Number 39882. You've robbed the Fatherland of a child with your weak womb and your bad blood.'

Naomi just sang on, a soft, lilting lullaby, and with another toss of her head, Klara was gone. The door of her room slammed and peace fell across the barrack. Slowly, Naomi wound up her song and gently placed the dead baby down on the stove.

'Thank you, little one,' she whispered and covered the tiny corpse with a scrap of blanket before sinking down next to it and weakly calling, 'Ester?'

'Coming.'

The women in front of her parted and, thanking them, Ester crawled out with Isaac still sucking on her finger, as if he'd somehow known how to save himself. Naomi held out her hands and Ester placed her son carefully back into them. For a moment it was like handing Pippa to the SS all over again but Naomi was no Nazi and this baby had a chance. It was a slim chance but a chance all the same and Ester vowed that, as this dark war battered its way to a conclusion, she would save baby Isaac for her friend. And for her own sanity.

TWENTY-EIGHT

30 NOVEMBER 1944

ANA

Ana paced outside Block 24, trying to get some feeling back into her feet. She had acquired a pair of boots, tenderly removed from a dead woman by a grateful mother, or, rather, ex-mother. Why, Ana had wondered so many times over this last, vile year, was there no word for a mother who had lost her child? If you lost your husband, you were a widow, if you lost your wife you were a widower, but a parent who lost a child...? Ester called them lost mothers and Ana could see why but Ester, at least, might find her baby again – if they could just make it out of this hell.

Every day they prayed for liberation, actually believing that their prayers might finally be heard. The SS guards were increasingly listless and, miraculously, the crematoria stood empty. The gassings had been stopped suddenly a couple of weeks back and since then the skies had been blissfully clear of human smoke. No trains roared into the station any longer and the only whistle came from the bitter winds that brought snow sweeping in from the east, though not yet any Russian soldiers.

The guards huddled into their watchtowers, took roll call later in the morning and earlier in the evening, and could barely even get up the energy to administer a short rap with a baton. The immediate danger of murder was, it seemed, gone, but its creeping fellows, starvation and exposure, were stalking the camp at will.

And yet still babies were born.

Still, somehow, in the mass of transports across the summer as the Nazis had made a last-ditch attempt to clear Europe of 'racially inferior' peoples, women had arrived with buds of new life within them and escaped even Mengele's practised eye at selection. Perhaps the babies in their wombs gave them an energy, a radiance that made them look fit for work, but increasingly as winter had crept in, more and more women had come to Block 24 for Ana to examine. At first, they'd had to keep working to avoid Mengele and the other doctors who'd roamed the barracks looking for people to dispatch as if that small act of cruelty would bring them some relief from their own fears. But now the crematoria were being blown up in a feeble attempt to hide the terrible crimes that had been committed in Auschwitz-Birkenau so it was safer for the women to declare themselves, and Ana's maternity ward was fuller than ever.

There was a certain delicious irony to the knowledge that, for the first time in its history, Birkenau would most likely be bringing more lives into the world than it dispatched. Keeping the new inmates alive, though, was still a huge problem. Food was scarcer than ever and the weather harsher. More clothes crept out of Kanada in what were, surely, the dying days of the camp and most prisoners had at least a jumper and a coat to bolster their thin uniforms. But with no fuel to light the stoves and mere scraps of food coming into the kitchens, it was starting to feel like a losing battle.

It made Ana want to scream in frustration. The secret radio sets across the camp were reporting that the Allies were within a hundred miles of Auschwitz, so they must surely be close to the end, which only made it more painful to feel survival slipping through their increasingly bony fingers.

'Ana!' The hoarse, pathetic cry did not even make her turn. Klara had fallen ill last week and called her name endlessly. Or, if not hers, then Ester's. 'Help me. Nurse me. Save me.'

'Why?' Ester had asked her the other day.

'Common humanity,' Klara had croaked, and Ester had laughed.

'Humanity is not common around here, Klara, and I have certainly never seen it from you.'

'But why bring yourself down to my level?' Klara had choked, pushing sweat-soaked hair off her fever-tinted cheeks.

It had been ridiculous but had carried a certain dark sense and Ester had taken Klara water to soothe her fever but not lingered to mop her creased brow. The kapo had TB, far too well advanced for there to be any hope of recovery, even if there had been anyone to hope for it. It was taking her longer to waste away than most, her big body kept slightly padded with SS 'gifts', but she was wasting away all the same.

'Ana, please,' Klara whimpered. 'I thought you were a Christian.'

'I *am* a Christian.'

'So be a good Samaritan and bring me some vodka, just to ease the pain.'

'We have no vodka, Klara.'

'No, but I do.'

'It will not help you.'

'It will.'

'Let me put it another way then: *I* will not help you, not like that.'

'I think you should.' The menace in the remnants of Klara's voice made something prickle ominously within Ana and she moved closer to the kapo's doorway. Klara sneered at her from her bed. 'I *know*,' she croaked. 'I know about the baby. The secret baby.'

Ana felt her heart skip a beat. They had kept Isaac hidden for a month now, the women in the barracks taking it in turns to play with him and soothe him and hold him while he slept. Word had crept around the camp and many whose own children had died in Block 24 found time to come and help out, as if baby Isaac had become a symbol of hope for all the lost mothers. One or two of the political prisoners were battling to keep nursing their newborns, but no Jewish mother had been able to save her own baby. If, together, they could get just one Jewish infant out of Birkenau it would be a tiny victory for nurture over neglect, but if Klara knew, she could wreck it all. Ana fought to keep her face calm.

'What secret baby, Klara?'

'The one...' Klara's words were lost in a fit of coughing but when she finally surfaced she managed two words: 'Naomi's baby.'

Ana gritted her teeth.

'Naomi's baby died,' she said fiercely. 'You know that.'

Klara pushed herself up on her pillows and sucked in a deep breath.

'I'm not stupid, Ana, whatever you think. I worked it out. I was going to tell Irma, but she never comes this way any more, Schweinhünden, and then I got ill. But I can still tell on you, even from here.'

'The Nazis don't come near the hospitals, Klara, you know that.'

'Not at the moment, no. But they will when... when...'

Again the coughing. Ana stood watching, hating the impassivity she was capable of in the face of a woman dying. But this was not just any woman. This was a woman who drowned babies in a bucket without a second thought, a woman who laughed at mothers without the milk to feed their wailing newborns, and who would have flayed Ester's daughter out of her belly if it had not been for Naomi's stolen diamond.

'When they move us,' Klara spat out at last.

'Move us?'

'Any time now. Maybe even today. They're closing down this part of the camp, moving the women across the tracks to keep the last miserable Jews and degenerates together. They will come and, unless you help me, I will tell them.'

Ana looked down at her. Klara's eyes were narrowed in anticipated triumph, poor fool. Slowly, she shook her head.

'Delusions,' she said, tutting gently. 'Sad but common enough amongst TB sufferers, so Ester tells me. You poor woman, you've been so surrounded by wailing babies that you hear even them in your broken mind.'

'I do not,' Klara protested violently, making herself cough again. A droplet of blood splashed onto her blanket. 'There's a baby. I know there's a baby. I'll tell them there's a baby.'

'And when they find no baby, they will know that you are delusional.'

'But they *will* find one.'

'Not now they won't,' Ana said, shooting her a wink. 'Thanks for the warning, Klara.'

With that, she spun out of the room and back to the barracks where Naomi and Ester were huddled into the back of a lower bunk singing to Isaac.

'We're being moved,' she hissed in at them. 'We need a plan, and fast.'

Ester frowned, then said, 'Lipstick.'

Ana and Naomi stared at her.

'Lipstick?' Naomi questioned. 'That's your plan? That I slick on some scarlet gloss and seduce my way past the SS?'

'No! I wouldn't ask that of you even if it were possible, but *do* you have a lipstick?'

'You know I do.' Naomi produced the dark pink stub from

the hole they had carved out beneath the new brick tiles of the barrack floor and held it up. 'But I don't see how it will help.'

'Give it to me and take off your top.'

'What?'

'I'll be quick.'

Naomi looked to Ana but Ana could see steel in Ester's eyes and nodded the younger girl on. Naomi handed Isaac to Ana and, shivering, took off her jumper, her striped uniform top and then the silky shirt she wore beneath. Ana knew that Naomi had organised more jewels since they'd had to bribe Klara and held onto the precious garment, hoping the girl got a chance to use them. A diamond would buy a good start in life for a 'widow' and her son. But first they had to get out of here.

'Good,' Ester said. 'Now, hold still.'

Biting her tongue between her teeth in concentration, Ester lifted the lipstick and began drawing red typhus sores across Naomi's shoulders, down her arms and up her neck, dotting a few onto her lower jawline. Then she rubbed some of the pink into her upper cheeks and around her eyes to simulate fever before she finally drew back satisfied.

'You look disgusting,' she announced happily.

'Thanks!'

'This, along with some nice shallow breathing, a cough and maybe a bit of a stagger, and no SS officer will go near you. Get dressed again – carefully – but not the jumper.'

'What? Why?'

'Because you'll need a bigger one. Ana?'

She gave Ana an apologetic grimace but Ana nodded happily. The jumper that had been organised for her had been a man's one and hung off her like a dress. Handing Isaac across to Ester, she took it off and pulled Naomi's smaller one on instead. It was ridiculously tight across her saggy old chest but who cared? Everyone looked weird in Birkenau and there would be time enough for fashion after the war.

After the war.

It was the phrase on everyone's lips now, and not just the prisoners. The other day, while she'd been fetching water, Ana had overheard two SS guards talking in low voices to one another, discussing escape routes out of Europe. Poles beyond the fence, according to one, were doing a brisk trade in fake identity papers to help Nazis flee those who might bring them to justice. It twisted at Ana's guts to hear it. Her own dear Bartek had worked at great risk to offer the same to innocent Jews to escape a persecution far more dreadful than even they had been able to imagine and their whole family were suffering for it. Now some other unscrupulous locals might do the same to help the very men who had brought such horror to Poland, and all for money. She sighed as she handed Naomi's shirt back to her, feeling the hard jewels in the hem. Blood diamonds. Were they as bad as the enemy? Had this war eroded all morals?

She shook herself. Thinking about it did no one any good at this point. Her job was, as it always had been, to keep the mothers and soon-to-be mothers in Birkenau safe, and she would go on doing it until those gates were opened and the real world flooded back in. Time enough, then, to think.

Naomi had her jumper on now and with her 'rash'-covered arms and neck sticking out and her chest heaving with expertly shallow breaths, she looked every inch a typhus sufferer. There was just one small detail left.

'Isaac?' she asked Ester.

'Isaac goes underneath in a sling.'

'A sling...?'

'We'll figure it out.' There was a sound of shouting outside – an impromptu roll call. This would be it. 'Hurry,' Ester urged.

She grabbed some of the strips of cloth from their precious store. With Klara stuck in her bed, there was no one to supervise the removal of the sadly regular dead bodies and they were usually able to secure at least one article of clothing before laying them outside for collection. Those could then be torn into swaddling or, indeed, fashioned into a makeshift sling. Naomi lifted the big jumper and took Isaac against her chest as, fingers fumbling, Ana and Ester tied the bands as tightly around him as they could.

'Block 24 – report!' a voice snapped from outside.

Ana went to the door.

'Report, sir?'

'Roll call. You're being moved, prisoner. Now!'

'Yes, sir, of course sir. I'll get the others from their bunks but some of them are very pregnant.'

'They won't be for long if they don't hurry up.'

'Of course, of course. Others are very sick. Typhus is back.'

'What?' The officer recoiled instantly. 'In this weather?'

'We've had the stoves on occasionally. It's been lovely and warm but it seems the lice like it as much as we do.'

'You stupid woman!'

He raised his hand to strike her but didn't dare come close enough to deliver the blow. Typhus had always scared the SS. Even with their smart hospital block over in Auschwitz I, those unlucky enough to catch the nasty disease suffered with it, the rash being a particular insult to their proud Aryan skins.

'Perhaps we should send those infected to the...' He tailed off and glanced, rather forlornly, to the space in the sky where the demolished chimneys had once stood.

'Don't worry,' Ana said, summoning up her best bedside manner, although every part of her flesh crawled at being nice to this monster, 'we'll keep them well away from you.'

'Yes, well, see that you do. Now – out!'

Behind Ana, Ester was already marshalling the women out of Block 24. Those from the maternity end were large but perfectly able to walk, but some of the poor patients in Janina's hospital end were very weak and the expectant mothers had to help them along. Naomi was doing a good job of impersonating them, limping out, head low, breathing coming hard and fast in the cold air and her body, wrapped in not just Ana's jumper but a large coat someone else must have given up, hunched over to hide the baby strapped to her lipstick-marked chest.

Ana watched her move out, surrounded by her fellows, and saw the SS stare at her in disgust. The women were being asked to bare their forearms to have their numbers counted off on the Germans' precious list and Ana prayed that Ester's lipstick marks stuck. If they were found out, they would all be dead. The Nazis might not have their gas chambers any more but there were other ways to dispatch prisoners – bullets, injections, plain old clubbing. Over the last two years Ana had seen inmates die in more ways than she had ever wanted to imagine and was under no illusions about their safety. People were often at their most vicious when their backs were to the wall.

She held her breath but the officer in charge barely even leaned close enough to see Naomi's number before he ushered her onto the path. Klara had been right, it seemed, and they were to be sent across the tracks. That side of the camp had only existed, until now, on the horizon of their tiny world and Ana had to put a hand to the door frame of Block 24 as a sudden dizziness overcame her at the thought of going so far. She tutted at herself but still glanced back into the barrack with something close to fondness.

Ridiculous. This place was a hellhole of misery and suffering, where women and babies came to die. And yet... Ana had birthed nearing three thousand babies in here, and every one of them safely for both mother and baby. Her only reported still-birth had been a lie – a wonderful, important lie. True, of all those three thousand, only six were still alive in the camp– five born in the last month to non-Jews and one hiding beneath Naomi's jumper – but over sixty had been taken to be 'German-ised' and Ester had managed to tattoo most of them. Surely those numbers would stay inked into the babies' innocent skin?

Surely someone would question what they meant and raise them with groups like the Red Cross once the war was over? Surely they would provide an identification mark to match that on surviving mothers in the perfect pairing? And at least many of the mothers had survived – that, in itself, was a small victory.

She forced herself to look back to the women in her care as they gathered in the rigid lines their captors still insisted on, and that was when she spotted Klara, lying in bed in her room, unnoticed by the two young guards who had made a swift sweep of the block.

'Ana,' Klara croaked, holding out a limp hand.

She looked pathetic, a woman shrivelled almost to nothing, as if her own hate had sucked her body dry of life. If Ana turned away, showed her number to the guards and passed through the fence, Klara would be left here alone to die – no food, no water, no care. It was, Ana was sure, exactly what she deserved, but... Did Christ not exhort forgiveness? Did he not teach his children to turn the other cheek and treat others as they would like to be treated? It was a code enshrined in the Lord's own prayer and Ana would be betraying herself to forget it.

'Come on, Klara.'

Going over to the bed, she put her arms around the kapo and helped her up. Klara leaned heavily on Ana, her breaths rasping from her hollowed lungs.

'Thank you,' she managed.

'Common humanity,' Ana said drily, leading her out and past the SS to join the back of the line.

They were led at a thankfully slow speed up the road and across the tracks to the gates of their new sector, alongside that of the remaining men. It would be the first time Ana or Ester had left the confines of their own small section of Birkenau since they were marched in here, shaved and robbed of all they'd come with, two springs past. Even stepping onto the central path felt giddily like freedom and Ana was almost glad of Klara to cling on to as she passed through the great wire fence.

They were the last survivors. When Ana had arrived, there had been well over 100,000 people incarcerated in the camp; now they were down to what looked like at best a twentieth of that number. It was still a lot of people but it felt like a mere huddle after so long with great crowds moving around the place queueing for food and latrines – and gas chambers.

She glanced to the huge buildings, now collapsed in on themselves, with prisoners labouring to cover the traces of the barbarism they represented.

'Killing machines,' she muttered.

At her side, Klara looked too.

'I saw a little girl taken off to them once,' she said, her voice hoarse and sore. 'She came in on one of the trains this summer. She was just standing there...' She pointed to a spot on the path, 'her hand still held out next to her where her suitcase had been until someone snatched it away. She had brown plaits, tied with ribbons, and a pleated skirt beneath a lovingly fastened duffel coat. She looked like me, when I was young... I was young, you know Ana, once.'

'I'm sure.'

'I looked at her and I thought, if it had been me – and others like me – sent to the gas when I was that age, would this all be here? Would it have happened at all?'

Ana blinked at the kapo, astonished.

'You regret it, Klara?'

A sharp laugh turned into a bitter cough.

'This place? No – I was already too late for regret then. I turned bad in my early twenties, fresh out of midwifery college. Got pregnant, got abandoned, got smuggled to a woman in a back street to get rid of it.'

'I'm sorry.'

'Don't be. This is no sob story, Ana. My parents paid her a

lot of cash and I realised that killing babies was more lucrative than birthing them. No excuse. But, yes, if they'd sent me to the gas like that girl, it would never have happened.'

'Or, perhaps, if they'd let you keep your baby.'

Klara looked at her and for the briefest of moments her eyes seemed to clear, but then she shook her head and the shutters came down again.

'Don't be sentimental, woman. Ah – looks like we've reached my deathbed. How lovely.'

She waved ironically to the barrack in front of them, identical to the one they'd left. As they walked inside, however, Ana was surprised to see an open room, the walls painted white and pictures pinned to them – children's pictures in bright crayon, showing rainbows and swings and toddlers playing with dogs, like a vision from a world long-forgotten.

'Where are we?' she gasped.

'The former Roma camp,' the guard growled. 'This used to be their kindergarten. Mengele said it would be a good place for a load of pregnant sows, so here we are. You'll sleep on the floor.'

'Kindergarten?' Ana breathed. She'd not dreamed such things could exist here in Birkenau, but the evidence was before her eyes.

'Did all right, the gypsies,' the guard grunted. 'Got to keep their babies and everything.' Ana felt a stab of jealousy, but then the guard leaned in with a leer. 'Just like the family camp – remember them?'

Ana did. Once, it seemed like forever ago, they had hoped to smuggle Pippa into the family camp. The guard gave a dark laugh. 'Didn't do any of them any good though, did it? All went to the gas in the end. And good riddance, stealing bastards.'

Ana felt a thousand replies battering to be thrown at the Nazi whose own kind had stolen everything from so many –

their land, their freedom, their goods, their very lives. It wouldn't help though. Their only weapon was staying alive.

'Thank you,' she said instead, and stepped inside, laying Klara on the ground and going to find Naomi.

Janina and the worst of the patients had been hustled into the next block along, but the doctor had kindly shooed Ester into the maternity section and Ana blessed her for it. She was standing with Naomi, the other women clustered protectively around the pair and as the guards slammed the door shut on them, they gave a tiny cheer and stepped back. Ana watched, spellbound, as Naomi shrugged off the giant coat, removed the big jumper, then slowly unpeeled the makeshift sling to reveal Isaac, contentedly asleep against his mother's chest with nothing but a lipstick smudge on his cheek to show for his adventure.

'We did it,' Naomi said, her eyes shining. 'Praise God, we did it.'

And as Ana looked around at the women cheering under their breaths, for fear of their captors detecting their moment of happiness, she knew that whatever happened next, this moment was to be treasured. Love would, somehow, triumph over hate. They just had to wait and to pray, and one day, surely, it would be the main gates that opened and let them out into the rainbow.

TWENTY-NINE

17 JANUARY 1945

ESTER

'It hurts! Why does it hurt so much? It never did before.'

Ester looked at Ana in the dim light of a candle stub and was relieved to see that the midwife looked unruffled. The labouring mother before them had given birth twice already – to children who had been marched to the gas on arrival in the camp. The baby inside her had been the only thing keeping her going through her grief but now that the moment to greet her child was close, she was fading. Ana stepped in front of her and put a hand on each shoulder, speaking to the Hungarian in slow German, the only language they shared.

'It's hurting, Margarite, because I think Baby is facing forwards. That will make it more painful because you are spine to spine, but it doesn't mean there will be any problem with the birth. Do you understand?'

'Baby will come out?'

'Of course. I will make sure of it.'

'Alive?'

'I haven't lost one yet, even here in Birkenau.'

'Not one?'

'Not one, and I don't intend to start now.'

Ester saw Margarite nod at Ana's calm certainty and brace herself to endure the cramps that were wracking her wasted body. Ester certainly did not envy her this bit, but knew already that once the baby was born she would ache anew for Pippa. Her daughter would have passed her first birthday. Did her new 'parents' even know the date of it, or had they just made it up to suit, picked a convenient German date to go with a convenient German name and a convenient German identity?

It made her blood boil to think of them stamping their mark on her precious baby, but then she reminded herself that it was not necessarily their fault. She doubted the Reich had told whichever couple they'd passed Pippa on to that she had been born in a death camp, to a Jewish mother. Some glossy story would have been made up – a father lost on the Russian front, a mother dead in childbirth, all terribly tragic and designed to make the new parents feel good about their adoptive child. Certainly that's what she hoped, for the alternative was too much to bear – that Pippa had been taken into some household as no more than a servant to be spat on and reviled, like the Grimm brothers' Cinderella. She could see no sense to that, but the Reich, as she had learned time and again, worked on a very twisted logic and it dug at her like a screw to think of her daughter caught in its whorls.

Did Pippa have a soft cradle, in a warm room? Did her pseudo mother cuddle her and read to her and sing her lullabies? Ester could almost bear that the tunes would be in German if they were just sung with love. But then, usually in the coldest, darkest part of the night, she would wonder what this unknown woman made of the number she would certainly have found in her baby's armpit – and how it might affect her treatment of poor innocent Pippa. What if the very number

Ester had tattooed onto her baby to save her was the one thing that condemned her to ill treatment – or worse?

Don't, Ester, she told herself sternly, trying to focus on poor Margarite climbing the barrack wall with her cramps. There was no point dwelling on what might be going on beyond the fence. It had been nearly two months since they'd been moved across into the ex-Roma section; 1944 had ground into 1945 and still no one had come to liberate them. The Nazis had started shipping prisoners deeper into the Reich at the back end of last year but then the train lines had been bombed and even that had stopped. Those people remaining in Birkenau, prisoners and guards alike, were trapped on these windy, marshy plains until someone came to free them. Even once that happened, who knew what the war-ravaged world looked like out there.

Air raid sirens rang out more and more often these days and planes roared overhead, making for unknown targets with a bellyful of bombs. The guards barely even bothered searching for radios any more and the men in the next camp had the BBC on for all the key broadcasts, as well as illicit Polish stations offering information from nearer home. They passed the news through to the women in whispered bulletins and it was from one of those that Ester had heard the word 'Chelmno'. She'd grabbed at the man through the wire.

'What's happened at Chelmno?'

'They say it's totally disbanded.'

'Totally? What about the workers?'

'Gone.'

'Gone?'

He'd drawn a line across his throat and her world had spun, but then he'd added, 'Well, all save some poor group left to clear up. Fifty or so, they think. Blokes from Łódź.'

'Fifty?!'

Ester had snatched at this. Fifty men! And from Łódź! That

was enough for hope. She'd clung onto it amidst all the other news of Allied advances into Germany and Soviet ones into Poland. It had burned more brightly to her than thoughts of the liberation of Paris or Brussels. She'd imagined Filip, out in the forest at Chelmno, working with a group of friends. It would be hard, bitter work, she knew. She'd heard what the Sonderkommando had been made to do here in Birkenau and hated the thought of her poor, gentle husband having to burn endless broken bodies. But if he was alive, she would mend the hurt it had done to him, as he would mend the hurt that Birkenau had done to her. Together they would nourish their souls and their bodies. It would be slow, but it would be done.

Last week the men had come rushing to the fence to tell them that the Russians had taken Warsaw. Ana had cried at that and Ester had held her close. The last they'd heard, her friend's husband and oldest son had been in Warsaw, but she had no idea if they'd survived the uprising. They said some had managed to flee out of underground tunnels and down secret paths and that, too, was enough for hope.

Now the Red Army was marching on Krakow and from there, to Oświęcim, just three kilometres down the road. Germans who had moved into the village had been evacuated and the place was apparently a ghost-town. The Russians could be reaching it even now and Ester just prayed they did not stop there, did not rest in the nice, empty homes full of German comforts, but came on here, to hell. They'd heard that a camp at Majdanek had been liberated already, the departing Germans setting light to every building in the place as they'd fled, including the ones with prisoners inside, and they were all on alert. For now, though, there were more immediate concerns.

'This baby is tearing me apart,' Margarite cried. 'I swear it's tearing me right in two.'

She clawed at the wall, sending a pretty picture of a tree

fluttering to the floor, and Ester darted forward and picked it up.

'It isn't,' Ana assured her. 'It just feels that way. If it's any consolation, Baby probably isn't feeling it at all.'

'That's children for you,' Margarite said through gritted teeth, and Ester rubbed a hand up her arm as a cramp passed and, momentarily, she could rest.

'Maybe,' Naomi offered, sitting up from her bed on the floor, Isaac tucked into the crook of her arm, 'Baby doesn't want to come out until the world is free.'

'Then tell the damned Soviets to hurry up, will you,' Margarite gasped, as her body convulsed once more.

'Maternity block – report!' a voice rasped from outside and Ester looked to Ana, confused.

There had not been a roll call for days. Many of the SS had gone, snatching the chance to accompany inmates west. Mandel had shot off before Christmas and Grese just last week and those guards that were left lacked those women's commitment to active sadism. The only buildings that were patrolled now were Kanada, where Naomi and her colleagues still worked to sort the mounds of goods left from the last of the gassings in November, and the kitchens. Now, though, they could hear the unmistakably ominous sound of jackboots on the hard, snow-encrusted earth outside and those who had not yet been woken by poor Margarite's struggles blinked awake and sat up.

'Report! It's time to go, ladies – time to leave camp.'

Leave camp!

Suddenly torches were shining into the barracks, criss-crossing crazily over the pictures of children long since gone to the gas and illuminating the scared whites of fifty pairs of eyes. Ester saw Naomi scramble to cover Isaac, but the guards were in a hurry and lingered on no one.

'Let's go.'

'Where to?' Ester asked.

'West,' was the curt reply.

'But the trains aren't working.'

He leered at her.

'Then it's a good job your feet are, Jew girl. We're marching to the stations at Gleiwitz and Wodzisław Śląski.'

'But they're miles away,' someone protested.

'Which is why we need to get going – now!' He was losing patience, taking his gun from his back, but the air beyond the door was jet black and the ground lethally white and still the women hesitated. 'You don't like the cold?' he snapped. 'Well, tell you what, how about we warm you up instead, huh? Aufse- herin – the matches please.'

That got everyone scrambling. Ominous as the night was, no one wanted to burn like the poor souls in Majdanek and the women snatched up blankets to wrap around themselves as they were hustled outside. Ester looked to Ana, who looked in turn to Margarite, then stepped forward.

'This woman cannot march. She is in labour.'

The guard looked her up and down.

'Fine. She stays. And anyone else too weak to get up. The rest of you—'

'They cannot stay alone,' Ana insisted. 'I will tend them.'

'You?' the guard looked her up and down. 'You wish to stay here? With them?'

'They are my patients.'

'They are dead women. The electricity is being switched off, the water too. There is no fuel and no food and no one to protect you when the Reds come. Have you heard what they do to women? If you think they're going to save you, think again. You'll be far better off with us.'

Ana glanced to Ester and she could read her thoughts straight away – what on earth could be worse than this? But, then, who could have conceived of *this* until they'd been here, so who was she to judge? A shiver ran down her spine at the thought that their 'liberators' might bring a new sort of hell but then she reminded herself that this was a Nazi speaking. They were all built in Goebbels' lying mould and if this idiot guard could truly delude himself that he had been 'protecting' them, he wasn't worth listening to. Even so, she couldn't leave Ana here alone.

'I will stay too. I have patients in my charge who cannot leave their beds.'

'You? You're mad. I don't think—'

But at that moment there was a scuffle outside and someone barked: 'What's taking so long? Are these guards all incompetents?' The man looked around in a panic.

'Fine,' he snapped. 'Stay with the dead if you must. The rest of you – out!'

He jerked Naomi up by the arm and Ester had to step forward fast to kick the blanket back over a thankfully still sleeping Isaac.

'She's a nurse too,' she said, but the guard had had enough.

'No way. She goes. Out!'

Naomi looked frantically to Ester but the guard was ramming his gun into her back and she had no choice but to follow the others to the exit. Outside Ester could hear shouts and cries, the crack of whips and the bark of dogs. At the door, Naomi glanced back, her eyes signalling wildly to the blanket. Ester's eyes met hers and she tried to fill them with a heartfelt promise to look after Isaac, but it was all happening too fast. Why had they not thought of this? Why had they not made plans to meet again if they got separated? All Ester truly knew of her friend was that she came from some place in Greece called Salonika. It wasn't enough.

'Łódź!' she cried after her. 'St Stanislaus' cathedral.'

It was all she could think of but she had no idea if Naomi had heard her, for the noise of the mass of assembled prisoners was so great now that it masked even Isaac's sudden cry as he woke to find himself alone on the floor. Ester ran to him, gathering him into her arms and rocking him to try and hush him back to sleep but he had clearly picked up on the fear crackling in the night air and was not to be soothed.

'Take him there,' Ana said, pointing to the one-time kapo's room at the back. Klara had died just two days after they'd arrived in the former Roma camp, expiring quietly with a tear running down her cheek. There had been merely relief at her passing and no one had chosen to take on either the leadership of the hut or the solitary room. 'And don't come out until it's quiet.'

Ester did as instructed, shutting herself into the cubbyhole with the baby, who was now throwing himself backwards in anger.

'Please, Isaac, hush. I've got you.'

But she wasn't his mother. However much she loved him, however much he meant to her, she wasn't his mother. She didn't smell of Naomi, she didn't feel like Naomi, and she didn't have Naomi's milk – and Isaac knew it. What had they done?

Already she could hear people being driven out of the camp and, stretching onto her toes, she peered out of the cracked window. The sight was, if possible, one of the worst she had ever seen in Birkenau. It was still dark, and would be for some time, but the floodlights cast their unforgiving light onto the huddle on the road. People were being driven down it in ragged clothes and the remnants of shoes, so worn that many of them had bare toes. The wind was blowing, tugging at what meagre protection they did have and throwing snow into their bewildered faces.

SS guards, dressed in their thickest coats, hats and gloves, were whipping them out of the gates and into the barren countryside beyond. It had to be at least ten degrees below freezing and even the fierce dogs were cowering, but the guards showed no mercy. Anyone who fell was shot and the poor evacuees huddled closer and closer to each other, their combined breath rising into the black night like a primitive cry for help.

Ester stood, so shocked that even baby Isaac sensed it and whimpered quietly against her chest. How far were they going? They would never make it. Healthy, well-fed, well-clothed people would not make it, so what chance did this poor band of emaciated prisoners have? And Naomi was with them.

In the other room she could hear Margarite reaching the critical stage of labour but could do nothing more than stand there rocking Isaac and praying for Naomi as the camp drained away around them. For so long she had yearned to see the gates of Birkenau opened, but not like this, not with a forced march into the abyss. As the last stragglers of the agonising march shuffled, line after line, through the archway and into the dark night, she heard the gates being rattled back into place and chained. Next came a loud pop as the electricity snapped off and Ester knew, with terrible certainty, that they were being left here to die.

She went back through to the main room to see, in the thinnest of lights from a half-hearted dawn, Ana lifting a kicking baby from between Margarite's legs.

'It's a girl,' she said. 'A beautiful, healthy baby girl.'

Margarite took her daughter into her arms and kissed her with infinite tenderness.

'Hey, baby,' she said. 'Hey, sugar – welcome. You're here just in time to die with Mama.'

'Margarite, don't!' Ester protested.

In reply the weary mother waved a hand around the dark, empty barrack.

'Where will we get food?'

Ester wrapped Isaac tighter in his blanket and went to the door. The camp was eerily quiet. Row after row of snow-covered barracks stretched before her, hollowed out and abandoned. She could make out the shapes of a handful of guards on the perimeter and a small work party was still breaking up the crematoria in the trees at the back, but other than that Birkenau was empty.

The kitchen buildings and latrines were dark and the only noise was the pitiful whimper of the dying. Clearly the Germans had left all those they believed to be one step from the grave, plus Margarite, Ana, Ester and, of course, Isaac. Ester looked down at the boy. She would not let him die. Naomi might have been driven out into the cruel night but they were here, in the place they knew and they had a chance.

'Kanada,' she said firmly. 'We will break into Kanada.'

'Good idea,' Ana agreed, joining her. 'As soon as it's light we'll make our camp there and pray the Russians are close. They must be, surely, if the Germans have gone?'

Ester thought of what the guard had said about the Russians but cast it aside; they would cross that bridge when – if – they came to it.

'How do we get into Kanada?' she asked. 'I've never even been there.'

'We need Naomi,' Ana said.

Ester looked out across the snow-desert of camp, rocking Isaac up and down to try and hush his wails.

'So does this one,' she agreed sadly.

'Good job I'm still here then,' said an oh-so-familiar voice.

They froze.

'Naomi?'

'Give us a hand out of here, will you?'

To their side, the ever-present pile of corpses shifted and Ester jumped back, spooked. But then, from beneath their skeletal forms, Naomi came crawling out, alive and well and beaming fit to burst, and suddenly it felt as if the sun had come up over Birkenau.

'Naomi!' Ester ran to her, hugging her close and between

them, sensing his mother, Isaac gave an eager gurgle. 'How did you...?'

Naomi shrugged.

'Simple. It was dark and it was chaotic. No one seemed to be making a count, so I just, you know, dived sideways and crawled under... under...' She faltered for a moment as she looked at her macabre hiding place, then shook it off. 'Under these kind ladies. They kept me safe.'

'Safe?'

Ester looked around the dark, deserted camp.

'Safe,' Naomi confirmed, 'because I'm with you and I'm with Ana and I'm with Isaac. What more do I need?'

Ester could think of a few things, but with Naomi quite literally back from the dead, she had hope again, and with that, surely, they could endure.

THIRTY

20 JANUARY 1945

ANA

'No!' Ana clutched at Ester as, behind the fences, flames burst into the air and the riches of Kanada began to burn. 'They can't do that.'

She hammered furiously on the gates but the guards were too busy feeding the flames onto the next of the thirty barracks full of precious belongings. All that Jewish wealth had proved too much for the fleeing Nazis to resist and they'd left a handful of guards and some big padlocks to keep sorting through it. Trucks had even arrived to take the best goods after the marching prisoners into Germany. The jewels and furs had been treated with far greater care than the people, but that was the Third Reich for you.

For two days Ana and Ester had been trying to get in. They'd attempted to sweet-talk the guards, to dig under the fence, and even to force their skeletal bodies through its barbed gaps, but in vain. Now the Nazis were setting the whole thing on fire – just letting all the clothes and blankets burn while the remaining prisoners shivered in barren barracks, letting the sausages and the dried biscuits toast merrily while they starved. That was the Third Reich for you too.

Ana pressed her forehead against the cold concrete of the fence post and fought for sanity. The hunger was terrible. They had water from the snow coating the ground to assuage their thirst, but their stomachs were gnawing in on themselves and Isaac had sucked poor Naomi dry in the first day. They'd got into the barrack next door, hoping to find Janina, but she must have been forced out with those of her patients who could stand and her 'hospital' had held only corpses. It had seemed that there'd been nothing to do but huddle as many of the living together as they could and wait, but today the terrible sound of flames had drawn them out.

The last of the thirty barracks was on fire now and the heat was immense. For the first time since October had dragged winter into the camp, Ana felt warmth steal across her skin, but at what cost? The guards were moving away, picking up pace as the flames grew higher. They reached the gate and tumbled out, laughing manically. Ana and Ester fell back. If they left, they might be able to dare a run on the last of the barracks, snatch a few things from the inferno, but the guards just sneered at them and bolted the huge padlock fast.

'Look, we've lit a nice fire for you,' one threw at them and then they were gone, arms full of final steals as they made for the main entrance.

'They're leaving,' Ester said. 'They're all leaving.'

And it seemed that they truly were. Trucks were pulling up on the other side of the arched entrance to Birkenau and the last of the guards were leaping in and leaving all this behind as if it had never happened – as if it wasn't still happening.

'Bastards,' Ana breathed, then put her hand over her mouth. She never used to swear but, then, she never used to be left to die behind a merciless fence.

From their own block came a thin wail and Ester turned

instantly towards it, a haunted look on her face. Ana knew the young woman hated it when Isaac cried, that she felt every vibration of his distress as if it were an echo of her own, lost daughter.

'They're not going to defeat us,' she shouted, her voice echoing off the wooden barracks around. 'Not now, not when we've got this far. Go on!' she screamed after the far-off trucks. 'Clear off, take your dirty souls out of here. You won't escape. The Russians are coming. The Russians are coming and they're going to find us alive. They're going...'

Her anger convulsed in a series of coughs that shook her thin body and Ana put an arm around her but then, through the cold air, they heard what sounded like an answering shout. A very small, very young answering shout.

Ester fought down her cough and looked to Ana.

'What's that?'

Ana listened hard.

'Sounds like...'

'Children?'

The shouts came again, thin and surely childlike. Ester started running, darting from one barrack to another to seek out the voices, and Ana did her best to keep up. Her knees ached, her ankles ached, her spine ached, but Ester was right – the Nazis weren't going to defeat them now.

'Here!' Ester had reached one of the far blocks, identical to the others, save that it was echoing with shouts. She pushed on the door but it didn't budge. 'It's locked. It's bloody locked!'

Ester hadn't used to swear either. Birkenau had made barbarians of them all; but not such barbarians that they would lock children away.

'Help me!' Ana joined Ester at the door as she shouted at whoever was on the other side to stand back. 'Now!'

They kicked. They kicked all their fury and their frustration and their deep, dark fear right into that wooden door. The hinges groaned and from within came a cry of encouragement from what sounded like a hundred tiny voices.

'Again!'

Again they kicked and this time the wood splintered around the lower hinge. Ana's lungs screamed for mercy at the unaccustomed exertion and she had to stop to try and draw air into them but Ester kicked on until, with a shriek of protest, the wood gave way and she tumbled inside. Ana stepped in after her and looked at the hordes of youngsters stuck inside in disbelief. Birkenau still had the power to shock her. The ones nearest the door, pawing desperately at Ester, were clearly the strongest, but there were so many others beyond, lying weakly on the floor. Had they been in here for two days with no food or water?

She pushed the broken door open wider.

'Go,' she urged those still on their feet. 'Get snow to drink and bring it back for the others. We must all work together now.'

They looked at her blankly and she tried it again in German but at that they shook their heads.

'We understood,' one lad, the tallest of them all and clearly a self-nominated leader, said. 'We're just.... It's just...' He swallowed. 'Is it safe outside?'

Ana's heart went out to him. What brutality these poor things must have suffered.

'It's safe, I promise.'

He stumbled forward and gave her a hug so strong that it almost knocked her off her feet, then he was gone, scooping snow ravenously into his mouth.

'Only the fresh stuff,' Ana warned, hastening after them. 'Only take the fresh stuff from the surface.'

Below the innocent white were mud and rats and endless corpses; the snow might kill as readily as it might save. But Ester headed outside to supervise them so, filling her hands with snow, Ana edged into the barrack. There were not as many children as it had at first sounded. Their desperation must have made them loud indeed for there were maybe fifty in here and at least half of them not in a fit state to shout anything.

She knelt down next to a slight girl and offered her the snow in her hands. She lifted her head and licked delicately at it, like a kitten.

'Thank you,' she croaked in Polish.

'It's fine. Have more. Slowly now. That's good.' The girl licked up the rest of the snow and the ghost of a smile crossed her chapped lips. 'What's your name?'

'Tasha.'

'A lovely name. How old are you, Tasha?'

'Sixteen.'

The answer jolted Ana, for she looked little more than twelve, but she supposed that was what camp life had done to these poor young people, and fought not to show her surprise.

'And where are you from?'

'Warsaw.'

Ana's heart jolted.

'Warsaw?'

'They threw us all out when our parents were bad.'

'Bad?'

'That's what the Germans called it. Mama said it was "brave and strong and necessary" but the Germans didn't think so.'

She looked thirstily at Ana's hands and Ana eased herself painfully up and went to fetch more. There were so many children to get to, but first she had to hear more. Tasha lapped up the second handful and pushed herself up against the wall.

'They killed my papa.'

'I'm so, so sorry.'

'And they put us on a train with Mama. All of us. The whole city.'

'No one escaped?'

'I don't know. We tried. Papa had some friends who'd got out to the hills and he wanted to get us out too, but the Germans shot him. They found us hiding in a shed and they shot him right there in front of us.' Her eyes shone but there was not enough moisture in her poor body to cry. 'Then they shoved us on the train.'

Ana held her hand tight.

'I'm so sorry,' she said again, feeling bad for pushing, but she had to ask. 'Did you know a man called Bartek, Tasha?'

She shrugged.

'Several.'

'Of course, sorry. Bartek Kaminski and his son, Bronislaw. Did you know them?' Tasha frowned and Ana squeezed her hand. 'Did you see them? Do you know what happened to them?'

Tasha opened her mouth and she leaned in eagerly but then the shutters went down over the girl's eyes and she just shook her head.

'I don't know. I don't know what happened to anyone. And now Mama's gone too.'

Ana pulled her into her arms. She didn't even want to think about what that hesitation might have meant and it wasn't important now. The child was all that mattered.

'Where's your mama gone?'

'I don't know. They pushed her out into the snow, told her to march. She wanted to take us but they said no children. I told them I was sixteen so not a child at all but they wouldn't believe me. They just shoved me in here with the others and then locked the door. We tried to get out, I promise we did. Georg said we had to, for the little ones.' She nodded over to the first boy Ana had spoken to who was bringing snow in for the smallest of the children. 'We tried, we did. But it was too hard.'

'It would have been,' Ana soothed, hating that Tasha was

blaming herself for this. 'You did all you could. You were very brave.'

'But not very strong,' she said sadly.

'That's not true. It's strong to stay alive. It's strong to still be here.'

Tasha looked up at her, eyes wide and scarily trusting.

'Will we get out?' she asked.

Ana sucked in a deep breath.

'Of course,' she said firmly. 'Of course we will get out.'

The only question now, was how.

THIRTY-ONE

27 JANUARY 1945

ANA

Seven interminable days later, Ana sat in a very crowded barrack, stirring a pot of soup she was desperately trying to cook on the brick stove. Finding the children had been the incentive she, Ester and Naomi had needed to renew their hunt for supplies and, with the help of Tasha, Georg and the other older ones, they'd tried again to break into Kanada. Georg had shown an aptitude for lock picking that Ana hadn't wanted to question too closely and they'd burst into the compound, eager for goods.

Most of the warehouses had been smouldering piles of embers, but six at the back had still been largely intact where the flames must have blown out before they could engulf them. They'd carried out armfuls of clothing to keep everyone in the camp warm. Even better, it had been possible to retrieve half-burned wall planks and, with shovels full of the hot embers, they'd been able to stoke up the stoves at either end of their barrack and get some semblance of warmth into it.

Greatly cheered by this and the relief of finding company, Georg had organised his band to keep the stove going and they'd also helped Ester and Naomi carry some of the sick from elsewhere in the camp into the only warm building in Birkenau. They had fuel for days if they were careful, but they'd still needed food.

Their search of Kanada had turned up little and Ana had despaired, but then Naomi and Tasha had come back into the barrack with big boxes in their arms. Those who could had rushed to see and they'd proudly revealed that they'd found a laden railway car at the top of the tracks. It must have been intended to be shipped into the Reich before the tracks were damaged and then forgotten about. When Georg had bust the lock open, they'd found a couple of crates of dried sausage and packs of old biscuits, stale but perfectly edible. A feast indeed.

Excitement had been high and the fight for a scrap of the precious meat fierce. Ana had had to step in with her sternest midwife voice to stop the children beating each other for a mouthful, for while it had been a truly wonderful find, there were a lot of people in the barrack and it would not go far. Distributing biscuits to everyone, she'd taken charge of the boxes, sitting herself and Ester firmly on them to stop the fights, and sent the gang out to break into the kitchens as well. This had yielded a small stash of onions, potatoes and turnips – all way past their best but enough, with buckets of snow, to make a soup that would go far further than mere chunks of sausage – and be far kinder to hollow stomachs.

They'd been living on it ever since and supplies were getting dangerously low again. It was a week since the last guards had abandoned Birkenau, but still all that swept in from the east were icy winds. Why on earth did no one come?

Ana stirred the soup, round and round and round, watching the tiny bits of sausage spinning in the liquid. To her left a poor mother was in the first stages of labour and soon she would need to tend her, but for the time being she was lost in the simple swirls of the thin meal. These last days had been the first ones in two years in which she had actually cooked and it was both satisfying and surprisingly exhausting. Even if anyone did come to rescue them from their wasteland, would they ever be able to adapt to normal life again?

She thought of Tasha's hesitation when she'd asked after Bartek and Bron, and stirred the soup faster. Had the memories all just been too much for the girl, or had she known something she didn't want to share? And would it all matter anyway if they couldn't get out of here? Time and again she, Ester and Naomi had discussed whether they should try to break out of the main gates to find help, but the snow was still falling and they had no idea what was out there. It might take days and there were so many sick. Ester was kept busy all day trying to ease the suffering of the TB patients, and even with the meagre warmth from the stove, they were losing many. They had no choice but to place bodies in the snow behind the barrack, and it was impossible not to look at that growing pile and wonder how long it would be before they were all on it.

A cry from the mother pulled Ana out of her melancholy and she forced her creaking bones up to go and tend her. The labour was progressing faster than she'd expected and she bent to rub the woman's back.

'You're doing very well, Justyna. Come, lie on the stove.'

She shooed a few children away to make room. They stood around watching curiously as Justyna panted against the cramps that were clearly increasing in intensity, but Ana ignored them and focused on the one thing she knew best – bringing babies into the world. This would be at least the three thousandth child she had helped birth here in Birkenau and even with the Germans gone, she had no idea what chances it had. What sort of hellish midwifery was this? And yet the miracle of birth awed her every time; still it brought light into the darkness and hope into despair. While babies were being born, there was a future. So she set herself to helping the mother bring yet another life into their packed barrack in the middle of nowhere.

'That's good, Justyna. We're going to be pushing soon, I promise.'

She spotted Naomi going to tend the soup, Isaac strapped to her chest, and her heart lifted. Isaac would soon be four months old. He had lived and even thrived with so many 'lost mothers' to help tend him and this new baby would live too.

'Not much longer, Justyna,' she assured her. 'We're going to have baby out and then rescue is going to come and—'

A great shout went up from outside and everyone in the barrack jumped. Georg burst into the room with Tasha in tow, scattering wood in their excitement.

'They're here. Soldiers are here.'

Justyna looked at Ana.

'That was quick work,' she said with a tired smile but then another cramp came and Ana had to focus on helping her as everyone who could walk followed Georg out of the door.

Naomi was hot on his heels, but Ester paused next to Ana.

'Is this it, do you think, Ana? Is this liberation?'

Ana cocked her head listening.

'It certainly sounds like it.'

'I'm scared,' the young woman admitted. 'What if their intentions are, are...'

Ana squeezed her hand.

'If their intentions towards us,' she waved a hand around at the emaciated, exhausted women, 'are lecherous, then the world has truly gone to the dogs and we will be better off out of it. Come, let's go together.'

She pushed herself up. Justyna would be fine for the time being and she had to see this. Taking Ester's arm, she went with her to the door, took a few steps out into the white of the compound and stared.

The giant gates at the entrance had burst open and soldiers

were pouring in, dressed in the scarlet-trimmed uniforms of the Soviets. It was the fearsome Red Army, but the men and women coming up the great central road towards them did not look so much fierce as terrified. Their eyes were as wide as children and they looked around them constantly, taking in the vastness of Birkenau, the unremitting lines of the endless barracks, the harsh wire divisions, the skeletal corpses and the equally skeletal men and women crying out to them for help.

'Remember the first day we arrived?' Ester murmured, turning to her. 'I could not believe this place either.'

Ana did remember, vividly. She remembered being shoved onto that cattle train, bruised and aching all over from the cruel interrogation. She remembered more and more people being crammed in after her and she remembered her horror when Ester's sweet face had appeared in the battered crowd. She remembered poor Ruth dying in her daughter's arms and the long journey with no food or water, only to arrive here. In hell.

'Is this liberation?' She repeated Ester's earlier question, unable to quite believe it.

The soldiers were close to their section of the camp, attracted by the shouts of Naomi, Georg and Tasha, and Ana could see the horror on their faces, see their smiles as they bent to the youngsters, fishing what food they had out of the pockets to press it upon them and looking on the women with the tenderness of fathers and brothers. The world had not, it seemed, gone to the dogs yet and kindness lived.

'This *is* liberation,' Ester confirmed, and they both looked again to the gates of Birkenau, standing wide open for the first time in six years.

'We made it,' Ana said, clutching at Ester. 'We made it to the end.'

'We did,' Ester agreed, then she was pulling Ana into her arms and they were hugging each other so hard that for a moment Ana thought her too-thin ribs might crack – and didn't even care.

Through the snow and the wind and the cries of the exultant children she heard Ruth's voice: *She's your daughter now*. She dropped to her knees.

'I did it, Ruth,' she whispered. 'I kept her safe. I kept Ester safe for you.'

'Ana?' Ester tugged on her arm. 'Ana, look!'

Ana brought her eyes back from Ester's imagined mother to the girl herself. She was pointing to where trucks were coming through the gates. Behind them came an ambulance – a real, Red Cross ambulance, bringing not deadly gas but genuine help for the sick. Ester started to cry and Ana stumbled to her feet and held her close once more, but then a wail from inside the barrack made them both leap back.

'Justyna!' Ana cried and they dived inside to see the new mother red in the face and screaming.

'I think I need to push,' she shouted at them, through gritted teeth.

'I think maybe you do,' Ana agreed, rushing to her as a laugh bubbled up inside her and burst out into the barrack in a ripple of joy. 'For liberation is here and your baby wants to see it.'

ESTER

Ester looked around the ward, unable to believe she was nursing in a proper hospital again. They'd been moved to the Auschwitz I main camp last week and had been astonished to find smart brick buildings, now occupied by the Polish Red Cross and rapidly filling with such luxuries as blankets, mattresses and medicines. It was still very rough but palatial compared to camp life in Birkenau and Ester reached out to touch the newly delivered supplies of antibiotics, feeling as if she had crossed a century.

For two years she had lived the most basic of lives, no better than an animal in a cage save for the camaraderie and support she had found in the women around her. To be back in civilisation was like plunging frozen hands into hot water – both pleasure and pain. Bit by bit she was fully registering all that she had been robbed of in the last two years and with that tingling realisation came anger.

Clenching her hands into fists to stop herself hammering on the walls in frustration, she looked out of the window to the bustle of the one-time camp below. The Russians had moved east, working to secure the full German surrender, and Polish organisations had come in behind. More and more medics and volunteer helpers were arriving every day and for the first time in far too long, Ester found herself speaking her native language on a regular basis. The barked barbs of German orders had been replaced by the soft curls of Polish care and while she was hugely grateful, it also made her ache for home.

Home! Where was that any more?

The workers had told her that Łódź was liberated and the walls of the ghetto had been torn down. People were trying to return to their pre-war houses, or to new ones seized from fleeing Germans, and the city was in flux. Were her and Filip's fathers there? And if so, where were they living? Was Leah back from the countryside? Had she married this farmer she'd been courting? She remembered Filip's one letter with her sister's news and felt anew the ache of having his precious words pulped by Nazi disinfectant. But the war was over – she could go and find Filip himself. Was he alive? Had he got back to their hometown? Was he there, even now, looking for her? How would he know where to find her?

For a moment, she smiled. He would know – the steps of St Stanislaus' church, where they'd eaten their lunches across from each other six years ago. That very first time Ester had looked across and seen Filip sitting there, his long fingers playing with the crumbly pastry of his pasztecik, his gorgeous face creased in concentration on the newspaper in his lap, her world had shifted in ways that had felt important – that had turned out to be very important. The problem was that other, bigger forces had been moving the world too, and in far more seismic ways.

One thing Ester knew though – their love, and the daughter born from that love, was all that she had and she was going to fight for it. If she could only get back. Every time a snippet of information came through from the workers, she realised how cut off she'd been in camp and the hunger for news of her loved ones gnawed at her far more powerfully than any empty stomach.

Then there was Pippa.

Her daughter's name curled around Ester's heart, as it always did, and she moved closer to the glass, looking out over the gate to the world beyond. She'd gone nowhere bar the three kilometres from Birkenau to Auschwitz I, and although it had felt magical to drive out of the dark archway of the women's camp, in truth she'd made little progress. Somewhere out there was her daughter. Every time Ester thought about how she might find her, her body physically ached with yearning.

'Nurse, can you help me?'

She turned, pushing aside her own concerns to go and tend the wasted woman in the nearby bed. There were so many people in a worse state than she was and for the moment she had to make them her main concern. But, oh, the longing to get away from this place grew with every person she saw head out of the hated gates. The other day she had seen Pfani, dressed up in frills and furs, driving out in the back of a Polish officer's car. It was clear what her passage had cost but, even so, Ester had envied her. Pfani had spotted her, gaped, and then given her an enthusiastic wave, as if they were old friends; like a fool, Ester had waved back. But then, who was she to begrudge anyone their passage out of this place? Every evening she and Ana would sit and exchange memories of Łódź and vow to get back there as soon as they could, but with the world in transit, seats on trains, or buses, or even just carts were impossible to come by.

'Ester!'

Naomi came running in, Isaac on her hip, giggling away as he jiggled up and down with her every step. Ester went to meet them, taking the boy and lifting him high in the air so that he giggled even more.

'Hey, Isaac, sweetie. How are you?!'

Her answer was another laugh and a tug on her hair. Isaac was nearly five months old and starting to test his limbs. His clothing was permanently filthy from the rough floors of the hospital, but they had spares now and water to wash them in, so Naomi did not care.

'Let him free,' she'd said. 'Let him kick his legs around as much as he damn well wants. He's been restricted long enough.'

Now he squirmed to get down and, laughing, Ester set him on the floor and crouched next to him to watch him wriggle.

'He'll be crawling soon,' she said.

'Yes.'

Her friend was looking down at her with a strange expression on her face.

'Naomi? Is all well?'

'All is very well, Ester, but...'

She shuffled her feet and, attracted by the noise, Isaac turned and started to try and wiggle his way back to her. Ester pushed herself back up to standing.

'What is it, Naomi? What's happened.'

Naomi swallowed and focused on her son as he pulled at the laces of her new boots.

'We've got a train.'

She said it so low that at first Ester didn't think she'd heard right.

'A train?'

Naomi suddenly grabbed at her hands.

'A train, Ester, out of here. Not all the way to Salonika yet, but to Budapest. The Hungarians are working hard to get their people home and there's a space for me and Isaac to go too. From there we can work our way south to Greece, to... to home.'

'That's wonderful, Naomi,' Ester managed but the words clogged in her throat. She looked to Isaac again, trying to eat his mother's laces, and tears sprang into her eyes. Naomi was leaving and taking Isaac with her. Ever since he'd been born, Ester had poured her energy into making sure he was safe. And she'd done it. He was going home. So why did she feel so very bleak?

'I don't want to leave you, Ester,' Naomi said.

Ester looked at her through her tears and saw that the younger girl, too, was crying.

'Don't be silly, Naomi. You have to seize this chance. You have to go home.'

'I'm scared.'

'We all are. For too long we've been kept away from everything that's vital and real, so no wonder it scares us, but we can't let them do that to us. Remember how we used to say that our only weapon was staying alive?' Naomi nodded. 'Well now it's more than that; now it's finding our life – our real life.'

Naomi leaped forward to hug her, forgetting Isaac and sending him toppling. The look of surprise on his face as he rocked sideways made them both laugh and then cry all over again. Ester bent and scooped him into her arms, holding him so close that his soft baby skin pressed against her chaffed face.

'He'll miss you,' Naomi said, hugging them both.

'And I him. Ana too, I know. But we can write, Naomi. We can – we *must* – stay in touch and when we've found our families, when I've found...'

Her words tangled too much to get out and Naomi covered her face in kisses.

'When you have found Pippa,' she said firmly, 'we will meet again.'

'Oh Naomi,' Ester said, clutching her close, 'how do you manage such optimism?'

The Greek girl shrugged and Ester drank in the familiar gesture, trying to imprint Naomi onto her memory before she was gone. Birkenau had been a terrible place but it had brought her wonderful friends and her stomach already felt hollow at their imminent loss.

'It's quite simple,' Naomi told her easily. 'I manage it because without it I would fall apart. The world is a terrifying place. It became so from the moment the Nazis started stamping all over us and even now that we're stamping on them in return, it's still as frightening as before. They took our past, they still dominate our present, and who knows in what dark ways they've wrecked our futures. It's bitterly, bitterly unfair and if I let myself think too much about that I want to rage and scream and throw myself on the floor like a toddler. But what good is that? We only get one life and the Nazis have wrecked enough of it.'

Ester wiped away her tears.

'You're so right, Naomi. And so strong. I know you and Isaac will be just fine. When do you go?'

Naomi scuffed at the floor again and Ester's heart sank.

'Tonight.'

'Tonight?!'

'I'm sorry. They've got hold of an extra carriage for the train, so spaces have come available. They asked me if I wanted one and I felt I had to say yes.'

Ester fought the swirl of emotions inside her.

'Quite right. Of course you did. Of course you *must*. Oh but...'

She pulled back and they looked at each other. Ester drank in the sight of the younger girl, her friend and sister through this nightmare, and could not believe that by tomorrow she wouldn't even have her here. Somehow, whatever it took, she had to get herself and Ana home to Łódź.

It was two days later that the man came to the camp. He had three large wagons drawn by sturdy horses, and he walked the streets of the medical camp shouting a single word: 'Łódź'. Ester heard it through the hospital window and ran out to see him.

'I'm heading for Łódź,' he told her. 'I've been going round the local villages and I have these men and these carts and I'm happy to take whoever wants to come.'

'For what price?'

He looked offended.

'No price. I want to help people get away from this hellhole and I want company on the road, that's all. I'm Frank.'

He stuck out a hand and Ester took it, reflecting that it was the first time she'd touched a man in two whole years.

'Nice to meet you, Frank. It's very kind of you.'

He grimaced.

'I don't know about that. It will be a hard trip. Łódź is 250 kilometres away and we won't be moving fast so it will take weeks. But I'm fed up of waiting for trains and I figure the Polish people will help us along the way so... It's worth the risk.' He looked at her. 'You're from Łódź?'

'Yes.'

'And you want to get home?'

'Yes! So much.'

He shrugged and flashed her a sudden smile.

'Then what are you waiting for?'

It was a good question. Ester pictured her home city and, for the first time, it felt within touching distance. Glancing back up to the hospital, she thought of Ana. The midwife had been working hard in the hospital as more women gave birth to babies who'd escaped Birkenau by the skin of their as yet unformed teeth, but Ester knew that thoughts of home and family tormented her every bit as much as they did Ester.

'Can I bring a friend?'

'Of course.' Frank smiled again. 'I leave tomorrow morning, first thing, and, God willing, we'll be in Łódź in time to see the blossom forming on the trees.'

Ester closed her eyes and pictured the cherry tree by the steps of St Stanislaus' cathedral. It had rained its petals on her and Filip in the early days of their courtship and, if this kind man was right, she could be beneath them again to find him. Filip was alive, she was sure of it. The road ahead would be cold and hard but it was paved with hope at last. She was going to make it out of here and she was going to make it back to Łódź. She was going to find Filip and, somehow, they were going to find their daughter and be whole again.

'So,' Frank asked, 'are you in?'

'I'm in,' she said determinedly, and rushed off to find Ana.

The next morning, at first light, they were both there, wrapped up warmly, with new boots on their feet and Red Cross food parcels in sacks on their backs. There were about thirty in their bold band and they shuffled together, falling naturally into prisoner-style lines and then, with awkward laughs, pushing themselves out of them as Frank led them away from Auschwitz and onto the road.

A few minutes out, by unspoken mutual consent, they paused and looked back. Ester sighed. Bleak Birkenau, where she and Ana had spent the last two hideous years, was already out of sight, but the stark lines of the main camp were every bit as forbidding and she knew some parts of her were irreparably damaged by the horrors she had experienced in this unimaginably vicious Nazi construction. They'd been told they were lucky to be alive and, of course, they were, but it did not feel like luck. She did not even truly feel alive; it felt more like she had found the empty shell of what had used to be life.

'A curse on you!' Frank yelled at the dark, low buildings and the crowd gave a thin cheer and turned their weary backs resolutely on hell. There was a long, hard climb out ahead.

PART THREE
ŁÓDŹ

THIRTY-THREE

MARCH 1945

ANA

'Łódź!'

Ana heard the cry go up from the people at the head of their weary caravan and lifted her head from the wagon Ester had finally persuaded her into a few days back. She'd managed to walk for the best part of sixteen days but her poor old bones had been protesting and in the end Ester had put her foot down. She'd talked kindly Frank into letting her ride in the baggage wagon with people's meagre belongings and the Red Cross provisions and, ashamed as she'd been to give in, it had been wonderful. Most of the time she'd slept, cushioned in bundles of blankets and rocked by the motion of the horse, and she had to admit that the whole experience had been strangely childlike. She almost didn't want to arrive, dreading what she might find, but as she wriggled into the open air, she found Ester looking eagerly at her.

'We're here, Ana. We're home.'

Ana pushed herself to sitting and looked around, stunned. She'd forgotten how big Łódź was – and how beautiful. She'd never thought of it as a particularly striking city, especially compared to Warsaw, but after two years of seeing nothing but identical barrack buildings and barbed wire, she felt as if she were drowning in riches. As they turned onto the bottom of Piotrkowska Street she stared up at the beautiful palaces of the industrial pioneers of last century, standing tall and proud on either side with their elegant porticoes and long windows. It was a warm day and many windows stood open. Ana could see people within – here a maid dusting, there a man at his desk, and there a young girl sat engrossed in a book, activities that looked dizzyingly exotic.

'It's so... so...'

'Normal,' Ester finished for her. 'So wonderfully, thrillingly normal.'

She reached up a hand and Ana clasped it as Ester walked on at her side, their pitiful caravan moving even more slowly than the long, painful trip through the Polish countryside. It had felt, at one point, as if they would never make it and yet here they were and suddenly it was almost as if they had never been away. The city must have been spared bombing, for it was perfectly intact and, indeed, improved. The Nazis had clearly known how to create impressive structures when it suited them, for she could see several stunning new buildings. Anger spiked inside Ana and she felt a sudden longing to jump out of the cart and coat those impertinent new walls with blood-red paint, but then reminded herself that they were theirs now.

Poor Poland had been cowed but had not given up. They'd heard stories all along the road. Kindly housewives had brought them out bread and soup and even – unbelievable bliss on the tongue – cakes and pastries. They had sat with them as they ate, asking about the camp and telling tales of their men who had headed off to fight in Polish regiments under the British command, or with the Soviets. All were still fighting, closing in on Berlin where Hitler was somehow continuing to lead his forces as they shrank back in on themselves in the face of the oncoming armies of the rest of the world.

'We'll get him,' they all said, when it was time for the travellers to pick themselves off the spring grass and head on. 'We'll get him for you.'

They'd thanked them, tried to smile, but it had become increasingly obvious with every lovely family they'd talked to that their own experience of the war was going to be one that could never be fully conveyed. They had told people about sleeping on wooden slats, fifteen to one bed. They had described the hunger, the bone-chilling cold, the degradation of endless roll calls, the brutality of the guards and, of course, the horror of the great gas chambers, belching human smoke over them day and night like an unending curse. And people had listened and gasped and said 'how awful' and meant it, but still had not been able to understand. And perhaps that was good.

But it still hurt.

'You're not even a Jew,' people would say to Ana, as if that made a difference, as if the Jewish people were somehow hardened to suffering. But no one would ever be hardened to the horrors that had been endured in the camps and as Ana looked around bustling Łódź, full of people who thought twenty minutes waiting for a tram in the snow was a hardship, she feared she might never slot back into normal life again. If there was even a normal life here for her.

They'd met one couple a few days ago who'd escaped from Warsaw. Ana had seized on them, desperate for information, but their faces had closed up and they'd said they couldn't bear to talk about it. From the little they had said, Ana had gathered that the brave townspeople had been duped by the Russians into rising up to meet troops that had not, then, been sent in. The initial attack had been gloriously successful, claiming much of the city for the Poles and breaking down the ghetto, but the siege that should have lasted a few days had rolled into week after miserable week until eventually, starving and disease-ridden, they'd been forced to surrender to the Germans once more.

It had been a doubly bitter blow and their enemy had been characteristically sadistic, shipping the whole native population, Jews and non-Jews alike, out to camps. This family had escaped with a handful of others when their train had got stuck at a leaf-strewn siding and they'd broken out of their wagon. They'd known nothing of Bartek or Bronislaw and had admitted that casualties had been high, but the mere fact of their escape had given Ana a glimmer of hope and she had to cling to that.

'How will we ever find our families?' she asked Ester, sitting up and looking around the crowded streets in despair.

'We'll help.'

Ana jumped and looked around as a small group of men approached. They were dressed in the dark clothing of Hasidic Jews and, with their wide-brimmed hats smart on their head and curls either side of their bearded faces, they looked like a vision from the past.

'How?' she asked cautiously.

'Many ways,' their leader said. 'We have been busy since liberation. The CCPJ – the Central Committee of Polish Jews – is working hard in Łódź to help those returning home. You have been in the camps?'

'Auschwitz,' Ester told them, and they winced.

'You are, then, a living miracle,' their leader said, with a bow.

Ana saw the discomfort in her friend's face.

'You too?' she asked them.

They shook their heads.

'We hid. In the hills. It was a very tough life.'

'Was it?' Ester asked dully.

Ana squeezed her hand.

'How can you help us?' she asked gently.

They looked her up and down.

'Are you Jewish?'

'No.'

'But she has been with us all through our time in the camp,' Ester said hastily. 'She has helped us and cherished us and been a true friend to us.'

'For which we thank you,' the man said, with another funny bow. 'But we cannot help – we simply do not have the contacts to do so. You, though,' he looked to Ester, 'you are a Jew?'

'I am.'

'Then you must make your way to Śródmiejska Street. The Jewish relief committee is handing out apartments to returning Jews and there are many places to leave notes for your family and gain information.'

Ana saw Ester's eyes light up, but then she looked to Ana and faltered.

'What can my friend do?'

He shrugged.

'How should we know?' he said and then caught himself and added, 'Your church perhaps?'

He gestured across the street and Ana turned to see that they were passing St Stanislaus' cathedral. Instantly she was engulfed with images of its rich interior and something inside her swelled in response. She could almost smell the incense, hear the soft chanting of the priests, see the blessed Christ on the cross, calling her home. She could also almost see the young people in the Lady Chapel that time in 1941 when she'd gone in seeking respite from her anger at the Nazis and found the Resistance group that had helped her fight them – and taken her to Birkenau.

She shivered. She did not regret her calling for a moment, but God knew how hard it had been for her – and how hard it might yet be. She looked to Ester for reassurance, but the girl was standing stock-still, staring at the steps, and Ana remembered that this place held poignant memories for her too. Their religions, it seemed, like their fates, had become strangely entwined and she looked back to the cathedral, praying, as she knew Ester would be praying, to see Filip there, waiting for his wife. But the steps were empty.

Ana pushed the blankets off her legs and reached for the edge of the cart.

'I must get down, thank you, Frank,' she called, but Frank was gathered around the Jewish elders with the rest of the group, asking after friends and getting directions to the repatriation centre. Ana admired the Jewish community for their energy. And envied it. How was she to find a home?

'Let me help, Ana.' Ester had snapped out of her reverie and hurried to ease her from the cart.

'Thank you, my dear.' Ana put her hands on the younger woman's shoulders to get down and then found herself curiously reluctant to let go. 'I will miss you.'

'I'm not going anywhere.'

'I know. This city is both our homes and I hope it will stay that way and we can see each other often, but it will be different now. It—'

'I mean I'm not going anywhere right now, save perhaps into the cathedral with you.'

'No! You have to go to the Jewish centre. You have to find your family.'

'And I will. There is time. I have been on the road home for so long that one more day will make little difference. I'm coming with you.' Ana felt tears sting at her eyes and leaned in against Ester, who folded her close. 'I could not have got this far without you, Ana. You are not a Jew, this was not your fight, and yet you made it yours. You gave us help in the ghetto and hope in the camp. I will never forget that, and I want to see you safely back to your family in return.'

'Oh, Ester.'

Anything else Ana might have wanted to say was lost in a rush of emotion and she could only clutch onto her friend – her daughter – and try not to cry too noisily. She heard Ester give a soft chuckle and the sound rippled through her, louder than the sudden cry of the cathedral bells at their side.

'Come on, Ana – let's go and find your boys.'

Several long hours later, they nervously approached Zgierska Street. They had gone first to the apartment on Bednarska that the Nazis had assigned to the Kaminskis but had found it occupied by someone else, so now they were back at her original house – her one-time family home. The ghetto fencing was gone but an ugly scar still marked the land where it had been and they stepped over it with exaggerated care. They were both far too used to boundaries now and breaking them felt headily bold. They paused on the other side, but when nothing happened, they dared to walk on. The area was broken but teeming with life. People everywhere were clearing houses, repairing streets and carrying paint, furniture and carpets around in a hive of nesting activity. They passed one group of young men painting the exterior of a run of houses and singing their hearts out in a traditional Polish folk song.

'Afternoon, ladies,' they called down from their ladders, tipping their hats and barely skipping a beat in their song.

Ana felt her heart lift and tipped her own imaginary hat back at them, but the next street was her own and her knees buckled with nervous anticipation. Ester tightened her grip, sure and strong at her side, and they moved onwards together. Every house was familiar to Ana. Behind so many of those doors she had helped babies into the world in happier times, behind so many of them she had eaten with friends, or taken Bronislaw, Zander and Jakub to play. Just up the next turning was the school the boys had trotted off to every morning for years, and a few metres further on, the church they had attended every single Sunday. It had been shut off in the ghetto with the poor Jews and she'd heard tell it had been turned into a mattress factory.

'Hail Mary, Mother of God.'

Her fingers went to her waist and connected with the rosary Georg had found her in the burning remains of Kanada. She'd been so touched when he'd brought it to her with a gruff, 'Ester said you might like these beads, Mrs.' Where was he now? The children had been taken out of Birkenau almost immediately. One of the nurses had told her that orphanages were being set up all over Poland for them and that a 'rescue operation' had been launched to try and find them family once more. The Polish Red Cross were helping, alongside the Education Department of the Central Committee of Jews in Poland. Plus, a new American organisation called the United Nations Relief and Rehabilitation Administration was setting up a 'child search team', which sounded intimidating but promising. Ana glanced to Ester. She had quiet hopes that this rescue operation might help them find Pippa but had not said anything yet for fear of getting her friend's fragile hopes up before she knew more. One thing she was sure of – she would do everything in her power to find that little girl. First though, she had her own children to consider.

They had come to a halt in front of her old house and Ana felt another rush of memories, so strong that her senses were flooded with the sounds and smells of thirty years of family life. It was still standing, still with the same two steps up to the same dark green front door. The steps were chipped and the paint flaking but all that mattered was who might be inside. Ester guided her to the door but she felt herself start to shake all over and pulled back. On this side there was still hope; on the other there might only be sorrow.

'I can't do it,' she murmured.

'Then let me.'

'No, I...'

But Ester was rapping on the brass door-knocker that Bartek had so lovingly fitted when they'd first moved in as newly-weds, twenty-nine years ago. Ana heard the sound echo out on the other side and pictured the hallway, their coats just inside the door, her midwifery bag below them, always ready for the call. Nothing happened. They might not be here, she thought. Or they might be living here but out. They might be living somewhere else. They might not be living at all. The knock might bring no answers and then where would she go? What if...

Ana froze. There were footsteps. She could hear them coming down the tiled hallway, a little slow perhaps, a little uncertain, but footsteps. Ester hurried back to her side, taking her arm again, and as Ana glanced at her, Ruth's words seemed to echo down the railway line: *She's your daughter now.* She had that at least. Whatever had happened to her boys, she had Ester. Oh but, her heart did so ache for...

'Mama?'

Her world stopped. There was a man in the doorway. He was a thin, straggle-haired, surely middle-aged man, but the sweet sound of the word coming from his mouth made her look again and there in the sweet blue eyes, she saw him.

'Bron!'

Then he was bounding towards her and Ester was stepping back so he could sweep her into his arms. Ana felt him lift her like a child and spin her round, and he was saying it over and over again: 'Mama, Mama, Mama!'

When he finally set her down, she reached up and touched his dear face, but now there were two more men tumbling from the house and crowding around her and as she looked into their eyes, filled with joy and love, she was a young mother again, sweeping toddlers around her skirts.

'Zander, Jakub! You're here. You're alive.' The joy was

shooting around her weary body in such a rush that she felt as if it might burst her very veins. She hugged them all in turn. 'What happened to you? Where have you been?'

'Jakub and I were sent to a labour camp at Mauthausen-Gusen,' Zander told her. 'We've been lifting stones for the last two years – see how strong we are.'

He flexed an arm and Ana saw sinews stand out through paper-thin skin and knew he was not telling her everything but understood. There was time. Suddenly there was so much time.

'Bron?'

'I was in Warsaw with... with...'

His words drained from him and he looked to the ground and at that moment Ana knew. She looked into her eldest son's eyes, so very like his father's, and saw only sorrow within them. Her joy morphed into sick, dark sadness and she clutched at his hands.

'Papa didn't make it?'

'I'm so sorry, Mama. I tried to keep him safe. I promise you I tried. But he was so brave, so bold. He was a leader, Mama. He was in all the meetings, at the heart of all the plans for the rebellion. He led one of the initial charges and he was part of the group that seized the main post office as a base. He was jubilant, we all were. We thought we'd done it, Mama. We thought we'd won Warsaw. All we had to do was wait for the Soviet army to come in and back us up and we were there – freedom. You should have seen him, Mama. He was dancing on the tables that night, like he used to do at New Year when you would scold him and he would just laugh and pull you up to dance in his arms.'

Tears were flowing down Bronislaw's face and his brothers went to him, throwing arms tight around his shoulders.

'It wasn't your fault, Bron. There was nothing you could have done.'

Jakub turned to Ana. 'The Soviets never went in. They just

camped on the outskirts and let the rebels take the German army on alone, right, Bron?'

Bronislaw nodded darkly. 'Papa was there till nearly the end. He refused to let the Nazis take the Jerusalem Avenue, said he'd rather die than surrender again, but then the Germans started going from house to house, pulling civilians out and shooting them – men, women, children. They didn't care. Thousands they shot and our amateur army had to do something. Had to attack.'

'How did he die?' Ana managed.

'They shot him in the first charge. It was easy. He was out in front and they had machine guns. So many died that day. I should have died, I...'

'No, Bron! Don't say that. It would have been your father's greatest joy that you survived.'

'I got to him, Mama. I played dead and when the Germans were gone on to the next target, I crawled through the bodies and I got to him. He... he died in my arms.'

'Oh, Bron.'

She held out her own arms and he ducked his head into them, pressing against her so that she felt his poor body quaking with grief.

'He was calm, Mama. He said God was calling and he had to go to Him. He told me he loved me and he loved the others.' He glanced to his brothers, who smiled at him. 'Then he told me that, dearly as he loved us, he loved you above all things on this earth. He said you were the kindest, bravest, most beautiful woman he'd ever known and that being married to you had completed his life. He said just one day with you would have been enough and he'd been granted many wonderful years. He begged me to find you and take care of you and I had no idea how I was going to do that and yet... and yet here you are. I'm sorry I'm not him, Mama, I'm so sorry I'm not him, but I *will* take care of you. We all will.'

He threw his arms around her and she melted against him. Bartek, her dear Bartek was gone. He was with God, at rest, but somehow their boys were all here. Grief tumbled with the joy in her blood so that she had no idea which was ruling her, but she was here. She was free and she, like everyone, owed some part of that freedom to her brave husband and his peers and she must stand up and live a life that would honour their sacrifice.

'Come in, Mama,' Jakub was saying, tugging her to the door. She moved to follow him, but at the steps remembered.

'Ester.' The girl was standing back, smiling, though Ana saw the tears streaking her cheeks and feared that no joy now would ever be without its pain. 'Come in, Ester.' She held out her hand. The young woman looked at her blankly. 'Please,' she urged. 'Come in and be with us until you can find your own family.'

'Oh no, I...'

She was backing away but Ana could not have that. Ester had told her that she'd kept her going through the camp, but Ester had kept Ana going too and she was not going to abandon her. She tore away from her sons and went to take Ester's hands and pull her into the house.

'You have helped me, Ester, and I will help you. Boys,' she led Ester forward, 'meet your new sister, Ester Pasternak, the woman who brought me back to you.'

Still Ester hesitated, but her sons, without a moment's pause, held out their arms and said, 'Welcome.'

THIRTY-FOUR

APRIL 1945

ESTER

Ester turned the corner onto Śródmiejska Street and began to walk slowly up the long queue of people waiting to be registered with the Jewish relief committee. She scanned each face, as she had done every day for two weeks, praying she might recognise someone. There were few older men or women and she had little hope of seeing either her father or her father-in-law ever again, but she paused by any tall man, her breath catching in her throat every single time in case it was Filip. So far she had been disappointed, but still she checked.

Blond young women also drew her gaze. Only the day after her homecoming, Ana had sent Jakub out to the countryside to find her cousin Krystyna, who Leah had been hiding with, but both Krystyna and Leah were gone, the house shut up. The SS must have got to them and either shot them on the spot or taken them prisoner. For all Ester knew, her sister could have been shipped into Auschwitz and marched up the ramp to her death, barely metres from her, without her ever knowing.

Or she could have escaped.

It was beginning to dawn on Ester that she might spend the rest of her life not knowing what had happened to everyone she loved and that was almost the worst thought of all. So, every day she came down here to scan the queue and to wait in the court-yard with so many others, searching for connections in the crowd. She was lucky. Ana had insisted that she lived with her and her family so she'd not had to find a room, but she still felt rootless.

Spring had burst across Łódź; they had been there in time for the blossom just as Frank had promised. The open court of the relief committee offices was flooded with sun each morning, but it did little to light up the lives of those desperate to find their loved ones. Ester usually had to fight her way through to the long corridor leading to the repatriation department, which was lined with cork boards pinned with notes written on all manner of bits of paper:

Calling Moishe Lieberman – your wife Rachael and son Ishmael are safe and longing to see you. Find us at 18 Szklana.

My darling Abel. I pray that you will read this and can come and find me at 21 Przelotna. Your ever-loving, Ruthie.

Wanted, much-missed husband. I'm sorry we argued the night before the Germans came, my sweet Caleb Cohen. I have thought of you every day since. I am at the Grand Hotel and cannot wait to hold you in my arms again.

Occasionally one was snatched off the wall with a cry of joy and everyone else would turn jealously, but far too many of the hopeful notes were curling at the edges, unseen and unfol-lowed. Ester had placed her own on the board, written on a scrap of pink paper that Jakub had found in the old printing works:

Desperately seeking my beloved husband Filip Pasternak and precious sister Leah Abrams. Find me with Ana Kaminski at 99 Zgierska Street. I love you, Ester.

Even from the end of the corridor she could see it still there, curling like the rest. No eager hand had snatched it from the wall, no beloved husband or precious sister had seized upon her address and so the note hung on, as desperate as she was. She moved towards it all the same and that's when she noticed the man stepping up to it and reaching out to touch the corner. Her heart skipped and she pushed through the crowd to get to him.

There were too many bodies in the narrow corridor. She wasn't going to make it. He would go. She could see already that it wasn't Filip, for he was far shorter and stockier than her husband, but surely his interest meant something.

'Please – let me through!'

A kindly lady ahead parted the crowd and she squirmed through and put a hand out to touch his arm.

'Hello? Do you know Filip?' The man turned and looked at her and she gasped. He was so thin as to be barely recognisable but the mop of dark curls was instantly familiar. 'Noah? Noah Broder?'

He clasped at her hands and she felt the callouses of hard manual labour against her fingers.

'Mrs Pasternak! You survived – you're a miracle.'

She had to smile at that.

'Ester, please. And not, perhaps, a miracle, but definitely one of the lucky ones.'

He turned her hands over and over in his, as if struggling to believe they were real.

'My Martha didn't make it, my children either. Someone in

the Resistance got hold of a sheaf of records from Chelmno and their names are on the roll call of the dead, dashed off in a careless hand.'

His deep voice broke and he let go of Ester to scrub a hand across his eyes.

'I'm so sorry, Noah.'

He collected himself.

'Thank you. I used to wish I'd gone with them, died with them, but not now. Now I want to live and make something good in the world to show those bastard Nazis they didn't destroy us all, however hard they tried.'

'That's good, Noah. You're always welcome at our...' She stumbled on the word 'house'. There was no 'our house', not unless her husband came home. She swallowed a sudden lump in her throat and forced herself to ask, 'Do you know what happened to Filip?'

'I was with him,' he said, and she nearly fainted at his choice of tense, but seeing it he caught her under her elbow and guided her out into the courtyard. 'I was with him, Ester, in Chelmno. I escaped with him.'

'Escaped?!'

Sun burst, fire-bright across the courtyard, but he put up a warning hand.

'Let me be precise – I escaped at the same time as him. I'm sorry, I don't know where he is right now.'

It was a bitter disappointment, but the word 'escaped' still danced in her head and she sat eagerly down with Noah, begging him to tell her all he knew.

'It was back in April last year when a whole load of us were pulled off the streets of the ghetto. We were assigned to a new Sonderkommando and sent to Chelmno. Dear God, we were terrified. We thought we were being driven straight to our deaths. I could hear Filip praying all the way there, and it was only when I shuffled closer to him that I heard he was saying

"God bless Ester," over and over. "God bless Ester and keep her safe." Noah looked at Ester, a sudden smile breaking across his ravaged features. 'And God did. Filip will be so very glad.'

'You think he's alive?' she asked eagerly.

He pressed her hand.

'There's a chance, my dear. There is definitely a chance. We weren't sent to our deaths, you see, but to a run-down house in a normal village. Oh, the horrified looks on the faces of the locals! They must have thought they'd seen the last of the killing machine but here the Nazis were again, with us as their agents, being forced to build two huge huts in the woods which we knew would be to house our fellows on their way to their deaths. We wanted to stop it, truly we did, but what could we do? We were working at gunpoint.'

'I understand,' Ester assured him. 'It was the same in the camps.'

He looked at her gratefully and pressed on with his story.

'When the vans first started arriving it was terrible. We had to stand there and watch while the poor people were hustled into one of the huts to undress and then herded into the vans like cattle. Everyone knew what was happening to them. The stories were all over the ghetto by then and I swear their wails will haunt my nightmares until the day I die. But there was worse to come for us. We were forced to feed their poor corpses into two earth ovens and then to... to break up any remaining bones with flails on this big concrete slab. When night fell, we would have to dump their remains into the river Ner before we were allowed to sleep.'

'I'm so sorry,' Ester said. 'Poor you. Poor Filip.'

She thought her heart might break at the image of her gentle husband having to bash bones into powder, but Noah shook his head.

'Filip didn't have to do that. He was lucky. The Germans had put this large tent up on a farmyard in the village and set some prisoners to sorting the clothes for valuables. At first Filip was assigned to that but one day an SS officer brought his wife to see the tent and she took a fancy to a particular dress. It was a very fine one, I believe, but too small for her. She was bemoaning the "useless skinny Jew women" when Filip stepped forward and said that he could alter it.

'She didn't believe him – who alters clothing *up* a size? – but the officer found him a sewing machine and he did it. I don't know how. He tried to explain it that night – something about cutting up another dress to fill in the gaps on either side and adding matching trim at the hem and waist to hide the feature – but I wasn't clever enough to picture it. Either way, the woman was delighted and before you know it, Filip and a few other tailors were set up at one side of the tent altering the best clothing for the officers' families. They did not enjoy it, you understand, but...'

'We all have to find our own ways to survive.'

'Exactly. He was a talented tailor, your husband.'

'*Is* a talented tailor,' Ester corrected hotly, and Noah bit his lip and nodded.

'My apologies. I'm sure you are right.'

'I am, I know it. I would not be able to see the colours of the world if Filip were not still in it. Go on – what happened next?'

'Next...' He shuddered. 'Next came a month of killings. It was awful, Ester. They were all from Łódź and with every van that pulled up, members of our crew had to steel themselves to see their own families in there.' He put a hand over his eyes and Ester felt terrible for asking this story of him but he wiped them dry and pushed his head up, keen to bear witness. 'Finally, around the middle of July last year, the vans stopped. Just like that. One minute we were burning endless corpses and the next – nothing. No more vans. The SS told us we were useless and the brilliant Nazis had found a more efficient extermination method.'

'Auschwitz,' Ester said heavily, remembering poor Tomaz arriving there and dying right in front of her.

'So it seems, but we knew nothing then. We were terrified. We thought we'd be next to die but with the Russians advancing, the Germans were in a panic. They wanted the mass graves from the initial operations back in '42 dug up and burned. So that's what we did. It was gruesome work, but at least those poor skeletons had no discernible features.'

'And Filip?'

'Filip and his tailors sewed on. We all slept together, shut up in a brick storehouse behind the clothing tent, and the tailors would do what they could to make our lives more comfortable. They stole clothes for us and passed on treats that the German ladies gave them. Filip even tried to teach me to sew so that I could move into their easier work detail, but I've never been good with my fingers and I was too exhausted every evening to learn such a skill. I had to stick with the corpses.

'Even so, I thought I was lucky because I was still alive. We worked in two groups, one for each oven, and in autumn they took away the other group's oven and shot every single one of them at the edge of their own pit. The Germans were getting really twitchy by then and we had to burn in more and more of a hurry, but they still wanted that clothing, greedy bastards. We couldn't sort it fast enough, so somehow Filip got me a job in the tent, cutting coins and jewels out of hidden hems. It was just in time. The second oven was dismantled in the last days of 1944 and the tent in the new year. There were just forty of us left, tidying it all up, but then, on the night of January seventeenth, the remaining guards wanted out – and they didn't want to leave us behind.'

Ester stared at him, processing the date. She hadn't known it at the time, for dates had all merged together in Birkenau, but she'd found out since that January seventeenth had been the night the Germans had instigated the death marches out of the camp. While she had been fighting to keep Naomi and Isaac in the barrack, Filip had been fighting for his very life out in the woods of Chelmno.

'Tell me,' she urged Noah and, rubbing his forehead as if the memories physically itched, he did so.

'We were in the storage building for the night and the guards came banging on the door, telling us to file out in groups of five. Well, we knew exactly what they intended and we leaped to our own defence. About half of our group were sleeping on the ground floor, but Filip and I were on the first floor, thank the good Lord. They manhandled the poor lads down below out and shot them. We heard it – bang, bang, bang, bang, bang. And then again – bang, bang, bang, bang, bang. So cold, so efficient.'

'We knew we'd be next but they could only get to us through a trap door so we put everything we had over it to keep them out. They sent the local police chief in, but we overpowered him and grabbed his gun. Truly, Ester, I have never been so scared in my life – or so exhilarated. After months of soul-destroying routine, I was delighted to be actually doing something to stand up to them. They were furious and kept trying to shoot at the building, but we steered clear of the windows and the walls were made of good Polish brick and withstood all their assaults. I thought we were going to get away with it. I thought they were going to get fed up and go, but then came the tracers.'

'Tracers?'

'Fire bullets. Straight through the windows and into the straw we slept on. The place caught immediately – the flames took the beams and the floorboards, the room filled with smoke, and we were trapped. You could hear the bloody SS cackling outside – excuse my language. I swear I was ready to fall to my knees and die, but Filip wasn't having it. The Germans were on the front side, you see, waiting for us to come out the doors or burn before their eyes, but there was a window at the back. It was high up but looked onto a field and a wood beyond. All we had to do was jump...'

Ester held her breath, picturing the storehouse and willing the men on.

'So...?'

'So we jumped. Filip and I and maybe six or seven others. We jumped and we ran. It had been snowing and that cushioned our landing, though it also made it hard to run and brought far too much light. The flames danced off the white as we made for the trees, but we were almost there before they spotted us. They started shooting and from there on in it was every man for himself. I ran, dodging between the trees, pushing through the undergrowth. I was scratched to hell but I found an old badger sett. Thanks to the Nazis starving me for years, I fitted right into it, and there I stayed. For two days. I only crept out at night to suck down some snow, until I was sure that they'd gone. Finally I felt safe enough to get out, follow the woods down to the river and walk along it until I got to Grudziądz.'

'And the others?'

He gave her a sad smile.

'I don't know. I'm so sorry, Ester, but I just don't know. I pray they got away too but I haven't seen any of them since. I look every day, searching for new notes, but yours is the only one I've found.' He grabbed her hands. 'I'm sorry I can't tell you more but this much I can tell you – Filip loved you so much. If he's alive and well enough, he will come and find you. You must just pray and have faith.'

'Thank you, Noah. Thank you so much. Are you living in Łódź?'

'For now, yes. I was an actor before the war, believe it or not, and they've asked me to join a committee setting up a Jewish theatre.'

'Something good in the world?' she suggested.

'Exactly. There's so much art in the city at the moment. Warsaw is in ruins, which is a great sadness, but it means many people are coming to Łódź. We have a chance to make new creation out of the dust of destruction and I'm excited to be a part of that. It's not the same as family, but it's an act of creation all the same and we must find healing where we can.'

She smiled at him.

'We must, Noah. And I'm sure, with you involved, it will be wonderful. I will look forward to attending your first performance.'

'With Filip?'

'With Filip,' she agreed firmly, though doubt was creeping in once more.

What sort of arrogance was it to believe that she had the power to tell if her husband was still in the world when so many others were reeling in disbelief that theirs were not? Noah was the last person to have seen Filip, the last bar the German who may have shot him – or the kind people who may have sheltered him. She had to keep faith.

Taking Noah's address and saying goodbye to him, she turned her steps, as always, towards St Stanislaus' cathedral. If Filip were alive, he would come here in time for the midday chimes, just as he always had when they were young and shy and wasting time at opposite sides of the steps.

'Oh Filip, I miss you,' she said to the stone as she took up her place exactly where she'd always sat in her half-hour lunch-break from the hospital. She knew she had to start work again. People were sick. They needed her and she owed them her care, but not just yet. Not until she'd found Filip. Surely he'd come?

She looked across at his old place, trying to conjure the shape of him on the spring air, but it had been two full years since she'd been ripped out of Łódź and, to her shame, she could not see every precious detail of her husband any more. The glow of his love, though, that was still strong, and she stared into it, pouring every gram into the universe in the hope that it might deliver him back.

It had to. What if she spent the rest of her life sitting on blank steps every midday, waiting like a madwoman for a person who was never going to come? She shook herself. She'd rather do that than run the risk of missing out on even the slightest chance of finding Filip again, for that would be madness indeed.

'Ester? Oh God – Ester!'

She leaped up, spinning around madly to see who was calling her name.

'Filip?' The crowd on Piotrkowska Street seemed to part and someone stepped forward, wearing a big coat, a huge smile, and a jaunty ribbon in her blond hair. 'Leah!'

Pain spiked momentarily through Ester and then she was running down the steps and clutching at her sister. It might not be Filip but she had thought Leah dead too, so to have her here, in her arms, was a blessed release. And if one loved one had survived this hell, why not another? She held her sister close against her.

'We went to Krystyna's cottage,' she gasped out into Leah's blessedly well-rounded chest. 'There was no one there. I thought they'd taken you. I thought they'd, they'd...'

'Gassed me? No way. I think they did come but we'd moved house by then and I'd, erm, got a new identity.'

'Another new identity?'

Leah giggled.

'Yep. It's a bit of a story but there's time for that later. You're what matters now. I've been coming into Łódź as often as I can, Ester, hoping to find you here.'

Ester frowned at her.

'Why didn't you just come to Ana's house?'

Leah pulled a funny face, so achingly familiar to Ester that she wanted to burst into tears at the sight of it. Her sister was a woman now, that much was clear, but for just a moment she had looked three years old again.

'Krystyna couldn't remember the address! Imagine. She says she never used to come to Łódź because she hates cities. I had the address of their apartment on Bednarska but other people are there now, so all I could do was head to the Relief Committee looking for notes. And today...'

'Today you saw mine.'

'Saw it and copied it down. I didn't want to take it in case Filip...' She swallowed. 'You haven't found Filip yet?'

Ester shook her head and her little sister hugged her tight.

'Don't fret. There's plenty of time. People are scattered all over Poland and beyond. Some have joined the armies, some might be in hospitals, some are just in hiding or finding their way back. He'll be here, I know it.'

'I pray so,' Ester agreed, swallowing at the lump in her throat. 'Do you know anything of Father?' she asked. 'Or Benjamin?'

Leah looked down.

'They died, Ester.' Ester bowed her head, accepting the inevitability of this even as the pain bit, but Leah's next words made her head snap up in amazed horror. 'They were hung.'

'Hung? Both of them? For what?'

Leah wiped a tear from her eye.

'For killing a German officer. They waited for him outside the offices on Baluty Market and attacked him with broken bottles. They were wrenched off, of course, but not before they'd inflicted a fatal wound to his temple. They were hung that afternoon. One of the men who was left behind to clear up the ghetto told me that everyone gathered to watch, that their names were whispered around the crowd as heroes for daring to strike back. He said they clasped hands and held them high as the nooses tightened and that everyone cheered them into heaven.'

Ester's legs trembled and she sank to the steps, trying to take it in.

'But why?' she asked.

Leah crouched next to her.

'The officer's name was Hans Greisman.'

'Hans?' Ester stared at her sister. 'You mean...?'

Leah nodded.

'Father wasn't shipped off like cattle, or shot like an animal but went out in glory, wreaking revenge on the man who tried to rape me.'

'And Filip's father with him. An act of final defiance?'

'Exactly.' Ester heard Leah swallow and looked at her more intently.

'There's more?'

'Only that he wrote to me. He must have done it the night before he died and got someone to smuggle it out to me. It was short, Ester – you know he was never one for speechifying – but so beautiful. He said how proud he was of us both, how he prayed for us daily and begged God to keep us both alive for a happier future. He said that you and I, we carry him and Mother in our hearts and in our blood and that he hoped, one day, that we would have children to keep our family marching onwards.'

The tears were flowing from Ester's eyes now and she did not bother to hide them. Pippa had not just been taken from her but from Filip and from her grandparents, all four of them gone to God. She *had* to find her.

'Leah...' she started, but her sister had put up a hand to push Ester's hair off her face and the sun glinted on something golden around her finger. Ester grabbed it and stared in amazement at the plain gold band. 'You're married?'

Her sister flushed.

'I am.'

'That's your new identity!'

She nodded.

'Adam's a farmer up near Krystyna's cottage. He's Jewish but he's a mischling and his Prussian mother got him papers way before the war so he was safe. And when I married him – so was I.'

'Leah, that's amazing. When do I get to meet him?'

Leah looked suddenly shy.

'How about now?'

'Now?!'

Turning, her sister waved across the street and a ruddy-faced young man came bounding over.

'This is Adam Wójcik, my husband.'

She giggled again and Ester thanked God that someone, at least, seemed unchanged by the ravages of war.

'Pleased to meet you, Adam,' she stuttered, fighting to take this in.

'And you, Ester.' He shook her hand and put an easy arm around Leah. 'I'm so glad that you're back safe. Leah talks about you all the time. She adores you.'

'I do not!' Leah laughed, batting at him.

Ester smiled, letting the wonderful normality of the teasing wash over her. But it was at that moment that her sister's coat fell open and Ester caught sight of her belly – rounded and pushing ripely at the fabric of her dress.

'You're pregnant!'

Leah put her hands around her belly and leaned in to Adam.

'I am. Papa would be pleased, yes?'

'Very. When is it due?'

'I'm nearly eight months gone. Thank heavens Ana is back, hey? Is she still a midwife?' Ester nodded, unable to speak. Thoughts of Pippa washed over her again and she staggered and sat heavily down on the step. 'I hope she's not too rusty,' Leah was babbling on. 'There wasn't much call for midwifery in the camp, I imagine?'

Ester dropped her head in her hands.

'You have no idea,' she told her sister.

The enormity of all she had been through – and all she had lost – swept suddenly across her and she passed out across the steps of St Stanislaus' cathedral.

THIRTY-FIVE

JUNE 1945

ANA

'You and baby rest now.'

Ana smiled down at the mother, nestled into a warm bed with her baby nursing contentedly, and thought she might never tire of saying those words. She had always thought the miracle of birth a blessing, but never before had she realised that it was just as much of a miracle to have warmth and care and peace to look after Baby once it was born. This one had been a suspected breach, so Mother had been brought into the hospital for added security. In the event Baby had obligingly turned at the last minute and the birth had gone well, with no need for surgical intervention, but the very fact that it was a possibility filled Ana's heart with gratitude.

The three thousand babies she had ushered into the filth and hatred of Birkenau would haunt her forever more. There were the poor Jewish ones who'd been drowned in Klara's bucket or left to simply fade away in their devastated mothers' arms. There were those who'd been graciously permitted to be fed but whose mothers had been too malnourished to produce milk so had died anyway. Then there were the ones who'd been taken away...

Ana smiled down at the mother and went to tell the pacing father outside the happy news. His eyes lit up and he rushed to his wife's side, kissing her tenderly and touching wondering fingertips to the top of his son's head. This was how it should be – Mary with the baby in the manger and Joseph watching over her. This is what Ana had been blessed with three times and, although she still missed Bartek with every fibre of her being, having her sons with her was a precious consolation. Poor Ester, though, had no baby and no husband and it was tearing at Ana to see her friend wasting away. She could do nothing about Filip, save trust that if he was alive he would find a way back to his wife's side. Pippa, however...

Her stomach flipped as she came out of the maternity ward and saw the middle-aged man standing there in the khaki uniform of the Polish army, cap held respectfully in his hands and kindly eyes watching her.

'Rabbi.' She hurried forward, clasping his hands. 'I'm glad to see you safely back from your travels.'

Isaiah Drucker was a rabbi chaplain in the Polish army who had devoted himself to the near-impossible task of tracking down Jewish orphans who'd seen out the war in hiding and bringing them back into the community and the faith. An earnest doctor in the hospital had heard Ana asking about tracing lost children and suggested that he would be a good contact for someone seeking 'Germanised' Birkenau babies.

Ana had been introduced to him on the day, two weeks ago, that Victory in Europe had been announced. They'd met in a vibrant café in the middle of Łódź, with the streets full of people partying at the announcement of the final German surrender. It had made them both glad, but theirs had been serious business. The war might be over but its after-effects would ripple on for a long, long time, including the fate of the poor children taken from their biological parents and scattered around Europe. Children like Pippa.

'Do you have news?' Ana asked, running forward eagerly.

Rabbi Drucker put up a warning hand.

'Not perhaps the specific news you are seeking, Mrs Kaminski, but I have found three infants with the markings you describe.'

'Numbers in their armpits?'

'Exactly that.'

'What numbers are they?'

'They are 57892, 51294 and 47400.'

'47400,' Ana repeated – excruciatingly similar to Ester's number. 'You are sure it is a seven?'

'I have a photograph.'

He produced the sepia square and handed it to Ana. She moved to place it under direct light. Her eyes had been fading before Birkenau, and camp nutrition had only made them worse, but even her tired retinas could see the cross-line marking out the seven, carved into the tender skin with the same neat precision with which Ester had done all her tattooing, even on her own baby.

'The Polish authorities have the records,' Drucker went on, 'so we can find the name of the mother but then...' He gave a helpless shrug. 'I have had the children delivered to the orphanage here in Łódź and when the records come through we can attempt to find the mother.'

'And if we do not?'

He gave her a sad smile.

'If the records show the mothers to have been Jewish, I can take them to my new children's home out at Zabrze where they will be brought up in the faith.'

'But without a mother?'

He bowed his head.

'I can spread the word in the synagogues and put notices up in the Relief Committee corridors and hope that some relative comes forward, but other than that...'

He spread his hands and Ana nodded. She would visit the orphanage later, see those babies she had brought into Block 24 and who had, somehow, made it out. If she closed her eyes, she could picture the rough brick stove on which those mothers had laboured, she could see the look of total peace in the eyes of every woman who had held her baby, and the torment for those who'd had them ripped from their arms by Wolf and Meyer. Every one of those tattooed children had a bit of herself in them and she was determined to find the mothers' names from the rabbi and put out the word through every channel she could. She knew people in the Red Cross and the American UNRRA and her own boys were keen to help.

Bronislaw and Zander were working in hospitals now and in contact with Polish networks working to restore national pride. As for Jakub, he was training up in his father's printing firm but spending much of his time in political meetings. They worried, she knew, about the future of the country under Russian rule and they were right to do so, but her own, tired brain could only focus on one thing – getting babies back with their mothers. She was weary of politics, weary of being subject to the waves of the wider world, but this one thing she understood. If they could reunite even one mother with her baby, she would feel that she had somehow started to repair a tiny bit of the damage done by Birkenau and all the other barbaric camps. She just wished that one mother could be Ester.

Ana glanced at her watch – nearly midday.

'Here, Rabbi.' She took his arm and drew him down the corridor to a big window. Sunlight was streaming in, and down on Piotrkowska Street people were in bright summer clothing, sitting in pavement cafés, carrying bursting shopping bags home or stopping to chat to friends. But across from the hospital, on the steps of St Stanislaus' cathedral, sat Ester. She was all alone and very still, her eyes following the movement of the crowd with heartbreaking hope. She had a bajgiel in her lap but, although her fingers were crumbling it to bits, none of it ever made it to her mouth. Ana pointed her out to the chaplain.

'She's there every single day, waiting for her husband to come and find her. That's where they met. And where he proposed.'

'Will he come, do you think?'

Ana sighed.

'God willing. He was at Chelmno and made a break for it from a burning barn towards the end of the war, but that's all we know. We took Ester out to search the woods in case his body was still there, but we found nothing.'

Ana looked down on the young woman, remembering that dark trip. They'd seen the footprint of the wooden barracks, the site of the huge clay ovens that had been used to burn so many of the people of Łódź, and the burnt remains of the brick store-house from which Filip must have escaped. They'd combed the woods all day and Jakub had even borrowed a friend's dog, but none of them had turned up anything more than bluebells and rabbits.

'He's not here,' Ana had told Ester as gently as she could when dusk had started falling and she'd had to pull the girl from her search.

'I suppose that's good news,' Ester had said, but it hadn't sounded like she'd meant it.

Ana worried that she was starting to believe Filip was dead, and who could blame her? Chelmno was not so far from Łódź. Certainly it was closer than Auschwitz, so if they'd managed the journey back three months ago why had he not?

'He could be being nursed somewhere,' Ana always told

Ester when she raised this same point, but that idea was starting to wear thin. The war was over. Hospitals were open and welcoming refugees. Surely if Filip still needed nursing, someone would have got him to one and then his name would be recorded in the system. If, of course, he remembered it.

Ana pressed her forehead to the glass. They went round and round the possibilities all the time but whatever they could conjecture might have happened to poor Filip, one thing they knew – he wasn't here with Ester. And it was tearing her apart piece by tiny piece.

'I have word out with all the hospitals to let us know if a Filip Pasternak turns up but there's little else I can do,' she told the rabbi. 'If I could find her daughter though...'

Rabbi Drucker watched Ester sadly and nodded.

'I will do all I can, I promise.'

'You're a good man.'

He turned to her.

'I'm not sure about that, Mrs Kaminski, I just fear that in the last few years the bar for goodness has been set very low.'

Ana grabbed his hand.

'That's not true. The Nazis may have seemed to smother us with a blanket of hatred but as it is lifted, we are finding more and more examples of courage and kindness. These children you are tracking down have been sheltered and kept safe. So many Jewish people have survived thanks to brave citizens hiding them and it is that ability to care for our fellows that will see us forward.'

He smiled at her.

'I like the world you bring your babies into, Ana Kaminski.'

She smiled back but then her eyes were drawn again to Ester, still sitting rigidly on the cathedral steps.

'I just wish I could bring *hers* back into it, Rabbi.'

'Number 41400?'

'That's right.'

He pressed her hand.

'I'll keep looking.'

And then he was gone and Ana was left to watch as the clock struck half past the hour and Ester forced herself to stand and trudge away from her steps, head down and the crumbs of her bajgiel scattering around her for the eager birds.

THIRTY-SIX

1 SEPTEMBER 1945

ESTER

Ester sat on the cathedral steps staring at the birds pecking eagerly at the crumbs of her pasztecik. Ana had made the crumbly pastries fresh this morning to tempt her failing appetite and Ester tried to eat, really she did, but her stomach seemed shrunk these days, either by the privations of Birkenau or by the gnawing emptiness of life since she'd escaped its wires. She was lucky, she knew, to have a safe and caring place to live with Ana and her sons, and she loved her friend dearly for it, but it was not home.

They were all getting on with their lives and that was right. Bronislaw was moving to Warsaw to head up a department in the hospital there, Zander had passed his final medical exams, and Jakub was doing well at the printers and courting a lovely young woman. Even Ana was moving forward, working hard and bringing ever more babies into the world. Ester had felt privileged to be with them for the small memorial ceremony they'd held for Bartek in their local church, restored after its time as a mattress factory, and had sent up her own prayers for Sarah, who had been forced to work there in the ghetto years, and for Ruth. With the synagogues starting to run again she and Leah were planning their own memorial to honour Mordecai and Benjamin, who had died so bravely, but she was determined to wait until Filip could be there for it.

The clock struck midday and she looked up at it and into the blue sky beyond. It was 1 September, exactly six years from the day when Germany had marched into Poland, driving the cruel tanks and machine guns of the voracious Third Reich across all their lives. It was also exactly six years since Filip had dropped to one knee before her and asked her to be his wife and the 'yes' had exploded from her in a glorious burst of joy that was almost impossible to even remember now. Every day that passed without news of him eroded the edges of their too-brief marriage until she sometimes began to wonder if it had ever happened at all.

She touched her hand to her stomach. There were lines there, etched into her camp-ravaged skin, that spoke of the baby she'd borne him, the baby she had held in her arms for three beautiful days before she'd been snatched away to be 'Germanised'. Ester didn't want to hate, really she didn't, but Lord forgive her, it was hard not to.

She forced her mind away from Nazi darkness and on to sweeter things. She had had a letter from Naomi, sent via the Jewish relief committee. Somehow the girl had talked her way onto three different trains south and was home in Salonika and reunited with her father and sisters, all miraculously alive. They had been overjoyed to meet baby Isaac, she'd written, and were naming the restaurant they were opening in his honour. Ester must come and stay with them, as they'd discussed in Birkenau.

'You will have to come and visit when this is all over,' Ester remembered her dear friend saying to her the very first day they had met in the filth of Birkenau. She had stared at her then, amazed at her simple optimism.

'You think it will be?' she'd asked.

'One way or another it has to be, and what's the point in thinking the worst?'

Well, Naomi had been right and now it *was* over and Naomi *was* home and she *was* asking Ester to visit. But there was no way she was going to Greece without her husband. She let her eyes follow a white cloud as it drifted innocuously above the clock tower. It had been the same sort of weather on this day in 1939, but barely had she and Filip shared their first kiss than the planes had cut, dark and menacing, across the bright blue sky.

'Quick,' Filip had said, taking her hand and pulling her up the steps and into the cathedral, and Ester had had no idea whether it had been the happiest day of her life or the worst. It was a question she'd asked herself again and again over the dark years since, and one that she feared would haunt her forever more. Was it better to have known such beautiful happiness if its subsequent absence brought such pain? At least in the camp her emotions had been dulled along with all her other bodily functions, but here, in Łódź, where they had first been together, it seemed to stab at her constantly.

Ester reached into her pocket and pulled out her copy of the letter she'd found in Ana's bedroom last week. She hadn't been snooping, hadn't even known there was anything to go snooping for. She had just been looking for a dark ribbon to tie back her hair for work and there it had been, sat on the dressing table, wedged beneath Ana's hairbrush. Even then, she would not have touched it save for the stamp on the envelope: 'Society for the Recovery of Jewish orphans.' At those words, though, she had been unable to resist and, checking guiltily for any movement in the rest of the house she had edged it open.

The letter had been from a Rabbi Isaiah Drucker, reporting

back on a trip around Germany looking for Jewish children. Ana, it would seem, had asked this man to look out for infants with numbers tattooed in the armpits and he had found some. Five, to be exact, and this apparently on top of three from a previous trip – but none of them with 41400 written into their delicate skin. He had enclosed photographs, small and murky but still clear enough to see a run of tiny armpits with her own, careful tattooing tucked into the fold.

She had stared and stared at them, trying to picture which mothers had held their children while she'd carved such a hideous branding into their fresh new skin – all for this, all for the moment when they might surface again after the war and be found. And some *were* doing. Some truly were. The letter made it clear that Ana had written to this hardworking rabbi to tell him that one baby – 51294 – had been returned to her mother in Belorussia. Ester had been battling ever since to feel happy for her. Sometimes though, the only true emotion was screaming, raging jealousy.

'I'm sorry,' she whispered to the skies.

Another cloud drifted benignly past and she tried to see God's great goodness in it. The Nazis were gone. She'd heard that both Irma Grese and Maria Mandel had been captured and would stand trial for their crimes, along with so many others, and would almost certainly hang. It was kinder than they deserved, but what mattered now was that peace was here and families were being reunited. There was much to be grateful for, but, oh, how she longed to feel Filip's arms around her again, how she longed to tell him they had a daughter, how she longed to have him at her side to try and find Pippa. Without him, it all felt so pointless.

She forced her eyes down from the skies and across the road to the hospital. It was *not* pointless. There was her work and her patients and her fellow staff. There was Ana and her new 'brothers' and there was Leah. Her sister's baby boy had been born just two days after the German surrender, as if it had known it was now safe to come out. Leah had been back out on Adam's farm and sent word for Ana but by the time she and Ester had made it there in Jakub's cart, the baby had already been born and Leah had been tucked up in bed with Adam fussing proudly around her.

'Look!' he'd said excitedly. 'Look what she's made.'

It had been so sweet that Ester had burst into tears and Leah had held her and said she'd be a wonderful auntie and she'd not wanted to spoil the moment by talking about her own lost baby, so she'd just nodded and let it go. She felt bad about that now. Losing Pippa was not a shameful secret but a tragedy. It was not something she had done, but something that had been imposed upon her in the cruellest possible way. And yet... How could anyone who had not been there possibly understand? And why sully Leah's happiness with her own sorrow?

She could still picture the dread night when she and Ruth had stood in the shadows watching the cart ride up to the ghetto gates with Leah stashed beneath the sacks of Wehrmacht uniforms. She could still see the soldier produce his bayonet and still hear her mother's cries as she'd faked a fit to draw attention away. The bruises the SS had imprinted upon Ruth that night had weakened her so much that she'd stood little chance of surviving, but she had made that sacrifice to get Leah free, to keep her safe and innocent, and she had succeeded. Leah's continued naivety about the true ravages of the war was to be celebrated, not resented. But it sometimes felt as if there was only so much Ester's slim shoulders could bear.

A single dong above her rang out the half hour. Her break was over and she should get back to work. The stone of the steps was cold against her legs, just as it had been the day Filip had bounded down the street and proposed. There were no planes in the sky this September, but no husband at her side either. She scattered the last of the crumbs onto the stone and watched the pigeons land and peck, cooing gratefully, around her feet. How many more times could she keep doing this? How many more days could she sit here in the fading imprint of her former life? Perhaps it was time to call a halt to her foolish optimism? But if she did that, what would there truly be to live for? What—

'Ester?' She blinked, stared at the pigeons as if they might have spoken. 'Ester, is that truly you?'

Someone else's feet stepped into the line of her vision and the pigeons gave an indignant squawk and flew away. Still she did not dare look up. Too many times her hopes had been dashed and she couldn't take another disappointment. But then a hand reached out and oh so gently cupped her chin, lifting it so that she was staring into the dearest, warmest, most loving eyes in the world.

'Filip,' she breathed, then louder, 'Filip!'

She clutched at him, clawing at his clothes to pull him closer, to be sure that he was real, that he was here before her.

'Ester,' he said again and then he was bending and his lips were on hers and the world exploded into the brightest, most joyous colours.

'You're here,' she gasped, against his lips. 'You're alive. You're here.'

Tears were streaming down her face, mingling with his own. His arms were around her, his hands stroking her back, his lips kissing her face over and over and suddenly all the hurt was gone. The darkness of Birkenau was shoved into the shadows of the past and the light of love dazzled so that she would have staggered beneath it had he not been here, holding her up.

'Where have you been?' she stuttered when they finally pulled apart and she could look up into his dear face.

'Everywhere. I escaped from Chelmno. Oh Lord, Ester, it was awful.'

'I know,' she said, tenderly running her fingers down the war-sharp line of his jaw. 'Noah told me.'

'Noah? He made it too? He's here?'

'Right here in Łódź. He told me about breaking out of the storehouse, but he didn't know if you'd survived the German shootings.'

'Barely. One caught my leg but I wasn't going to stop running. I made it through to the other side and down to the river and I hid in the bushes by the water, worked my way downstream into some woods.'

'And then?'

He sighed and sat down onto the steps, pulling her in tight against him.

'I was weak, Ester, so weak. I might have died save that some Resistance fighters found me. They bound my wound and fed me. They kept me safe until I was well enough to walk again and then a recruiting officer came from the Polish army and asked us to join them in the final push against Germany. So we did. We fought all the way to Berlin – right onto the streets. It was glorious, Ester, but in the final battle for the Reichstag I was shot.'

'Again?'

'Sorry.'

He gave her a wry smile and she clasped his face in both her hands, laughing.

'Don't apologise, my darling, darling man. My husband. My Filip.'

He pulled her close, kissing her until she was almost too giddy with the touch of him to care what had got him here, but finally he drew away.

'I was in a Red Cross hospital for a while, unconscious. Even once I came round, it was a bit of a battle to get them to let me out to come and find you.' Nervously he pushed his hair back and she gasped. The top half of his ear was missing and a jagged scar ran back from it into his scalp. 'It's not as bad as it looks.'

'Thank God, because it looks awful!'

'I know. Can you still love me, Ester?'

She hit out at him.

'Loving you is the only thing that's kept me going all these horrible years. Well that and—' She cut herself off. 'One scar isn't going to stop me.'

She reached up and traced the line of it, marvelling. One millimetre deeper in and she knew she would have lost him. By such tiny margins had survival been decided in this bitter war but theirs, it seemed, had fallen on the right side of the line. Somehow, they had both made it through and the future was theirs once more.

'And you?' he asked with utmost tenderness, 'What happened to you?'

'I was at Auschwitz-Birkenau.'

His eyes filled with sorrow.

'All this time? You survived?'

She smiled.

'I survived. And so did Ana and so, perhaps, did...' She stopped herself. 'Filip, I have something to tell you.'

He looked deep into her eyes and she had to blink again to believe he was truly here.

'What is it, my darling?'

She swallowed.

'We have a daughter.'

'A daughter? Oh Ester – truly?' He looked around. 'Where?'

Ester let the tears flow once more, leaning in against Filip, daring at last to let her true sorrow envelope her.

'I don't know, Filip. I'm so, so sorry but I don't know. She was taken from me when she was just four days old.'

Filip's eyes filled with sorrow and he tried to draw her in against him again but this time she resisted.

'There is a way of finding her, Filip. Ana has been looking but I have not felt strong enough to properly help – until now.'

This time she did not resist when Filip pulled her close.

'We are together now, Ester. We have found each other and next we will find our daughter.'

EPILOGUE

APRIL 1946

There are cots everywhere. They fill the echoey, wooden-floored hall and from each one a small child peers, all eyes. There's not hope, the tiny infants aren't old enough for that, but there's a sort of longing that reaches deep into me and tugs, not on my heartstrings but deeper than that – right into my womb. It's been a long time since there was a child inside me but perhaps the feeling never quite goes. Perhaps every child I birthed has left a part behind, a nub of the umbilical cord that will always make it easy for a pair of wide baby eyes to melt my heart. And perhaps every child I've ever helped ease onto this earth in my twenty-seven years as a midwife has affected me in the same way too.

I take a few steps into the room. The cots are rough and old but they are clean and carefully made. In one of them a baby wails and I hear a woman's voice lift in a lullaby, soft and soothing. The wails hiccup to a stop and only the music remains. Like everything else in this big room, it isn't shiny or smart but it rings with love. I smile and pray this is the place we've been looking for.

'Are you ready?'

I turn to Ester, who hovers in the doorway, her fingers gripping tight at the whitewashed wood of the door frame, her eyes as big as any of the orphans within.

'I'm not sure,' Ester replies.

I reach out for her hand.

'It was a foolish question. You'll never be ready, but you're here and that's enough.'

'What if it's not...?'

'Then we'll keep looking. Come on.'

I tug her forward as a kindly matron clips her way between the cots, all smiles.

'You made it. I'm so glad. I hope your journey wasn't too hard?'

I can't stop the bitter laugh. The journey this morning was simple, but the years preceding it have been a tangle of hurt and pain. We have been on the sort of dark, dirty road that no one should have to tread to get to this run-down place of dwindling hope. It has weakened us both and I'm not sure – whatever I've just said – how much further either of us can travel down it.

The matron seems to understand. She puts a hand on my arm and gives a nod.

'The bad years are gone now.'

'I hope you are right.'

'We have all lost too much.'

I look to Ester, who has crept forward, drawn by the cot nearest the window. In it sits a girl, blond hair wisping around a serious little face in the sunlight shining in on her. As she sees Ester approach, she pulls herself up to standing, her legs wobbly but determined. Ester's own legs seem to crumple, as if in sympathy, then she crosses the last metres at speed and puts out a hand to the bar. The girl reaches through and my heart cracks at the sight – there have been too many bars, too many fences, too much segregation and division.

'Is this her?' I gasp out.

'She has something like the tattoo you described.' The matron shrugs awkwardly.

Something like... It's not enough. My heart sinks and suddenly it's me who's not ready, suddenly I want the dark, dirty road to wind on, for at least while we are travelling, we can travel in hope.

'Stop!' I want to cry but the word sticks in my throat because now Ester is reaching into the cot and lifting the child into her arms and the longing on her face is bigger than all these poor orphans put together. It is time to learn the truth. Time to see if the journey was worth it.

'Let me help you.'

I dart forward and together Ester and I take the toddler and lie her, very gently, on the changing table in the middle of the room. There is a wooden mobile above it and the girl smiles and reaches out tiny fingers towards the animal shapes. I see a flash of black ink in her armpit and swallow. We've been looking for so long, me, Rabbi Drucker, Ester and Filip. There have been many false leads and empty hopes, but this girl has given us all belief.

'Shall I...?'

Ester bites her lip. She glances across the room to where Filip is hovering in the doorway, fidgeting his hat round and round in his shaking hands, then she turns back to me and nods. Slowly I take the two-year-old's arm and place it gently above her head. She squirms, but the animals hold her attention and we are able to push up her top and reveal the number.

Ester gasps. My own old eyes are struggling but as a shaft of sun falls in on the child, I see it clearly: 58031.

Ester looked at me, eyes shining.

'It's her,' she says, 'it's Oliwia.'

I cross myself. It was a month ago that a lovely American woman from the UNRRA contacted Rabbi Drucker to say they'd found a blond girl, probably around two years old, with a tattoo in her armpit. The message lit hope in Ester's eyes, but when the number was sent through, we knew instantly that it wasn't Pippa. Even so, 58031 spoke to us both immediately – Oliwia, the first baby Ester ever tattooed. I remember her hand shaking as she applied the needle to the beautiful new skin. I remember the way she bit her lip and steeled herself to carve poor young Zofia's number into the tiny armpit with such determined precision. This is where it started, this is where the quest to reunite babies with those who love them began. It is not over yet, it is far from over, but it is properly begun.

Tears fill my eyes as Ester sweeps the child into her arms.

'Oliwia!' she cries, burying her face in the girl's hair.

She looks to me and for a moment we are both suspended, caught back in Block 24, between the packed bunks and the voracious rats and the disease-ridden lice. For a moment we are crouching over a newborn baby, a prostitute's needle in our hands, on a desperate mission to link mother and baby – a desperate mission that worked.

Zofia is dead and, as I look at Oliwia, I want to weep anew for all that they both missed out on, but this girl will have a mother. The day that number came through, I saw the wobble of Ester's lip as she remembered the baby, snatched from her mother's arms by Wolf and Meyer, just as Pippa was snatched from her own. I saw the tears sparkling in her eyes as she spoke to me of Zofia, robbed of first a husband and now a child, wasting away from grief in her arms. And I saw the determined set of her chin when she said, 'We have to go to her, Oliwia has no parents.'

Or rather, she had none until today. The adoption papers are ready.

'I am taking you home, Oliwia,' Ester tells her in Polish.

The girl struggles to understand the words.

Ester gives me a small but meaningful nod, then she is

running to the door where Filip still hovers, watching nervously.

'Filip,' she says, her voice clear and bright, 'it's time to meet Oliwia, our new daughter.'

She holds Oliwia out and for a moment the two adults stare at each other over the head of the innocent girl. I see tension shimmer. I see the tangible hurt that this is not Pippa – not yet. They will keep looking, we all will, but for now Oliwia needs parents and these parents need her. Hurts can be healed in many ways and this adoption of the very first baby Ester worked to save is the start of it. The tension breaks as Filip reaches out and strokes the little girl's blond curls.

'Hello, Oliwia,' he says. 'I'm going to be your papa.'

'Papa?' the girl echoes wonderingly, and her new parents laugh out loud and clutch each other close, sandwiching her between them.

I sink back against the changing table, my old legs suddenly weak with relief, and send up my own thanks to the Lord above. That beautiful child was born in Birkenau, the darkest place on God's earth, and ripped from her mother's skeletal arms after only two days of love. But love cannot be ravaged by guns and tanks and evil ideologies. Love cannot be cut off by distance or absence, by hunger or cold, by beatings or degradations. And love *can* reach out across blood, whatever the Nazis believed, and make connections that are worth a million sick ideologies.

I smile, remembering myself and Bartek with our own sons, and send up a prayer to the dear husband that I lost and that I miss every single day. I'm so glad Ester has been spared such grief, and bless this daughter that was gifted to me amidst the horror of war. Ruth cannot be here to stand as grandmother to this new gift for our skewed but happy family, but I can. I will.

Matron is hovering and, wiping away a tear, I motion Ester and Filip over. Fingers shaking, they sign the adoption papers to turn them into a family that will hopefully grow to one day include Pippa and more beautiful babies besides. I watch them sign their names with a flourish, kiss Oliwia, thank the matron. They press money into her hand – money donated by church and synagogue alike to try and ensure that more of these poor war orphans find a way back to their homes – then they add a piece of paper of their own.

There is a number written clearly across it: 41400. *Pippa Pasternak.*

She is out there somewhere and we will continue to search for her for as long as we all draw breath. Matron squeezes both their hands with her own endlessly caring ones, then pins the paper to her wall. Ester reaches up and touches her fingers to it for a moment, then Oliwia does the same and, with a choke of a laugh, Ester takes the girl's fingers in her own and turns away. She looks to me.

'Thank you, Ana. We are ready now, ready to go home.'

I nod, button up my cloak and pick up my bag. I will take this new family home to learn to be together and then I must get back on duty. There are babies waiting to be born and the world, at last, feels a fit place for them once more.

A LETTER FROM ANNA

Dear reader,

I want to say a huge thank you for choosing to read *The Midwife of Auschwitz*.

From the moment I first read about over 3000 babies being born in a death camp, I knew it was a story that had to be told. I really hope my fictional version spoke out to you, and if you want to keep up to date with all my latest releases, just sign up at the following link. Your email address will never be shared and you can unsubscribe at any time.

www.bookouture.com/anna-stuart

This wasn't an easy book to write. The subject is obviously harrowing, but my research led me to inspiring stories of fellowship and courage within the mire of Auschwitz-Birkenau, which provided a little light. Even when I visited Auschwitz and saw the site of the myriad crimes against humanity, it was hard to truly imagine how anyone survived. I can only assume that, despite those crimes, the humanity remained amongst the prisoners and that is what got those few survivors through the Nazi hell.

I recommend a visit to Auschwitz. It will not be a happy day, but it will be a moving and important one. In a turbulent world, we must fight for humanity, decency and tolerance, and I hope *The Midwife of Auschwitz* stands testimony to those virtues and is a story that will stay with you.

If so, I would be very grateful if you could write a review. I'd love to hear what you think, and it makes such a difference helping new readers to discover one of my books for the first time. I also love hearing from my readers – you can get in touch on my Facebook page, through Twitter, Goodreads or my website.

Thanks,

Anna

www.annastuartbooks.com

 facebook.com/annastuartauthor

twitter.com/annastuartbooks

HISTORICAL NOTES

Writing about the holocaust is an honour and brings with it a huge responsibility to the truth. While this novel is a work of fiction, I have worked hard to ensure that all details are as close to reality as possible to faithfully represent the terrible suffering that was endured by those, like my characters, who were interred in ghettos and camps by the Nazi regime.

Real people in the novel

Many of the characters are real and I feel it's worth more detail on some to be clear about the true stories that inspired my own:

Stanisława Leszczyńska was the original inspiration for this novel and, while *The Midwife of Auschwitz* does not follow her true story, many details of her astonishing life inspired key scenes.

Stanisława was a midwife in Łódź when war broke out and she and her family worked to help the Jews stranded in the ghetto and were sent to the camps as a result. Her husband and older son, both called Bronislaw, escaped capture and made it to

Warsaw, where her husband died fighting in the tragic rebellion there towards the end of the war (see below).

Stanisława was sent to Auschwitz, where she stood up to Sister Klara and Pfani, refusing to allow them to murder those babies she could save, and it is a recorded fact that she delivered around three thousand babies in Birkenau and that not one of them died during the birthing. Tragically, given the horrendous conditions and the fact that the Nazis did not allow the babies any rations, very few survived for long afterwards. Stanisława is known to have cared for all mothers with calm professionalism and to have stood up to the camp authorities, including the fearsome Josef Mengele, to enable her to do her job to the best of her considerable abilities in terrible circumstances.

Having returned to Łódź after the war and worked as a midwife until 1958, Stanisława barely talked of her experiences in Auschwitz-Birkenau until she was persuaded by her middle son to give a brief report of her time there (which can be found in full on the internet). In it, she details the terrible suffering of mothers and babies, and states that from May 1943, blond-haired, blue-eyed babies were regularly taken for the Lebensborn programme (see below) and that she devised a way of secretly tattooing them in the hope of one day reuniting them with their mothers. This gave me the seed of Ester's fictional story.

As I've said, many of the details in this novel are based on what we know of Stanisława's life but my character Ana is fictional. There are some elements of her story that differ and I wanted to highlight the following:

Stanisława had a daughter, Sylwia, who was captured and sent to Auschwitz with her. This young woman was a trainee doctor and worked with her mother to help deliver babies, as well as nursing in the hospital. She served as the inspiration for Ester, and I hope that the relationship between Ester and Ana goes some way to demonstrating Stanisława's care for her real daughter. One survivor's story reports that Sylwia was once so weak with TB that she was selected for the gas chamber but was saved when her mother clung to her tightly, refusing to let her go without taking her too. It must stand as testimony to the regard that the doctors at Birkenau had for this remarkable woman that Sylwia was saved and survived.

Details of exactly which blocks Stanisława worked in are unclear, but I found testimony that she worked in both Block 17 and Block 24 so chose to use those two for simplicity. Interestingly, there is a hut still standing at Birkenau that visitors are told was her maternity section, but it has no brick stove down the centre and Stanisława testified herself that it was this stove she used as a primitive birthing bed. I therefore used that hut as Ana and Ester's initial Block 17 and then had them move into the fuller 'maternity section' in Block 24 shortly after arrival.

Stanisława's prisoner number was 41355. I chose not to use that number to honour her own identity compared to my fictional midwife; instead I used 41401 for Ana and 41400 for Ester. Those numbers, like most, are on record to other Jewish Poles – Mayer Szac and Abraham Sukerman – both of whom were sadly murdered in Auschwitz. I hope that using their numbers to tell this vital story shines a light on the bravery of those who endured the horror of the concentration camps.

Stanisława Leszczyńska was a truly inspirational woman. She is honoured in Poland – the road running along the front of Birkenau is named for her – and is a candidate for sainthood in the Catholic Church. She stands as a wonderful example of kindness, professionalism, modesty and bravery.

Irma Grese came to Birkenau from Ravensbrück women's camp in March 1943, aged just 20, and was a woman as beautiful as she was sadistic. Reports tell of her extreme vanity, her promiscuity with various camp doctors, and her enjoyment of tormenting prisoners. One survivor reported her slashing prisoners' breasts open with her whip, a story I used in the novel to illustrate the horrific sadism of this young woman and her ilk. She left Birkenau with the death marches but was captured by the British, stood trial, and was executed for war crimes in December 1945.

Dr Josef Mengele has gone down in history as a particularly evil Nazi in a heavily populated field, perhaps because of his coldly scientific use of the Jews in his 'care' as lab rats. Known as the 'Angel of Death', he is infamous for his cruel experiments, especially on twins. He was also reputedly the only doctor who could perform the ramp selections sober and who, indeed, appeared to relish it. He seems to have had several brushes with Stanisława and perhaps respected her (as much as he was capable) for standing up to him. Contrary to popular perception, he was not the only, or even the main doctor in Auschwitz-Birkenau. He was initially head physician (if such a word can be used) for the Roma camp and was not put in charge of the women's camp as a whole until the Roma were all sent to their deaths in August 1944.

Mengele lived out his life in Brazil, dying of a stroke while swimming in 1979, aged 68 – a far kinder death than that he afforded so many of his poor victims.

Mala Zimetbaum was a Belgian Jew, brought to Auschwitz in September 1942 as prisoner number 19880. A talented linguist, she worked as an interpreter and courier, which gave her privileges such as wearing her own clothes, keeping her hair and being relatively well fed. Despite that, she devoted herself to helping other inmates, getting them assigned to easier work if they were unfit, warning of upcoming selections, and sneaking photographs that inmates' relatives had sent to them – such as I show with Filip's letter to Ester.

She had a 'courtship' (in the sense that they talked enough

to fall in love) with **Edek Galiński,** a mechanic in the women's camp. The story of their escape is faithfully told in the novel. They truly did manage to get out with Edek dressed as an SS guard and Mala as a prisoner going to install a washbasin before pretending to be an SS guard and his girlfriend on a walk. The plan worked for three days until Mala was caught trying to buy bread and arrested. Edek, watching from a distance, turned himself in as they had promised not to separate and there are stories, as told in the novel, of them singing to each other in their cells in the Auschwitz main camp.

Edek was hanged shouting 'Long Live Poland!' and later that afternoon Mala was marched out to hang in front of the camp. Instead, taking a razor blade from her hair, she slit the veins on the inside of her elbows. Amidst some rioting, she seems to then have been put on a wheelbarrow to be wheeled to the crematorium, possibly to be burned alive. The nurses in attendance reportedly bandaged her arms slowly to allow her to die. Some said she bled to death on the cart, some that she also took poison, and others that a guard shot her. I chose to synthesise these accounts into something that I felt fitted with her character and did not prolong the action too far and I hope that it represents a bold and brave ending to a noble woman.

Auschwitz-Birkenau

I approached writing about Auschwitz with some trepidation, very aware that it is almost impossible to truly convey the horrors of life for the prisoners – the vocabulary simply does not exist. I endeavoured, instead, to show readers what happened there and would like to assure you that, while some characters and all dialogue may be fictional, every incident in this novel comes from research. It is perhaps worth listing a few to make it clear that I have not in any way exaggerated the barbaric cruelty of life in Auschwitz-Birkenau:

The food supplied was, as many witnesses have testified, truly as limited and terrible as described – ersatz 'coffee' for breakfast, thin soup for lunch and a crust of bread for supper. How anyone survived on that while working long days in hard physical labour remains impossible to conceive.

Conditions in the barracks were as barbaric as I have shown, with prisoners often sleeping piled together, at least ten to a bunk on hard wooden boards with a scrap of blanket each. Uniforms were not adequate for the freezing conditions in winter and one especial cruelty was taking away prisoners' socks and shoes and forcing them into hard wooden clogs. Like the numbers and the shaving of heads, it was all a way of dehumanising them, and it is little wonder that a rampant black market, usually involving 'organised' goods from Kanada, developed.

The hospitals were even worse. The prevalence of sickness and diarrhoea and lack of latrines, water and disinfectant meant that patients were often left to lie in their own bodily fluids and, if they were on one of the lower bunks, to have those of others drip onto them. Rats as big as cats proliferated, nibbling on patients both alive and dead, and lice were impossible to get rid of. Again, how anyone survived is testimony to human endurance and spirit.

A Christmas tree really was erected by SS guards who made the prisoners stand before it and revealed a pile of naked corpses as a 'Christmas gift', although the defiant singing of the carol is my own invention.

'Selection' is another well-documented but still almost impossibly horrific truth about Birkenau. Built as a killing camp, from the start new arrivals were selected into two columns with the fitter ones being put to work and the weaker being dispatched straight to die in the chambers. They were usually lured in with the deception that they were going for showers (for efficiency, not kindness) but those working in the camps were under no such illusions. Periodic and seemingly random 'selections' also happened at any time and any inmate selected knew they were going to their death.

The trains: When my characters Ana and Ester arrived in April 1943, the train was still dropping people off outside the gates of Birkenau, but from May 1944 the train track was extended into the middle of the camp itself – as shown when Tomaz arrives – to speed up the process. The internal 'ramp' can still be seen by visitors today.

The death marches are a well-known final horror in the Auschwitz story and show the depths of both Nazi cruelty and delusion at the end of the war. Some of the sickest patients were left behind to die and Stanisława, along with several others, persuaded the Nazis to let them stay to tend them. Having agreed, the Nazis turned off the electricity, locked up the kitchens and set fire to Kanada to pointlessly deprive those left behind of any final comforts. Children were left, though it is hard to discover how many of their mothers might have been with them, and there is testimony of people avoiding the marches by hiding under piles of corpses as Naomi does in the novel. The only thing I altered slightly was the timeframe. It took two full days to hound all the remaining prisoners out onto the frozen roads but I shortened it for dramatic simplicity.

Sundays: It does seem to have been true that prisoners had Sundays 'off' in the camp, in the sense that they were not sent out on official work duty.

News of the camps: When the two escapees shown in the novel reached Slovakia in Spring 1944, they told the Jewish council the truth about Auschwitz-Birkenau. Their report was sent to the World Jewish Congress but not acted on, even when information was added to it by two more Slovakians who escaped that May. The dossier reached the Allies in mid-June 1944 and even got to neutral Sweden and the Vatican. The BBC, Swiss press and American papers and radio stations reported stories of atrocities in the camp increasingly from mid-1944 and American surveillance planes photographed Auschwitz, but the Allies still took no direct action.

The camp was not bombed and neither was the clear railway link into it. Why? It is not my place to comment but it is certainly a tragedy that the killings could not have been stopped sooner than they were. Perhaps, despite all the evidence, the inhuman crimes being perpetuated at Auschwitz and the other concentration camps were too terrible to truly be believed until we actually saw them with our own eyes.

Beyond Auschwitz-Birkenau

Beyond the dreadful confines of Auschwitz-Birkenau there are a few other aspects of the world portrayed in this novel that warrant further elucidation:

Łódź Ghetto

To my shame, until researching this novel, I did not know very much about the ghettos into which the Jewish people of so many cities across Europe were forced, especially in Poland. Łódź (pronounced something like Wudge) was one of the largest and longest lasting – mainly because of their leader, Chaim Rumkowski's, fierce policy of work – and was in place from February 1940 to August 1944. Life in there is well documented from an official ghetto record as well as several personal diaries, survivor interviews, and some astonishing photographs. I urge people to look up those sources, as they are more eloquent than I could ever be.

Although most of the characters I present in the ghetto sections of the novel are fictional, I have done my best to ensure that conditions and events are truthful. Food was in short supply and of terrible quality, fuel was so sparse that people were forced to burn their furniture to cook and keep warm. The initial overcrowding was made immeasurably worse when more people were shipped in from smaller, less profitable ghettos. Schools were closed and people forced into workshops and, from late 1941, many, many Jews were shipped out, first to the gas vans at Chelmno and then to Auschwitz – a few to work but many straight to their deaths.

The only good thing is that my representation of the people working to help those in the ghetto are also true to life, with Stanisława and her family being among a number brave enough to join the Resistance against the Nazis.

The Lebensborn Programme

This brutal programme sought to put children with Aryan traits into German homes to ensure that they were brought up in the Nazi way. Thousands of children were kidnapped from their parents, especially in Poland, and ruthlessly shipped to the Fatherland to be handed to German couples or put into special homes. Many were so young that, after the war, they had no recollection of their real parents or life.

To add to this, in an astonishing programme of state-sponsored prostitution, young Aryan women across the German-occupied lands were lured into big houses where they were encouraged to mate with 'good' Aryan men (usually soldiers) to provide children for the Fatherland. They were usually kept there until they gave birth, and sometimes after, with the children either being brought up in the homes or given to married couples to adopt. Tragic numbers of these children were rejected and horribly stigmatised after the war, especially in Norway where they were seen as living evidence of shameful collaboration, and had terrible lives.

Taking 'suitable' babies from the concentration camps was a relatively small part of the Lebensborn programme but no less distressing for the mothers involved. Originally only non-Jewish babies were taken but there is clear evidence that as the German authorities became increasingly concerned about the number of young men being slaughtered on the Eastern front, conditions of acceptance were dropped with the tacit agreement that anyone blond could not be truly Jewish.

It is hard to track the fate of many of the adults who survived Auschwitz-Birkenau, and even harder with children. Despite my best efforts I did not find a concrete story of any of the babies who were tattooed by Stanisława and her helpers being directly reunited with their mothers. There are, thankfully, some touching stories of other babies on the wider programme finding their parents so it is not impossible that it happened. But, dearly as I would have loved to reunite Ester and Pippa at the end of this novel, it did not feel true to the terrible loss of the mothers in Birkenau, so I chose to trace Oliwia instead. In my heart I hope my fictional character did, eventually, find her daughter but that is perhaps for the reader to decide for themselves.

The Warsaw Uprising

This brave Polish uprising began on 1 August 1944, the aim being for local rebels to take central Warsaw to prepare the way for Soviet troops to break in from the east. The Poles did their bit but the Soviets ignored their attempts to make radio contact with them and did not advance beyond the city limits. It's unclear exactly why and theories range from them being taken by surprise by the Polish action, to them deliberately allowing the Poles to be slaughtered to make way for Russia to take the country after the war. Whatever the reasons, it resulted in a protracted siege for the Varsovians, with lack of food and water rapidly becoming a serious problem, and in September the Germans retook the city with horrific loss.

The entire civilian population of Warsaw was expelled, many of them to labour camps across the Reich, and the city was decimated. The brave rebels, of whom Stanisława's husband and oldest son were truly two, were badly let down by their supposed allies and their brave and ultimately fruitless rebellion is one of too many tragedies of the Second World War.

Going home

It only truly struck me when researching the ending of this book, quite how many lost people were in transit across Europe in the months and, indeed, years after the war. There were so many refugees, evacuees, prisoners of war, internees and troops trying to get home and so many people who had no idea if they had a home – or a family – to come back to.

I was heartened to discover a large number of charitable organisations doing amazing work to try and match people up with their loved ones. One thankful feature of the hateful Nazi regime was the meticulous keeping of records which meant the masses they shipped into concentration camps could be traced. Some attempts were made to destroy those records as the Germans retreated but, in the scramble, many survived and helped groups like the Red Cross, the Jewish relief committee and the American United Nations Relief and Rehabilitation Administration to do their work.

Most cities had repatriation offices and the Jewish groups

were a focal point for this. Łódź was a vibrant city in the months after the war – a replacement capital for devastated Warsaw – and one thing that surprised me was that much regeneration of even things like theatres was already taking place by May 1945. The end of the war came earlier for Poland than it did for Britain but, oh, they needed it. The poor country suffered terribly and the stories I read of the notes all along the walls of the offices of the Jewish relief committee in Łódź were heart-breaking. Too many people never had a reunion and remained torn apart by war forever.

It felt important to me that readers were able to find out the fate of various characters, perhaps most vitally that of Filip. Like Ester, he is a fictional character but what he experiences at Chelmno towards the end of the war is based on known fact. A number of men were taken there when it was restarted as a killing operation in April 1944 and were kept on as workers to burn the corpses. It's also true that a marquee was set up to sort the prisoners' belongings and that a handful of the more talented tailors were taken on to alter items that took the fancy of the SS officers' families. This kept a few men alive until Chelmno was shut down in the face of the advancing Russians.

The story of Filip and Noah's dramatic escape from the barn is also based on survivors' testimonies with those prisoners on the lower floor being shot and those on the upper defying the Nazis and escaping into the woods. It is a small story of hope amongst so much tragedy and I was very glad to borrow it to get Filip back into Ester's arms at the end of the novel.

ACKNOWLEDGEMENTS

This has not been an easy book to write. There were times when I questioned if it was my place to tackle it, but I knew this was a story that had to be told and I would like to thank all the amazing people who have helped me to tell it.

First in that long queue must be my editor, Natasha Harding, and my agent, Kate Shaw. Both these fantastic women helped me to develop the concept of *The Midwife of Auschwitz* and to fashion the narrative in a way that would stand testimony to the terrible suffering endured by so many in the Holocaust whilst also telling an individual story. Although this novel is inspired by Stanislawa Leszczyńska, Natasha and Kate helped me to find a fictional interpretation of what she went through that would honour her without pretending to be a biography, and also to create Ester to run alongside her and open up the amazing true story of tattooing the babies in secret in the hope they might be found after the war. Thank you to both of you from the bottom of my heart – this would not be half the novel it is without you.

Heartfelt thanks must also go to the rest of the talented team at Bookouture for helping with the editing, sensitivity reading and fabulous cover design that has also helped bring this story to readers in its best possible version. I'm so pleased and proud to be working with you all.

A big shout out to my writing 'crew', most notably Tracy Bloom and Julie Houston, for all the advice, encouragement and wine... We went on our first writing retreat last year, with the lovely Debbie Rayner, and it was a genuinely inspiring few days. It's amazing how much you can get done with others working around you and wise people to consult when you're banging your head on the adjoining wall! Thank you, ladies, and roll on the next one...!

A huge thank you to my 'research assistants', Brenda and Jamie Goth, who very kindly came to Krakow with my husband and I. They were invaluable in our probing of Polish beers, food and – most memorably – electric scooters! On a more serious note, they came with us to Auschwitz and together we walked the camp where so much suffering took place and came away both saddened and enriched by the experience. May nothing like that ever be allowed to happen on this earth again – and may we, please, all remember that as the hideous events unfold in Ukraine.

We were blessed with our guide at Auschwitz, David Kennedy. He was hugely knowledgeable and kind enough to answer all my questions on the day and via Messenger afterwards and to point me to some excellent sources. He really helped me to step into the shoes of the thousands of poor women interred in Auschwitz-Birkenau, and I thank him for that.

I've saved my biggest thank you for last, and it goes to my husband, Stuart, who has been with me all the way on this one and for every book I've written. He's the one who gets the late-night wobbles, the research frustrations and the could-I-run-this-idea-past-yous. He's the one who has to listen to me banging on about new ideas, or 'fascinating' things I've read about, or plot tangles I've got myself into, and he does it with endless patience and good humour. He is my sounding board, my reality check and my rock – thank you, Stuart.